"Action-packed and twisty! With d̶a̶———————————————————————-ous setting, *The Off Season* is a decidedly modern take on *Rebecca*."

ROBYN HARDING, bestselling author of
The Drowning Woman

"With her signature atmospheric setting that will chill you to the bone, Amber Cowie has once again written a terrifying, exceptionally structured, mesmerizing suspense. *The Off Season* is an exhilarating thriller that will electrify you."

SAMANTHA M. BAILEY, *USA Today* and
#1 bestselling author of *A Friend in the Dark*

"In a style reminiscent of Ruth Ware, Cowie transports the reader to a stunning but isolated resort full of twisted menace and dark secrets. It's a gripping and addictive read!"

DANIEL KALLA, bestselling author of *Fit to Die*

"Amber Cowie has done it again—*The Off Season* is hauntingly atmospheric, claustrophobic (in the best way), and deliciously twisty. Impossible to put down."

SUZY KRAUSE, author of *Sorry I Missed You*

"Nobody writes haunting isolation like Amber Cowie. Fans of Lucy Foley will love *The Off Season,* a riveting tale of deceit and regret where no one should be trusted, nothing is what it seems, and even the weather might kill you."

S. M. FREEDMAN, author of *Blood Atonement*

"From the remote and eerie west coast setting to the stunningly unpredictable ending, *The Off Season* had me riveted to the page. Cowie's masterful use of misdirection as she weaves a tapestry of long-held lies and buried secrets makes this atmospheric thriller a stay-up-all-nighter."

K. R. DODD, author of the award-winning
Scare Away the Dark and *Everybody Knows*

"A well-written book with references to some good Golden Age mysteries. . . . Just who and why and what is happening to the people who went to the Point and who will be the last person standing is as clever a twist as Ms. Christie ever envisioned."

The Globe and Mail

"A riveting, irresistible locked-room mystery reminiscent of Agatha Christie, *Last One Alive* is endlessly entertaining and fiendishly clever. So jam-packed with tension and suffused with dread, you won't be able to put it down!"

CHRISTINA McDONALD, *USA Today* bestselling author of *The Night Olivia Fell*

"A haunting, claustrophobic, unpredictable thriller for fans of Agatha Christie, *Last One Alive* showcases Amber Cowie's extraordinary talent. As a violent storm rages outside a remote lodge, a group of strangers are stranded in a terrifying cat-and-mouse hunt for the murderer among them. Cowie writes with such skillful description that I could feel the cold and rain seep into my bones and my pulse spike as the exhilarating story reached a breakneck pace. A bewitching read jam-packed with fascinating characters, this book is an absolute standout."

SAMANTHA M. BAILEY, *USA Today* and #1 bestselling author of *A Friend in the Dark*

"An abandoned lodge. A group of suspect people. An old mystery to solve. And then the guests begin disappearing one by one. Can they figure out what is going on before it's too late? Fans of Agatha Christie and Ruth Ware will want to pick this book up immediately!"

CATHERINE McKENZIE, bestselling author of *Have You Seen Her*

"Cowie has done Agatha Christie proud in this stay-up-all-night, keep-all-the-lights-on mystery. With a setting that's remote, creepy, and possibly cursed—and a story both haunting and harrowing—*Last One Alive* will entertain you from the first disappearance to the final dead body."

MEGAN COLLINS, author of *The Family Plot*

ALSO BY **AMBER COWIE**

Last One Alive
Loss Lake
Raven Lane
Rapid Falls

THE OFF SEASON

AMBER COWIE

PUBLISHED BY SIMON AND SCHUSTER
NEW YORK   LONDON   TORONTO   SYDNEY   NEW DELHI

SIMON &
SCHUSTER
CANADA

A Division of Simon & Schuster, LLC
166 King Street East, Suite 300
Toronto, Ontario M5A 1J3

This Simon & Schuster Canada edition May 2024

SIMON & SCHUSTER CANADA and colophon are trademarks of Simon & Schuster, LLC

Simon & Schuster: Celebrating 100 Years of Publishing in 2024

For information about special discounts for bulk purchases, please contact Simon & Schuster Special Sales at 1-800-268-3216 or CustomerService@simonandschuster.ca.

Manufactured in the United States of America

10 9 8 7 6 5 4 3 2 1

Library and Archives Canada Cataloguing in Publication

Title: The off season / Amber Cowie.
Names: Cowie, Amber, author.
Description: Simon & Schuster Canada edition.
Identifiers: Canadiana (print) 20230552374 | Canadiana (ebook) 20230552382 |
ISBN 9781668023518 (softcover) | ISBN 9781668023525 (EPUB)
Subjects: LCGFT: Thrillers (Fiction) | LCGFT: Novels.
Classification: LCC PS8605.O9256 O34 2024 | DDC C813/.6—dc23

ISBN 978-1-6680-2351-8
ISBN 978-1-6680-2352-5 (ebook)

To all my parents, by birth and marriage

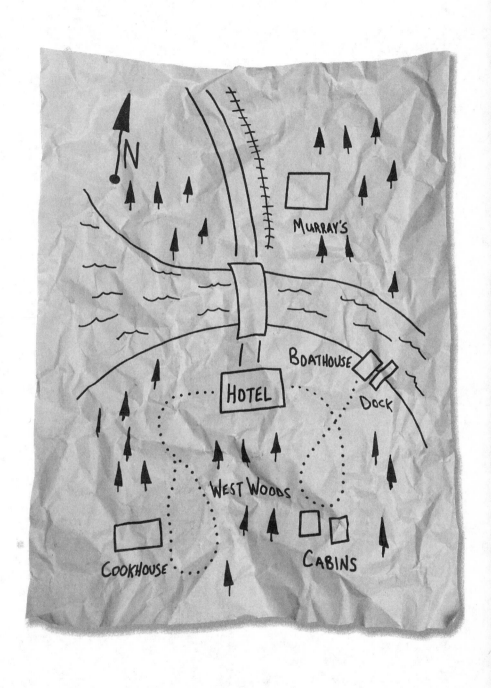

FIRE EVACUATION PLAN

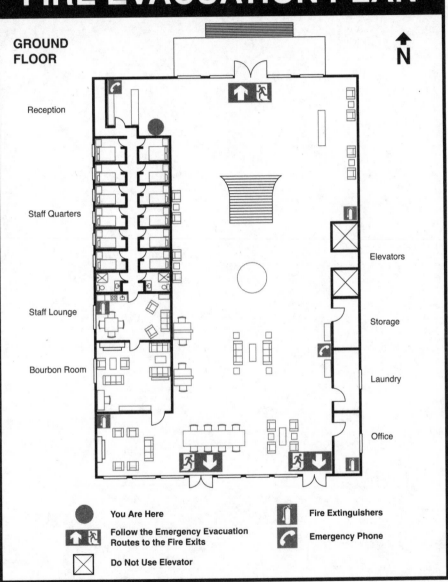

GROUND
FLOOR

N

Reception

Staff Quarters

Staff Lounge

Bourbon Room

Elevators

Storage

Laundry

Office

You Are Here

Follow the Emergency Evacuation
Routes to the Fire Exits

Do Not Use Elevator

Fire Extinguishers

Emergency Phone

CHAPTER | ONE

THE FIRST THING JANE SAW ON HER WEDDING DAY WAS A TEXT MESSAGE.

tell him

She dropped her phone face down on the nightstand. The clunk woke her fiancé, Dom, whose half-lidded eyes, tousled hair, and sleepy smile made the advice completely unadvisable. God, he was beautiful. And he loved and trusted her. Why throw that all away?

"You okay?" he asked, as she sank her head back down on the feather pillows. He laid his large hand flat on the rise of her hip.

She paused before answering. His palm was warm, the crisp hotel sheets smelled faintly but not unpleasantly of industrial detergent, and the room was luxuriously shadowed by the thick floral curtains the maid had pulled across the floor-to-ceiling windows the night before. Behind the fabric, the late September sunrise would be beginning to play on the pointed peaks of the Lions, Vancouver's most celebrated mountain view. Below their hotel, the gray-blue waves of Burrard Inlet would be gently bumping the boats docked in the harbor as the leafy urban Japanese maples rustled in the breeze. Inside the honeymoon suite, though, the darkness was comfortingly complete.

No one could ruin this day.

Not even Mickey.

Though she hadn't answered their text, Jane had formed a response in her mind: *some secrets should be kept.* Of all people, her friend and business partner should understand that.

Turning to Dom she whispered, "Absolutely perfect. Mickey wrote to wish us luck."

Dom smiled. "That's nice." He kissed her. His lips were soft with sleep.

As her body responded to his touch, Jane was reassured about her decision not to reveal everything. Four months ago, she had been hesitant to start a fling with a half-Chilean guy from the suburbs of the Lower Mainland. On the heels of a disastrous breakup and a devastating professional blow, her holiday was meant to be about recovery—not romance. But she had said yes, and now she was ready to promise Dom a lifetime. More than ready.

Their friends and family would come around.

The warnings and doubts from her inner circle were endless. So many red flags, they said, with worried expressions. As if Jane couldn't list them herself.

They had known each other for less than six months.

He was thirteen years older.

This was his second marriage.

He had a teenage daughter.

She'd never been remotely interested in having children.

She was rebounding from a bad breakup, and her last film had nearly killed her career.

She understood why everyone was confused. For the last several years, her course had been unwavering. Her work had been her focus, though she'd been seriously dating Chien, a talented designer and producer who was gathering accolades as an edgy voice from the second-generation Chinese diaspora. Both of their careers were taking off precisely according to Jane's plan—until it had all gone wrong.

Chien dumped her at the Hot Docs festival, the biggest documentary event in Canada, where she and Mickey were pitching a new project from their company, Ember Productions. The festival had started well. She and Mickey were in talks with Netflix to distribute their powerful new film, *Failure to Thrive*, and other distributors had expressed interest in the project too. They were heading into their screening when the story broke on CBC.

SPEED INVESTIGATED AS FACTOR IN
FATAL CAR CRASH INVOLVING WOMAN ON DVP

Chien had unceremoniously yanked his arm from her grasp as her phone pinged with the first condemning messages. Jane wasn't sure if it was a performative gesture of solidarity with the "victims" of Ember Productions or a preemptive self-preserving romantic breakup, but it made little difference. Chien left the theater before the screening began. After the boos from the audience and the hurtful accusations during the Q and A had died down, it took all of Jane's integrity to convince Mickey—and herself—that they'd done the right thing. That they'd conducted themselves *ethically*.

The next morning, it had been harder to stand strong. Chien scrubbed her from all his platforms. Meanwhile, the media eviscerated Ember Productions; the review in the *Toronto Star* was particularly scathing. She and Mickey were called "heartless, cruel, moral criminals who should be serving time rather than accepting accolades." Netflix killed the negotiations and canceled the rest of their meetings. Mickey texted that they should stop pitching the film. When Jane didn't respond to a single message, Mickey had left her a voice mail dripping with accusation.

I told you that you pushed her too hard.

Jane had wanted to scream at Mickey for abandoning her, that they were the only person she had left. Instead, she'd booked a solo flight to Barcelona.

If Mickey was going to leave her all alone in the world, she might as well enjoy it.

As she trudged through security, she was resolute. What had happened on the project hadn't been a bad choice—it had been the *only* choice. On the flight, after watching *Imitation of Life*, she scribbled furiously in her journal about removing toxic, shallow people like Chien from her life. She vowed to never again be so poisoned by other people's actions—or their *reactions*—that she couldn't control her own. Jane committed to a life of courage, authentic communication, and artistic conviction unbothered by the superficial judgments (or approbation) of small-minded critics. Her first week in Spain had been both lovely and intensely lonely. Then, she'd met Dom.

Talking to him had been like a balm to her blistered skin.

He was chivalrous, down-to-earth, good-natured, solid. And he was so far outside the industry that, to him, her career woes were remote and nearly undiscoverable. He wasn't a CBC/NPR/BBC kind of guy—and he didn't exist on a single social media platform beyond LinkedIn, which he sheepishly admitted he hadn't updated in twelve years. He worked with his hands, he told her, holding them up for inspection, while explaining he was a contractor with his own business who preferred to talk to his clients on-site and in person. For him, computers were nothing more than a means to send job quotes and the occasional email—and even then, his brother handled the admin side of the business. Dom's antiquated request to get to know each other the old-fashioned way was exactly what she needed, when she needed it. (From her own late-night doomscrolling, she knew a simple Google search of her name would reveal the ugly truth. The story behind her last production was the first link that appeared.)

So, they agreed. A fresh start for both of them.

She had never dated someone without searching their name at least once, so her pact with Dom created a relationship different from any she'd experienced before. There was no online prelude. What they had was real—no filters. From the first night, Dom made her feel new and safe. As they grew closer, he got to know her, not her history. He loved that she was a filmmaker. Accomplished. Intelligent. Admirable, even. But he showed little curiosity about her work. Someday, she'd tell him what had happened on *Failure to Thrive*. But for now, what was the point in opening old wounds?

Her marriage was the beginning of the rest of her life. All the doubters were forgetting who *she* was. This wasn't a flighty white-knight fantasy. Jane was not the kind of woman who had spent years dreaming of her wedding day. At thirty-two, she was an independent, urban professional who had always eschewed the easy route of marriage to live alone and make documentary films. She rented a ground-floor studio apartment in a converted Victorian house at Fraser and Eleventh in the dynamic and diverse East Van neighborhood, only dating when someone truly remarkable came along—usually writers, actors, musicians. People who, like her, treasured experiences and art instead of Ikea furniture and mass-produced decor telling them to *live, laugh, and love*. Dom wasn't her type, but maybe that's why it worked. At his core, he possessed all the attributes she loved and respected. He was honest and loyal. A creator, not a consumer.

And he turned her on like no one ever had before.

He liked to rope his fingers through her hair when they kissed, pulling back as his mouth moved down the line of her jaw to her ear. The things he whispered were flattering and shameless—coarse words softly spoken that made her warm and restless. She liked the look in his eyes when she had no clothes on. Half-lust, half-wonder, like she was better than he had ever imagined—and he couldn't wait to put his hands all over her. When she laid on her stomach, he drew lines down her back with fingertips roughened by work. Every time he touched her, she felt like she mattered.

Jane had to believe in herself and her choices. If she couldn't do that, she had nothing left.

tell him, Mickey had texted.

I will, Jane thought back. *Just not now.*

A discreet knock on the door was room service with a complimentary mimosa cart. The hour that followed was a blur of white lace and sweet champagne. After a final coat of mascara, she applied lipstick, blew a kiss in the rosy-bulbed glamour mirror, then emerged from the huge bathroom in her department store dress with off-the-shoulder sleeves and a tea-length floating skirt.

Dom's eyes shone as he crossed the room to take her hand.

"If I asked you something, would you say yes?" It was the same thing he'd said before proposing.

She nodded.

"Marry me?"

She tilted her face up to be kissed. Gentle at first, then deeper, harder, urgent. She broke away, a flush heating her cheeks. He grinned as she answered him the same way she had the first time he'd asked the question.

"Yes."

The officiant met them in a small room on the ground floor of the hotel. He was a tall Black man with thoughtful brown eyes and a wary expression, who stood beside the two witnesses he had provided at their request. One was an elderly Chinese woman with penciled-on eyebrows, whose smile failed to reach her eyes. The other, a young white man with a jaw that jutted forward at the same angle as his brow sloped back, was sheened with sweat though the room was air-conditioned. There was no one else.

Jane's parents had died when she was a teenager. She had no siblings.

Mickey was boycotting.

Dom's brother, Ted, was running a big job for the company and couldn't get away.

Dom's daughter, Sienna, was in France on an exchange program.

The ceremony was simple and short: seven minutes from start to finish. When the officiant pronounced them husband and wife, unexpected tears pricked Jane's eyes as she thought of her mother's face. The memory flicked away like the silk handkerchief Dom whisked from his pocket to place in her hand before kissing her again. When they parted, Jane caught the older woman carefully dabbing at the corners of her own eyes. Her expression had changed from placid neutrality to open admiration.

As Jane and Dom rode up to their floor in the velvet-walled elevator, her stomach flipped. Married. She was *married* now. She kissed Dom again to dissolve her doubts. In the hallway outside their room, Jane fumbled for the key card in the small white clutch that Dom had insisted she carry—something borrowed!—as he nuzzled her neck.

His phone rang.

"Is it work?" Jane asked as he gave it a glance.

"It's Sienna," he said with a look of relief. "She probably wants to see how it all went. You go ahead. I'll meet you inside."

"You can take the call in here," she said, nudging him with her hip before turning to the door, plastic card pinched between her finger and thumb.

But Dom was already walking down the hallway with the phone pressed to his ear. "Hello, sweetie," Jane heard him say as he turned the corner at the T-junction.

Inside the room, Jane leaned against the wall and lifted her left hand to eye level. The thin, rose-gold ring on her finger shone brighter than any piece of jewelry she'd ever worn. Much to Dom's chagrin, she had refused to let him buy her an engagement ring. It was too traditional, too ostentatious, too transactional. As a result, he had chosen a wedding band inlaid with tiny diamonds.

She walked over to the ivory couches embroidered with a white leafy design and fluffed out her full skirt before sitting down. It was nearly lunchtime. The sky was the hazy blue of a climate change–altered summer overstaying its welcome before the rains of autumn returned. Burrard Inlet glittered below, and Jane spotted a few joggers slogging through the heat on their way to Stanley Park. She couldn't remember feeling so content.

The door to the suite opened and she turned to her husband. Her *husband*! Her heart jumped.

"How is Sienna?" she asked brightly, full of optimism. "Was she thrilled for us?"

He smiled, but something dark danced in his eyes and he rubbed the heel of his hand under his clean-shaven jaw. "Yes, she was very happy for us. Just a little . . . distracted. She's kind of going through something over there."

Jane's stomach dropped. Had Sienna discovered what she'd done? "What do you mean?"

"Oh, you know teenagers. She wants me to change her ticket." Stress wrote lines on both sides of Dom's mouth, signaling his concern.

The champagne and orange juice gurgled inside her. She wasn't much of a drinker, and she had overdone it this morning. She kept her voice calm. "She wants to come home early?"

Sienna was scheduled to return the following week from France. Jane had hoped to have a proper honeymoon with Dom at an oceanfront resort they'd booked in Tofino, but that could be rearranged if necessary. The last thing she wanted to do was alienate her new stepdaughter before their first meeting. Or worse, have Sienna bombard her father with details about her new stepmother that Jane hadn't yet shared.

Dom frowned more deeply. "No, actually. She doesn't want to come home at all. She says it's too boring here."

Jane paused. Her stomach unclenched. Of course. Sienna was a teenager in Paris. Her summer exchange-program credits allowed her to take the fall semester off. It was no surprise that she wanted to stay in Europe.

"So, what did you tell her? Are you okay with her taking a little more time to explore?"

Dom's mouth quirked into something close to a small grin.

"Of course not. We've only got one more year together before she graduates high school and leaves for good. We need to bond as a family before she moves out."

She nodded, but worry rippled through her body. She didn't want Sienna to resent her before they met. Jane had never wanted a child of her own, but she had lots of love to give to Dom's daughter. And like

Dom, she wanted to unite their family as soon as possible. She wanted to be Sienna's friend and confidant in a way her own parents had never been able to do with her—the worst way to start was being complicit in curbing Sienna's freedom and ending her European adventure. "We do need to connect, and you know I can't wait to meet her, but I don't want to cut her travels short. I don't want to be a killjoy."

Dom joined her on the couch. His body was heavy beside her, and he put a muscular arm around her shoulder. "I love how much you care for her already." He lifted her chin and kissed her mouth.

Jane was surprised by another wave of emotion at his kindness. "I'm eager for us to be a family too, but we need to find a way to make coming home seem better than staying there."

"That's exactly what Peter said."

Jane tilted her head in surprise. "When did you speak with Peter?"

The name of Dom's closest friend felt unfamiliar in her mouth—she'd yet to meet him as well. The two men had become close ten years ago when Peter hired Dom to reconstruct the façade of the aging Venatura Hotel he'd recently purchased in the wilderness of the Fraser Valley.

"He called while you were putting on your dress. To wish us luck."

Jane placed her newly ringed finger on top of Dom's. "That was nice of him. How's the hotel?"

Dom flipped his hand over and clasped hers before kissing it. "Funny you should mention that."

She couldn't quite read his expression. Hope and possibility, but something else too. Concern? Before she could nail it down, he spoke again:

"If I asked you something, would you say yes?"

CHAPTER | TWO

THREE WEEKS LATER, THE NIGHT BEFORE THEIR DEPARTURE, JANE looked around the rented studio apartment that had been her home for seven years. It was hard to see her beautiful place stripped bare of its furnishings and washed clean of every trace of her presence, and she had mixed feelings about leaving it. The small space had been a haven *and* a prison throughout the dark days of social distancing. At first, the closed door had protected her from the unknown virus. She'd happily kneaded sourdough on the counters and hooked a bulky rug to lay on the floor. She'd finally read the novels she'd been meaning to get to for years in the gold armchair she'd reupholstered herself, and on YouTube she'd rediscovered her adolescent love of the turgid beauty of Neutral Milk Hotel.

But a year into the shutdown, the freshly painted walls had borne witness to her isolation-driven panic and the boredom of creative frustration. Crawling into the bed each night, sweaty with loneliness and fevered by lack of human contact, Jane tossed and turned. Her apartment had been like an overbearing mother who stifled and protected in equal measure.

Moving on was the best thing to do. Even though she still loved this version of herself, she knew her next act would be even better. A deeper romantic love would inspire deeper documentary work and maybe even a deeper engagement with the world. And now she had the opportunity to nurture a teenage girl—the daughter of the person she loved most in the world—who'd lost her mother at a young age just as she had. Jane could make a real difference in both their lives. Dom and Sienna were going to be the family she'd never thought she'd have and—until now—had never let herself consider. She wanted to throw everything she had into fostering a fully realized and incredibly fulfilling relationship with her stepdaughter. Then, after a winter of bonding with her new family, licking her wounds and recalibrating her production company, Jane was going to come back to Vancouver stronger than ever.

This was a good decision—no matter what Mickey said.

The bronze rays of the October sunset reached corners of the bleached hardwood floor that hadn't seen light since she'd moved in. Her dusty-blue, crushed-velvet couch—a miraculous find at the Value Village on Hastings four years ago—had already been picked up by a Vancouver Film School student who'd interned with Ember Productions the year before. The black milk crates that had doubled as her side tables and bookcases were in a storage locker she'd rented in South Vancouver.

Everything would be waiting for her when she and Dom returned after a much-needed break from the pressures of their careers. She knew their new life together would require a little reconfiguring when they returned to the city. But she wasn't worried. Loving Dom was the easiest thing she'd ever done.

As they had wolfed down a room service lunch on their wedding day, her new husband proposed a wild idea. He told her that Peter had called to offer more than congratulations; he had also made a surprising plea.

Peter needed Dom to take the role of caretaker for the upcoming off season, beginning in mid-October after Canadian Thanksgiving and lasting until the first of May when the hotel would open. The person Peter had hired had backed out at the last minute and he was desperate.

Built in the 1950s, his riverfront hotel—roughly two hours from Vancouver—had been catering to wealthy hunters, anglers, and wilderness enthusiasts for nearly seventy years. Peter had owned the hotel for the last ten and had been carefully renovating it with the help of contractors like Dom, to reflect both its storied past and enhance its contemporary appeal. His dedication meant hiring an off season caretaker during the fall and winter to ensure that the increasingly unpredictable and violent winter storms didn't undermine his efforts. Usually, the hotel would be open until late November to accommodate the hunting season for mule deer. But the catastrophic effects of climate change had forced Peter to change course.

Apparently, the area was highly susceptible to flooding during the recent onslaughts of autumn rain meteorologists described as "atmospheric rivers." The low-lying bridge that connected the property to the highway often washed out during the heavy weather. The storm events required someone to stay on-site to take care of the facilities and repair the damage. If Dom was that person, he could also take on some of the interior jobs that needed a contractor's touch.

"It's a lot to ask," Dom had said to her. His frown sketched two vertical lines in the space between his eyebrows.

Jane balked. Dom's brother, Ted, was already working overtime to allow Dom time off for their wedding and honeymoon. Dom's side of the phone calls with his brother sounded tense—sometimes hostile.

"How is Ted going to feel about this? Is it possible for you to take a break from the new job?"

He stood up and walked to the window. From across the room, she could hear his heavy sigh.

"Honestly, Ted would probably like me to get out of the game for a bit. Things have been . . . rough lately."

"What do you mean?"

"Working with family isn't always easy," he said with a slight grimace. "But hey, I can show you what the place looks like. Give you a feel for it before we make a decision."

He handed her his phone, and she scrolled through an album he had curated from his earlier visits to the hotel. On a remote property northwest of Chilliwack, the large, chalet-style resort hotel was nestled in a green valley watched over by snowcapped mountains. Higher up on the steep slopes, crystal clear water shimmered as it flowed through leafy green forests. Everything looked clean and fresh—she could almost smell the sweetness in the air and hear the gentle trills of birds. Lower down, closer to the hotel, the river widened and darkened to a slate gray. It was gorgeous. Best of all, in the photos Dom showed her there wasn't a person to be seen on the smooth boulders and sandy beaches that lined the Fraser River. The hotel seemed like the perfect place to rest and heal. A break from the grind of the city—and the cynical faces of her colleagues and peers—would be incredible. Returning to production with a kick-ass idea for a new film would be even better.

Jane's thoughts raced.

She stood up to join him and placed her hand on his chest. Exhilaration and fear swirled in her body like a gambler about to double down on a wild bet. "This could be a good thing for both of us. I'm at a natural pause in production. It would be wonderful to have the space to write and dream up a new project."

"You think so?"

The eager tone in his voice spurred her on. "My dad used to say that not pursuing an idea is like spitting in the face of fate. And this time with Sienna will be the perfect way to start our life together."

Dom smiled. "I've never heard that one. Your dad must have been an interesting man."

"He was," she said. At least when he wasn't drinking.

"It's a lot to juggle. We'd have to cancel the honeymoon. And what about your apartment? How will Mickey feel about this? We're talking about hitting the road in less than a month. And it's remote, Jane. The Wi-Fi is unreliable. The phones can be knocked out by storms for days—sometimes weeks—on end."

"Fortune favors the bold," she said. "We've got this far running on chance and good luck. Why should we stop now?"

Dom raised his eyebrows in an unspoken question.

She smiled. "Let's do it! Let's spend the winter at the Venatura Hotel!"

Dom closed his eyes and shook his head. He inhaled sharply, then he opened them wide.

"God, I love the way you make me feel. Let's do it, baby."

The details fell into place easily.

Dom changed Sienna's ticket and arranged for her host family to continue providing accommodation for three more weeks, slightly mollifying her after the denial of another full semester in Europe. Rather than traveling to Tofino for their honeymoon, Jane and Dom had used the time to hastily empty her apartment and restructure the operations of both their businesses so they could work remotely. The weeks had been beautifully frantic, filled with an incredible number of tasks to complete before they could depart. Jane woke up every day fueled by an energetic rush of longing for a new beginning in a place she had never seen.

Now, they were almost ready. Tomorrow was the big day. Though a tiny part of her still dreaded the feeling of waking in an apartment that was no longer her own, her trepidation was tempered by her excitement about the end of the preparations. She would meet Dom at the airport, greet her new stepdaughter, then travel together to the grand old hunting lodge where they would spend the next six and a half months. Following that, she would move into Dom's enormous home in the suburb of Langley, where she would liberate her belongings from storage and begin the next part of her life in love and acceptance.

There was only one obstacle left to overcome: Mickey.

Her oldest friend and valued production partner had not taken the news well. Jane walked slowly to the restaurant, hoping their farewell dinner wouldn't be a disaster.

"Are you seriously doing this?" Mickey asked in a deadpan drawl shortly after Jane arrived for their late-night dinner at Sushi on Main. The restaurant was nearly empty; only one other table was occupied. "You're throwing away any chance we have to redeem our reputation to go chop wood for the winter and cosplay *The Shining?*"

"I thought you hated drama," Jane retorted. "And I'm hardly 'throwing away' our reputation."

"No, I guess you already did that."

Jane glared at them. "I chose the truth."

"You *forced* the truth. On Carol and on me," Mickey said, raising their voice. "You don't think about other people's feelings in your hunt for this righteous truth you so revere."

The woman at the table across the restaurant glanced at them, then looked away quickly when Jane gave her a dirty look.

"You're one to talk! After what you texted me on my wedding day? What happened with *Failure to Thrive* changed me. I pushed someone too far and I will never do that again. Sometimes I don't make the right call—but at least I'm not too scared to try."

Mickey narrowed their hazel eyes. After eighteen years of friendship, Jane knew she'd gotten under Mickey's skin. "I don't want you to get hurt again. Keeping this from Dom is a mistake."

"I know what I'm doing."

"So, you're just going to leave me to pick up the pieces while you move into a McMansion to be all *Don't Worry Darling* in the 'burbs? What's next, baby showers and multilevel marketing schemes? Ember is going to flail and die if we don't get something going soon."

"This is a good move. Nothing will change with Ember. Everyone works remotely now. I'll be available online"—*so long as the Wi-Fi holds out*, she thought—"the entire time I'm at the hotel, and I can come into the city if we need to meet with anyone seeking reassurance about our value."

"So, I should just field the phone calls and schedule your appointments?"

Jane ignored them and continued. "This is a fresh start. For both of us and for Ember. The Fraser Valley has a ton of potential material for us to consider for our next project. Have you ever heard of the Hemlock Valley murders? Three women, all drug-involved, all found dead within three months of each other in the same area in the mid-nineties. Could be another Robert Pickton."

Mickey's bespectacled white face remained uncharacteristically dull at the mention of BC's most prolific serial killer. "You want me to wait for your direction from the sticks while people talk shit about us? About what you did?"

Jane heaved an enormous sigh.

"No one's still talking. You're being paranoid. But all right, fine. Get it out. Put me on blast."

Mickey broke eye contact. "You already know how I feel about what happened."

"But you won't let it go. We have to move on, and you most definitely are not. First, you refuse to be a witness at our wedding—"

"I had plans! You didn't give me any notice."

"I shouldn't have to! You're my closest friend. And why so much disdain for my marriage?"

There was an uncomfortable pause as Mickey eyed Jane. "You want the truth? You're using him to get away from yourself, from the mess you've made. And I don't like him, okay? He's basically the definition of toxic masculinity. He reminds me of every yo-bro loser who bullied me in high school—the ones you hated too."

"You're being so ridiculous—"

"Give me a break, Jane. Dom is a fucking caveman. He couldn't wrap his head around my pronouns when we met—it was like talking to my seventy-two-year-old dad. I don't know what you see in him. He's like the opposite of everything you value. I'm sure he votes Conservative. Plus, he has a mustache. He's practically a sitcom character."

Heat rose in her cheeks. Mickey's response was over-the-top and under the belt.

"You don't know him at all, and the fact that you're saying this makes it clear you don't know me either," she said, slamming her chopsticks down beside the bowl containing the last piece of spicy Agedashi tofu. "Everyone stumbles on new pronouns at first. Most nonbinary folks can extend a little grace, but not you. And I stand behind every choice I made on that film. You were with me all the way too, until—"

Mickey hammered their palms onto the table, making the tuna rolls jump. Their features were rigid. The woman turned in their direction again, but Mickey didn't back down.

"What we did was wrong, Jane. You know it and so do I. And regardless of how I feel about Dom, he deserves to know the truth."

Jane met Mickey's calm words with fury. "I did what I had to do."

"And is marrying Dom an escape route from the consequences of that choice? A chance to play wifey and let someone else make the decisions from now on?"

Jane swore. "Come on, Mickey. Am I not allowed any happiness? Should I be punished forever?"

Mickey shook their head. "It doesn't take a therapist to see this is textbook avoidance—"

"What is wrong with you? Why can't you be happy for me? I fell in love. He's loyal and kind. He is the opposite of every man I've ever dated—including Chien—who, by the way, you *adored* before he canceled me. Admit it, you're not the best judge of character either. Dom would do anything for the people he loves. You don't know him at all."

"But I know you."

Mickey reached across the table to touch her hand. Jane jerked away.

"Not as well as you think," Jane said. "He's incredibly encouraging of my career. He wants me to work while I'm at the hotel."

"His name is DOM! What other sign do you need? Should I start calling you Sub now?"

"Sure, if you want me to never speak to you again."

Mickey ignored the hollow threat. "So, you're not going to tell him the truth about our last film?"

"Why should I? The past is the past."

"So, what, pray tell, does the future hold?"

"We are both moving forward. He's working remotely on his contracting business too."

"Doesn't sound like a very strong business if he can just walk away from it."

Jane rolled her eyes. "There's not a lot of new builds in the winter. That's why he's taking this job. He's finishing the interior reno. And his brother is going to take care of any business in the city while we're gone."

Mickey raised one eyebrow. "The brother who chose not to come to the wedding?"

Jane bit the inside of her cheeks to stop herself from shouting. The stares from the other diners were making her skin crawl; she had to fight the urge to tell them to mind their own business.

"As you know," Jane said through gritted teeth, "we had to plan it fast."

"Did you though?"

"Can't you understand that I need to do this? Dom is my husband now. We've got one year with his daughter before she graduates high school and moves away. This is my only chance to connect with her!"

"How do you know she's going to leave home next year?"

"She's already told Dom her plan."

Mickey didn't respond. Instead, they looked at Jane doubtfully. Jane knew it was an interview technique to keep her talking, exposing things she didn't intend to share. She'd used it dozens of times and couldn't believe Mickey was trying it on her. Mickey should be supporting her, not attacking her. Their recrimination had been the reason Jane went to Spain. She would never have met Dom if Mickey hadn't blamed her for everything. She let the silence stretch and met their gaze.

Mickey caved first. "So, this is a family thing? You're going to be a mother now?"

"Stepmother," Jane said. The word was foreign yet thrilling.

"Wicked?" Mickey asked, with the hint of a smile.

That made Jane smile too. "I guess. Why shouldn't I get to have a family like everyone else? And it's not just that. Peter, the owner of the hotel, is a friend of Dom's. He's in a real bind—the person who was hired to work during the off season quit on super short notice. We're helping him out. Dom shows up for the people who count on him. I trust him and so should you."

Mickey exhaled loudly. "Fine."

"Fine?"

"I've never been able to change your mind before. I don't know why I thought I could start now."

"Okay," Jane said. "Good. This is going to work out. You'll see."

"It better," Mickey said. "If this is what you need, I'm here for you. You're not over it, you know. I can see it on your face. Telling yourself you are good and being good are two different things."

Jane clenched her fists under the table to keep herself from snapping back. She didn't need to ruin the fragile peace. Past events had never dictated her future, and she wasn't about to let that change now.

They signaled for the check; the server seemed relieved to deliver it. Before Jane could continue, Mickey picked it up with a conciliatory nod. "This one's on me. Consider it a late wedding gift, okay?"

Jane flushed from the effort of swallowing a retort that it should be an apology. This was hardly the first time she and Mickey had disagreed—they'd been friends since eighth grade, when they'd worked backstage on a hilariously overwrought high school production of *A Streetcar Named Desire*—but this time Mickey's criticisms were too personal. Maybe familiarity had bred contempt. A few years after graduation, they had cobbled together their documentary production company with nothing more than the small life insurance policy Jane had collected after the car accident that had killed both her parents, and the meager earnings from Mickey's short-lived tree-planting career. They'd been inseparable ever since—until the public shaming began.

"Truce. But you're wrong about him. Dom's different than you think.

He is a good guy. He set his daughter up with a trust fund so she can do whatever she wants after graduation—that's why she's leaving right after she finishes school. He wants everyone around him to succeed."

Mickey sucked in their cheeks then nodded. "I hope so. Unlike you, I can admit when I'm wrong."

"Um, didn't we just declare a truce?"

"Yes. But you know me. I can never resist getting in the last word."

"Ha. And you know me. I can never let you have it."

After a grudging but genuine hug, Jane walked home along side streets, to skirt the oddly diagonal intersection of Grandview Highway and Fraser Street.

She took a deep breath. The early fall air was warm and still smelled like the last of the late-summer lilies. The pleasant temperature and warm glow from the streetlights filled her with a peculiar future nostalgia for the moment she was living right now. She vowed to never forget the feeling of being satisfied with herself *and* eager for Dom. Jane loved Vancouver and the life she had built, but he was the right next step. Chien's cruel lack of support when public hatred rose against her had reinforced the idea that it was easier to stand alone than to stay upright when someone was pushing her down. Then Dom had arrived—the first man she could trust as much as she trusted herself.

But as she turned the key in the door of her empty apartment for the last time, the needling doubt raised by Mickey's last question wormed its way into her thoughts. Shortly before their goodbye embrace on the sidewalk, Mickey had looked her dead in the eyes.

"Dom's a widower, right?" they asked.

Jane nodded once.

"So how did his first wife die?"

"It's hard for him to talk about."

"What do you know about her? What was her name?"

Now was not the time to tell Mickey about their internet embargo.

"Her name was Melissa. And he's still not ready to talk about her. But we'll get there."

Mickey glanced pointedly at the ring shining on Jane's left hand, then back to her face.

"Soon, I hope."

Jane hadn't bothered to respond. Mickey was always like this when she came up with a big new idea, but they always came around. Of course, last time, it hadn't worked out well for either of them.

Her anxiety spiked as she set her keys down on the immaculate countertop. She didn't like admitting how little she knew about Melissa, Dom's first wife and the mother of his daughter. It was clearly painful for him to speak about—every time she asked, he changed the subject—and she chose not to press. For now. She had to trust the magic he brought to her life for a while.

What they had was special and not to be second-guessed. Because of him, she had shrugged off the lingering effects of pandemic isolation, her bad breakup, and skeptical friends. She was moving past the scouring reviews and withering public accusations. Mickey was right about one thing. Being with Dom made her feel brand-new, and that was what she needed more than anything. The past was the past. History could only hurt if you didn't know how to let it go.

CHAPTER | THREE

AFTER LOCKING HER FRONT DOOR AND LEAVING THE KEY UNDER THE
frayed welcome mat, Jane wheeled her large suitcase down the dark street
toward the Commercial SkyTrain station. She wasn't used to starting
her days before sunrise, and her underarms were damp with sweat before she'd settled into the molded plastic seat of the train. She transferred
to the Canada Line at Cambie, relieved to be running slightly ahead of
schedule. In an hour, she was set to convene with Dom at the airport
shortly before Sienna's arrival from Paris.

Though she was twenty minutes early, Dom was already waiting
underneath the Haida carvings that greeted visitors in the Arrivals
area. At the sight of her, his face brightened. She could feel his joy as
she approached. His sparkling eyes, tall frame, and dark hair finely
threaded with silver made it seem as if she were the one being wel-
comed home.

After wrapping his arm around her waist and kissing her cheek, he guided her up the winding ramp to the bustling baggage claim area. Unlike most airports, the domestic luggage carousels at YVR were unofficially open to the public. Dom and Jane slipped through the opening between two half walls made of dull gray stone, scanning the overhead screens to confirm which conveyor belt would hold Sienna's suitcase.

"Right here," Jane said, pointing to the second baggage claim area with rotating tracks empty of both luggage and surrounding claimants. "The flight must still be disembarking. They haven't got the bags off yet."

Dom slung his arm around her neck. "Good—I'm glad we got here before she did. I didn't want her to think I forgot about her."

Jane nodded, though she doubted Sienna would believe that. His ideas about what Sienna would need and want over the course of the off season had been both touching and out-of-touch—she'd had to talk him out of purchasing an unnervingly lifelike toy dachshund to assuage her potential longing for the pet owned by the Parisian family. His outlandish suggestions had become slightly grating as the number of shopping items increased. Jane didn't begrudge Dom—she could already tell he was an amazing dad—but she was also aware of how independent a sixteen-year-old really was. After all, Jane had been only two years older than Sienna when she'd lost both her parents, and she'd managed fine on her own.

She shifted her body closer to his while she scanned the travel-worn faces at the adjacent carousels, wondering if Sienna would be weary from her flights. From the photos Dom had showed her and the fuzzy connection during their video chats, she knew her stepdaughter was a smooth-skinned teen with long light-brown hair highlighted by strategically placed honey tones. Pulling away from Dom's warmth, Jane ran her hand through her bleached-white choppy shoulder-length bob, hoping it looked less disheveled than it felt. She'd always favored an edgy, asymmetrical, Scandi-punk vibe, but for the first time, wondered if she wasn't due for an image overhaul. She rolled her shoulders to ease the tension down her spine, then curled back toward her husband.

"There she is!" Dom cried.

He kept one arm around Jane as he waved enthusiastically to a pretty girl with a messy bun coming down the escalator. Sienna noticed her father when she was about halfway down. She smiled and waved back. The moment her gaze cut to Jane, she dropped her hand.

Jane pressed closer to Dom as Sienna, clad in a cropped blush-pink sweatshirt and matching high-waisted sweatpants, approached them. She looked back and forth at Dom and Jane.

"Hello," she said quietly.

"Welcome home, honey!" He removed his arm from Jane's shoulder and swept his daughter into a tight embrace, lifting her off the floor.

Sienna responded in kind, and the two held each other for a long moment with their eyes closed. Jane stood beside them in silence, trying not to feel awkward. Sienna was the first to release. She stepped back from her dad, scrubbing tears from her eyes with swipes from the heel of her hand. Jane recognized the gesture as Dom's, and her heart swelled for Sienna. Dom gathered Jane's shoulders in a warm, possessive gesture that she took as her cue.

"Hello, Sienna," Jane said. "I'm Jane. It's lovely to finally meet you. I've heard so many wonderful things."

The girl looked toward her with eyes ringed by teary streaks of makeup. "Hi, Jane."

"How was your flight?"

"Long," she replied curtly.

Jane looked at Dom for assistance. This was going to be harder than she had thought.

Dom chuckled. "Well, rest up. Still got two more hours until you can plant yourself for a while. Are you ready for a new adventure?"

"Is that what we're calling canceling my entire life to drag me back to the Venatura?"

Dom's eyes filled with concern. "It's only for a few months, Sienna. It's going to be great for both of us." He held his daughter's unwavering gaze for what seemed like minutes.

Jane grew uncomfortable. There was a current of tension running between Dom and Sienna that she didn't understand. She cleared her throat and Dom glanced at her with a surprised expression, as if he'd forgotten she was there. Her throat dried in irritation, and she swallowed hard.

"It will be great for *all* of us," Dom corrected, squeezing Jane's shoulder.

Sienna sniffed. "I guess." Suddenly, her eyes were glassy again, and Jane caught a glimpse of what Sienna must have looked like as a child. From the tender look on Dom's face, he had noticed the same thing. She wondered if a parent could ever see their grown child without the layers of every age they had passed through, realizing this was the first imprint she would have of her stepdaughter's face. She wondered how long it would take for Sienna to warm up to her.

Sienna moved toward him and hugged his waist. His face pinched with indiscernible emotion. This was clearly an enormous moment for them, and Jane wanted to respect it. When they broke apart, Jane smiled at Sienna.

"I'm looking forward to it too," Jane said. "Mostly to getting to know you better."

Sienna looked away and Jane kicked herself for being so corny. Teenagers and young adults usually responded well to her—she was often invited to speak at the Emily Carr and Vancouver Film School career day about her work—and they liked her cool, indie-filmmaker vibe. The smaller age difference between her and the audience gave her an advantage over other professionals on the panels, but Sienna was no ordinary teenager.

Jane pulled out her phone. "Can I take a picture of you two? A welcome home snap?"

"I'm so grubby. Hard pass," Sienna said.

"Of course, sorry. I'm just too used to being behind the camera, I guess."

"What do you mean?"

She tried to hide her dismay that Dom hadn't mentioned it—and her relief that Sienna hadn't found out anything on her own.

"Oh, I own a production company. I make documentaries. It's called Ember—like starting a fire, you know?"

Sienna's face lit up. "Whoa—really? I've always wanted to make movies."

"Maybe I could show you one of my films when we get to the hotel. It's not like we have anything else to do."

"Yeah, maybe," Sienna said, her sudden tone switch signaling anything but enthusiasm, making Jane regret her suggestion. "Dad, can you grab my bag? I have to go to the toilet."

"You got it," said Dom, already training his eyes on the bags that had started to slip onto the belt in front of them.

"Is she okay?" Jane asked, grateful for the chance to talk to him one-on-one.

Dom's tone was distracted as he scanned the luggage. "Yeah. Long flight, I guess."

"Sure—she must be exhausted," Jane said. "She just seemed a little . . . off. Or maybe she's always like that?"

Dom was too preoccupied to answer. He darted forward to lift an enormous black suitcase from the rack with one arm. Despite how many times she had seen him in action, his strength always impressed her. She took a deep reassuring breath. Their family wouldn't be built in a moment, or a day, or even a season. Jane wasn't a patient person by nature, but for Dom and Sienna, she could learn.

As soon as Sienna returned, Dom led them out of the airport with swift strides toward the main exit. Outside, the light wind and budding sunlight revived Jane. She debated making another attempt at conversation with her stepdaughter but decided it was better to give her space. Sienna kept her eyes fixed on Dom's back as he cut through a small group of dazed travelers milling about just outside the terminal, walking fast to keep up with her father. Jane had to push hard to remain alongside. They climbed the stairs into the open-air parking lot where Dom located their vehicle with admirable precision.

"Let's go," he said, heaving the suitcase into the back of the SUV beside his and Jane's. "Peter's meeting us at the hotel at two p.m. It's time to hustle."

Sienna reached for the door to the back seat without comment. Jane had been prepared to offer her the passenger side, though long drives often nauseated her. Sienna's choice would save her from witnessing Jane retching into the emergency paper bag she had packed. Jane slid into the front seat. Dom immediately tuned the radio to a local oldies station that she usually hated, but the muted sounds of Guns N' Roses were oddly comforting. She watched the combination of warehouses, fast-food restaurants, and newly constructed high-rises on Marine Drive fly past the window while trying to think of something to say to Sienna.

"Did you get to see the Louvre?" she asked as Dom pulled into the left lane to turn onto Boundary Road, which would lead them back to the Trans-Canada Highway.

No response. Jane looked over her shoulder. Sienna was fast asleep, her head lolling on a pink travel pillow circling her neck. Despite the immaculate contouring and expertly applied (though slightly smudged) eye makeup, the teenager's face was vulnerable. Jane turned back toward the road in front of them, and Dom placed a reassuring hand on her thigh. He stopped a generous distance behind the Evo car ahead and indicated to a truck turning right that he was letting them into the flow of traffic. She loved that he was a respectful driver—there was nothing she hated more than an aggressive man behind the wheel.

"She asleep?" he asked softly.

"Yes."

Dom smiled. "She's been like that since she was a baby. Get her in a car and it's lights-out."

"I'm the same way," Jane said. "Unless my motion sickness gets the better of me."

"Oh, Sienna gets that too."

So, they had something in common other than Dom, though it was hardly a conversation starter.

"Yeah, I've had more than a few close calls." She chuckled. "My first road trip with Mickey was a doozy. We were heading to Oregon, so we had to cross the border. We got into the line-up—you know the spot when you can't pull over?"

Dom nodded.

"My stomach was going wild with all the stopping and starting. I couldn't get it under control, and we had no bucket, nothing. I had to throw up in Mickey's favorite toque."

Dom laughed. "That's a good friend right there."

"Yes, they really are."

"Peter saved my butt like that too. Long time ago, back when we first met, I had a few too many drinks on the job site after work. I was supposed to drive home, but he offered me a room for the night instead. Kept me from making a bad choice. It was the moment I realized he was a true friend."

"That's nice," Jane said, forcing down a wobble of unease at his casual mention of substance abuse with a deep yawn. "I'm looking forward to meeting him."

"Yeah, he feels the same way. How about this? Let's avoid any nausea-related catastrophes. You rest, I'll drive."

"Deal."

She closed her eyes and let the road lull her to sleep.

CHAPTER | FOUR

SHE WOKE UP TO THE CHIRP OF THE TURN SIGNAL. DOM HAD POSI-
tioned the car to exit on the right-hand side of the highway. Jane stretched
and Dom looked her way.

"Gotta fill up," Dom said. "This is the last gas station before the hotel."

"Sounds good," Jane replied with a sleepy smile.

Their small SUV was now in a narrow, wooded valley. Dom navigated
them onto an exit road flanked by steep, treed mountains crowding out
the lemony sunlight that had been shining in early morning Vancouver.
Here, the light was blue and dim as if someone had added an ambient
filter to the world. She glanced at the clock on the dashboard. It was just
past noon, but the gloom made it seem later. Dom eased the SUV to a halt
in front of the one free pump at a small but busy gas station.

A harried white woman with a stain on her stretched-out, oatmeal-
colored top stood at the pump beside them, eyes closed as the gas gurgled
into her tank. In her back seat, Jane could see two screaming toddlers,

red-faced but (mercifully) silenced by the closed car windows. At the pump in front of the tired woman was an Indigenous man in a baseball cap, T-shirt, and jeans, filling up a large late-model Ford truck with two enormous ATVs strapped to the bed by orange cords.

Directly in front of the pumps, cars and trucks were parked between faded diagonal lines on a slope that was steep enough to appear vaguely threatening. Jane imagined gravity coaxing the parked vehicles to roll over the low curb across the narrow two-lane road before being dumped into the grassy ditch beside the highway. She shook her head to remove the intrusive thought.

Sienna was silent in the back seat. Jane turned to see if she was still sleeping. As soon as her gaze hit Sienna, the girl jerked her seat belt off.

"Why are we stopping?"

Dom, who'd been checking his phone, angled his torso to face her.

"We always stop here."

"I know, Dad. That's why I'm asking. Doesn't it seem disrespectful?"

Dom stiffened. Jane looked back and forth between the two in confusion.

"Do you even care?" Sienna pressed.

The hollow expression on Dom's face was unmoving—nearly frozen.

Sienna lunged for the door. "Fine. Don't answer. Just forget it. I need coffee anyway."

Her voice was too loud for the small SUV, and it jolted Dom from his stupor. He nodded and handed her a twenty from his wallet.

"Go in and get what you want. I'll fill the tank."

Sienna slammed the door hard enough to rattle Jane's teeth, but Dom seemed unfazed. He exited the vehicle as Sienna entered the low, cedar-shingled building containing a convenience store and a folksy-looking restaurant.

Jane got out of the vehicle and rolled her neck and shoulders. "Are you okay?" she asked, standing on tiptoes to see Dom over the roof of the SUV.

He seemed more relaxed now. His jaw was less tight and his face had regained color. She wondered if Dom and Sienna were always that strained with each other, or if Sienna was just tired from the flight.

"Bit stiff," Dom said. "Long time to sit in one place. You know what my back is like."

Jane murmured her agreement, though they'd never discussed any old injuries. "How do you think Sienna is doing? What was she talking about? She seems upset."

Dom's gaze moved to the storefront at the mention of his daughter. Once again, Jane found his expression difficult to parse. Concern? Fatigue? Regret? She was surprised when a smile cracked through the lines on his face.

"No, no, she's fine. Just a bit cranky from the travel," he said. "This is all going great."

"It is?" It didn't feel great. The disconnect between them twisted her stomach.

"Yeah," Dom said as the pump clicked aggressively to indicate the tank was full. "I think she really likes you. Listen, if you need a bathroom break, there's a couple washrooms inside. Grab us some coffee too, okay? I'm going to pull into one of those spots up ahead. I'll text Sienna your number in case she needs to contact you."

Jane nodded, keeping her misgivings to herself. Perhaps Sienna was a restrained person with most adults. Teens favored their peers, didn't they? And she'd just been ordered home from Paris, so she was likely to be a bit resentful. Jane entered the store, only realizing when she smelled coffee that she had no idea how Dom drank his. Had he added milk when they were in Spain? In the honeymoon suite at the hotel? Nothing jogged her memory.

She nodded at the clerk's half-hearted greeting, then followed his instructions to the toilets. She saw Sienna facing a long, neon-lit fridge full of bottled drinks, but the girl didn't notice Jane pass behind her. The toilets were at the back of the store on the right-hand side of a little hallway that connected to the restaurant. On the way, she dodged a wobbly rack of sunglasses placed next to a large display of Canadian bric-a-brac and camping supplies. Flag-emblazoned shot glasses, polished stones, and bags of Wonder Bread sat forlornly beside sun-bleached boxes of crackers.

Directly across from the door to the bathroom was a corkboard covered in home-printed posters. Amidst the ads for used lawnmowers and available babysitters, a missing-person notice caught her eye. A photo of an olive-skinned young man with piercing brown eyes stared back at her. Elijah Stanton, age twenty-one, whereabouts unknown, hadn't been heard from since October of the previous year. The sound of the fridge door opening and closing reminded her she needed to pee.

Inside the washroom, Jane was unsettled by the washed-out face and limp hair reflected in the mirror. She fluffed up her bob, pinched her cheeks, and debated adding lipstick before deciding against it. Makeup always made her feel as if she was wearing a disguise, and she wanted her new family to see her exactly as she was.

When Jane came out of the washroom, the store was empty, save for the clerk. She poured two hot coffees into paper cups—opting to keep Dom's black, but adding milk to her own—then paid and returned to the SUV. Sienna stared pointedly out the window as Jane slid back into the front seat and handed the coffee to Dom. She watched as he took a sip.

"Thanks, hon. That's exactly what I needed."

She let out a quiet sigh of relief as she lifted the cup to her own mouth. Despite her suspicions, it was rich and strong. Dom winked at her before pressing the starter button.

"Next stop, the Venatura Hotel."

Dom pulled out onto the highway. Out the window, the dark valley blurred past like a half-erased storyboard, its early potential obscured by the haste of the director to start something new.

CHAPTER | FIVE

DOM MANEUVERED THEIR VEHICLE NORTH ALONG THE SIDE ROAD that hugged the main highway.

"There used to be a dinosaur park here. We took Sienna there when she was little. Remember that, See?"

Sienna sighed loudly. "So now we want to talk about old memories?"

Dom didn't respond. There was another huffing sound from the back seat, which made Jane's neck prickle.

"What was I, like three?" Sienna's voice had softened. It was more curious than combative.

"Something like that," Dom said.

Sienna didn't answer. Jane dared a quick glance back and saw her staring out the window with a placid expression. Judging by their reactions, Jane assumed that Melissa had still been alive during the visit. They must have come here as a family—the memories had clearly affected them both. Jane's curiosity bloomed.

"A dinosaur park?" Jane asked. "Beside a highway?"

Dom smiled. "Yeah, it was odd for sure. We could see these colorful statues of big cartoon dinos from the road. Sort of like a cross between a low-rent Flintstones and a very tame Jurassic Park? From far away, they seemed like they'd be these awesome and immense creatures, but up close they were a lot less intimidating. Actually, they were kind of falling apart, and the dinosaurs had chipped paint on their toenails. We joked that I should come help them with dino repair, and Mom could give them pedicures."

Jane laughed, though the mention of his deceased wife made her wonder if the reaction was inappropriate. Dom grew quiet again. She turned quickly and saw Sienna had pressed her forehead against the cold glass of the window. She was biting her lip like she was trying not to cry. Jane wished she could think of something to say to make Sienna feel better. Dom broke the silence.

"Anyway. There's an RV park there now."

He flicked the signal to indicate a left turn, then maneuvered onto a road that ran perpendicular to the busy highway. A black-and-white sign indicated they were on Highway 9. The lanes narrowed down to two. Traffic thinned to nearly nothing—only a large white work truck chugging forward about a kilometer ahead. On both sides of the road were lush green farms bordered by white-capped mountains. A large green sign to Jane's right announced the town of Agassiz in six kilometers.

The interior of the SUV was as quiet as the traffic. Jane was sure Sienna and Dom were thinking about Melissa; she certainly was. She guessed they would feel more comfortable talking about her if Jane weren't in the car. But their tiptoeing around the topic made her feel alienated and awkward, like an outsider—and a foolish one at that. She should have anticipated that Sienna would resent her for trying to replace her mother. The sixteen-year-old probably wanted her dad to stay single forever.

Jane and Dom had fallen in love so easily; she had felt perfectly accepted by him almost at once. She'd assumed that winning over Sienna would be just as easy. Jane leaned back in her seat and closed her eyes.

The night she'd met Dom she'd already fended off several overzealous ex-pat suitors while dining alone at an outdoor café in the Plaça de Catalunya. He had been sitting a few tables over from her and his flawless order in Spanish had made her raise her eyes from her reading. She had smiled at his sheepish shrug and perfect grin, but had dropped her eyes back to her true-crime book about a spree of domestic airline terrorism in the 1970s. Unlike the others who had approached her, he had taken the hint and left her alone. After finishing her drink, she'd paid her bill then made her way back toward her hotel, swaying slightly due to her strappy sandals, the uneven cobblestones, and the sangria.

About a hundred meters from the café, a young man with shining black hair, glassy eyes, and a slender build stopped her.

"Oh, señorita, you are so beautiful tonight. You must dance with me. Please." He smiled, angled his body uncomfortably close to hers, and grabbed her wrist and the small of her back with sweaty palms.

She yanked her hand away. "No. Get off, don't touch me."

When he ignored her, she stomped down, just missing his sneakered foot. Before she could regroup, he grabbed her again and spun her in a quick circle, once then twice, fast enough to disorient her. As she tried to escape his strong arms, he thrust her into a dip. She smelled alcohol and unbrushed teeth on his breath. Repulsed, she turned her head away. The strap of her purse slipped off her shoulder and touched the ground. The man suddenly released her. She landed hard on the dirty sidewalk alongside her bag. She had barely registered she'd been dropped when a swift blur darted in to grab her purse. The thief sprinted through the crowded square.

Her passport! Her Airbnb key!

She scrambled to her feet and raced in the direction of the thief. Tourists standing by the brightly lit fountain stumbled out of his way to give him a wide berth. Unblinking faces turned from her as she shouted in English to stop him. When the heel of her shoe wedged between the smooth stones, she tripped and landed hard, swearing. Looking up, she realized the man was too far away to catch, and her chest compressed with despair.

Another shape raced by. A large man in a white shirt tore past—was it the man from the café? She squinted. It was. As she watched, his long legs helped him gain on the robber. Within seconds, he leapt forward and tackled the man to the ground.

She unbuckled her strappy shoes with shaking fingers and rose to her feet. Her breath was ragged and her ears were still buzzing. The man from the café approached, gripping the thief's arm in one hand and her purse in the other.

"This belongs to you," he said, breathing hard.

Intense relief flowed through Jane's body. She blinked once as the man met her gaze with a clear, dark-eyed stare. His cheeks were flushed with exertion and good health. Her eyes flicked down his large, well-muscled frame. His chest was straining against the thin weave of his linen shirt as he worked to regain his breath. She rushed to speak.

"Oh my god, thank you," she said. "You have no idea—"

The thief interrupted her by spitting what she could only assume were Spanish curse words at them both before looking toward a loud noise behind her. She spun around to see two uniformed officers striding across the plaza with whistles tweeting. When they arrived, the younger of the two roughly seized the thief. The café man released him without hesitation, keeping his eyes locked on her.

"Pickpockets," said the older of the two officers in heavily accented English. "They're everywhere. This is no place for a woman to walk alone."

Jane bristled. "Way to blame the victim."

The officer's expression soured. His eyes raked over her before turning back to the café man. "You can take her home, yes?" the officer asked her rescuer.

Jane was about to speak again when the café man stepped between her and the officer. He gave her a wry look before answering in what sounded like perfect Spanish.

"Estaría feliz de hacer eso," he replied. Turning to her and translating, he said, "I'd be happy to take you wherever you need to go. If you want me to. I'm Dom, by the way." He reached out his hand and she shook it.

The pulse of attraction diminished her frustration. "Jane."

He flashed a shy smile. "It's short for Dominic, but no one ever calls me that. Would you like me to take you home? I mean . . . um . . . walk with you?"

His clumsy invitation was as endearing as his bravery had been impressive, and the dump of adrenaline was making her legs weak.

"I'd like that very much."

After a terse exchange of information with the Spanish police, aided by Dom's translation skills, she gratefully accepted his offered arm. She walked barefoot beside him on the rounded stones that covered the moonlit streets. His presence made being shoeless seem romantic and not repellent.

"Your Spanish is excellent," she said. "I'm hopeless."

He laughed softly at the compliment.

"Thank my mother. She moved to Canada from Chile when I was young, and learned English well, but she only spoke Spanish at home."

"Good mother," Jane said.

"She was," he replied.

"That's important," she said. She'd had a good mother, too. Long-suffering, but good. And she should have lived longer. The professional turmoil and ensuing isolation had prompted Jane to think a lot of her mother since she'd left Vancouver, but as the light from the streetlamp above them turned Dom's dark eyes to gold, suddenly, all she could think about was kissing him. Though it was close to midnight, the air was still hot and sultry, and music drifted down to them from mosaic-tiled balcony windows. . . .

In the SUV, Jane shifted to a more comfortable position, comforted by the fond memory. She did not second-guess herself—it was a point of pride to hold true to her convictions—but she realized that her initial assumptions about the Spanish city and her now-husband had been flawed.

Both were much more magical than she'd realized. Here she was, about to be whisked away by him again.

Outside her window, the cultivated farms were slowly giving way to wild forest. She imagined an aerial shot of their sleek vehicle snaking through the rugged landscape—jarringly diminished by the enormity of the valley. Green leaves on the trees were curling and browning at the edges, the beginning of autumn decay. Fall was coming faster here than in the city. On either side of the highway were short cement barriers that seemed too insubstantial to stop a full-sized vehicle from going over the edge. Beyond the guards, Jane could see pools of brown water through the gaps in the trees. As they moved forward, the water grew deeper and wider, and the trees became sparse. The cement barrier was replaced with a steel fence as the murky ponds joined together to become the churning waters of an enormous knife-gray river directly before them.

Jane was transfixed by the scenery. She had never been this far from the city before, but she recognized the Fraser River from her preliminary research about the area. It was the longest and hardest-working waterway in the province. Of course, she was familiar with its southern stretch in Vancouver, relentlessly productive with chugging tugboats and high-priced condos piled on its shores. But here, the Fraser was raw and untamed.

A massive metal bridge arched before them like a modernist version of a covered wagon, robotic ribs caging them from the fierce rapids below. It made her think of early settlers, colonizers really, and how that history would have to be addressed in any local project she might find. Especially one that involved missing and murdered Indigenous women. The SUV hurtled over the rattling structure, and her stomach bounced along with the rivets. The smell of stale coffee in the small interior made the air feel close and cloying. Jane willed her nausea away.

"Almost there," Dom said as their tires touched asphalt again.

He turned right onto a narrow country road. On their left, Jane caught a glimpse of a low split-rail farmer's fence beside a cornfield before Dom

drove them over the smaller one-lane bridge connecting the hotel property to the mainland. The four storeys of the Venatura Hotel loomed before her like a citadel, positioned on a curved section of riverbank cut off
from the mainland by a surging flood decades before. Though it had once
been possible to drive directly to the Venatura, the charging, changing
river had cut off access—creating an island carved by storms.

The magnificent northern façade of the hotel was composed of ash-
gray wood beams faded by time and wear. The planks were impossibly
long and wide—and the immense grandeur of the trees that had been
felled to provide them made her gasp. An enormous wraparound deck
jutted out from the second floor, with smaller balconies on the east side of
the third and fourth levels. The churning river flowed around the three
visible sides of the hotel, promising spectacular views from the higher
vantages. Behind the hotel was a massive forest of looming Douglas fir,
towering spruce, and quivering aspen: deep, dark, and shadowy.

"Wow," she said as their SUV crunched to a halt on the gravel stones
of the circular driveway that looped back onto itself to lead guests out.
"This is gorgeous."

Dom looked at her with his head cocked to the side.

"I'm glad you like it. It's a pretty special place."

Sienna made a choking sound from the back seat before her door
opened and slammed shut with the same ferocity as before. Jane flinched
but tried to hide it by reaching for the handle of the passenger side.

The roar of the river drowned out her thoughts as she stepped from
the vehicle. Overly oxygenated air flooded her lungs, and her scalp prickled with the bite of sharp wind cooled by the glacier-fed current flowing
meters away from her body. She shivered. It was colder than she expected,
and her boiled wool coat wasn't as effective here as in the shielded streets
of the city. Half a dozen stairs beckoned them toward huge French doors
flanked by driftwood sculptures. The thick glass panes were framed
with wood. At the top of the stairs—which were carpeted in a tasteful
rough-woven dark-brown fabric—was a tall white man wearing a long
charcoal-gray overcoat.

"Peter!" Dom said as he closed his car door.

Sienna didn't bother with a verbal greeting. Instead, she rushed into Peter's arms. His somber face cracked into a wide smile, but he held her awkwardly. When the embrace ended, Sienna positioned herself at Peter's side, facing Jane and Dom as if battle lines had been drawn. Dom bounded up the steps to shake Peter's hand with two sure pumps; Peter clasped Dom's upper arm with his free hand.

Jane followed Dom, bristling at his lack of inclusion. When she got closer, she realized Peter was older than she had first assumed—likely ten to fifteen years Dom's senior. The wrinkles bracketing his eyes and mouth were permanent grooves on his otherwise smooth skin, while Dom's lines were still faint. Though Peter was handsome in a gray-eyed, thin-lipped patrician sort of way, he was not warm or hospitable. A strange quality in a hotelier.

"I'm Jane Duvall," she said, extending her hand in greeting, though the icy wind blowing off the water had already made it uncomfortably cold to touch.

Peter didn't register any discomfort as he shook it. "A pleasure to meet you, Jane. I've heard wonderful things. Congratulations on your marriage." His crisp British accent was as elegant as his simple firm handshake.

"She didn't even bother to change her name?" Sienna muttered to her father, in a voice pitched to be heard by all.

Jane addressed her directly. "I chose not to, Sienna. It didn't make sense for me to do that. I'm at a critical point with my production company, and I don't want anyone to get confused when they're deciding to fund my next project."

"Jane is a documentary filmmaker," Dom said to Peter with a smile in her direction.

Out of the corner of her eye, Jane thought she saw her stepdaughter roll hers, but she focused on Peter, who was nodding agreeably.

"I believe you mentioned that on the telephone. And what kind of stories do you tell, Jane?" he asked.

"Mainly true crime."

"Ah, I see," Peter said with a glance at Dom. "I suppose we'll have to be on the lookout for any untoward activities, then. Fodder for your next project. But no bad press, please. This renovation won't pay for itself."

Dom chuckled good-naturedly. "I've already told Jane to start investigating who keeps chewing on all the garden hoses." He flashed her a winning smile.

But Jane wasn't so easily swayed. "Surely a hotel as old as this one has *some* stories to tell."

"Indeed, it does," Peter said. "And I'll leave it to Dom to tell you the very best ones."

His gray eyes burrowed into hers before he tipped his head toward the door. "Shall we?"

He placed his hands on the polished nickel handles of the front doors and opened them wide.

CHAPTER | SIX

JANE'S HEART QUICKENED AS SHE FOLLOWED PETER INTO THE VENA-tura Hotel, with Dom and Sienna close behind. She took one step inside, then stopped short. The exterior of the hotel had been stunning, but the interior took her breath away. She had been expecting a slightly dated design reflecting the hotel's history and primary purpose as a hunting lodge—gun racks and wine-colored carpet, green glass banker lamps and a mounted deer head or two. Instead, she found herself in a different aesthetic entirely.

To the right of the enormous lobby was an exquisitely sanded front desk made of bleached wood that begged to be touched. The whorls of the natural grain created an elegant, subtle façade polished to the sweet creamy beige of crème brûlée. In front of the desk was a huge burl of swirling orange-and-peach-colored wood, hollowed out to hold half a dozen hotel-branded golf umbrellas for guests.

The floor beneath her feet was solid charcoal stone—huge, irregular slabs of dark granite seamlessly hewn together. The rock had been treated with something and was warmed from underneath—it maintained a trace of its original rough texture yet felt welcoming as a carpet.

But the incredible focal point of the lobby was a sweeping staircase that united the dark stone and light wood as the run and the rise. Its intricate yet commanding beauty urged her forward. She walked toward it, admiring the way its prominent positioning conjured grand entrances by beautiful women in gorgeous gowns. The staircase was clearly made for momentous events, like wedding receptions, costume balls, and exclusive cocktail parties. Even touching the gleaming wooden banister—seemingly carved from a single wrist-thick sapling that ran the entire length of the staircase—made her wish she had a camera in her hand. It looked like a movie set.

"It's quite something, isn't it?" Peter said with pride.

He stood beside Dom and Sienna by the front desk. All three of them seemed quietly awestruck by the West Coast elegance too. The fact that they were entranced by the beauty of their surroundings despite their familiarity made her feel better about her effusiveness.

"It's astonishing," Jane replied. "This is beyond my wildest dreams. Your designer is incredibly talented—who do you work with?"

Peter blinked and coughed.

"Let's get into all that later, hon," Dom said as he took a couple steps forward to stand alongside Jane.

Sienna scowled and shook her head. "Oh my god, Dad."

"Wait until you see the dining room on the second floor," Dom said, putting his arm around Jane's waist. "Incredible views of the river and the mountains."

"The first and second floors have been completely redone," Peter said in a measured tone. "Between the third and fourth floors there are forty-eight guest rooms in total. The fourth floor is where our grand suites—the most luxurious of our rooms—are located, alongside our higher-end guest rooms. They have all been completely refurbished, but Dom will be redoing the hallways up there. The third floor—featuring our most affordable rooms—has not been redecorated since the late 1990s, and Dom will be tackling those too. We had plans to pursue the entire project last year, including finishing the fourth floor and completely overhauling the third, but we had to pivot."

Sienna huffed again. "Don't need the tour. I'm getting my suitcase."

Peter looked at her departing form with concern. "Sienna, I'd be happy to help—"

Dom interrupted.

"It's okay, Peter. I've got this. She's still a bit unsettled from the trip. It might take her a while to get used to being here." Dom was gracious enough not to mention his marriage to Jane, which Jane suspected was the real reason behind Sienna's bad attitude.

"Ah," Peter replied, pursing his lips. "Well, that's to be expected, isn't it? It's always difficult to see a child without her mother. Especially a mother as talented and lovely as hers."

Jane blinked incredulously. Why would Peter say such a thing in front of her? Did he assume that Jane was trying to take Melissa's place? Did Sienna? Dom also seemed taken off-guard. His eyes widened at Peter, before following his daughter without a word.

Peter clapped his hands and turned to Jane. "Well, as you can see, there's much for you to discover here. I only ask that you temper your innate curiosity with respect and courtesy. As you've noted, this hotel does contain a few secrets. From my experience, most are best left unearthed."

Jane paused, unsure how to reply to the man's strange words. Part of her agreed, but she followed her instincts.

"What kind of secrets?"

Peter's eyes darted to the spot where Sienna and Dom had been. He turned to Jane and gestured to an open corridor to the left of the stairs with a pleasant but pasted-on smile.

"Should we continue our tour so I can show you?"

It was too much to resist, so Jane nodded. Her concern about Sienna's behavior and Peter's cold demeanor were momentarily forgotten as she followed him through the lobby. The designer had combined the rustic feeling of an old-fashioned inn with the clean lines of high-end Pacific Northwest design. Her gaze drifted up to the thick, white-washed wooden beams along the top of the high ceilings. They ran the length of the main floor, beckoning her toward the open areas beyond the grandiose staircase.

"The ground floor is where we invite guests to experience our elegant yet accessible comfort. Previously, this area was compartmentalized into the music room, ladies' parlor, reading room, and sun parlor. Our designer, uh, wanted to modernize the space. We knocked down the walls and opened the entire area to create a lounge. Notice the multiple arrangements for small groups and for individuals seeking a quiet place to read or rest."

As he spoke, he led Jane past the staircase into the main area. The lounge was huge—at least the size of a school gymnasium—but the floor-to-ceiling windows on the front wall made it appear almost infinite. It was like there was no division between the stone floor under their feet and the rocky beach of the Fraser River that swirled and dipped wildly around three sides of the hotel. She had to tighten her jaw to keep it from dropping.

Soft armchairs, couches, and love seats upholstered in tasteful tones of oatmeal and caramel were placed in conversational settings or reading nooks throughout the expansive space. A long, bleached-wood table with the same finish as the front desk ran half the length of the west wall, about five meters from a large wood-burning fireplace surrounded by inlaid river rock. It was surrounded by matching wooden chairs like an immense reading room in a modern library. A stack of beautifully cut kindling and firewood rested in a low-lying open shelf beside it.

Jane drew in a breath.

"Peter, this is . . . indescribable. Have you ever thought about organizing a media tour? I have a few friends who freelance. A piece on the design choices might give business a boost."

Peter was too focused on his description of the hotel to hear her question.

"The only vestigial room in the hotel is one our long-standing guests couldn't bear to part with—and it's a clue to those secrets I mentioned before. On the west side of this floor"—he gestured to a door on their right—"is the Bourbon Room. Intact and unchanged from the fifties, much to our designer's chagrin."

He chuckled, deprecatingly, leading Jane to suspect the designer had left on bad terms. He stepped back after opening the door so she could peer inside. The imposing masculine decor could have been lifted straight out of *Citizen Kane*—exactly what she had envisioned the whole hotel would look like. She edged past Peter into the room painted a deep forest green. A loamy must of cigars and scotch infused a thick but worn Persian carpet swirling with a bloodred and mustard-yellow design. The heavy leather furniture was as brown and worn as an old saddle. The walls were predictably adorned with mounted animal heads: a stag with a massive rack of antlers, a snarling wolf with yellow eyes, and a bighorn sheep whose horns were thicker than her forearm. Carefully placed under each trophy were sturdy gun racks. All of them empty.

"Where are all the guns?" she asked.

"I had them removed last year," he replied.

"A hunting lodge with no guns? There's a dark secret in that, I bet." She smiled, inviting him to elaborate.

He didn't return it. "Perhaps those can be left alone for now." He pointed to an adjoining door on the opposite wall. "The Bourbon Room also connects with the staff rooms on this floor. Lots of unexpected servant passages in old hotels. It's never a bad thing to respect history, wouldn't you agree?"

"Yes, absolutely. You've done an incredible job of marrying the old and new."

Peter made a small noise in the back of his throat. He gestured for her to leave the room, then shut the door behind them.

"Have we now? How interesting that you noticed. On the west side of the second floor, we have the working rooms in the hotel—the kitchen, scullery, and linen rooms, accessible to staff only. You of course have the run of the place, but you will likely be preparing food and dining in the staff quarters."

An image of a tawdry room unbefitting guests came to her mind. "Staff quarters?"

Peter paused.

"I've just realized that it really should be Dom who shows you around the rest of the hotel. When he called to ask about the caretaking role, he was quite enthusiastic about being able to share this with you. Exuberant, even."

Jane looked at Peter in surprise. "Wait. Dom called *you?*"

Footsteps from the lobby made them both turn in the direction they'd come. Sienna marched across the granite floor, suitcase in tow. Rather than acknowledging them, she headed directly to a bank of elevators on the western wall of the lobby that Jane hadn't noticed before.

"Everything all right?" Peter called.

Dom nodded as he crossed the wide expanse to join them. The room was so large that he had to pitch his voice to reach them.

"Just a little jet lag. Sienna is headed up to the fourth floor to get settled in her room."

Peter shifted uncomfortably in his impeccable clothes. "The fourth floor? I had expected you to stay in the staff sleeping quarters."

"No, we'd rather be on the top floor," Dom said once he was close enough to speak in a normal tone. "Jane and I will be in the Sunset Suite."

"Not the Sunrise?" Peter asked, feigning surprise.

Jane wondered at the significance. And how close were Dom and Peter if Peter expected them to occupy the rooms for the help? Was this some kind of throwback to the British class system? She reached for Dom's hand and gave it a reassuring squeeze. His rough calluses were as comforting as a cat's tongue.

The older man locked eyes with Dom, who returned the hard stare.

Peter gave a tight nod. "Of course," he said smoothly. "I have a few papers to go through with you before I take my leave—tedious but necessary, I'm afraid. Is that all right with you, Jane?"

Jane murmured assent, and Dom looked down at her with a weary smile. Jane was surprised to see his eyes were hazed with red.

"Are you okay?" she whispered.

"Never better," he said with a quick squeeze of her hand.

As they followed Peter, surrounded by the unexpected beauty of the Venatura Hotel and the knife-gray waters of the Fraser River, Jane felt another current: the strained friendship between the two men.

CHAPTER | SEVEN

WHEN THEY RETURNED TO THE LOBBY, SIENNA WAS NOWHERE TO BE seen. The three of them made their way to the front desk, where Peter produced a stack of paperwork for both her and Dom to sign—a liability waiver, a lengthy contract of employment, and tax forms. Jane gave it all a cursory glance but didn't belabor the process; she normally left that kind of thing to Mickey. She was eager to begin exploring their new—albeit temporary—home. Upon completion, Peter gathered the papers into a tidy pile, which he tapped on the front desk to align.

"That's me done and dusted. We are officially in order now." He smiled officiously. "But I must warn you, Jane. The winters are long and hard. No Uber Eats up here. I hope you are mentally prepared for the isolation." Peter paused and caught Dom's eye again before continuing in a brisker tone. "In any case, I've laid out sandwiches and some cold sides for your dinner in the dining room upstairs."

Jane shifted uncomfortably at Peter's words. What was he implying?

Dom grinned. "Peter, you old softie. You take better care of me than my abuela did."

Peter gave Dom the warmest look she'd seen since they arrived. "It's the least I can do. Now, I'll be staying in Chilliwack for a brief period to ensure you get settled. If there is anything you need—and I mean anything—my cell number is on this card. Please put it in your phone and be sure to reach out if you need me."

He handed Jane a simple black card.

"Cell service here is generally strong, but a storm can knock out the lines. Come to think of it, I should show you the radio in the scullery and the main control panel in our utilities room downstairs to make sure—"

Dom cut him off. "I've got it, Peter. I'll give her the grand tour."

"Of course. You have it under control. As you always do."

The two men shared a solemn handshake.

"I do," Dom said. "You can trust me."

"Indeed. You know I do. With so very much," Peter said. He cleared his throat. "Jane, please enjoy your stay at the Venatura. I know you will be safe and sound, but if you need me, you know where to find me."

Jane clasped the older man's arm. "I do. And I promise to take care of your beautiful hotel. You can trust me too."

"Trust is something that must be earned," Peter said.

Jane's jaw tightened and she responded in a clipped manner of her own. "And I will do exactly that."

He stared at her for a beat before responding. "Excellent. Goodbye to you both for now, and I look forward to seeing you again soon."

He slid the signed papers into his leather briefcase, then exited through the lobby doors.

Finally, Jane and Dom were alone.

Her husband raised his thick dark eyebrows. "Are you ready for your official guided tour, madam?"

A thrill tickled all the way down her spine. Now that Peter was gone, the Venatura Hotel felt like Christmas morning, New Year's Eve, and a year of birthdays all at once.

"I don't think I've ever been more ready for anything in my life."

He winked. "Wonderful. It begins in the bedroom. Jeeves will bring our bags up shortly."

Jane estimated it to be close to four p.m.—roughly two hours before the sunset. It was the midpoint of October, the moment in the year when darkness began to last longer than the light. Late-afternoon sunshine burnished the front desk, the staircase, and the walls.

Jane laughed as Dom led her by the hand to the elevators. "Everything okay with Peter? He's a little . . . formal."

"He loosens up when you get to know him."

He pressed the button to call the carriage and the doors opened immediately. Jane had only a moment to take in the mirrored walls and bleached-wood paneling that echoed the grain of the front desk before Dom closed the distance between them. In a smooth motion, he pressed the button for the fourth floor then placed one hand on her lower back and cupped her head with the other. He pulled her in for a soft, slow kiss. She closed her eyes and leaned into his body's work-built muscles, rocking onto the balls of her feet to stand tall against his height. He pulled her closer and the weirdness of the day melted away.

A gentle ping announced their arrival on the top floor. Jane smoothed her hair before stepping out of the elevator into a small open area with a bank of guest rooms directly in front of her.

"Where's Sienna? Should we tell her about the sandwiches in the dining room? She might be hungry."

"She's fine for now, safely tucked away in her usual room. Suite 412, right down there," he said, pointing to the left. "But we're heading this way. Come on."

She followed him in the opposite direction. Peter hadn't been wrong about the dated styling of the hallway on this floor—it was clearly in need of Dom's handiwork. The carpet was a garish '90s print with deep jewel tones. Royal-blue patches of sky peeked between twisting olive-green vines bursting with crimson berries and thickly outlined pine cones. She could smell its age, too. Years of damp and dust were trapped in the fibers.

Gone was the tasteful wooden wainscoting of the elevator and main floor. Here the walls were covered in a nubbly beige fabric, and the wall sconces were chunky and black, no doubt meant to echo the snarled vines underfoot. Dom turned to the left again at a T, then hurried her down a shorter hallway that had only one door. Number 402.

"This is it," he said as he turned the handle.

"Don't you need a key?"

"Peter digitized the entire locking system last year. It's all on the cloud—we can turn it on and off at will with the Wi-Fi. I've got all the rooms open for now. I'm going to be in and out of them during the restoration."

Jane followed him into the room and was astonished by what she saw. The tacky '90s had been erased. She had entered a whole new world, and it was gorgeous.

The room was enormous—easily the size of four standard hotel rooms, and twice as big as the honeymoon suite they had stayed in on their wedding night. Everything in the spectacular suite was bright and light. Just like on the main floor, floor-to-ceiling windows lined the exterior wall to showcase the sparkling waters and magnificent landscape below. The river seemed close enough to dive into. Behind it, the endless rows of tall trees blurred into a rich green and brown velvet of branches, needles, and leaves. Pops of orange, red, and yellow marked the last dance of the deciduous. A sliding glass door led to an inviting balcony, which she knew would offer an even more incredible view of the river and the valley beyond. At the west corner of the window wall, she could see the bridge they'd passed over to reach the island. The silvery water shimmered and undulated like a living painting. The gathering clouds and lilac sky no longer seemed ominous. Instead, the river stretched out before her like a watery kingdom.

Inside the room, the textiles and furnishings were inviting and tasteful. The wainscoting was the color of river-sculpted driftwood, providing a slight contrast with the off-white textured wallpaper above. The tempting duvet on the enormous bed was the color of the fluff on a pussy willow. The headboard echoed the wood panel on the wall—etched with shades of gray and white and silver.

"Dom, I—"

He cut her off with a kiss, hard and longing. When he pulled away, his eyes shone with lust and his voice was rough.

"There'll be plenty of time for conversation later. But right now, there's only two things you need to do." He started unbuttoning his denim shirt with one hand as he pressed his palm against her cheek. He kissed her lips softly as he let his hand drift down to gently encircle her throat. "Take off your clothes and lay down on that bed."

He didn't have to ask her twice.

CHAPTER | EIGHT

AS THE SUN SET, RAYS OF HONEYED LIGHT SHONE ON HER HUSBAND'S sleeping form. The room glowed soft and golden as if lit by a thousand candles. Jane could see every pore on his face, mark the growth of his stubble in the hours that had passed since his morning shave, trace the strong line of his jaw with her eyes. For the first time, she saw the vulnerability underlying his handsomeness. His eyelashes were long and dark—an unassuming semicircle of beauty on his rugged skin, and his faint snores rumbled like the purr of a sleeping cat. Jane smiled. She hadn't owned a pet since she was a child, but she fondly remembered Puff, the long-haired calico her parents had given her on her ninth birthday.

Puff had outlived her parents.

She slipped out of bed, had a quick shower in the en suite bathroom (outfitted with exquisite Le Labo products), then made her way back down the hallway.

While Dom sprawled across the bed, Jane opened the door to their suite as quietly as possible and slipped out into the corridor. She saw another door at the end of the hall that ran the length of the front of the hotel. She assumed it was the twinned suite Peter had mentioned: the Sunrise. Now that the sun had lowered, the hallway was mostly lit by the wall sconces, which threw warped shadows onto the carpet. She quickened her pace to retrace her steps toward the elevator. She heard a faint hum—the heating had kicked on. The low noise murmured like quiet conversation from inside the guest rooms she passed.

Jane continued through the open area by the elevator bay down the hall. She tapped on the door of room 412. No answer. She tried again, louder this time. Still nothing. Maybe her stepdaughter was in another part of the hotel? She took a tentative step back, wondering if she should return to her room or go to the second-floor dining room alone. She had put nothing in her stomach but gas station coffee since breakfast; as far as she knew, Sienna hadn't eaten since getting off the plane.

The door handle moved, and Jane startled. Sienna peered out from a small crack. Her face was bare of makeup and she looked fragile and tired.

"Hi," said Jane.

"Where's my dad?" Sienna replied.

"He's still in our room."

Sienna gave her an appraising once-over, taking in her wet hair and change of clothes. Jane became aware of the pleasant ache between her legs and felt a blush rise on her cheeks.

"Huh. And what room is that?"

Jane smiled. "We are in 402 at the end of the hall to the left."

Sienna didn't smile back.

"Mom and Dad always stayed in 401 because it faces east. Dad likes to watch the sunrise."

There was an odd challenge in Sienna's eyes that Jane wasn't sure she understood. She wanted to ask Sienna more about their history in the hotel—had they stayed here frequently as a family? Was it a place Melissa enjoyed?—but she knew the teenager wasn't offering an invitation. Instead, she donned an expression she imagined a mother would use when encouraging a small child.

"That's interesting. Maybe your dad wanted to try something new. See the sunset instead. Fresh perspective is always good, right?"

Sienna shrugged. A beat passed.

"Are you hungry? We should get some food into you." Jane cringed inwardly at the folksiness in her voice.

"I've got snacks in here," said Sienna.

The door was open four inches at most, making it impossible for Jane to see beyond the girl's small frame. When Sienna moved to shut it, Jane blurted, "Peter left us sandwiches in the dining room. I was wondering if you'd like to have some with me. We could get to know each other a little more."

"No thank you."

"Oh."

Sienna began to pull the door closed again.

"It's probably better to have something solid in your stomach before you go to sleep."

"I'm good."

"I know I get really shaky if I don't eat—"

"It's fine, Jane. I don't want any."

"All right," Jane said, raising her hands in mock surrender. "I just thought I'd let you know."

"Thank you," Sienna said. "Good night."

She shut the door before Jane could respond in kind.

Her stomach rumbled. Turned out even rejected attempts at motherhood burned through a lot of calories. As she walked back toward the elevators she gave herself a pep talk. Sienna was adjusting to the new life that had been thrust upon her. She was still getting used to the idea of her father being remarried. Jane had to give her time. It was natural for her to think of her mother, and to be offended at the idea of a replacement. But she wished Peter had been less odd about it, less confronting. So what if Sienna wanted to stay in the same room as she had when her mother was alive? Grief had its own schedule. Hadn't she driven past her childhood home for years after her parents' death, stopping the car at the curb to weep? She had to give Sienna a little space, a little grace.

Jane pressed the call button. Once again, the elevator arrived within seconds to carry her downstairs. It was going to be difficult not to be spoiled as the only guests in a huge hotel—no waiting, no hassles. She stepped inside the elevator and, in the mirror, saw her cheeks were flushed with a mild rash from Dom's mustache, and her lips were reddened and chapped. Sienna had seen the sex written all over her face. No wonder she wanted nothing to do with her. She had to be less brazen with her stepdaughter—she couldn't flaunt her honeymoon bliss with Dom. The elevator doors opened, and Jane stepped out onto the second-floor mezzanine.

Between the rungs of the golden cedar plank railing in front of her, Jane looked down and saw the front desk and a side view of the sweeping staircase. On her left was a wall blocking off what she presumed was the food preparation and laundry areas Peter had described. She followed the walkway running the length of the railing toward the open dining room that spanned the back half of the hotel.

Once again, the wall facing the river was made of glass. The views of water curving around the three visible sides made it seem like she was looking over the bow of a luxury ship setting out to sea. Inside the grand room were dozens of round tables made of light-colored wood. Chandeliers hammered from slender strands of bronze glowed above her. To her left was a coffee bar and, past that, a swinging door that surely led to the kitchen. A huge bar to her right was covered in subtle light blue and gray glass tile, which winked and gleamed as the last streaks of sunset poured through the windows. As promised, a covered tray of deli sandwiches and containers of assorted salads were laid out on the surface. She walked toward it, her stomach growling, before something out the window caught her eye.

Dom stood on an enormous wraparound deck dotted with elegant patio furniture and potted plants, looking out at the river. She made a beeline toward the glass doors that connected the indoor and outdoor dining areas.

"You woke up," she said.

He turned at the sound of her voice, his troubled expression relaxing into a peaceful one.

"You wore me out," he said, reaching an arm around her shoulder to fold her body against his. "But I recover quickly."

"For an old man," she teased.

"Hey, I took the stairs and I still beat you, Little Miss Elevator. Besides, I didn't hear any complaints earlier." He ducked down for a light kiss.

After a lovely moment or two, Jane turned to the landscape before them. The light in the western sky was an extraordinary red, underpinning dark magenta clouds, slowly shadowing the horizon and the farm across the river into velvet charcoal. Below their feet, the waves and rocky shoreline were in conversation. The water pushed forward as the gravel whispered its consent. She leaned into him and sighed. He had spoken a lot about his love for this old hotel. Now she knew why.

"It's a beautiful place."

"It is."

"Full of happy memories?"

"Some. I'd kill for a nice steak right now," he said. "Those little sandwiches aren't going to be enough if we keep at it like that."

"So how about rustling up something more substantial? The fridge must be stocked for us."

Dom chuckled. "Yes, Peter made sure of that. We may need to pick up a few things—I noticed we are woefully low on hot sauce—but we're covered for the most part. You're going to be in good shape to keep us fed for the winter."

Jane pulled out from under his arm and cocked her head. "Me?"

"Yeah, hon. I'll be busy with the renovation. Peter emailed me a long list of things that need to be dealt with. Unless you're ready to pick up a hammer, I'll be doing the labor while you keep the home fires burning."

Jane blanched at the antiquated sentiment. "Dom, I'm really not much of a cook, you know that. More of an Uber Eats kind of girl, like Peter said."

"Hey, I'm not fussy. If it's warm and fills my belly, I'm happy."

Jane stared at him for a moment, then nodded slowly. She supposed the division of labor made sense, for now, but she really wasn't into the domestic thing. She thought he'd have figured that out by now. "Okay, I'll give it a shot, though I can't promise it will be anything like what's usually prepared in this place. What kind of stuff does Sienna like?"

Dom hesitated. "She can be a bit picky, but I'm sure she'll be fine once you get the hang of it."

Jane frowned. Not only was she in charge of the kitchen, but she also had to grapple with a fussy eater? Dom smiled and pulled her back toward him. In the comfort of his embrace, she pushed away her doubts. Sienna had been anything but easy to please so far, but Jane wasn't going to shy away from trying to win her over. She'd make Sienna believe in their new family just as strongly as she and Dom did.

It was going to take time. But they had all season.

CHAPTER | NINE

THE NEXT MORNING, JANE STOOD IN FRONT OF THE STOVE IN THE EX-pansive industrial kitchen on the second floor. Custard-colored sunlight gleamed off the hanging copper pots and stabbed at her eyes. She was momentarily blinded, like an animal caught in headlights.

Dom had been irritatingly vague about what he wanted for breakfast. "Like I said last night, I'm easy. Cook me up your specialty!"

Jane had laughed at his naïve assumption that she had one, but he had been distracted by another call from his brother before she could tell him. *Mickey* would have understood how funny it was. They knew Jane had only ever used her oven in East Van as a storage place for scripts. She and Mickey lived on takeaway sushi, sandwiches, and salads. The thought of a banh-mi baguette and her friend's company filled her with a pang of homesickness.

"Don't expect much," she said to Sienna, who was still sitting at the dining room table her father had left. Jane was surprised to see her up early. Weren't teenagers nocturnal?

"I'm not really hungry," Sienna replied.

The dismissal in her voice had made Jane frown in determination. Fifteen minutes later, after a chilly search through a massive walk-in cooler, she had a chunk of steak thawing on the butcher-block counter. She poked at it, wondering if it was possible to cook meat from frozen. She pulled a frying pan off a large metal hook and approached the stove. Immediately, another problem presented itself. Jane had no idea how to ignite the gas burner.

She cranked the dial and examined the face of the appliance for a way to light it. The faint smell of propane seeped into the air. She turned the gas off and went in search of an old-fashioned lighter. A drawer close to the stove was full of miscellaneous and puzzling items: twine, long metal skewers, a deck of cards—and yes, a shiny red Bic! She was brandishing it close to the burner, keeping her face cautiously averted from the gas source, when she heard a low grumbling.

It sounded like it was coming from outside. Dom had told her that the exterior door on the west wall opened to a set of stairs that led straight down to a side road off the driveway. It seemed like an awkward way to receive deliveries during the peak season; staff were forced to lug deliveries up a flight of stairs. Now something was out there—and it didn't sound like the UPS carrier. Another growl, this one accompanied by aggressive scratching. Jane tried to remember what she'd learned about wildlife during a camping trip with Chien. They'd hung their food high in a tree to outwit bears. Could one be attracted to the smell of thawing steak in the kitchen?

The growl came again, and the scratching increased. Whatever it was wanted in.

"Shoo!" she called, cringing at the weak word. She rallied more strength and raised her voice over the scrabbling of the claws. "Get out of here! Go away!"

The wild noises continued. The hair on her arms rose in an unpleasant ripple. She grabbed an enormous metal ladle from a hanging stand behind the stove, then took a step toward the door. Had she angered the animal? Was it strong enough to get through the door? She flinched as a bang on the door made it shudder. Scuffling noises followed.

Then, a sharp knock and a voice.

"Hello?"

She dropped the ladle, hurried to the side door, and opened it to see a big, raw-boned man—taller than Dom but rangier in limb—wearing a dirtied flannel jacket and an orange baseball cap advertising chain saws. His light brown skin was weathered, and his eyes were kind. Jane placed him in his late sixties, early seventies. In one hand he carried a dozen eggs. Wedged under his other arm was the ugliest cat she had ever seen.

"Your neighbors are here to introduce themselves," he said with a fleeting sideways smile. "This is the local stray. Half-feral, half-willing to eat anything you give it. My grandson used to feed him when he came around the farm. Looks like he's been getting fed here too. They spoil him all season—a little too much this year, judging by the size of him. He's ready for his breakfast, I guess."

He unceremoniously dropped the muddy-brown tabby—the spitting opposite of her sweet little Puff—who hissed at his work-booted feet before darting away.

"I'm Murray Jack," he said. "You drove by my place on the way in. I own the farm across the river."

"Nice to meet you, Mr. Jack. I'm Jane," she said. "Jane Duvall."

He handed her the eggs, then shook her hand with a firm grip like worn leather.

"These are for me—for us?"

He nodded. "Call me Murray. Sort of a welcome wagon, I guess. It's something we like to do in this area, like leaving keys in the wheel well of our trucks in case someone needs a ride home. Consider it a housewarming gift from my chickens."

"Well, thank them on my behalf."

The man dipped his head again. "Heard you're recently married. Congratulations."

Jane smiled and looked down at the band on her left hand. It was starting to feel like it belonged there. "Thank you," she said. "Still getting used to it."

"I'll bet. So, there's just the two of you here for the winter?"

"Three of us. Sienna, my husband's . . . my stepdaughter is here as well."

The older man looked thoughtful, as if wondering why she'd garbled the description. She hoped that Sienna was far enough out of earshot not to have heard her clumsy words.

"Well, if there's anything I can do to help, you can reach me on the short-range."

"The radio?"

"Yeah. I've got one too. If the cell towers go down—and they usually do at least once a winter—you can get in touch with me on that. Range doesn't go much farther than a mile, but you can call me and I can relay a message beyond that during an emergency. Or you can walk over the bridge—so long as it's not heavy weather. Don't ever go out there in a storm, okay? This section of the river can surge unexpectedly."

"Okay," Jane said. "Thanks for the advice."

The last thing she planned to do was step onto a narrow bridge during a huge storm—she'd read *My Cousin Rachel* far too many times as a teenager—but it was nice of him to warn her.

"Anything else you need? Farm's slowing down now so I've got some time."

Jane hesitated. But she dreaded the look on Sienna's face if she was forced to admit she had no idea how to turn on the stove.

"Any chance you know how to light a gas burner? I'm having some problems with this one."

"Sure, I can help with that. I've got a beast like that myself. You don't see them in homes as much these days. Too dangerous, I guess."

Jane sighed in relief. Murray stepped inside, wiping his boots repeatedly on the mat before entering the kitchen. She followed him to the stove.

"Never worked on one this fancy, but I'm assuming the principle is the same."

He waved off the lighter she tried to pass him and showed her the ignition switch. As he pressed, it clicked impatiently before he gently turned the dial. A huff of blue flame immediately appeared under the burner.

"There you go," he said. "Ignition first or you'll lose your eyebrows. Smells like you've tried it a few times before I got here. Best to open a window and clear out that remaining gas or the whole hotel might blow up."

Jane chuckled alongside him. "I'm not the domestic type, so I appreciate a man with kitchen wisdom," she said. "I'm glad to have you close by."

Murray looked pleased. "Well, I'm happy to help."

They walked to the side door together.

"Thanks again for the eggs and the lesson."

"Yep. You're here for the season, I'm guessing?"

"Until March or so. The first thaw." She laughed a little at the unfamiliar term. After a lifetime of living in Vancouver, she had never experienced a true winter.

"Well, be careful. Last season was a rough one."

"What do you mean?"

Murray's eyebrows pinched together. "They didn't tell you when you took the job?"

Jane shook her head.

"Caretaker went missing last year. Far as I know, they never found out what happened."

Jane remembered the poster from the gas station. Her mouth dried as she tried to recall the man's name, but it hadn't stuck. She wondered if it was the same person—or if there'd been more than one unusual disappearance in the area. Her curiosity was piqued. Could this be the story she and Mickey were looking for? The one to turn the page on their last, disastrous film?

"What was his name?"

"Elijah. Elijah Stanton."

The name triggered her memory. It *was* the same man from the poster.

"What happened to him?"

"No one knows. Here one day, gone the next. Happens sometimes. Some people think he ran off, others worried it was something else. You might hear some rumors. Best to pass anything on to me, let me help you sort the wheat from the chaff. People get a bit bored around here during the off season. It can ratchet a suspicion into fact quicker than you think."

He put a hand on the door, clearly ready to get on with his day.

"Well, thanks for letting me know," Jane said. "I'll definitely tell you if I hear anything else about it."

"You're welcome. You take care. The storms aren't coming in for a bit. But best to learn that radio before they do, okay? Oh, and in the meantime, this might come in handy."

He reached into the back pocket of his thick jeans, removed a folded piece of paper, and smoothed it onto the stainless-steel counter beside the door. It was a hand-drawn map of the entire property.

"Wow. This is amazing, Murray. Thanks—I haven't seen anything like this yet."

"I always say that the best way to know where you're headed is to see what's in front of you. Good luck to you, Jane."

He touched his forehead with two fingers and walked outside into the crisp morning air. Jane heard his heavy steps thump down every stair.

CHAPTER | TEN

JANE PLACED THE GRILLED STEAKS ON THE TABLE IN FRONT OF DOM
and Sienna with a flourish. The meat smelled good—if slightly charred—
and she had added scrambled eggs and a few pieces of sliced kiwi to the
plate to give it a festive touch. This was their first breakfast in the hotel,
and she had tried to make it special.

The skies had cleared overnight, and it had become just warm enough to
sit outside at the round tables, which overlooked the majestic dips and whirls
of the Fraser River. The trees on the riverbank were still flirting with fall colors. Hints of red, orange, and gold waved among the green as the wind whis-
tled a gentle song. A solitary bird—white-chested with brown wings—dove
toward the waves, then rose seconds later with a jerking fish in its talons. Jane
stared in awe at the scene. Set against the stunning landscape, the successful
hunt could have come out of central casting for a documentary celebrating the
Pacific Northwest. She could almost hear David Suzuki's narration.

"And you said you couldn't cook?" Dom beamed at her. "This looks fantastic."

He plunged his steak knife into the meat.

Sienna pushed her plate a couple inches away from her.

"Is everything okay?" Jane asked.

Sienna didn't meet her eyes. Her long hair was loose now, hanging in painstakingly rolled curls down her shoulders. Her middle part was immaculate. Jane tucked her own hair behind her ears, realizing she'd forgot to run a comb through it that morning.

"It's fine."

"Are you not hungry?" Jane asked.

"Come on, Sienna. You've got to eat. We have a big day ahead of us," said Dom.

He was nearly half-finished with his steak. The interior was redder than Jane had anticipated—likely a result of its frozen state, which she had done her best to rectify in a massive microwave. Cooking oil and meat drippings pooled onto his plate. Jane stared at her own meal with far less enthusiasm than she'd had a moment before.

"I can't eat this," Sienna said in a low tone.

"Why not?" Jane asked. "Too rare?"

Sienna didn't look up. "I'm a vegetarian."

Dom laughed with his mouth full. "Since when?"

"Since . . ." Sienna trailed off.

Something meaningful passed between father and daughter. Jane could only guess it had to do with Melissa, but she dared not ask. Discomfort bubbled inside of her. Had her agreement with Dom—the internet embargo—been a mistake? How long would they tiptoe around the topic of Melissa? She pressed the tops of her thighs under the table and willed herself to have patience. She would learn what she needed to know when the two of them were ready to tell her. Like Peter had said, trust was earned.

Dom set down his fork and knife. The serrated edge had a pinkish sheen.

"Okay," he said. "Well, maybe Jane can whip you up something else."

"I'm so sorry, Sienna. I had no idea," Jane said. "I rarely eat meat too. I should have asked."

Sienna faced her. "That's okay. Don't worry about it. Like I said, I'm not hungry."

"Please, I really want to—"

"No, it's okay. I'll eat something later."

Seeing another opportunity with Sienna slipping through her fingers, Jane blurted, "Maybe I can show you one of my videos this afternoon?"

Sienna looked away. "Yeah, maybe." She pushed her chair back with a painful scrape against the wood decking. Dom and Jane watched her go.

Dom ran his hand through his hair, tousling it more than before. "I'm sorry. It must be a European thing," he said quietly. "She was never this fussy before. She'll get over it."

Jane swallowed hard to clear the lump in her throat.

"Don't worry, honey—you'll nail lunch and she'll forget all about it!" Dom said with a smile.

"Maybe you can give me a hand with it? I really can't do all the cooking on my own. I'm just not equipped."

"No can do. I've got to get down to the boathouse this morning. You'll figure it out. Women have instincts about these things."

Some women, Jane thought, frowning as he dug back into his food. She stared at the far shore, wondering how to shake him out of the 1950s without hurting his feelings. On the far horizon, a line of rounded blue mountains bumped up against the sunny sky. In the near distance was a tangled line of dense foliage. Though the balcony they sat on was a storey up, the tall trees on the far side of the riverbank still loomed above them. Through the thick forest, she could see the faint outline of buildings and vehicles and remembered the map Murray had given her. She wondered idly what Murray was having for breakfast. The man's comfort with the stove suggested that he could cook for himself.

"I met our neighbor this morning. Murray Jack."

"Oh yeah? The guy who owns the farm across the bridge, right? What was he doing here?"

"Delivering eggs. You're eating some of them right now," Jane said. "He called himself the welcome wagon."

"That's nice."

Dom wiped his mouth with a linen napkin the same gray-blue color of the tiles on the bar and the water rushing below.

"He mentioned something about the previous caretaker. He went missing last year. Did you hear about that?"

"Huh," Dom replied, rising to standing. "Well, off to get started. Peter gave me a list as long as my arm. There was a lot that didn't get done last year."

"Probably because the guy went AWOL. Did Peter mention the caretaker's disappearance? Were you here last year? Did you meet him?"

"Caretakers leaving is not uncommon. Peter's never been able to get someone solid in this role. Like the guy who bailed this year at the last minute. It's a seasonal job in a place not many people have heard of. It attracts an itinerant sort of person—the kind that can slip away without anyone knowing where they've gone. Doesn't mean you've got a murder mystery on your hands. But I'll keep my ears open."

A shaft of sunlight shone on the surface of the bleached-wood table, making their knives and forks wink.

"Great. If you hear of anything, let me know. It could be an interesting topic for my next doc."

"You got it," Dom said, pressing a kiss on the crown of her head. "But in the meantime, why don't you take it easy? Didn't you tell me that part of your creative process is a period of rest before you begin something new? Enjoy this beautiful place and let the ideas come to you, okay? No need to force them."

Jane nodded. "You're right. It's just . . . something about the caretaker story is intriguing me. Synchronicity, you know?"

Dom smiled. "My mother always said the best idea is the one you haven't had yet. Maybe this is how your wheels get turning." He rocked on the balls of his feet.

Jane took the hint. "Don't let me keep you. I'm fine on my own. I'm going to take a walk this morning—get to know the grounds a little."

"That sounds perfect. The east side trails and cabins are in a bit of disrepair though. I'd stick to the west side for now until I can get out there and get the others in better shape. Sound good?"

"Sounds great."

She rose to kiss him. As the length of his body met hers, his arms circled her, and he lifted her effortlessly.

"Don't be too long," he whispered in her ear. "After lunch, I'd love to spend a little quality time with you."

"I can't think of a better way to relax than that," she said.

She gave him a final slow kiss before reluctantly pulling away.

CHAPTER | ELEVEN

IF THIS WAS WHAT DOM CALLED A GOOD TRAIL, SHE HATED TO THINK of the state of the bad ones. With the help of the map, she'd found the trailhead easily on the west side of the hotel. Beyond the area that had been cleared for the driveway, the forest began—a wall of twisted branches and waist-high brush. Two enormous cottonwood trees, grayed and stripped of their greenery, flanked the gap where the path began. She passed between them respectfully. A whiff of sweet decay was the only similarity to the spindly versions she was used to seeing in the city. The little leafy trees were a pest to many gardens and parks in the spring. Their fluffy seeds coated the ground like snow, littering prepared soil with eager saplings determined to root. But these trees were different. Their height and age gave them a solemn, almost disapproving air. Even the trail immediately surrounding them was clear and flat, as if no plant dared grow within their grasping shadows.

As Jane moved deeper into the forest, the bushes and undergrowth seized their chance to run wild. The narrow dirt path soon became crowded by thick weeds and fallen branches. Had no one walked this path all summer? Every few steps, she was forced to stop and clear the way. Her shoulders ached in protest as the trail narrowed again about five hundred meters from the hotel.

Here the weeds were taller and wet with morning dew. The sleeves and chest of her lightweight sweater grew uncomfortably damp. She should have worn a coat; a breeze had picked up after their lovely breakfast on the deck and now the damp chill in the air was finding its way into her core.

She pulled out the creased map Murray had given her. The wind poked it from behind until she found a thick stump with a surface flat enough to lay it on. Despite its uneven texture of crumbling red rot, Jane was able to pin it down and get her bearings. The sketch was rudimentary and amateurish, but it followed the basic parameters of mapmaking: oriented north, buildings blocked out in squares and rectangles, trails drawn as simple lines. The handwriting was distinct and unique—the stylized lettering brought Mickey's well-formed script to Jane's mind with a pang of longing. Murray's farm was in the northern position, placed at the top of the page with the bridge connecting the property to the grounds of the Venatura Hotel. The trail that ran along the western edge of the island—labeled West Woods—was the one Jane had followed from the hotel. It began close to the kitchen stairs, then headed south into the deep forest before looping back onto itself.

On the east side of the island, a similar but seemingly shorter loop followed the river, then went past two rectangles drawn on the edge of the bank and a cluster of small squares nestled between the trees. The larger of the two rectangles, which stretched out into the water, was labeled *Dock*. The smaller—perched on the bank—had the name *Boathouse* scrawled over the top. The small squares were labeled *Cabins*. Dom had told her that the eastern trail and cabins were in rough shape, but she made a note to ask him for more detail. How bad were they? It might be fun for her and Dom to stay a few nights away from the hotel once Sienna felt more settled.

She traced the loop of the trail she was on and found another blocky square had been rendered at its southern edge called *Cookhouse.* Unfortunately, the creator hadn't included a sense of scale. Jane couldn't be sure if the trail she was on was five kilometers or fifty. She imagined Mickey's aghast expression at the idea of following a handwritten map into the forbidding woods. The thought made her lonely. As she folded the map back up, she saw a tiny tree—no thicker than her thumb and no taller than her knee—had sprouted from the red ruins of the stump she'd used as a table.

A nurse log, she recalled suddenly from Chien's attempts to lecture her on forest ecology during their camping trip. Once a tree dies, its remains provide nutrients and soil matter for new seeds to take root. Jane had found the idea of a baby sustained by the decomposition of its mother's body horrifying. Chien had told her to stop being so macabre.

A shadow passed over her and she looked to the sky to find its source. The largest trees in the forest—three stories high at least—stood in a towering circle of grooved bark, wide branches, and boughs with long, flat, spirally arranged needles. *Flat means fir, Douglas fir,* she thought. Chien had attempted to drill tree identification into her mind as well. Despite her disinterest, some information had stuck. The sky was visible only through a small gap in the center of their circle. The height and magnitude of the trees made her dizzy. She looked down and steadied herself on the gnarled bark of the nearest trunk. The blistered surface was reassuring. Perhaps the spectacular growth around her was worth the gift from the mother tree. Jane didn't know enough about ecology to call it a sacrifice. Was the mother already dead when the saplings began to sprout? Or did the tree die to give its offspring what they needed to survive?

Jane continued forward, the air sweet and cold against her face. The leaves high in the canopy shivered in the wind, overtaking the sound of the rushing river. A large red maple leaf, its edges withered by cold, floated down in front of her. In the distance she heard the chatter of birds, but she couldn't see any.

The ground cover erupted.

A loud thumping pounded the earth, and the air beat against her ears.

She cowered. An animal burst out of the loose brush, hammering at the twigs and grass as it fought to get free. A fat, brown-speckled bird rose from the ground and flew into the fall forest. Jane gasped, leaning forward with hands on her knees to regain her breath and quiet the rolling thump of her heart in her chest. On her last ragged breath, she tasted earth as if she'd drawn deep enough to suck in the soil under her feet. Tentatively, attuning to the quieter forest sounds, Jane continued around the curve in the needle-strewn path, kicking at the fallen leaves to ensure that whatever was nesting within would hear her coming and retreat before she arrived. With each step, the trees grew thicker, denser, and darker, the blanket of leaves underfoot heavier.

After half an hour or so of walking, Jane spotted something that seemed entirely out of place in the wilderness.

The cookhouse.

The rough-beamed, open-walled, wooden shack had been built in a cleared area beside the trail. Uneven stumps and rotting forest debris marred the site. The huge trunks of the surviving trees edged inward toward the building as if bowing to those that had been felled for its construction. Jane moved closer too. The ground beneath her feet became spongy and soft until she found footing on the concrete slab foundation for the roofed cooking area that fit three long wooden picnic tables with benches attached. In comparison to the earth, the built surface was cold and impermeable. At the head of the building was an enormous concrete-encased outdoor oven. Beside it squatted a rusted metal burn barrel. Jane saw a small pond just beyond the oven. Water-logged, leafless trees splayed fingerlike twigs to the sky along its edge. Their whitened trunks made them look like bones. One had formed a burl on its trunk. The dark maw at the center was a screaming mouth.

Her ears tuned into a quiet but unfaltering sound unlike the birdcalls and ground rustling of the wind.

Squeak, squeak, squeak.

It was unnatural and grating in the richly layered melody of the forest. Metal on metal. Her gaze landed on the cast-iron door of the gray-walled oven. It was wider than her shoulders.

Squeak, squeak, squeak.

She took another tentative step forward, half expecting to see the handle turning slowly. The wind blew off the swampy water, colder this time and smelling of old eggs. She reached out a hand to the coiled metal of the handle, intending to jerk it open, when she realized the sound was coming from somewhere else.

She turned to her left where a collection of corroded metal cooking instruments hung from the side of the burn barrel. An enormous set of tongs, a wide spatula, and a thick metal hook swung lightly back and forth in the breeze. The metal ring that attached them was rubbing against the jutting nail, shrieking in protest. Though the discovery made it clear that there was nothing to worry about, leftover dread prickled her shoulders. This place felt wrong.

The snap of a twig close by made her jerk her head toward the sound. She peered into the twisted branches that clung together, blocking her view.

Another snap.

"Hello? Is someone there?"

Blood pushed against her temples, pounding hard as she scanned the forest. Her body stilled as she heard footsteps. This was no panicked bird. The ground crackled with the weight. She grabbed a metal spoon and raised it above her head, its rusty edges digging into her palm. She breathed deeply, trying to force the lump out of her throat.

One snap, two snaps.

It was getting closer. Her lungs wouldn't inflate. The forest closed in on her. Dark green needles and mottled brown bark were all she could see as she took a faltering step forward, then another quick step back.

Snap, snap, snap. The branches quivered.

It was here.

An enormous beaver emerged from the underbrush and poked its head toward her. Its startlingly yellow teeth jutted out from its narrow jaw, and its dark shining eyes took her in casually before widening in alarm. It retreated with a shambling gait.

Her laughter was deep, loud, and humbling. The bird and the beaver were both signs, weren't they? Signs to wake up and get over herself. To let go of her ego. Nothing was ever as bad as it seemed at first. She sat down on the knotty surface of the picnic bench closest to the oven, pulling out her phone. She checked the comments that continued to pile up on her social media—vicious, all of them, though they'd started to dwindle in number as netizens migrated to other, fresher offenses—before dialing a familiar number. It rang once, twice, three times. Jane was about to send a text instead when a voice answered.

"Are you okay?"

"Yeah. Why?"

Mickey exhaled loudly into the phone. "God, Jane. I thought you were in trouble. You know I hate getting phone calls unannounced. It's so aggressive. What's up?"

Before Jane could respond, the wind picked up again and billowed into the receiver.

"Yikes. Are you calling from the top of Everest?"

Jane laughed. "No. But it kind of feels that way. It's really remote out here. I . . . miss you."

She expected her friend to hesitate but they didn't. "I miss you too. It sucks working all alone. You're the ideas person. I'm just the grunt who lugs the cameras around."

Jane smiled. "But you were the one who found and followed the Lindsay Buziak case. And I seem to recall lugging a camera or two."

The first film they'd made together at film school was about a real estate agent who'd been lured to a showing on Vancouver Island, then was fatally stabbed. Her murder had never been solved.

"I guess that was me," Mickey said. "So, how's married life treating you? Any new information about the mysterious first wife?"

"No," Jane said, swallowing irritation. "Except she was a wonderful person, according to Dom's friend Peter. But I do have a lead on something else. I met a farmer who lives nearby."

"Why does this sound like the beginning of a horror movie?"

"Shut up and listen. He told me that the last caretaker of the Venatura Hotel went missing. I was wondering if you'd want to do some digging. See if there's a story there."

"Yes! And in the meantime, can I look into what's-her-name? Which you honestly should have done a long time ago."

A mournful whistle came from somewhere in the boggy area beyond the cookhouse. It sounded like a bird . . . a loon? Jane had never been great at birdcalls, and their names never stayed in her head despite her father's best efforts. Before he disappeared into the bottle, he used to lift her up to watch the small creatures gather at the bird feeder in the backyard.

"No. Please don't do that."

"Why not? You obsessively research everyone you've ever dated. And now there's real information to unearth and you stall? You need to know what happened to Dom's first wife."

Jane steeled her shoulders. "I haven't been totally honest with you. I made a promise to Dom, okay?"

"What do you mean?"

It had happened in the afternoon the day after their meeting on the street in Barcelona. Jane had been lounging on a reclining chair on the balcony of Dom's hotel, wearing nothing but his old Rolling Stones T-shirt. The fabric was worn enough to feel like a nightgown, and it smelled like him too: pine trees and salt. He came to join her with two beers in his hands, dripping and cold—a welcome reprieve from the humid heat of the late Spanish spring.

Her entire body was wet with sweat. They had just had sex for the fourth time in less than twelve hours. She couldn't take her eyes off his bare chest, strong and thick, corded with the results of hard work. She stretched out her foot to rest on his thigh after he sank down in the chair across from her. He used his thumbs to rub the tight spot at the arch. It had felt so good.

"I want to make a pact," he said.

She took a swig of beer. It was light and sweet and tasted better than champagne.

"You want to form an alliance with me?" she had said with a laugh.

"Ha ha. No, more like a promise."

"Okay," she said, drawing the word out. "I'm listening."

"I don't know if you use dating apps or whatever. I've tried them out but it's all so sterile and weird. Women show up to a date armed with all this intimate knowledge of my contracting firm, my daughter . . . one even tracked down my street address and told me she was going to drop off cookies. Call me old-fashioned, but I'd rather get to know someone more organically. In person."

Jane nodded. "Yeah, I understand what you mean."

"So how about this? Let's make a promise, okay? No online searches of each other. No internet research, no social media. I want to get to know who you really are. Not your online persona."

Jane hesitated. She was more than ten years younger than Dom. Everything she'd ever done was online—her work, her friendships, her love life. She had never dated anyone without digging into their history first. But it felt right to eschew her past ways. After all, they'd never yielded anything but shitty relationships.

"Okay," she said. "I promise." The fact that their pact conveniently shielded her from Dom's inevitable rejection when he discovered what *she'd* done had been icing on the cake.

Mickey's stony silence on the other end resonated judgment.

"That's the stupidest thing I've ever heard," they finally said. "Like dangerously stupid. This is a man with a past, Jane. He's not like Chien, who failed to tell you about his obsession with women waxing off everything below their eyebrows. This guy's a widower. You need to know what happened to his first wife. You're married to him. He can't keep you in the dark."

Jane's cheeks flushed and she stood up, rubbing her backside where the chill from the wood had seeped through the fabric of her pants.

"It's not stupid," she said. "It's romantic. It's the old-fashioned way of getting to know each other."

"It's idiotic."

"It's what I promised him. And I keep my promises. You know that."

"Jane—"

"Maybe I don't want him to know everything about me either."

Another pause.

"Well, there it is, then. I thought you believed in what you—what *we* did to her. You said it was worth it."

Jane bit her lip so hard the flesh felt like it no longer belonged to her.

"It was. We had to do it—she gave us no choice. But that doesn't mean I want to tell my new husband all about it. I have to find the right time. And that's how he feels about Melissa."

"So, the right time is *after* you promise the rest of your life to each other? Got it. Hey, listen, I got a used car. Wanna buy it, sight unseen? Don't ask me what happened to the last owner, by the way, they're dead."

Jane held the phone away from her face, her thumb hovering over the red circle, seconds from disconnecting. The bird called again, a mourning cry. Jane brought the phone back to her ear.

"Mickey, why can't you respect me? I've given you something to delve into. You don't have to drag Dom's history into this."

The wind picked up at the same time Mickey's voice dropped. Jane had to strain to hear them.

"But what if Dom did something bad in his past . . . like we did?"

Jane gritted her teeth hard enough to feel sand in her mouth. "We made a choice. What happened next was beyond our control."

"We made a lot of choices," Mickey said. "And our choices hurt someone."

The speaker crackled unpleasantly as the air moved Jane's hair. She narrowed her gaze to a long deep crack in a trunk—the split was so deep that yellow beads of sap had bled beyond the edges. What caused that kind of damage? And how was it still alive?

"I don't want to have this fight again, Mickey. We have to move forward. There might be a story here. Look into the caretaker. His name is Elijah Stanton."

"Stop trying to distract me. You promised your new husband a publication ban, but I choose for myself, and since I made no such promise, I'm free to proceed. I *will* look into the caretaker thing, Jane. But I'm also going to find out what the hell happened to Melissa. Dom's last name's Lawrence, right? Just checking my wedding invite. Aha."

"Don't you dare—"

But it was too late. Mickey had already hung up.

CHAPTER | TWELVE

AFTER AN UNINVENTIVE LUNCH OF CANNED VEGETABLE SOUP AND grilled cheese sandwiches—which Sienna hardly touched, leaving most of it in her bowl and plate for Jane to clear—Jane convinced Dom to show her how to use the short-wave radio.

"That's not exactly the quality time I was hoping for," he said huskily.

She smiled innocently into his smoldering eyes. "Safety first."

"Always. Your wish is my command."

He led her into a small room on the second floor, attached to the kitchen, which she had assumed was the laundry. The industrial area was lit with harsh fluorescent tubes and had two long utilitarian stainless-steel counters running parallel to each other. Two deep sinks and a commercial dishwasher with a stack of thick plastic dish racks took up most of the space on the counter lining the shared wall with the dining room. At the end was a cart with shelves so high she would have to stand on tiptoes to reach the top. Each shelf contained a clean bus pan. There were several large heavy-duty plastic garbage cans beside it and another door beyond them, presumably to the dining area.

"The scullery, my lady. Also serves as the office for the front-of-house team."

He pointed to the corner of the other counter on the exterior wall. Tucked under a cupboard full of silver teapots was an old-fashioned-looking radio and a hard-sided black case. On top of the counter was a computer that was at least ten years old. A small filing cabinet was placed neatly underneath.

She headed to the workstation and picked up the radio. She knew her way around most cameras and had always been able to figure out fine machinery, but the radio had numbers written on it in a pattern that didn't make sense to her.

"Why does this look like Radar is going to start yelling that the helicopters are coming?"

Dom snorted. "You're much too young to make that reference."

Jane grinned. "My dad was a devoted fan. *M*A*S*H* just seemed like something you'd understand too."

He scoffed. "You think I'm like your dad? Should I start dyeing my hair?" Dom ran a finger through the slight dusting of silver at his temples.

"You're nothing like him . . . except that he probably knew how to work this radio. Come over here and show me all the secrets."

He joined her at the counter, but instead of beginning a tutorial, he brushed her hair behind her ear and kissed the sensitive skin. He spoke in a soft, low voice. "I was just thinking about how much you liked that thing we did in Barcelona."

The memory flooded her body. His lips moved from under her ear to behind it, trailing light kisses down her neck. Then he spun her and kissed her full on the mouth, teasing her lips open. She gave in, laying her hand flat against the front of his work pants.

He groaned, then whispered in her ear, "You don't need the radio. Peter stopped by and told me the satellite phones bring emergency services here faster than messing around with the radio ever would." He kissed her again, cradling her lower half with his hands before hoisting her onto the counter.

"I've never used one of those either." Her words were breathy and she was having trouble focusing. But her brain snagged on the mention of Peter.

"Sat phones work just like cell phones," he answered, burying his face in her breasts. "No radio lesson required. Which means we have time for this."

He sank down to his knees and kissed her inner thighs. She could feel the pressure of his lips through her thin canvas hiking pants, but something he'd said distracted her.

"When did you talk to Peter?"

"He came over while you were on your walk."

He snagged two thumbs under her waistband and began coaxing the elastic lower on her hips. When he gazed up at her from his kneeling position, his eyes seemed deeper than usual, pupils dilated, face flushed. It was hard to focus. He pulled her pants below her hipbones. The cool air and his hot breath made goose bumps rise on her skin. He sighed softly at the sight of her.

"You are so beautiful."

Blood rushed from her lower half to her cheeks.

"Oh, Dom."

"I mean it. You are the one for me. And don't mind Peter. He's lonely and cranky. His wife left him years ago."

"That's too bad," she said, the words choppy and low. "I don't think he approves of us, Dom."

His mouth was close enough to her body to make her ache.

"He's just jealous. Maybe he didn't do this often enough for her."

She laughed. "What? Teach her how to use the radio?"

His breath puffed against her most tender skin. "Big Poppa to Little Momma. Do you read me?"

She laughed again, tossing her hair back and succumbing to the delicious sensation. "Ten-four, Big Poppa."

He laughed softly and opened her with deft fingers. "Got plenty of time for radio play, darling. If Elijah could figure it out, you'll have no problem."

His tongue pressed into her, and she struggled to respond to what he'd just said.

"Eli—" she began.

The swinging door to the dining room burst open and Jane glimpsed honey-highlighted hair and a beige tracksuit.

"Jane, do you want to—" Sienna's face contorted into pure disgust as she took in the scene.

"OH MY GOD, DAD! EW!!!!!!!"

Sienna rushed from the room as fast as she had entered.

CHAPTER | THIRTEEN

JANE STUMBLED DOWN THE STEPS OF THE GRAND STAIRCASE TO ESCAPE the red-hot humiliation burning her face and chest. As she flew through the front doors, Sienna's cries still rang in her ears. Dom had hastily reassured Jane that everything would be fine, before hurrying after his daughter. Jane had been left with her pants down, wondering if she'd ever gain Sienna's trust.

At the thought of walking in on her own parents, she shuddered. To avoid getting lost in the past, she set her gaze at a point across the manicured front lawn sloping gently downward to the bank. Scratches and bruises were surfacing on her forearms after her earlier adventure in the woods. Rather than explore another trail system, she headed straight to the river. It was decidedly cooler now than it had been during her walk, but the sunlight was sparkling invitingly on the moving water about a hundred meters away.

The well-tended grass turned to sand then rocky beach under her feet.

Closer to the edge, the river was a more complex color than the flat blue it appeared to be from the hotel. Here, glimmers of blue, green, and silver rolled and rippled in the water. It was colder, too—a chill seeping off the glacier-fed waves. The incessant murmur of movement was comforting, like the gentle hum of tires on the road. When small whorls appeared on the surface of the water, she wondered what was below.

Jane wandered upriver toward the bridge they had crossed to get onto the property the day before. No wonder Murray had warned her about its frailty. From underneath, she could see how the wooden trestles had been aged and worn down by the relentless water circling the pilings. She spotted a large flat rock bathed in golden sunlight close to the shore and settled onto it before pulling out her phone. Might as well begin her research. She had no desire to return to the hotel anytime soon.

She typed *Elijah Stanton* into the field of a search engine. The first hit was a brief bulletin from CBC with little more than the facts about Elijah's disappearance—name, age, and contact information, with the same photo she'd seen on the gas station bulletin board. The next was a local newspaper, the *Chilliwack Progress*, dated August 2019. She clicked on it and enhanced a grainy image, which accompanied a short caption: *Local youths Elijah Stanton, Dylan Musgrave, and Randeep Gill cool down from the stifling heat.*

The three boys—Jane estimated they were in their late teens—were captured in frenetic action. The young man she recognized as Elijah from the poster was in midair, hurtling toward a body of water while his two friends looked on, frozen in a perpetual high five. She zoomed in to the finest detail her phone could handle, viewing the photo a piece at a time. In the bottom corner, she saw a wooden trestle that looked identical to the one she was sitting beside.

She resized the photo back to its original scale and confirmed the three young men were on the same bridge she was facing. The discovery made her scalp tingle—Elijah had spent time at the Venatura before taking on the caretaking role. There were two others in the photo as well, watching the antics from the bridge deck. Two women. No—a woman and a girl, both laughing. The tingle returned when she recognized Sienna. Her body was softer and her face less formed than it was now, but it was definitely her stepdaughter. Beside her was an older woman with similar features. Her hand was on Sienna's arm.

Melissa.

She'd been alive in 2019.

For the hundredth time, Jane wondered how she'd died. And when.

She zoomed in on the woman's face, her hands trembling, flooded by an odd mix of guilt and thirst. She'd never seen Dom's former wife and she couldn't help but compare herself. Melissa, of course, was gorgeous. Same high cheekbones and glowing skin as her daughter. Thick, beautifully dyed, light hair. Even in the black-and-white image, it shone. But it was her smile that captivated. Both Sienna and her mother had an open-hearted, picture-perfect expression of joy on their faces. Anyone who saw the photo would immediately know how they were related. Beautiful, connected, and loving—the perfect mother/daughter relationship. Jane's heart sank as she recalled how Sienna had just seen her. A tawdry, male-centered, oversexualized stepmother with half an inch of dark roots and blotchy skin.

Jane stopped that train of thought and diverted her mind to another: *You cannot compete with Sienna's mother. You are Jane Duvall. You are cool, you are successful, you are everything you need to be.*

It was hard to reconcile the idea of her worth with the reality of what had happened on her last film and the public vitriol it inspired. Jane could only hope there truly was no such thing as bad publicity. Otherwise, Ember Productions was doomed. Finding a riveting new story was critical.

She closed the browser and opened her camera app, standing up to ensure the entirety of the bridge was captured in the frame of the video. It was B-roll at best, but she always thought better when she was filming. Questions swirled through her mind like the whirlpools in the choppy surface of the river. Why had Elijah been on the property years before he was hired as the caretaker? Was he a local? A guest? Did Sienna know Elijah? Had Melissa?

The back of her neck bristled. The light changed as something behind her blocked the sun. She whirled around with her phone still recording.

"Hello, Jane."

She sucked her breath in with surprise, then dropped her phone to her side. The older man's eyes caught the movement.

"Hello, Peter."

Today he was clad in a cable-knit sweater and a pair of jeans that looked stiff and freshly purchased.

"I'm sorry to startle you. I missed you earlier when I popped in. I thought it would be good for us to have a chat. But you seem to be immersed. Dare I ask what you're filming? Are we to be the subject?"

"What? No, of course not," she said, wondering if Dom had mentioned that she was curious about the previous caretaker.

He continued to stare at her, clearly expecting a more detailed answer.

"I'm not recording anything specific. Just wanted to capture the fall sunshine. I've been told it won't last long. You don't have a problem with that, surely."

He smiled, but his eyes remained locked on hers. "The sunshine certainly does not last. Did Dom mention I stopped by earlier?"

Jane nodded.

"Oh good. I was hoping to see both of you, but it's fortuitous to catch you out here on your own."

He took a step forward, and she instinctively retreated. Her ankle rolled on a loose rock, but she kept her balance. His smile broadened, like he was happy to see her off guard.

"I've always liked this spot myself. Most of the time, the water is too high to see this rock, but in the late fall, it's a lovely place." He cleared his throat and paused before speaking in the smooth voice of an experienced hotelier. "How are you finding your stay so far? Are things going well with Dom? It must be wonderful to be newlyweds in such a grand location."

"Absolutely. We really appreciate the opportunity. What a coincidence for Dom to reach out to you just after you'd learned of your caretaker leaving."

He eyed her, seeming to understand what she was fishing for.

"Indeed," Peter said. "Though as I noted, it was Dom who put the idea forward when I mentioned it."

She seized her chance.

"Have you had that happen before? A hire suddenly falling through, or disappearing?"

Peter met her eyes in an unblinking gaze that gave nothing away.

"From time to time. Seasonal workers can be unreliable."

Jane nodded. "I heard you lost your caretaker last season too."

Peter raised one eyebrow. "My, you are a good investigator. Did Dom tell you about that?"

"I never reveal my sources," Jane said.

The words were meant to be playful, but they had an unintended edge.

A squawking crow flew past using the river as a flight path. Peter looked up, then back to her before answering. "Yes, that was unfortunate. But it's part of this business, I'm afraid. That's why I'm so happy to have you here for this season. A family is more reliable. If you don't mind me asking, how are you getting along with Sienna?"

This time, it was Jane who broke eye contact. "It's an adjustment. She's been through a lot."

"Indeed. They both have. Losing a mother like Melissa . . . well, she's not someone who can be easily replaced."

"I'm not trying to replace her," Jane said tightly.

"No, no, of course not. Excuse me. I misspoke. So, all is fine with your newly blended family? No troubles?"

"What could go wrong? It's been lovely. The fourth-floor suites are truly incredible."

"Ah yes. So, Dom showed you both the Sunset Suite and the Sunrise on the east side of the building?"

Jane shook her head. "We're staying in the Sunset. There really hasn't been time for a full tour yet."

"I see. Well, I'm happy to hear that you are enjoying them while you can."

"While we . . . can?"

"Didn't Dom mention it?" The smile returned to Peter's face. "We don't heat the entire hotel in the off season. It will likely make much more sense for you to move into the staff quarters on the main floor once the temperature begins to drop. Have you by chance seen that area of the hotel yet?"

"No, not yet."

"Ah. Well, the rooms are certainly more rustic than our premium suites. But they'll have everything you need to live . . . comfortably."

Jane looked down to hide her dismay. She could only guess at the state they were in.

"One more thing. Given your talent and expertise, I'd like to invite you to send me any particularly striking images you take during your stay here. Our marketing team is always looking for seasonal shots to include in their materials and the fall colors are beautiful this year."

"I'm not really that sort of photographer. I focus on the stories of a place—not the sentiment."

"I see," he said with a twitch of his mouth. "Well, I certainly hope any stories you find won't tarnish the reputation or standing of the hotel."

Jane squared her shoulders. "Depends on what I find. As I mentioned, I'm quite curious about your most recent off season caretaker."

A cloud moved across the sun, darkening the landscape. Peter's smooth cheeks grayed slightly.

"Ah, that's a question for our human resources department, I'm afraid. He held the position for a very brief period. Well, it's time for me to press on. I'm hoping to have a quick word with Dom before I head back to my hotel."

He turned and walked up the rocky beach before Jane could ask any more about Elijah Stanton.

CHAPTER | FOURTEEN

THE LOBBY WAS EMPTY WHEN JANE RETURNED TO THE HOTEL.

"Hello?" she called.

Her voice echoed through the vastness of the main floor, introducing an eeriness to the space she'd not noticed before. Her studio in East Van may have been cramped, but it had always been cozy. The space that surrounded her suddenly felt too large for three people. She craned her ears as rustling sounds came from behind the front desk.

"Is someone there?"

She approached the desk and popped her head around it only to find it empty. Her eyes trained on the closed door behind the golden wood of the desk, wondering where it led.

"Sienna? Dom?"

No one replied. She remembered her overreaction to the harmless beaver. Perhaps there was a draft somewhere, moving papers around. It was nothing creepy, she assured herself. Shaking off her trepidation, she walked past the desk toward the diagonal sun slanting through the enormous windows on the far wall. The clouds had passed, and the day was blooming like a flower; the sunshine, blue skies, and fall colors made the lounge more spectacular than it had been upon their arrival.

She ran a hand along the polished surface of the long wooden table, which likely functioned as a workspace for hotel guests who didn't have the kinds of jobs that stopped when they were on vacation. (After a quick search of room prices, Jane had realized that described *most* people who stayed here, minus the lucky few who had inherited or accrued enough wealth not to have to work at all.) The surface of the table was warm beneath the pads of her fingers. Yesterday, her attention had been focused on the rushing waters of the river beyond the glass. Today, an art piece hanging above the gorgeous stone fireplace on the west wall caught her eye.

It was huge—easily two meters across. In the center was a circle of sapphire-blue concentric layers wheeling around and around until an exterior ring of earth brown interrupted the beautiful sea of blue. There was a perplexing depth to the piece—a mesmerizing three-dimensionality. She got closer. Once she was standing near enough to catch a blurry glimpse of her own face in the glass, she realized that each ring of the circle had been made from overlapping pieces of nearly uniform, seemingly organic items that had tiny patterns of their own. Were they feathers? The artwork rippled with texture. She drew in a breath as she realized what she was looking at.

The gigantic design had been made with thousands of butterfly wings.

"Do you like it?"

She jumped at the deep voice from her right.

"Dom! I was looking for you." She took a step away from the piece, feeling unnerved. "I'm not sure 'like' is the right word. It's breathtaking . . . but a bit . . ."

"Gross?" he offered, breaking into a grin. "I hate it. Someone told me that it's a good reminder to never let anyone clip your wings. But it's a backward way to send a message like that."

A burst of laughter escaped her chest. "I hate it too," she admitted.

She and Dom both broke into guilty giggles and she walked into his open arms. Looking up, she loved the way the skin around his eyes crinkled when he laughed.

"Just wait until you see the Bourbon Room," he said.

"Peter showed me that yesterday. The one place on this floor that hasn't been changed?"

"Yeah, the old-timers made quite a fuss about no one altering their sacred man cave. Come on, I'll give you a better look."

He took her hand and led her past the sectional couch that faced the fireplace and the artwork. They threaded through the armchairs that had been strategically placed to look directly out the windows, capturing the best of the view, then moved to the door Peter had showed her the day before.

Dom opened it and gestured for her to enter. Once inside, she took in the details that Peter's haste had prevented her from fully absorbing. Unlike the rest of the ground floor, which embraced the interface between the inside and outside, there was only one rectangular window placed in the upper section of the west wall, resulting in the stuffy and dark feeling she'd noticed the day before. All the furnishings seemed to have been selected for their imposing, heavy quality, making them compete with each other for mastery of the space. A chunky brick fireplace and mantel dominated the northern wall, and a large, imposing black chandelier hung in the center of the room. To her left was an old-fashioned, heavy-legged rolltop desk, which was closed.

Hanging above it was a movie poster for one of Hitchcock's first films, *Suspicion*. It wasn't well-known, and in Jane's opinion, for good reason. Her main takeaway after a film school viewing was the absurdity of a wife being charmed by a husband who consistently called her "Monkeyface" before becoming convinced he was trying to kill her. A dark scrawl at the corner of the frame caught her eye.

"Is that an autograph?" she asked.

Dom smiled. "One of Peter's prized possessions. It came with the hotel. I guess good ol' Cary Grant was a big fishing buff. He came here once after the Venatura reopened in the fifties."

The empty gun racks on the dark walls distracted her from the movie star.

"Why did Peter get rid of the guns?"

Dom frowned. "He thought it was a bad idea to have weapons at hand. It wasn't an easy decision. He's a great marksman and loves target practice."

"That must have annoyed some of the guests."

"It did, but it's Peter's hotel. He made the call. There's a safe downstairs where the guests who come to hunt can leave their own firearms, but honestly, most people come here to fish now. The fall storms are getting bigger every year. The dwindling guest numbers were what convinced Peter to close the hotel during most of open season over the last few years."

The mention of negative emotions brought her stepdaughter to mind.

"Did you talk to Sienna?"

"I did. She's . . . not happy," he said. "Can't really blame her. That was not ideal."

"That's one way to put it."

The two of them shared a look that was part tender and part ashamed.

"Should I go to her?" Jane asked.

"Definitely not," he said quickly. Her expression made him backpedal. "I mean, not right now. She's in her room. She needs a little time."

"Oh. I thought I heard her downstairs when I first came in. Was that you behind the front desk?"

Dom frowned. "No, I've been upstairs. Just came down now. Maybe it was the heater? It can be a bit noisy. Old hotel."

"Maybe it was Peter. I saw him down at the river earlier," Jane said.

Dom shrugged. "I thought he was on his way out, but he might have forgotten something."

"Yeah, probably. Dom, I think I can really help with Sienna. I lost my parents when I was about the same age as she is now."

"I think the grief is kind of a side issue at the moment."

She nodded. The silence was as heavy as the stale air. It was the first awkward moment they'd had.

"This room is something else," she said finally.

"Yeah, it doesn't get used much. Through there"—he pointed to a door to the right of the fireplace, which mirrored the one they had entered from the lounge—"is the staff quarters."

"Peter mentioned that's where we'll be sleeping once it gets cold."

"Yeah, it will be the best option. The rooms aren't all that nice, but they're serviceable. Might as well show you those, too."

He crossed through the Bourbon Room and opened the door for her. She entered a nondescript common room with a worn floral couch, matching armchairs, and a kitchenette with a hot plate and microwave— presumably a place for the staff to hang out after hours. They went through the room to another door that led to a long hallway. The floor was covered in a bland beige linoleum that reminded her of a hospital. The two of them moved along the hall, past doors counting down from twelve until they got to the end.

"That goes to the front desk," he said, pointing to the opposite side of the door she'd been wondering about earlier, before turning back the way they'd come. "Want to see what the rooms look like?"

Jane peered at the door. Now that she knew what it led to, she was more certain that someone had been moving around back here, but she could see no sign of it.

"Sure."

"This is the biggest one. Reserved for couples."

Dom pushed open the door labeled eleven and they entered. As he'd said, the room was plain but functional. Beige walls, a double bed, and a small closet. It looked like a dorm.

"And Sienna will be down here with us?"

"Yep, probably as far away as possible from whatever room we choose," he said with a sigh. "Hopefully she'll have forgiven us by then. It's going to take a lot of effort on both our parts to help her through this. It's not easy for her, being here."

"She misses her friends?"

"Yeah."

"And Melissa?"

"Yes, of course." He shifted uncomfortably. "Listen, I know how curious you are about the hotel's history. I mean, who wouldn't be? It's a crazy place with a lot of old stories to tell."

"I'm not just curious about the hotel's history. I want to know what it means to you. The time you spent here with your family. With Melissa."

He flinched. "This isn't a good time to talk about Melissa—"

"Then when is? You know I'm not just here to take care of the hotel or create a bond with your daughter. I need to learn more about you. Your past, what you've been through. It matters to me."

"Of course, I know. I guess I'm feeling a bit overwhelmed. It's been a lot, with Peter's instructions and Sienna's needs. Then that thing this afternoon got me rattled. I want more time to focus on you. All of you."

He moved forward and brushed her waist with his hand. She felt the touch throughout her whole body. Despite the abrupt and embarrassing ending to their last encounter, it was enough to make her fondly remember the feeling of his mustache on the inside of her thighs.

"I feel the same way. I know Peter is your friend, but I wasn't expecting him to be around this much. I thought it was going to be just the three of us."

"You and me both. I talked to him about it today. He's heading back to the city this afternoon. We won't see him again until March."

Jane's shoulders relaxed.

"That's a relief. Though I wouldn't mind having a call with him if we can arrange it. I want to ask him about Elijah, the caretaker who went missing last year. I think Melissa knew him, and I think Sienna did too. When she gets over what happened this afternoon, I'll ask her about him."

He reached around her body to lay his hand flat on the small of her back. "What's with this obsession with Elijah?"

"Not an obsession. I just think there might be a story there. I've got a feeling that it's something worth pursuing."

"I know what I'd like to pursue," he said, moving closer. "You look so pretty right now. The light . . . it's perfect."

She smiled, her body responding.

"Better make sure that door actually locks," Jane said.

Their lips were an inch apart.

"I already did."

He half lifted her, half pushed her onto the double bed, kissing her neck and her chest after slipping off her shirt. She reached for his buttons as he unzipped her jeans. His mouth was hot on her skin. She yanked on his belt, hard and leathery in her hands, and then she freed him, arching her back to meet him halfway.

Afterward, she propped her head on her elbow and turned to her husband, who was tracing the line of her body with a gentle finger. The afterglow of intimacy made her bold. She returned to her earlier questioning.

"How often did you stay here with Melissa? Was this a summer vacation spot for the family?"

He let out a puff of air through his nose. "Yeah. We came a few times. Sienna made friends. Melissa loved the Sunrise Suite. She was high-class all the way." He smoothed the worn bedspread. "Wouldn't be caught dead in the staff quarters."

Jane rolled onto her back and stared at the ceiling, feeling less confident than she had a moment before. So that was why Peter had acted so oddly about the Sunrise Suite. And what did Dom mean by high-class? Was Peter's insistence that they stay in the staff accommodation an insult? Did he consider her low-class?

Dom sat up and swung his legs off the bed.

"I really don't want to talk any more about Melissa. Not now."

"Okay," Jane said, biting her lip. "But whenever you're ready, I'm here."

"I know why you're curious, but sometimes . . . the past can grip us in a way that I'm not sure is entirely healthy. I'm working on it . . . but I know you understand. You lost your parents. Grief pulled me down when Melissa died, too. It took all my strength to pull out of it, and I'm just not sure I'm strong enough to do it again. Not yet."

She raised her body and hugged his back. His skin against hers was a comfort, softening jagged memories.

"Oh, Dom. I know what you mean about burying the past. We can't change it, so why dwell there?" She leaned around to kiss him.

He smiled. "I knew you'd understand. It's a lot to ask, but can you set aside your curiosity about Elijah for now? Just focus on us and building the relationship between you and Sienna?"

Jane moved to sit beside him on the bed.

"It *is* a lot to ask, Dom. I mean, you all knew him, right? I found a picture of Melissa and Sienna with Elijah and two other guys jumping off the bridge. It's possible that we can figure out what happened to him if we put our heads together. Kind of like a family project!"

He rubbed his hand through his hair.

"See, that's what I love about you. Dog with a bone. You don't give up. All right, how about this? I'll tell you what I know, and then you drop it?"

"Depends on what you tell me," Jane said playfully.

A flicker of exasperation entered and left his eyes. Jane recognized it from her past relationships. She knew her persistence could be charming to men . . . until it wasn't. She hated the idea of jeopardizing what she'd found with Dom for a story, but she couldn't change herself for him. Curiosity was the root of her success. Mickey called her Kittycat when she got like this. They used to love it about her.

"Okay. Elijah was around some summers, mostly doing work with Peter and his ex-wife, Lucy. Scrawny kid, kind of broody, but nothing stands out. Sienna met him a few times, but she probably barely remembers him—he's a lot older than her."

"Why did Peter hire him as the caretaker?"

"No idea. You'll have to ask him."

"I will."

"Okay. Hey Jane?"

He touched the underside of her chin with his first knuckle, lifting her face before continuing.

"What I really want to tell you is that Elijah is not the important thing, okay? We're here for us—all of us. And Sienna is struggling. Maybe it's too much to expect you to become a mother overnight. But that's what she needs."

She stiffened at the insinuation of her failing. "I understand, and I'm trying. But Sienna's pretty shut down right now and I want to give her space. In the meantime, there's a story here and that's what I do."

"I'm hoping you're willing to also 'do' this family. Just give it a season and then dig into whatever story you want."

There was a pleading note in his voice that Jane had never heard before. She swallowed hard. Dom needed her to be a good stepmother.

"You're right. Our family is the most important thing."

They exchanged a tender smile.

"It's getting late," he said. "What are your plans for dinner? I'm hungry."

She blinked. "I don't have any plans."

"Well, something simple is fine with me. You'll get the hang of this kitchen soon."

"Do you really expect me to make all the meals every day?"

"Hey, I fulfilled my end of the deal. I told you what you wanted to know about Elijah. But I've got work to do. Unless you want to haul furniture around in the dark, I'm hoping you can honor your side too. I'll be the caretaker if you can be the cook. I always find being in that kitchen awkward. It's hard for me to use a lot of stuff in there."

She rolled her eyes. "Because you're a man? Are you weaponizing your incompetence?"

He laughed. "No, it's hard because I'm left-handed."

She blinked. It was something she should have known. Her embarassment made her relent, though she found the excuse feeble at best.

"Fine. But I can haul furniture too."

"With those skinny little arms?"

She attempted to swat him with an open hand as he jumped off the bed and pulled on his clothes. She followed him all the way back down the hallway, across the lobby, then up the stairs to the entrance to the kitchen on the second floor. The sun was low in the sky now. Late-afternoon beams shot through the dining room like arrows of light.

"I'll be outside pulling the tables in. The forecast looks like rain for tomorrow, and Peter wanted me to store them before it begins."

As he crossed the room to the exterior doors, she entered the kitchen. The counter nearest the door was piled high with dishes from breakfast and lunch. She sighed at the domestic drudgery awaiting her, then moved toward the scullery. On the way, her phone pinged with a message from Mickey.

I was a jerk

sorry

She hesitated, then replied:

I was a jerk too

Jane saw three dots appear, to show Mickey was responding. She entered the scullery and grabbed a bus pan, blushing when she caught sight of the stainless-steel counter. It needed a thorough cleaning.

Another text from Mickey arrived:

I want you to be happy. But I'm worried that you're becoming someone else for a man

something you told me you'd never do

A swear word escaped Jane's lips. Mickey was so wrong. She texted back quickly:

I'm still the same jane married or not

I want you to get to the bottom of this Elijah Stanton thing

Peter is divorced but his ex knew Elijah too

Full speed ahead

She hit send.

CHAPTER | FIFTEEN

ON THEIR SECOND MORNING AT THE HOTEL, JANE PUT THE FINAL
touches on an elaborate breakfast for Sienna. She had found a room service cart in a storage area in the kitchen to carry the fully vegetarian
options—cold cereal, warm oatmeal, and a stack of toast with a choice
of jam or peanut butter—directly to her room. She knew Sienna had to
be hungry. She had picked at her lunch and skipped dinner the night
before, though Dom had tried to coax her to join them for baked beans
and buttered bread.

Jane wheeled the cart carefully to the elevator on the second floor and
called the carriage. It arrived within seconds, and she navigated the bump
with ease. This area of the hotel was already beginning to feel familiar
though there was still so much left to explore.

Outside of Sienna's room, she took a deep breath then tapped on the door.

"Go away," Sienna said loudly.

"I made breakfast for you; I was hoping we could talk."

"Go. Away."

Jane slowly inhaled and exhaled. She knew Sienna was angry and hurt after seeing her father and Jane in such a compromising position the day before. Defusing her emotions was going to be more complicated than she'd realized.

"Sienna, please. You need to eat."

"GO AWAY!"

She reached out a shaking hand to turn the knob. As she gently pushed the door inward, she heard the thud of footsteps. Sudden pressure slammed it back into her face. "Sienna, please."

"I said GO AWAY. I don't want to talk to you. Leave me alone."

The closed door muffled the words but not the rage behind them. Jane stared at the number plate. She could hear her stepdaughter's forced breathing and the faint buzz of the lights in the ceiling above.

"I'm really sorry about yesterday."

No response.

"I know this isn't easy for you."

"GET OUT OF HERE!"

Jane flinched. The hum of the lights seemed to grow louder. "Is there anything I can do for you?"

"ARE YOU DEAF?"

"Is everything okay here?" Dom called from down the hall.

Jane jumped. The noise hadn't come from the lights. It was the elevator.

Sienna opened the door a tiny crack. Her eyes were wide with panic. "Jane, please, don't let him in here," she hissed.

But it was too late. Dom had arrived. Sienna shut the door quickly.

"She won't open the door," Jane whispered.

"I can still hear you," Sienna said.

"Hon? Let us in, please. Jane made you breakfast."

"No, I don't want you to come in."

"Sienna. This is unacceptable. We need to talk to you," Dom said.

They both fixed their eyes on the door. Jane sighed in frustration. Then, she saw the doorknob turning. The door opened a crack.

"Fine, I'll eat," Sienna said. "Leave the food outside."

"No way," Dom said, forcing the door open.

Jane pushed the cart into the room as Dom held the door for her. It resembled the suite she and Dom were sharing, save for the fact that it was half the size and ten times messier. The bathroom door on her left was ajar. Mounds of wet-looking towels were heaped on the floor and the counter was covered in eyeshadow palettes, makeup brushes, lipstick, moisturizer—like a drugstore had exploded. The shower curtain hung half off the hooks.

On the large chest of drawers opposite the king-sized bed, Jane saw a half-eaten black forest cake that looked as if it had been clawed. A tub of profiteroles had been spilled all over the carpet. Several were squashed, imprinted with dirty footprints. Whipped cream oozed onto the expensive weave. Crumbs crunched under her feet and the wheels of the cart. Several boxes of crackers and bags of chips were open, their contents spilled across surfaces.

Jane tried to find a place for the cart amidst the chaos. The shock of Sienna's clearly disordered eating made her heart swell with compassion—she had assumed the girl's lack of appetite was due to stress, not something deeper. She darted a quick look to Dom, whose face was drawn. Did he know Sienna had these kinds of issues with food? How could he not have told her?

Sienna tearfully glared at them from the corner of the room. The anger on her face could not disguise the pain underneath. Her arms hugged her slight body. Jane wrapped her arms around her own torso.

"Honey—" Dom began with a catch in his voice. "We've got to clean this up."

"It's my room. I'll clean it up when I'm ready."

"But surely you don't want to live like this," Jane said, gratefully nodding at Dom as he repositioned a shriveled shrimp ring so she could slide the cart beside the chest of drawers.

Tears streamed down Sienna's face. "What's it to you, Jane?" she yelled. "You're only here to bang my dad. You don't care about me. I asked you not to let him in because I didn't want him to see this! But you don't care."

"Sienna, that's not true. Of course I care about you. I'm worried about your health."

"Oh, so you're the expert on health, right? Like it's sooo healthy to marry a man less than a year after his wife dies?"

Jane's stomach dropped. *Less than a year?* She whipped her gaze to Dom, but her husband was staring intently at his daughter—seemingly unaware of the impact Sienna's words had on Jane. Dom hadn't told her how recent Melissa's death had been, but like a fool, she had assumed a larger span of time. Mickey's words rang in her ears; the pact between them did seem idiotic now.

"Sienna, that's enough." Dom had adopted a stern "dad" voice Jane had never heard before.

"Okay, fine, I've got the stupid breakfast, Dad. Can you please get her out now?"

Dom looked between his wife and his daughter for a long moment. Then he turned to Jane.

"Can we have a minute?"

Jane was crestfallen and took a step forward. "Dom, please, don't shut me out." She turned to Sienna, whose eyes burned. "I lost my mom and dad too—I was close to your age when it happened. I know how awful it is. How empty you feel inside. I'm not trying to replace your mother—"

Sienna's face contorted in rage. "Dad, GET HER OUT OF HERE!"

"Jane, this isn't the right time—"

She drew in a deep breath. Empathy, frustration, concern, and anger balled in her chest, making it hard to breathe.

"Okay," she said. She took two steps toward the door.

"Wait," Dom said. She turned back, hope bubbling. "Can you take these with you?"

He handed her a stack of food-spattered plates topped with the lolling remains of the layer cake. Deflated, she took the dishes without a word.

Dom finally seemed to register the effect of his request. His eyes brimmed with worry. He followed her to the door. "She's in such a tough phase right now. I just need a minute to calm her down. I'll meet you back downstairs, okay?"

Jane nodded though the muscles in her neck were tight enough to make the gesture painful. "Sienna needs help," she whispered.

"I can hear you," Sienna called in an angry singsong voice.

Jane relented. Dom held the door for her, and she exited into the hallway. Before it could fully close, she pressed the flat of her hand against it to ensure it didn't latch. Carefully, she leaned into the fractional opening. Sienna spoke again the moment she thought Jane was gone.

"I want to go home. Now."

"Sienna—"

"I do. I hate being here," she sobbed. "It was mean to make me come back. I don't care what Dr. Abebe said! All I can think about is Mom. And Elijah. I miss them both so much. Don't you?"

Jane closed her eyes. Sienna didn't hate her; she hated the fact that her mother was no longer alive. And, underneath her new understanding, Jane felt a flare of triumph. She had been right—Sienna did know Elijah.

"Sienna, that's the reason we're here. To try and get through that loss. I know it seems harsh, but your doctor believes that exposure is necessary to help you process. I'm here too. And Jane can help—"

"UGH! NO! I wish she wasn't here. I wish we had never come here. I wish you had never married her!"

Jane leaned in. The hinges squeaked.

"What was that?"

Footsteps rushed toward her, and the door was yanked open.

Sienna wore an expression of blind fury. "OH MY GOD! She's fucking eavesdropping on our private conversation, Dad!"

Red-faced, Jane sputtered, "I just want to help—"

"You are not my mom! You will never be my mom! Never!"

The slam of the door made Jane's ears throb like a broken heart.

CHAPTER | SIXTEEN

IN THE EARLY MORNING LIGHT, THE KITCHEN WAS QUIET SAVE FOR THE sound of the feral cat lapping milk from a bowl Jane had used to coax him inside. As Murray had noted, he was very food motivated. He had even let Jane rub his rounded side after she'd shown him the bowl. The scruffy guy was better-fed than she'd realized—his tight belly had a lumpy shape when viewed from above. On top of that, his mottled fur was matted and he was missing an eye. The poor cat was ugly as sin, but he was quickly growing on Jane. It was nice to not feel so alone. Especially after seeing another round of hateful messages on Ember's social media feeds.

Dom had spent the rest of the previous afternoon with Sienna, then stayed the night in the room beside hers in case she needed anything. Meanwhile Jane had explored the third floor, installed a padlock on the walk-in cooler, (unsuccessfully) attempted to make a call on the radio, and (successfully) fought the urge to search for more information on Melissa or message Mickey to pass on what she had learned. It seemed wrong somehow to feed Sienna's words into their investigation after her step-daughter had reacted with such fury to her eavesdropping—yet the new information pressed like a hand on her back. Jane had never been so conflicted about a story. Dom's absence hadn't helped.

If Melissa had passed away the year before, Dom was in a much more vulnerable state of mind than she'd imagined when they first met five months ago. In her experience, the first year of grief was a fog of sorrow and uncertainty. His swift proposal had seemed romantic at the time. Now it made her uneasy. They'd both been on the rebound. Worse than that, though, was the odd coincidence of Melissa's death and Elijah's disappearance happening in such proximity. It raised a red flag for Jane. Was it possible the two incidents were connected? Was that why Dom was so cagey whenever she asked him about Elijah?

She tugged the padlock to make sure it held. It was a rudimentary solution to a deep-seated problem, but she wanted to keep Sienna safe and ensure their supplies lasted. And she needed to do something productive. She wasn't planning on making more than a trip a month into Chilliwack to replenish produce and perishable items. There were enough dry goods and frozen food to see them through the season—so long as they could help Sienna regain control over her intake.

A knock on the door interrupted her thoughts. Jane opened it to see Murray standing outside, this time brandishing a bouquet of silvery-blue flowers with the slightest hint of brown at the edges of the petals. Jane was thrilled to see his friendly weathered face.

"Good morning, Jane. My wife loved hydrangeas, so I've got lots to spare. You like 'em?"

He pushed them toward her as if suddenly embarrassed. She accepted and stepped to the side.

"I love them, and I'd love some company," she said. "Please come in. I've just made coffee."

The cat darted out between his legs as he diligently wiped his feet on the mat.

"Looks like you've made a friend," he said.

"Something like that. I suspect his affection only lasts as long as I'm feeding him, but it's nice to have him around."

Jane led Murray through the kitchen and into the dining room where she'd been making the most of the elegant serve yourself coffee station stocked with supplies for pour-over, French-press, and percolated coffee. She poured him a cup then invited him to sit down at a table near the window. Fog had settled in the valley, but the mountaintops were still visible. A dusting of snow had fallen on them during the night.

"Thanks for this," Murray said. "It's chilly out there this morning, but no frost on the pumpkins yet." He tipped his mug toward her.

Her attention was caught by a band of trees on a high eastern slope, glowing bronze and gold as the sun's rays reached it.

"That orange patch is so striking—so much deeper than the others."

Murray squinted. "Those aren't fall colors. That's the effect of the pine beetle—nasty little bug that's been feasting on the trees for the last few years. It's insidious—doesn't get cold enough here in the winter to kill them off. Bugs burrow deep inside the tree through holes that are so small you can barely see 'em. Tens of thousands of them kill the tree from the inside. It's almost impossible to tell they're there until one day the needles change to show you the tree's dead."

She thought of the haggard tree near the cookhouse and pictured it teeming with burrowing beetles. "That's terrible—"

She was interrupted by a sound from behind. She tensed, expecting Sienna, and turned.

Dom stood at the entrance to the dining room, showered, dressed, and ready to start his day. He hadn't shaved—his dark beard had begun to cover the sharp line of his jaw, making him look more handsome. Jane smiled and felt a stirring. She gestured with the pot to a cup. He nodded gratefully before stretching his hand out to Murray, who had stood in greeting.

"Hello there. I wasn't expecting to see a guest. Dom Lawrence," he said.

Murray gave Dom's hand a firm shake then dropped it. "Murray Jack. We've met. I own the property across the river."

Dom nodded. "Oh, right. Sorry. Nothing really registers until I've finished my first cup of coffee. Good to see you again."

"I suppose I knew your wife better," Murray said. "May she rest in peace."

The dining room fell still. Jane kept her eyes trained on Dom. Her husband dropped his gaze to the floor before returning it to Murray's face.

"Thank you for that. So, what brings you around this morning bright and early?"

"He brought me flowers," Jane said, gesturing to the blue hydrangeas.

"Is that right?" Dom looked over at her. "Should I be jealous?"

"If there's anyone who should worry you, it's that old cat who keeps coming in the back door," she teased.

"Yep, Fraser can be a real mooch," Murray said. "He comes around my farm too, but by the sound of it, you're a lot more generous than I am. Better watch out or he'll never leave."

Jane laughed. "Fraser? He has a name?"

"Sure does," Murray said. "In fact, I think it was Melissa who named him. Isn't that right, Dom? She spent a lot of time out here."

Jane swallowed her coffee carefully.

Dom looked out the window before answering. "Yeah, that's ringing a bell."

"With Elijah, right? And those other fellas Elijah used to pal around with? That big crew?"

Jane stayed silent, watching Dom's reaction. Curiosity buzzed through her body. She was right. Melissa had known Elijah. From what Murray was saying, they'd been closer than she'd initially guessed.

"Sounds like you know more about that time than I do. I was in the city—had a few big jobs over the last few years that kept me distracted." He turned to her, his face passive. "Jane, you know I love your fancy pour-over coffee, but I'm going to make an old-fashioned pot if that's okay with you. I need more than these little cups to get the third floor in shape. I can smell snow in the air this morning. Murray, you must have a lot to get back to on the farm?"

"I'm on top of it," Murray said with a nod.

Dom moved toward the kitchen. "Well, nice to see you. Always good to have neighbors close by."

Jane squeezed Dom's hand on the way by. Murray tipped his hat then leaned forward.

"Feeling comfortable with that short-wave radio yet? I'd be happy to give you a quick rundown. Weather report showed the rains are coming early this year. It's good to be prepared."

"Yes, actually. That would be great. How about now?" She pushed aside the memory of her previous lesson. As they moved past the coffee station, she noticed Murray's troubled expression reflected back from the beautifully beveled mirror behind the counter.

"You all right?" Jane asked.

"What? Oh sure. It's just an old superstition my grandmother used to tell me. Never look in a dead person's mirror."

Jane was confused. "Dead person?"

Murray looked surprised. "That was the mirror Melissa picked out, wasn't it?"

Jane looked into the mirror at her own bewildered eyes. Her hands had grown cold. "I don't know."

"Oh, don't mind me. It's just a silly old story. My grandmother was full of them."

"Sounds like you knew Melissa well."

The older man rocked on his heels. "Pretty well, I'd say. She was a great woman. Fierce and smart. A lot like you."

"And she knew Elijah Stanton? The caretaker who went missing last year?"

Murray eyed Jane. "She did. Your husband knew him too. He's likely a better source of information than me."

Jane hesitated. Murray seemed trustworthy, but she wasn't ready to disclose to him how little she knew about the man she'd married.

As her pride trumped her curiosity, her questions—when exactly had Melissa died? And how had it happened?—went unasked and unanswered.

"Yes, definitely," she said.

In the scullery, Murray fiddled with the top of the radio.

"Two things to remember—frequency and band," he said, while rotating the analog dials. "You're probably too young to remember transistor radios, but it's the same kind of deal. Reception is often better after the sun goes down, but you should be able to reach me at this range at any time of the day or night."

At his insistence, Jane performed a call to his frequency.

"Okay, seems like you're all set. Now you know what to do. If you need anything, just call."

Jane nodded as he locked onto her with a direct stare.

"You know Melissa was the one who drew the map I gave you? Always organized, always on top of things. She was a helluva woman."

Jane remembered the handwriting on the map and shivered. "You liked her?"

"I liked the fact that she didn't take any shit. Pardon my French." Murray winked.

Jane laughed. "I speak French. She sounds wonderful."

Murray eyed her. "That's one word for her. Seems like you and your new husband have a lot of talking to do."

She smiled. Murray was perceptive. "He's not much of a talker."

"Is that so?"

"He thinks that the past is better left in the past. And I agree. Moving forward is the only available option."

Murray crossed his arms over his chest. His face turned solemn. "Jane, when you get to be as old as I am, you'll realize the things that have come before have a way of catching up with you. I often think it's better not to let them take you by surprise."

CHAPTER | SEVENTEEN

THE TEMPERATURE DROPPED THROUGHOUT THE DAY. DOM CAME INTO the kitchen for lunch, ruddy-faced and red-knuckled, prompting Jane to exit the walk-in cooler where she'd been working.

"It's cold out there. Looks like our days of warmth have come to an end."

Jane shivered with agreement and anticipation. She was making sandwiches for lunch and wondered if she should put a can of soup on. Something warming. She patted a stool and Dom came and sat by her. It was time for a conversation.

"Let's talk, Dom. Tell me about Sienna. Is she struggling with bulimia? What do I need to know?"

"I'm so sorry. That must have been hard to see," he began. "I should have warned you."

"Yes, you should have. There's a lot you should have told me about. Like Melissa dying so recently. Like what Murray said about her spending a lot of time out here with Elijah."

"You're right. I just get so distracted when we're together. I'm crazy about you, Jane. I can't be in a room with you without thinking of taking off your clothes." He moved toward her with a familiar look.

"Dom!" she said. "Talk. Not sex."

Dom looked cowed and Jane found herself closing the distance in response to his sweet smile. *No*, she told herself. It was time to listen. She gripped the underside of the counter to anchor herself in place.

"Of course, yeah. Like I said before, Sienna is going through a really tough phase. She's struggled with disordered eating for three years. It's gotten worse since her mom died."

"Last year," Jane said flatly.

"Yeah." He ran his hand through his hair. "I should have told you that too."

Jane drew a line in the air on an imaginary tally sheet. "Adding it to the list."

"Are we ready for joking now?" he asked.

"Not even close. I want to know when Melissa died. And how it happened and where. But first, I want to know why you told me that Peter was the one who called you, instead of the other way around."

Dom sighed and swore. "I should have realized nothing was going to get past you. I lied. Sienna's therapist, Dr. Abebe, prescribed exposure therapy for her emotional problems and eating disorder. She recommended a controlled, familiar environment where Sienna could explore memories of her mother and face her difficulties. I thought you were going to think it was too out there for us to hunker down in this old hotel, and I wanted to protect Sienna's privacy. I needed to get you here so you could see it. So you could see how good it would be for us."

"So you were going to be caretaker all along? And you and Peter made up a story about this year's caretaker crapping out so I'd go along?"

Dom nodded.

Her chest was tight but she tried for levity. People tended to be more

THE OFF SEASON | 123

honest when they didn't feel attacked. "Don't lie to me again, Dom. I can handle the truth. That's what I'm here for. I have to say I'm relieved to hear that the Venatura doesn't lose a caretaker every year. I was starting to question what I signed up for."

He drew an imaginary line of his own. "Add it to the things I'm sorry for?"

"Yes."

He looked at her under the lids of his lowered eyes. "Is that it?"

"No," Jane said. "You haven't answered my other questions."

The door to the kitchen swung in fast, whacking against the wall.

"I don't know where you want me to put these," Sienna said, holding out a load of soiled laundry at shoulder height.

"Hello, Sienna," Jane said.

"Hello, Jane," she replied. "Since you want to be my mother so badly, might as well start now."

Jane recoiled, then laughed. "You've got to be kidding. You want me to do your laundry?"

"Uh-huh."

"But I'm still finishing the inventory on the food."

Sienna narrowed her eyes, and Jane realized her error too late. "That's so offensive."

Dom broke in. "She didn't mean it like that, See."

"I think she did," Sienna said with a hurt expression. "She hates me. She thinks I'm disgusting. She thinks I can't be trusted around food."

That's about right, Jane thought, remembering the shrimp ring.

"Don't blame Jane. It was my idea—"

Dom's phone rang from his pocket and the argument stopped. Sienna's expression was poisonous, though Jane could see the pain in her eyes. He fished out his phone, glanced at the screen, then answered.

"Hello, Peter. What's up?"

Sienna and Jane were silent as Dom listened.

"No, I haven't checked the weather today, but I'll get on it. Sounds like

I need to push a little harder." He paused again and held one finger up at the two women. "Okay, thanks for letting me know."

He ended the call and addressed them both in a low voice. "That was Peter. There's a big storm moving in tonight—it's a winter front. Lots of rain, maybe even some snow if the temperature gets a few degrees colder. I've really got to get to work. Most of the outdoor dining stuff is still on the deck. It's going to get pummeled if this storm is as big as they're predicting. Another atmospheric river."

Jane remembered the year before when East Eleventh flooded.

"Sounds like you need to eat this fast."

Jane hastily assembled the egg-salad sandwiches. Yellow mixture spilled from both sides when she plopped a piece of bread on top. As she added a dill pickle to the plate and passed it to Dom, she realized she'd forgotten to heat the soup. Out of the corner of her eye, she saw Sienna shudder.

"What would you like to eat?" she asked her stepdaughter as Dom began wolfing down the food. She passed him a torn piece of paper towel to wipe the egg mixture from his fingers.

"Nothing," Sienna said, her voice dripping with disgust.

Dom stopped chewing and looked at her sternly. "Sienna."

"Fine, ugh. A piece of fruit. Banana or something?"

Jane made eye contact with Dom, who nodded.

"That sounds like a good place to start. Then maybe a piece of toast."

"Later," Sienna said. Her tone warned of a pending emotional explosion.

"Not much later though," Dom said. He wiped the last traces of egg from his mouth before demolishing the pickle in two bites.

Sienna scowled.

"I'll be checking on you, okay, Sienna? Let's get that food diary going again."

"I'm happy to make you anything you like," Jane added.

"As long as it's out of a can," Sienna sneered. But Jane noticed a catch in her voice that undermined her vitriol.

Jane decided to ignore her. Nothing she said came out right, and the girl was clearly sensitive.

Dom brushed crumbs off his gray wool sweater, then passed the plate to Jane with a quick kiss on her cheek. "I'm going to be a few hours out there. In the meantime, we need to get our rooms ready in the staff accommodation area. Sounds like those suites are going to be too cold to sleep in tonight. You okay to take that on?"

Jane nodded. "Sure."

He patted his daughter on the arm on his way by. "Try to get back into a regular pattern of eating, okay? I'll get in touch with Dr. Abebe tonight."

"Okay, Dad." Her tone was sweet, signaling a sea change.

Jane turned to her after Dom left the room, about to try again, when Sienna dropped the clothes on the floor along with the kindness she had shown her father. "Can you take this on as well, Jane?" she asked, mimicking Dom.

Never had Jane heard her name spoken with such contempt. "Let's talk about chores and responsibilities. I want to build your independence as a nearly grown woman. I'll show you how to use the laundry machines so you can wash your own clothes."

"Please. Doing laundry is what you're here for."

Jane balked. "No. That's hardly why I came here. We are building a family—that's the point of this whole thing."

"A family? My dad only brought you here to take care of us. Didn't he tell you? We needed someone here to do all the housework so we could properly grieve."

Jane bit the insides of both her cheeks. "I'm sorry for everything you've been through, Sienna—"

"Good. Then do my laundry."

The urge to tell Sienna what she really thought burned in Jane's chest, but her commitment to Dom made her swallow it. "Come on, Sienna. You're being so difficult. Let's just break this down and start again. We're trying to build a new family on the foundation of what has come before."

Sienna huffed. "A new family? What makes you think we want a new family? You still don't get it, do you? This place *is* her. Everything about it. It used to be a gross and tacky hunting lodge, then she came along and made it this incredible space. *That's* why my dad wanted us to come. To be near her."

Jane, remembering Peter's reticence about revealing the name of the designer, felt the egg salad curdle in her stomach.

"Your mom designed this place?"

"Thanks for keeping up," Sienna said. "Finally. The Venatura is her hotel. She's part of every room. She brought it all to life. Dad's just finishing the job they started together."

Shocked, Jane moved backward, right into the edge of the workstation behind her. It stabbed her hip, bruising the muscle. Pain seared her lower back and her head swam. Melissa had decorated the entire hotel from the staircase to the artwork.

"So, laundry?" Sienna said as if she was talking to a five-year-old.

"Just put it in the linen room," Jane said with gritted teeth. She had run out of compassion for her stepdaughter, and she needed a minute to regroup. "I'm going to move a few things down to the first floor. The laundry is right through there. I can give you a hand when I get back." She pointed at a small hall that led off the back of the scullery.

"Thank you!" Sienna sang.

"You should move your stuff down to the staff quarters tonight as well."

"Maybe. I'm pretty busy right now," she said as she moved to the swinging doors. "By the way, you don't have to worry about showing me your films. I've been doing my own research." She left the room before Jane could answer.

Jane took a long slow breath to calm her lurching stomach. It was hard to shake the chill caused by Sienna's parting words. Their stupid internet ban didn't apply to her stepdaughter. Had Sienna discovered the controversy surrounding her last film? Was she about to share what she'd learned with her father? Jane walked quickly to the elevator bay.

The elevator responded immediately to her call, and she slipped gratefully into its mirrored confines. Inside, she took a long hard look at her face. There were lines across her forehead that she hadn't seen before. Jane wasn't vain, but she didn't like the idea of the Venatura leaving a mark on her. On the fourth floor, she stepped out of the carriage. Through the window, the sky had become a uniform gray broken only by storm-whipped branches tossing their leaves to the ground.

She hurried through the hall to the corridor that led to the two luxury suites. Steps away from the door, a sound came from the right. The image of identically dressed twin girls popped into her mind, but she forced it away. She looked down the hallway. Standing outside room 401 was her husband, swaying slightly as he stared at the closed door.

"Dom? What are you doing? I thought you were going outside?"

He jerked around as if she'd yanked his body from behind. "I—"

His eyes were glassy. She took several tentative steps toward him, then stopped.

"Are you okay?"

"I was going to the dining room deck." He shook his head, once, twice. "I had to grab a warmer layer. Stopped here for a moment. Got distracted." He brushed his hair from his forehead and his eyes sharpened. "I'm fine. Going to head outside now."

"You seem . . . a little off."

"I'm okay now. Just got distracted like I said. Been an emotional morning, I guess." He took a few steps toward her, then embraced her quickly before moving down the hallway. She heard the elevator ping its arrival. Her phone buzzed in her pocket, and she tugged it out. It was a text from Mickey.

elijah stanton is peter's son

Jane's eyes widened. Another message arrived.

found out what happened to melissa

you ready to know yet?

Jane didn't hesitate:

tell me everything

CHAPTER | EIGHTEEN

IN THE SECONDS BEFORE MICKEY'S RESPONSE CAME THROUGH, JANE reeled. Peter's nonchalance about the unreliability of seasonal workers and Dom's throwaway description of Elijah working at the hotel took on a sinister cast. Of course Elijah had been here with relatives. His father was the owner! So why did Peter act unbothered by his son's disappearance?

Why had he and Dom lied?

As she read Mickey's next texts, Jane's thoughts grew wild. She tugged open a door marked *Stairs*. Her speed down the two flights was close to dangerous: her footsteps paced her heartbeat. The moment her feet hit the cement on the second-floor landing, she hammered open the heavy door that led to the dining room and flew around the top of the grand staircase. Her phone was still lit up with Mickey's words:

melissa drowned at the venatura hotel last
year on october 27

creepy right????

call me and I'll tell you more

Dom was standing on the deck facing the river with his phone at his side. His broad shoulders were stiff. At least half of the outdoor dining furniture remained in place around him. She opened the door and the wind gusted in. When she reached him on the eastern edge of the deck, she followed his gaze to the river carving out the landscape with an unrelenting rush. The dead and dying trees on the far vista shook and bent. From this side, she could see a building hulking down by the muddy waves. The boathouse.

"Dom!" She rounded on him.

Once again, his eyes were unfocused. "Jane. I was just about to—"

"Is that where it happened?"

She pointed to a narrowing in the river that dropped in elevation before sluicing down into a sucking flow of water. The river rolled back onto itself to form a churning whirlpool at the base of the drop. A hydraulic, she remembered suddenly from the one and only kayaking lesson she'd taken years ago. A place where water forces itself into an unceasing cycle that is nearly impossible to escape.

"Where what happened?" Dom's voice was clearer now.

"Is that where Melissa died?"

He threaded his fingers and put both hands to the back of his head. He dropped his eyes. "We had a deal. We promised not to investigate each other."

Jane searched Dom's voice for a tone to indicate that Sienna had told him about Jane's last film, but his words were without guile or subtext.

"I was an idiot to promise that. I didn't know at the time that the only way I could learn about you was through online research!"

"I haven't had enough time to explain it all."

Though she hated to admit it, she knew what he meant. She hadn't had enough time to explain everything either.

"But why did you bring me here? Why didn't you tell me what happened? Why would you bring Sienna back here after what happened?"

"I told you. It was Dr. Abebe's idea. Sienna was so stuck. Her eating got worse in France—the host family was worried about her. I was getting calls almost every day. I didn't know what to do. Her doctor recommended we return here for a visit to help her get closure. You were so excited about it . . . It seemed like what we needed. Now I'm not so sure."

"Why didn't you tell me Peter was Elijah's father? Why would you both lie about *that*?"

"It's complicated. And it wasn't a lie, it was an omission."

"We were just talking about it! Peter said seasonal workers were unreliable." Jane paused. "About his own son. And your first wife . . . she died here, Dom. You should have told me the moment you mentioned this hotel. I don't know what to do. Mickey was right. We got married too fast. I don't know enough about you. I trusted you too soon." All this time, she had been worried about losing his faith, when she should have been thinking about protecting herself.

When he finally raised his head to meet her eyes, his expression was fierce. "Don't say that! I love you!"

"But what if this was all a mist—"

"It wasn't. This was exactly what we both needed. We found each other for a reason." He grasped her upper arm. His face was imploring, and she was struck by the suffering under the surface. She took a deep breath, then slid her phone into her back pocket. She placed her hand on top of his.

"Then tell me what happened to your first wife. I need to know."

He broke eye contact again and settled his gaze on the slate-gray water downriver from the churning rapid.

"It happened down there, past the boathouse."

She leaned forward on the railing to get a better look at the large rectangular building with its long side facing the river. It was perched on pilings about two meters above the water and had four bays, all closed.

Though the long ash-gray planks echoed the hotel's West Coast façade, it looked newer than the hotel.

"We had both kayaked this river more times than I could count. We never put in above the rapid." He gestured to the violent water she'd noticed earlier.

"The water moves fast in this section, and the river will take you straight into the whirlpool if you launch near the bridge. Melissa knew the river well. She used to take the kayak out all the time."

"Alone?"

"Yeah, she'd been paddling since she was a kid. She needed time to herself—hated being cooped up with people all day long. She'd go out every morning if she could. Then one day, she just . . . didn't come back. I was in Vancouver. I got a call that she was missing and rushed out here as fast as possible. We found her kayak first, then"—he swallowed hard—"her body late in the day."

"You found her?"

He nodded once, eyes still on the river. "Me and Peter."

"Peter," she repeated. "Elijah's father."

Dom sighed. "Yeah."

"Keep going."

"Elijah was like a son to me too. When he went missing on the same day Melissa died . . . I don't know, Jane. Something inside me went wrong. I was numb. It was hard to function. I guess when you started asking all those questions . . . I froze. I really didn't want to revisit that time." His voice broke.

She softened, but she knew there had to be a connection between Elijah's disappearance and Melissa's death. Mickey was on it, she told herself. For now, she had to figure out if her marriage would survive.

"But you have revisited it. Literally. You've come back to the place where it all happened. And you've brought Sienna and me too. How am I supposed to help her with all this going on? And it's all so recent. Dom, you've lost so much in the last year. I don't think you were ready to marry me. If you were, you would have told me everything."

He squeezed her hand as she tried to not apply the words to herself.

"It's not like that, Jane. I lost a lot, but I found a lot too. Be patient with me. I'm not trying to hide it. But I don't have the words to talk about it just yet."

She smiled though tears pricked her eyes. "I can help you through this. But you need to find a way to let me in. You have to be honest."

"You're right," he said. "No more secrets."

"I'm glad you told me," she said. "It's a start."

"So am I," he replied, intertwining his large fingers with hers. His hand was cold.

"You should put gloves on. It must be close to freezing out here."

"You're right—I've got 'em in my pocket. It's also too cold to be outside without a jacket. Get back in and warm up," Dom said with a smile that made him seem more like himself. "I'll be done later this afternoon."

"Okay," she said. "Good luck with all this. You sure you don't need any help?"

"Getting our new bedroom sorted and putting a warm meal on the table is all the help I need."

She kissed his hand then pulled him toward her. "You got it. But listen—you can trust me, okay? No more lies and half-truths. Tell me everything."

"Always."

Their cold lips met. When they broke apart, she returned to the welcome warmth of the glowing dining room. But inside, shadows cast by the darkening sky made it seem as if the sun had already set. The corners of the room were thick with gloom.

A clanging sound from the kitchen made her jump. She turned to the deck. Dom was lugging furniture into a roofed area close to the windows.

"Sienna?" She craned her ears to hear her stepdaughter's voice. No response. Her body had been cold before. Now her hands were clammy with unease. Another bang came from behind the wall.

"Sienna? Is that you?"

With a thumping heart, she pushed open the pass-through doors and burst into the kitchen, half expecting to see a distraught Sienna struggling to open the padlock to the cooler. Her mouth tasted like nails as she surveyed the empty room. In eight bounding steps, she made it to the exterior door to track an intruder. No one was there. The door had been bolted from inside. She sped to the scullery. Again, the room was empty. She got on her hands and knees and peered into the cupboards to see if something had toppled over. Everything was in order. It was only when she returned to the kitchen that she noticed the hanging pots by the stove.

They were swinging.

The numbness from her hands spread throughout her chest and an uncontrollable shiver wracked her upper body. She was getting really tired of chasing ghosts in this creepy hotel—particularly since she now realized it was her stepdaughter sneaking and hoarding food. She took the elevator to the fourth floor and entered their suite, puzzling over how to address Sienna's forays into the kitchen. The teenager's behavior was strange. Was it a prank or a cry for help?

Her anger eroded to sadness. Dom had mentioned Sienna had a therapist. Perhaps it was time to work with them on a care plan? She wasn't sure what kind of therapist recommended exposure therapy to a teenage girl still grieving her mother, but she had to do something. Dom was trying, but clearly Sienna needed more.

She surveyed the room. Unlike Sienna, after two nights they had barely moved in. Lifting the nearly full suitcases onto the bed, she gathered the few clothes they'd unpacked and returned them to their luggage, then headed to the bathroom to collect their toiletries. As she reached for her hairbrush, she knocked over a bottle of the muscle relaxants Dom took for his old back injury.

The vial landed on the bathroom tiles with a clatter, its contents spilling onto the floor. She gathered several pills in her palm. Each was stamped with a name.

Seroquel.

She sat down hard on the bathroom floor, remembering a terrible ex-boyfriend from years before. He'd been the lead singer in a band, deeply involved in drugs, legal and otherwise. Over the course of their awful relationship, he'd been diagnosed with BPD—borderline personality disorder. She could still remember the night she left for good, when he'd grabbed her hair and ground his forehead against hers, screaming that she would never understand him. He had been prescribed Seroquel too.

An antipsychotic.

Why was Dom taking an antipsychotic?

With shaking hands, she dialed Mickey.

CHAPTER | NINETEEN

"TELL ME EVERYTHING YOU KNOW ABOUT HOW MELISSA DIED," SHE said as soon as her friend answered.

Mickey didn't waffle.

"Drowning, super close to the hotel. Local police called it an accident—kayak washed up alongshore. Looked fairly cut-and-dried. She wasn't wearing a life jacket, and the coroner was quoted talking about how hypothermia can occur in water that cold in seconds blah blah blah. Her body got really banged up—coroner attributed that to rocks and floating debris. She was underwater for a while. Sounds pretty grisly, actually."

"That's awful," Jane said, her voice trembling at the thought of Melissa's body on the rocky shore just outside the window. "Dom told me she was an experienced kayaker. Weird to not be wearing a life jacket."

"Yeah," Mickey said. "The thing that makes it weirder is the sudden disappearance of Elijah Stanton right after. And get this? It's not his dad who's putting those posters up all over the place. It's his mom, Lucy. Nice tip about her, by the way. I spoke with her earlier today—she's agreed to an interview. Disgruntled wives always do."

"Awesome work. I love disgruntled. When does she want to meet?"

"Tomorrow. She lives in Maple Ridge."

"I'm coming. That's like . . . an hour and a half from here."

"Yes! That's my Jane. Okay, sweet. I think you are going to like her. She is . . . um . . . eager to talk."

"Perfect, text me the address and time."

Jane and Mickey ended the call. With the phone down, she heard rushing water. She quickly checked the toilet and faucet in search of the leak but found nothing. She stepped out of the bathroom, alert to the source. As soon as she looked outside, the cause became clear.

The windows had become walls of water. Rivulets streamed down the glass with a volume that obscured everything else. In the time it had taken to speak with Mickey, the entire world had blurred. The chill she had taken outside returned. Her feet and hands were icy as she finished packing their suitcases—divvying out a small overnight bag for the next day. She lugged everything downstairs to the slightly dingy but noticeably warmer staff quarters on the first floor, off the Bourbon Room. At least Peter hadn't lied about that.

There was no sign that Sienna had moved from the fourth to the first floor, but Jane decided not to push it. She settled on the bed, itching to plug Melissa's name into a search engine. The only thing that stopped her was the idea of Dom doing the same thing to her. Better to hear it from him and let Mickey do the deeper investigation. Trust went both ways, she reminded herself. That's what good marriages were built on. Her own parents hadn't had it. But she still believed it was possible with Dom.

A door slammed shut in the hallway and she breathed a sigh of relief that Sienna had done what she was told.

The thought of her stepdaughter prompted her to redirect her researching urge to the subject of bulimia. Helping Sienna was another commitment she'd made to her husband. Prior to this, the closest personal experience she'd had with the disorder was a year spent in a ballet class as a preteen. The restroom in the studio had smelled perpetually of vomit. After reading about eating disorders and the connections to trauma and troubled mental health, she left her room and scanned the hallway to determine which room Sienna had chosen.

All the doors were open. There was no sign of either Sienna or her belongings. The back of Jane's neck rippled with the feeling of someone watching. She spun on her heels.

The hallway was empty.

The unease stayed with her as she returned to the kitchen to prepare a dinner of spaghetti and canned tomato sauce. She was jerky and unsettled, flinching when Fraser scratched at the door and gasping when the stove timer chimed. Movement in her peripheral vision made her grip a knife, but it was only Dom at the exterior door, dripping and cold. He was unaware of the quavering breath she took while he removed his soggy outer layer and hung it on a hook.

"Smells good," he said.

"It's nothing special. I'm kind of running out of ideas. I have a pretty limited repertoire."

"Practice makes perfect," he said.

She bit her lip to keep from rolling her eyes. Was she going to have to start reading food blogs? They took their plates into the dining room. The pasta was overcooked and starchier than Jane had expected, but Dom seemed too hungry to notice.

"Thanks for this," he said between large bites.

"You're welcome. I texted Sienna to tell her it was ready, but she hasn't answered."

Jane had wondered if the ping of her stepdaughter's phone would help her to find the girl's location, but she'd heard nothing all afternoon.

Dom grimaced. "Okay. I'll try to get her to eat something after we finish up. She texted me from her room this afternoon. Says she needs alone time."

Jane pushed her food aside at the information. Her appetite was lost to the underlying feeling that someone—or something—was sneaking around the hotel. "Peter left yesterday, right?"

"Yep."

"I ask because I keep hearing strange noises around the hotel. I don't think it's my imagination, but maybe I'm wrong. Anyway, just so you know, you're going to be on your own for meals tomorrow. I'm going to meet Mickey for a bit of work."

Dom paused, fork halfway to his mouth. A noodle lolled off the edge. "What are you doing?"

She steeled herself. "Mickey has a meeting set up with Peter's ex-wife. She's the one who has been putting up all the posters for Elijah. We want to get a sense of what she thinks happened to him. Where he went. It could be helpful."

Dom tried to speak but she rushed on.

"I know Melissa's death was incredibly painful, and you don't like to talk about it. And losing Elijah right after is more than any person should have to deal with. But maybe if Mickey and I can find out what happened to him, things will . . . seem clearer." She bit her lip, wondering if now was the time to ask about his prescription medication. It was private, something she would prefer he volunteer rather than be forced to disclose, but she deserved to know what she was dealing with. She was also aware that her dogged research was getting under his skin. How far could she push him before he began asking questions of his own?

Dom shoved the forkful of spaghetti into his mouth. He chewed for a long moment while Jane waited for his response. Finally, he swallowed. "Maybe you're right," he said. "You're welcome to take the car. But I warn you. Lucy isn't going to be a reliable source of information. Her divorce from Peter was extremely acrimonious. He almost lost the hotel."

Jane was surprised and buoyed by his show of support. She had expected more of a fight. But she couldn't help feeling that he had granted her permission when she hadn't needed or asked for it. She might have to nip that in the bud.

"Noted. That's a great piece of information to have. Any chance you want to record an interview with me tonight before I talk to her?"

His fork scraped against his plate as he worked to clean up the last of the sauce. "I'm bagged, Jane. Not sure I'm up for it."

"That's fine. Let's talk about it when I get back. You might know more than you think. Missing persons cases are often solved using a bunch of loose details—not a single lightning bolt moment."

"Sure thing. But try to be on the road home before dark, okay? That rain doesn't look like it's letting up anytime soon. This is another 'river from the sky' that everyone keeps talking about. The weather report looks bleak for the next few weeks."

"I will. Thanks, Dom."

He smiled, finished his plate, then stood up. "I'm going to go check on Sienna. I'll see you in our new room."

"Room eleven," she said. "I liked the time we spent in it earlier so I thought we should move in."

A glitter in his eye gave her a lovely thrill. "I liked it a lot too. Okay, see you shortly."

After clearing up and washing both their plates and the accumulated dishes from the day, Jane was also hit with a wave of fatigue. Between the endless chores, the cold weather, the revelations about Melissa's death, and the discoveries about Elijah's lineage, she was exhausted. She made her way to their new room, got into pajamas, and curled into the (surprisingly comfortable) double bed with a book.

Hours later, she woke with a start. The book was on her chest, the room was dark, and Dom was lying on his back snoring heavily beside her. Had his snoring woken her? No, there was another noise. It was coming from outside. She got out of bed and peered out the window. The only break in the darkness was a glowing light from the front of the hotel, faintly illuminating leaping and bucking waves hammered by rain.

Dom stirred and she turned back to the bed. Filtered by the window, the light was too dim to fully reach the deep shadows pooled on the white bedspread around him. She squinted, then took a step closer and gently pulled the sheet toward the thin beam. The patches were almost black; they weren't shadows.

They were bloodstains.

She approached Dom in a panic, pulling out her phone to scan his body for injury. No sign of a nosebleed, no marks on his neck. It was only when she saw his right hand that she realized the source.

The knuckles of his middle and ring finger were split wide open like a boxer's.

She fumbled for the phone's flashlight for a better look. On the screen was a message from an unknown number—a screenshot of an old Tinder profile she recognized. Her heart seized with shame.

HAILEY • 29

University of British Columbia

12 kilometers away

• Recently Active

MY INTERESTS

- Hot Yoga
- Skincare
- Trying new things
- YouTube
- Road Trips

- Loving, kind, silly mom of one amazing kiddo seeking rad partner to stimulate my mind . . . and/or other areas.

- I'm still looking for my path, but enjoying everyone and every thing I find along the way. I never know when a good connection will come along, so I don't say no to anything.

- Kindness, love of children, and a fun heart required.

The screenshot of the profile was accompanied by a terse message:

You've got secrets too.

CHAPTER | TWENTY

"WAKE UP, WAKE UP!" DOM SHOOK HER HARD.

Jane opened her eyes in the gray morning light. Her husband stood above her, his hands gripped around her arms. The skin around his frantic eyes was pale and wrinkled like fingertips shriveled after a long bath. Patches of red rose high on his cheeks.

"Why? Wha's goin' on?" Sleepiness made her consonants slur, though her pulse was racing. Something was wrong. Dom let go of her arms and she sat up abruptly.

"It's the bridge. It's gone."

"Gone?"

She struggled to focus. Dom's voice was tight. He sounded scared.

"Last night, the water rose fast—probably a beaver dam or something upstream let loose. It happens sometimes—a surge comes in too hard to be held by the banks and it blows away everything in its path. The river is coming up quicker than I've ever seen it. It could flood us out."

"What do you mean?"

Dom's mouth turned down in a grim line. "We're cut off. There's no bridge, no way out. We can't get off the island until rescue crews can repair it."

"What?" She ran to the window and threw open the curtains.

Squinting past the pouring rain, she saw the torrent of brown frothy water had overrun the bank by the boathouse. The river was level with the building now—a rise of at least two meters overnight. Water flowed over the dock rather than underneath. It was nearly impossible to comprehend how much of the bank had already been consumed by the driving current of the swollen river.

"We can't leave?"

Jane felt stupid with shock, but Dom was patient.

"That's right. There's a better view from the deck. Get dressed. I'll show you."

She pulled on a robe and hurried after him through the door that led to the front desk. They crossed the lobby to the stairs, climbed them to the second floor, and headed to the dining room deck. Outside, the wind was icy and the cold rain felt like shards of glass. Within seconds, her flimsy silk robe was a clinging, frigid, second skin.

Dom was right. One side of the bridge's moorings had been ripped from the earth and it bobbed frantically in the rapid flow, the force tugging it from the bank. A near-constant metallic groan suggested it would soon succeed. The place where she had stood with Peter during her conversation two days before was now a mess of mud and churning water. As she watched, a large wave flung the tattered steel bridge up, then down. Murray's warnings returned to her.

"What are we going to do?"

Dom came behind her and put his arms around her shoulders, letting them rest above her pounding heart. Despite the cold rain, she could feel the heat of his body. His chin touched the top of her head.

"I know this is scary. I know this is more than you signed up for, Jane. I'll make some calls. Our phones are still working. I'll figure this out. I'll protect you."

"You can't fight a storm," she shouted, shielding her eyes from the rain.

He spun her around by the shoulders. "But I can find a way through one."

His brown eyes were fierce and earnest. Her heart slowed. She was still terrified, but at least she wasn't alone. Together they ran back inside to shower and change into warm clothes.

Back in the kitchen, Jane stared morosely at her corn flakes, dragging her spoon through the mush in her bowl. The storm had initially pushed the memory of Dom's bloody knuckles and the ugly text message from her mind, but now she had time to ruminate on both. She was furious that an internet troll had managed to find her private number—the possibility that Sienna had sent the message was an ugly suspicion she refused to harbor until she had proof—but more than that, she was pierced by guilt all over again. Would this film haunt her forever?

She could hear Dom in the dining room on a call, his agitated voice coming through the walls. Sienna was nowhere to be seen, which was fine with Jane. Dom had said it was best to wait until she was up before delivering the bad news, and she wasn't looking forward to the conversation. Jane ate another soggy mouthful before setting the bowl aside. Mixed with her fear, the thrashing of the rain and the roar of the river outside was almost unbearable. The swinging door made her twitch. Dom came in with a foreboding face. Her stomach sank.

"Just got off the phone with Peter and the Abbotsford and Chilliwack RCMP detachments. They know about the washout but can't guarantee crews can get on scene anytime soon. Apparently, there've been floods all over the region and it's not over yet. The forecast is calling for more rain over the next few days."

"Murray radioed while you were on the phone," Jane said. "He told me that he'll check in with us every day to make sure we're okay. Said if we were brave enough, we could swim over and have some of his whiskey."

Dom stared at her.

"Sorry. That was insensitive. Gallows humor. I'm just scared."

The wind picked up again and Jane saw a flurry of leaves fly past the window. The trees within view were all but skeletons now, flailing their stripped limbs.

"Don't be scared, Jane. We'll get through this."

"But how long is it going to be until we can leave?"

Dom shook his head. "The sergeant I spoke with wasn't hopeful. He's never seen a storm this big before, but even on a good year, this area's low priority for them—sometimes it can take until spring before they send anyone. It's triage time, basically, and they're going to start with the regions that serve the most people. Most of their crews are in Vancouver dealing with felled power lines and trees on houses; the rest are focusing on the sections of washed-out highways. And there are emergencies all over the province—mudslides, power outages, sewers backing up. It's a mess. Merritt has no drinking water. We're on our own for the foreseeable future."

Jane took a deep, calming breath to smooth out the spikes of fear that were drilling into her shoulders. She offered Dom a wan smile. He responded in kind.

"So, we just wait it out?"

"For now. The important thing is that we're safe. We've got food, we've got heat. We're better off than most."

Jane nodded, trying to follow his lead. "You're right. We're lucky. And we can keep working. You've got everything you need to keep the renos going, and I won't let a little weather stop me from finding out the truth about Elijah."

"But you'll have to cancel your meeting with Lucy, right?"

"I called Mickey to let them know what was going on. They're fine to do it alone on the phone."

"Good. I'm glad Mickey can pick up the work for you. We have to focus on keeping Sienna safe and getting through this in one piece."

"Do you need to call Ted too? Let him know what's going on?"

"What? Oh yeah. I've already taken care of that."

He rubbed the new growth on his jaw with a flat palm, pulling focus to the gouges on his knuckles. In the light of day, they looked deep and sore.

"What happened to your hand? Are you okay?"

He held it out in front of his eyes, squinting as if surprised to see the damage.

"Caught it between a couple tables when I was storing the deck furniture yesterday. I didn't think it was this bad."

"There was blood all over the sheets last night."

He frowned. "Sorry about that—think it'll come out?"

The kitchen door opened before she could answer. Sienna entered.

"Good morning, hon. How'd you sleep?" Dom asked.

"Fine."

"Good. I've got some bad news, but I don't want you to worry. The bridge washed out last night."

Rather than the expected rage, Sienna's face fell in sorrow. Jane fought the urge to go to her side and comfort her.

"So we can't leave?" Sienna said.

Her father shook his head. "Not for the time being. I'm sorry, See. I'm going to take a walk out there in a minute and get a few more details to pass on to Peter. You two going to be okay here on your own?"

"You sure you don't want a hand?" Jane asked.

"No, no. It's going to be rough out there. You stay here. Keep warm."

Dom gave them each a quick kiss before donning a bright yellow slicker and heading out into the rain. After he left, Jane eyed Sienna cautiously. The teenager looked down at the floor for a moment before raising her head.

"Damn. Well, I guess that makes my idea for tonight a little weird."

"What idea?"

Sienna raised her eyes. "Well, I know this has all been a lot for you to get used to, and I've been a bit of a pain. I wanted to plan something cool for you to make up for it. I was thinking that you and my dad can have a special romantic dinner. Just the two of you. But that seems dumb now."

Jane was touched. Almost enough to tamp down her doubt about the girl's true motive.

"That's so thoughtful. I think we can make that work. There's plenty of food and our power's still on. Why not fill the hours with something special?"

Sienna beamed.

Jane felt encouraged enough to try something else. "You'll make something for yourself as well, right? Your father said Dr. Abebe really wants you to work on eating three meals a day."

"Of course. I'll eat too." Sienna's eyes were shining.

"Sienna, this is so kind. It's been a crazy morning—a crazy few days, actually. It's nice to have something to look forward to. Thank you."

"No problem. I have a gift for you as well. A wedding gift."

Jane was stunned. Was Sienna finally beginning to thaw? She didn't know what had changed Sienna's mind, but she was grateful. Her coldness had been so off-putting. Which was a pity, really, because Jane understood Sienna better than the teenager thought—she reminded her of herself, after all. It would have killed her to see her dad having sex with a woman besides her mom. Even now, the thought of it made her gag.

Before she'd met Dom, Jane had never wanted to be a mother. Since she'd learned that Dom had a teenage daughter, she'd harbored secret doubts that she would be able to fulfill the role. But now, in the midst of a chaotic storm, her chosen family was finally beginning to come together.

They were starting to heal. Together.

"A gift? Sienna, you didn't have to do that."

"I wanted to! I'll leave it in the Sunset Suite. And make sure to keep your outfit secret until the big reveal with my dad. Dinner at eight?"

"Perfect," Jane said, aglow with maternal feeling for the very first time. She didn't bother to mention that she and Dom had already moved to room eleven in the staff quarters.

CHAPTER | TWENTY-ONE

AS EVENING FELL, JANE OPENED THE DOOR TO THE SUNSET SUITE. GONE
were the amber shafts of sunshine from their first evening in the hotel;
instead the room was steeped in a dim bluish light. The reflection of the
rain pounding against the windows patterned the walls. A wan beam of
warmth came from the soft yellow glow of a low lamp on the night table,
like a beacon.

Laid out on the bed like a display in a jewelry store was a simple gold
pendant. Jane picked it up with shaking hands. Three delicate letters
intertwined to form a word she never dreamed Sienna would associate
with her.

M-O-M.

Just holding it made something inside her shimmer. Something she
hadn't been sure even existed. A desire to accept the role Sienna had chosen for her.

She clasped the cold metal chain around her neck. The sleek links and smooth letters rubbed against her bare skin. In the bathroom, she carefully applied pale-gold eye shadow, a coat of mascara, and a deep-red lipstick. The sweet taste surfaced a long-forgotten memory of her mother dabbing her favorite shade—Cherries in the Snow—on both their lips as she prepared for a night out. Jane shoved the memory back down as she recalled her mother's tight expression when her father had stumbled in the door later that night, his sweat reeking of acrid whiskey as he struggled to pay the babysitter. She smoothed her pale bob, touched the ridges of her collarbones, and smiled at her reflection.

She was ready.

The rain outside gave the hotel a storm-battered feeling, like a scene from *Rear Window*. She entered the elevator and took it down to the second floor and the dining room. In a way, this was better than the honeymoon she and Dom had postponed. She'd been looking forward to cozying up with him during one of Tofino's monumental, open-ocean storms, but the touristy location had nothing on this remote hotel at the edge of an immense forest, nestled between the soaring peaks of the Rocky Mountains. Tonight, here at the Venatura, with a raging, elemental storm outside, Jane had all she could ever want. A passionate marriage to the man she loved. Multiple months to develop a new film project with Mickey. And a chance to nurture a teenage girl whose grief mirrored her own adolescent wounds.

Her heart thudded with happiness.

Her marriage to Dom had finally been blessed by his daughter—which made the moment feel special and more meaningful. Dom had been right. All Sienna had needed was time. Time to adapt, time to test Jane's commitment and patience. And she had passed! Dom was right about the storm, too. No matter what happened, the three of them would make it out together.

When the elevator doors opened onto the second floor, Sienna was standing outside waiting for her with a shy smile.

"Sienna! I cannot thank you enough," Jane said, touching the pendant. "I love it. I am so honored." She rushed forward and gathered the girl to her in an embrace.

The teenager returned the hug stiffly.

"You're welcome. Great dress! Is it okay if I record your entrance?"

"Oh, thank you," Jane said, patting the bodice of the deep-blue cocktail dress with a sweetheart neckline she had chosen to offset the jewelry. "That's a great idea. It hadn't occurred to me. I'm so used to being on the other side of the camera."

Sienna trained her phone toward her and Jane followed her stepdaughter's backward walk into the dining room. The sight of the glimmering dining room took her breath away.

Sienna had outdone herself. In the time Jane had dressed, she'd created a magical scene. A large round table in the center of the room flickered with dozens of white votive candles floating in glass bowls. The light bounced off the dark windows and shining surfaces, making the entire room glitter. She took a deep breath.

"Oh, Sienna. It's so beautiful!"

From behind her phone, Sienna smiled. "My dad's right over there," she said, pointing to the bar on the western wall. She motioned for Jane to join him.

"Hi, Jane." Dom leaned against the bar with a cocktail glass in hand, wearing a fitted black suit and a crisp white shirt open at the neck. His tall frame seemed longer and leaner than usual, and his newly grown dark beard, threaded with hints of silver, lent him an elegant sexiness. A brooding, modern-day Cary Grant—minus the blatant misogyny. A black silk band had been tied around his eyes.

She had never seen him look so handsome. Something stirred deep within her.

Jane felt like she was at a glamourous masquerade ball—exactly what this gorgeous room had been designed for. She offered a silent word of gratitude to Melissa for her incredible talent and sacrifice and vowed to never forget that her death had given Jane a new life. She would take care of this family no matter what. She was a wife and mother now. She was needed.

She was loved.

Jane walked toward Dom, her heels clicking on the hand-scraped cedar floor.

Sienna put her hand up to halt Jane's movement when she was about a meter away from her husband. Her stepdaughter steadied the camera to ensure they were both in the frame.

"Dad, you can take the blindfold off now."

Dom reached up and pulled the fabric down while Jane struck a pose, as still as a statue, anticipating his pleasure.

But at the sight of her, he winced and looked away.

Sienna whirled so the camera was on Dom. "What do you think, Dad?"

Dom's eyes flashed with pain as he focused on the pendant at Jane's neck. With a shaking hand, he lifted his glass full of amber liquid and took a long draw. He wiped his mouth with the back of his hand before lowering the glass. The wounds on his knuckles had scabbed over.

"What's wrong, Dom?" Jane whispered, panic swirling in her belly.

She was uncertain and confused. It was clear that she'd done something wrong, but what? Finally, he met her eyes. In the twinkling light, his stare was glazed. Blotches were rising again on his cheekbones.

"Yeah, Dad," Sienna said. "Is something *bothering* you?"

Jane broke eye contact with Dom for a moment to look at Sienna. The teenager's eyes glittered with malice, and Jane struggled to understand.

"I'm . . ." Dom took another gulp of his drink. There was nothing left in the tumbler when he set it down on the polished surface of the bar. "I don't know what to say."

"Why?" Jane asked. "What's making you so upset?"

Dom's eyes raked over it. "How can you ask me that? Where did you find it?"

Jane's hands fluttered to her neck. "What do you mean? Sienna, what's going on?"

Her bare arms prickled with cold tension as his brown eyes locked onto hers.

"Why are you wearing my dead wife's necklace?"

CHAPTER | TWENTY-TWO

MIDWAY THROUGH THE MORNING OF THEIR FIFTH AND INCREASINGLY miserable day at the hotel, Jane's phone buzzed. She jerked her hands from a sink full of soapy water, then quickly dried them with a rough dish towel. The notification was a huge relief—the crews must have fixed the telephone lines. Their cell service had gone down during her ill-fated date night, and she'd been unable to tell her closest friend about what Sienna had done. Jane had been terrified that Peter's prediction about being cut off from the rest of the world had come true. Her relief about her phone eradicated any apprehension about another unwanted text from the internet troll. Even an awful message was better than no contact with anyone besides Dom and Sienna.

After Sienna's stunt the night before, neither she nor Dom had any appetite. He'd thrown back three tumblers of whiskey and they'd gone to bed without making love. Dom had turned away as she'd undressed, like he couldn't bear to look at her. When she'd awoken, he was already up and gone.

Fortunately, the text was from Mickey.

why aren't you answering my texts? are you on tiktok?

Jane gave her phone a dirty look. She was right about the phones but wrong about any distraction being a good one. Mickey's obsession with new social media platforms was a running joke between them, but Jane was in no mood for laughing. She sent a perfunctory reply.

Phones were down—sorry. Have an account. Never post. How did the interview go?

Instead of an answer, Mickey sent a TikTok link, and Jane clicked through to a feed that belonged to Sienna. To her horror, she saw herself on the small screen wearing the hateful gold necklace Sienna had tricked her into wearing. White text scrolled across the top of the video as the image of Jane walked through the glowing dining room while the chorus of a catchy pop song played in the background. The camera zoomed to the sparkling gold pendant. Jane shuddered as she read the caption.

Not my stepmother wearing my dead mother's jewelry! #noshame

The camera panned to Dom's face. In the golden light and sharp suit, he looked better on-screen than he had in real life. Jane watched the color drain from his face as he looked beyond the frame. At her.

Watch the moment when my dad's heart breaks

The light caught a sheen of sweat on his graying complexion. He looked ill. The TikTok ended, then began playing from the beginning. Jane scanned the text below.

My dad deserves better #ember #chilboyz #fyp

Even with her limited knowledge of the platform, Jane understood that including the last hashtag (ForYouPage) meant the video would be highly searchable and distributed widely. She didn't recognize the second tag, but knew TikTok had a constant rotation of trends that could increase traffic to a post. The first hashtag angered Jane the most: Sienna had directly called out her production company. This latest stunt was worse than her cruel prank the night before. Jane shoved her phone into her back pocket and entered the dining room. She approached the table where Sienna and Dom sat.

"How could you do this?" Jane asked, holding her phone out to Sienna. Her throat was tight with fury. "This was a difficult, private moment for us as a family."

Sienna shrugged. "What family?"

"What are you talking about?" Dom asked.

Shadows darkened the hollows under his eyes. She had felt him tossing and turning all night.

"Sienna posted . . . this." Jane brought it up on her phone and put it into Dom's hands.

His eyebrows stitched together. "Take it down," he growled.

"What? Oh my god, Dad. That's not how it works."

"Of course that's how it works. No video, no one can see it."

"It's already been duetted hundreds of times," she said, leaning back in her chair. "People are worried about what I'm going through here. They want to help."

She glared at Jane, who absorbed the blow like a punch to her stomach. What had she done to make Sienna hate her so much? Catching them having sex had been horrifying, but surely it didn't justify this.

"Please, Sienna," Jane said. "This matters more than you know. It's my livelihood."

She hated to think what a video like this would do to her already soiled reputation.

"I don't have to listen to you."

"This is not a request," Dom said.

Sienna rolled her eyes. "It's not going to change anything. I have a following now. I'm planning to do a series."

"No! Do not put me or tag Ember in another TikTok. I mean it." Fear and frustration made her volume rise. She looked to Dom, but his eyes were fixed on his daughter.

"Sienna, this is a mess. I know that we rushed this marriage. Didn't know . . . everything about each other"—he glanced at Jane—"but we have to try. See it through. At least for the season."

The season?

Jane's heart sank at the hopelessness in Dom's voice. She'd never heard him speak of their marriage like that. Just the day before, he'd refuted all the doubts she'd expressed. Now he thought they'd only last a season? "Stuff like this can ruin a person, Sienna. I know you are going through a lot, but this is not an acceptable response. Maybe it's time to talk to Dr. Abebe?"

Sienna flinched dramatically. "I'm not insane just because I'm bulimic." She pulled her phone out of her back pocket and began filming herself. "My stepmother is ruining my life, check."

"Stop recording," Dom said.

Sienna wheeled the phone around to film Jane. "Why? Why should I stop?"

Dom was staring at his daughter in disbelief. "Sienna, come on."

Sienna held the phone steady.

"Sienna!" Jane cried.

"I need to make sure this is captured. Why are you so worried about being on camera? Do you have something to hide, Jane?"

The words cut her. Without thinking, Jane grabbed the phone out of her stepdaughter's hand and hurled it. It hit the mirror above the coffee counter like a rock on a windshield. All three of them stared in disbelief at the fist-size point of impact. Glass spiderwebbed around the break.

The room was still. Then Sienna spoke. "Nice one, Jane. Maybe *you* should talk to Dr. Abebe."

I'm not the one hoarding rotting shrimp rings in my bed, Jane thought.

Sienna stomped over to retrieve her phone, tossing spiteful words over her shoulder. "Lucky for you it's not broken. My TikTok followers would find me if I stopped posting. They would assume my evil stepmother hurt me."

Jane met Dom's eyes. His face was guarded. Sienna stomped toward the elevator bay.

"What are we supposed to do with her?"

"Not that," Dom said with a frown.

Jane closed her eyes. "I'm sorry. I lost my temper. She was being—"

"She's been through a lot," he said, interrupting. "Might want to try going easy on her. On both of us."

Jane took a deep breath. "She was being vicious and vindictive, Dom. And she wasn't just cruel to me. She filmed *your* pain for her followers. She has every right to be angry with you—for marrying me so soon after Melissa's death, and for dragging her back to this hotel. But Dom, she tagged my company—"

"I know, and we'll deal with it. But not through tantrums."

Jane looked at him with reproach. "I need you to be on my side on this, Dom. It isn't just my job—it's Mickey's too. Ever heard of cancel culture? This is my career we are talking about. She's out of line with her awful antics last night and this stunt today. You need to do something about this right now."

"And this"—he gestured toward the door that Sienna had left through—"is your family. That should count too." Dom's expression was expectant and slightly hostile.

"To quote your daughter: What family? And your defense of her—" Jane stopped herself before she said something she'd regret. After a moment, she nodded. "There is a limit to what I'll tolerate, Dom, but you're right. I'll talk to her later."

"Good. Thank you. Listen, I've got a bunch of work to do on the third floor today. Don't worry about making lunch for me—I'll eat upstairs. It's probably good for us to spend a little time apart. Cool down."

Unease made her throat feel dry. "Any word on the bridge repair?"

Dom looked to the large windows at the front of the dining hall. Rain filmed their surfaces. Beyond the blur, the raging river was higher than it had been the day before. "Nothing yet."

Jane dropped her gaze, trying to hide the tears welling up in her eyes. To her surprise, she heard Dom rise from his chair. He wrapped his strong arms around her. She breathed in his scent, trying to ignore the faint whiff of old whiskey that reminded her of the few times her dad had been sober enough to tuck her in.

"I know you're scared and confused. So is Sienna. She's struggling with this washout just like you. But remember—we're in this together."

"I'd appreciate if you reminded her of that too. Ask her to give me a break. I'm trying my best here."

"I know." He sighed heavily, kissed her on the top of the head, and left the room.

Jane began to clear the table. As she gathered the plates, she fought the urge to smash every single one of them onto the floor.

CHAPTER | TWENTY-THREE

JANE WAITED UNTIL SHE WAS BACK IN THE SCULLERY BEFORE PULLING out her phone. Her stomach churned when she saw another text from the unknown number. It was a YouTube clip from a relatively well-known personality named Rascal Rococo—one of the subjects of *Failure to Thrive*. She'd viewed it many times before as part of her research, and an edited version had ended up in the final cut of her documentary. A scan of the latest comments sickened her.

RASCAL ROCOCO
96.7 thousand subscribers

2022 was a massive year for my crew and my fans. My work, my drive, my hype is all for you guys. Everything I make and share is because of you guys. I ain't ever stopping. Shout out in the comments about your fave moment of this crazy year.

Subscribe to RascalRococo http://bit.ly/Rascalrococo MERCH! http://Rascalrococo

FOLLOW THE FAM

HAILEY SIMON: https://instagram.com/haileysimon
TOMMY SHINE: https://instagram.com/tommyshine
FERGLE THE DERP: https://instagram.com/fergle
CHILBOYZ: https://instagram.com/chilboyz
MAESTRO MAN: https://instagram.com/maestro

889 comments

Chloe| Mama Power

You can see the kid's dimples. He is clearly having the time of his life.

sarah prett

that kid is being abused. someone call the police.

Chris THE MAN

This dude looks like he's about to kill that kid. Is it even his baby?

sarah prett

Right?

BrownSuga

Everybody so creative

SweetChildOMine

I'm on mama's side here. That baby is fine and needs to learn his lesson.

Zara Long

Can we get the authorities in to check on that poor child? This is not normal.

ZingerDinger

LOCK 'EM UP

She called Mickey.

Mickey picked up on the second ring. "Finally!" they cried. "I texted you like a hundred times. This rain is unbelievable. Are you still cut off from everything? Are you okay with that fucking little weasel? I can't believe she did that to you."

Jane looked from side to side to ensure she was alone.

"Honestly, I want to kill her. But it's not just the TikTok. I'm getting harassing messages from some online loser. It might be Sienna, but I wouldn't be surprised if she gave out my cell number." Paranoid thoughts crawled like maggots in her brain. Sienna had unfettered access to the internet, and she'd been heavily hinting that she knew what Jane had done. Was her stepdaughter spiteful enough to tell Dom? To send these messages herself? The gnawing guilt that Jane had lived with since the documentary festival had formed a hollow pit inside her.

"Stay strong. Maybe she'll choke to death binging on a cheeseburger, and you can have Dom to yourself."

Jane laughed softly. God, she loved Mickey. "She's definitely a . . . challenge. Did you see that she tagged us on the post? Luckily, some candle company called Ember has been trending on TikTok, so they're probably getting weird buzz today. Nobody seems to have connected the dots to us."

"Yet."

"Yeah. It's not the comeback tour you were hoping for." Jane exhaled a puff of rage. "I have to get her to take it down."

"That won't change much at this point. TikToks are pretty tenacious. That one's already been picked up by a bunch of influencers, but even viral stuff can die down quickly. Users on that platform are not exactly documentary film lovers. Fingers crossed some other dum-dum makes it big today and we avoid ugly blowback. Want to hear some good news?"

"Desperately." Jane tried to shake off the lingering anger she had about Sienna. She had to focus.

"I've got a new lead from Peter's ex-wife. Lucy is no fan and she was eager to talk shit. According to her, Peter is a cold prick. He was a workaholic who spent more time at the hotel than at home."

"Sounds about right. The guy had a hard time leaving us here alone. I thought he was going to stay for the season."

"Lucy said Peter had a hotel back in London that failed miserably. He's got family money, so he moved to Canada to try again. She thinks it's an ego thing—he desperately wants this hotel to be a success, to show all his initial investors that they shouldn't have dropped him. Apparently, he's got a bit of a revenge complex."

"And the workaholic thing was the cause of his divorce?"

"Seems like it. Major alienation of affection. He became obsessed with the renovation and poured all their money into it. Elijah was volun-told every summer to work on the property. Lucy said it was the only way he could spend any time with his dad. Even after Elijah went missing, Peter couldn't stop thinking about the hotel. Lucy said he barely seemed to care that his own son was gone. Was more worried about what it might do to their reputation. After a few months of searching, he basically gave up and went back to obsessing about the hotel."

Jane's mind raced as she recalled Murray's conversation with Dom.

"If Elijah spent the off season out here the year before he went missing, he would have been working with Melissa. She was the head designer on the project. They definitely knew each other—and likely pretty well."

The line rustled in her ear. Jane could picture her friend eagerly nodding. "Yes—totally! That's the link. Apparently, Melissa and Elijah spent *a lot* of time together before she died. They were tasked with"—Jane heard more paper rustling—"an interior redesign of the main floor, guest rooms, and an exterior refurbishment of the boathouse. Does that make sense?"

"It does. They did an incredible job on the main floor. I haven't seen the boathouse up close yet. And won't for a while if this rain keeps up." The mention of the renovations brought Dom to her mind. Her heart ached with new sympathy. No wonder he was being so guarded and protective of his daughter, and cagey about Elijah—it had to be excruciating to have to finish the job Melissa had started with the missing young man. And Sienna was clearly channeling her grief into misguided rage. Their tense conversation about Sienna's maliciousness at breakfast suddenly seemed petty in the face of their pain.

"What did Lucy have to say about Melissa?"

Mickey exhaled. "Kind of a dead end there. Sounds like Melissa came on the scene as the designer when Lucy and Peter were on the outs. Lucy said she made a point not to come to the hotel for the last few years of its operation. Before that, she and Melissa hung out socially a few times over the years when the families would get together. Lucy liked her well enough, but they weren't close. Lucy said she was fun and a little flirty—just like Sienna."

"Sienna?" It was difficult to imagine her surly stepdaughter flirting. It was also a strange way to describe a teenager.

"Yeah, I guess Peter had to step in a couple years ago to keep Sienna from hanging around Elijah and his friends too much."

Peter? Then Jane did some quick math. "Sienna would have been barely fourteen then, and Elijah would have been in his early twenties."

"She seems pretty feisty though. Fourteen isn't exactly a baby."

"No, but it's a vulnerable age." Though there was nothing she'd put past Sienna now, Jane didn't like the idea of a younger Sienna hanging around grown men. "Anything else?"

"Lucy said Dom was nice. Kind of jealous at times, but only when he drank too much. Apparently, Melissa had a tendency to get handsy with other men after a few glasses of wine. Lucy said she saw the two of them arguing a few times but nothing extreme. Couple stuff, I guess. Is he like that with you?"

An unpleasant flare of jealousy made her palms sweat. "No, not at all. We've never fought. But then again, I haven't flirted with anyone in front of him." Jane bit her lip. Did his stern instructions this morning count as a fight?

"Okay, but um—"

Mickey's pause grated on Jane's patience. "What?"

"Don't get mad."

Jane didn't respond.

"I just . . . How did he feel when he saw you wearing Melissa's necklace? He did not look happy."

Jane gritted her teeth hard enough to make her jaw hurt. "I one hundred percent do not want to talk about that."

"Okaaaaaay, got it. But let me know if he goes all Jack Torrance. Let's focus on the story. Go check out the boathouse when you can—get some footage. I'd like to see it. And take photos of the inside of the hotel too. There might be something there for us to dig into."

"So you think there's a story?"

"Absolutely! An experienced kayaker drowns in a freak accident at the Venatura, and the hotelier's son goes missing right after? This is juicy. And I dug up another connection between Melissa and Elijah. Lucy said that Melissa had a small crew—Elijah and three other guys. Dylan Musgrave, Randeep Gill, and Joseph Jack."

"Joseph Jack? He must be related to my neighbor, Murray. And those other guys—I saw a photo of them with Elijah."

"Put the photo on the shared drive I set up. And yeah, that makes sense that they were palling around. All these guys are local."

"So Peter and Melissa hired them as grunt labor?"

"Pretty much. Dylan and Randeep were working at the hotel already. I guess the two of them ran a guided fishing tour for guests during peak season. Peter asked them to stay on to help with the renovations. Not sure how Joseph Jack came to be on the crew, but if he lived nearby that would explain it."

"Let me follow up with that. I should be able to find out more from Murray."

"It looks like the five of them worked together throughout the off season of 2021, the year before Melissa died and Elijah went missing. There's videos of them spending a lot of time together at the hotel."

"And stayed on until May?"

"Yep. From what I can tell, they were a tight-knit crew who formed a COVID bubble so they could work together without masks or whatever. They had a YouTube channel. At first, it seems like they were going for a fun 'ruins to renovation' kind of vibe, but it devolved into stupid pranks mostly led by Elijah. Some of them are kind of funny, but most are dumb. The channel is called ChilBoyz."

"Oh god," Jane groaned. She made a mental note to watch the videos on the channel later.

"I know. But here's where it gets really weird. The following summer, 2022, Dylan and Randeep went out to meet someone about buying a truck. I guess the whole group had a thing for vintage Fords. They planned to meet the seller on a rural property. Police tried to track down the seller, but they couldn't find the online ad, if there was one."

"Police?"

"Yeah. After twenty-four hours, the two of them still hadn't come back, so someone reported them missing. I haven't yet tracked down who called the police, but I will. The search went on for weeks—I sort of remember hearing about it."

Jane's mouth was so dry that her lips stuck to her teeth when she spoke. "Did they find them?"

"Nope."

For a moment, neither of them spoke. Jane worked hard to organize her thoughts.

"So a few months before Melissa drowned and Elijah disappeared, two other men they knew went missing?"

"Yep. See what I mean about us being onto something? The Venatura is a true crime gold mine."

CHAPTER | TWENTY-FOUR

JANE BRACED HERSELF BEFORE WALKING DOWN THE GRAND STAIRS. The soup she was carrying sloshed up the sides of the bowl and she gripped the tray to ensure it wouldn't spill. When she reached the main floor, she glanced outside. The massive windows of the hotel's façade were no longer framing a beautiful tableau. Instead, all she could see was the furious river and the endless rain.

A quick scan of the news headlines as she prepared lunch had been unnerving. To the east of them, a pulverizing landslide had taken out a section of a secondary highway and dozens of cars were trapped until rescue vehicles could get through. To the west, less than twenty kilometers away, farmlands and houses were underwater. People and livestock were being airlifted out of areas where overflowing rivers and creeks had breached homes and farms. The disappearing banks of the river suggested the water was coming for them as well. A shiver ran down her spine.

Now that she knew Melissa had been the creative force behind the redesign, Jane saw the main floor with fresh eyes. The clean elegance of the open area now felt cold and unwelcoming. She headed to the seating area near the fireplace where Sienna was glued to her phone.

"Hi," she said when she reached the couch where her stepdaughter sat.

The teenager had her legs drawn up beneath her and she looked small on the enormous sectional.

"Hey," Sienna said without looking up.

"I brought you some lunch."

Jane set the tray down on the coffee table in front of Sienna.

"Not hungry."

"You need to eat. And we need to talk."

"About what?"

Jane set her jaw. "About the TikTok."

Sienna dropped her phone onto the soft cushion beside her. "Or we could talk about you destroying my property."

"Or we could talk about you filming your father's grief for the validation of strangers, and tarnishing your mother's memory. What would you prefer?"

Sienna scowled.

"That's a good look for you. Very attractive. Listen, Sienna, I lost my temper and I'm sorry. But you could have ruined my production company."

Sienna smirked. "As if you aren't doing a pretty good job of that yourself."

Goose bumps rippled up Jane's arms. "What's that supposed to mean?"

"You know."

"I don't," Jane said, a little louder than she intended.

"Is this what you think being a mother is? Losing your shit whenever things don't go your way?"

"Please don't swear."

"Why the fuck not?"

Jane fought to rein in her temper. "This is never going to work if you keep acting like this."

Sienna smiled. "I know."

Jane stared at the girl in disbelief. Her heart pounded and she clenched her fists, once, twice, digging her nails deep into the flesh of her palms. Her mother had once told her she hoped Jane had a daughter just like her one day. Was this what she had meant? Had she ever been this bitter and mouthy? The powerlessness was nearly unbearable. Jane took a deep breath. "Fine. There's soup there if you want it."

"No thanks." Sienna pushed the tray with her big toe. The liquid lurched over the lip of the bowl and spilled onto the surface of both the tray and the table.

Jane resisted the urge to take it away and leave Sienna with nothing. Instead, she turned on her heel and walked out the main doors. There were few places to go, but she had to be alone. She couldn't trust herself not to lash out. The hollow sound of her steps across the stone floor wasn't loud enough to drown out Sienna's chuckle.

Miserable little bitch.

The outside air smelled like campfire and cold. Jane tugged the hood of her coat over her head to protect herself from the driving rain. The sides of her hood obscured her peripheral vision, but through the curtains of rain, she saw a waterlogged landscape. The raised lawn that had stretched toward the sandy shore of the river was now overrun by the water, and the beach beyond it had disappeared. A fast-moving muddy froth replaced the land she had stood on only days before.

Jane turned to the right and followed the gravel path that hugged the hotel. The mulch of wood chips that had covered the flower beds beside the building was a mess of standing water and brown muck. She avoided the gathering puddles on the side of the trail as best she could, but her suede Blundstone boots were soaked in minutes. The damp fabric of her socks rubbed on the back of her heel, promising blisters. She tried to console herself by imagining this part of the property on a warm summer's day. She could picture the gentle slope of the green lawn drifting toward the enormous trees standing tall on the curve of the riverbank. But the high water levels had engulfed their trunks, making them appear dwarfed and helpless in the push of the powerful currents. It was unnerving to see their strength overcome by the river.

Her boots squelched with every step as she turned the corner and saw a covered deck lining the eastern side of the Venatura. She ducked under it for a brief respite from the relentless patter of rain on her hood. Streams of water sluiced from the corners of the covering like she was trapped behind a waterfall. She squinted at the foreground where the massive trees were shaking in the wind. Between their wet trunks, she could see the vague outline of a path and the large white building perched on the edge of the river. The boathouse. She willed herself to return to the rushing rain, but as she moved forward, another sound registered.

It was deep and mournful—a cross between a moan and a cry, barely audible above the falling water. She searched the length of the deck to find the source of the anguished noise, listening intently, but could see no sign. There it was again. The long sad wail raised the hairs on the back of her damp neck. She moved toward what she thought was the source, taking one step at a time to determine if she was any nearer. The low cries turned into a sharp yowl—loud and fierce.

She halted.

It sounded like a dying animal. Another howl, shorter and louder than the last, plucked at her core need to protect the weak. No matter the danger, she had to help. Jane took another step. The howling was louder now but she couldn't find the source. In desperation, she jumped off the edge and back into the storm to search underneath. Maybe something had sought refuge in the dry space under the decking. The ground was spongy and streams of water pounded her back. She laid down on her stomach. Using her phone's flashlight, she shone it toward the sound, illuminating a flash of eyes.

Without thinking, she shoved her hand into the darkness, crying out when she touched something warm and wet. The creature screamed at her. She yanked her hand back, fearing a bite or worse.

Another wail came from the spot under the deck, but plaintive and softer than before.

Again, she reached into the dark space, turning sideways to extend her reach, willing to risk pain to save whatever was suffering. But instead of a nasty bite, Jane felt a tiny, sandpaper lick. With a flat hand, she patted the area and found fur. She moved her phone. The weak beam allowed her to get a good glimpse of the ugly one-eyed cat blinking warily at her. Fraser! But why was he so upset? Surely a feral cat knew how to weather a storm.

A low growl came from the depths of the cat's throat, but he didn't threaten to scratch when Jane petted his flank. Using her feet for leverage, she shoved her head and shoulders as far as she could into the tight space. Small cries filled the musty, dank air. She repositioned her phone again and saw three newborn kittens, still wet, nuzzling into Fraser's shivering body. Another little one lay unmoving a few inches away from the others.

Jane spoke tender words to the frightened, exhausted animal as she gently stroked his—no, her—wet fur. Fraser was a mama cat. And Jane needed to protect her little family.

CHAPTER | TWENTY-FIVE

JANE LOOKED AROUND FOR SOME WAY TO CARRY THE MOTHER AND kittens inside where it was warm and dry. At the edge of the long deck, she spotted a rectangular planter with a neglected grouping of flowers that had browned and withered in the cold weather. She dumped out the dirt and did her best to scrape it clean using her bare hands and the edge of her raincoat. She knelt on the sopping ground once again and began the heart-wrenching job of separating each kitten from its mother. Their tiny meows were difficult to hear—harder even than the anguished cries of Fraser, whose growls became more mournful than menacing.

Once the three surviving kittens were safely placed in the box, she shoved both her arms under the deck to capture their mother. Fraser hissed and clawed at Jane's raincoat, but calmed the moment she was reunited with her babies.

The adult cat sniffed each of them in turn before she began howling again. Jane gathered the stiff body of the runt of the litter—small enough to fit into the palm of her hand—and gently placed it beside Fraser, who licked it vigorously. As Jane rushed toward the main entrance of the hotel, the kittens squirmed toward their mother, pressing to protect themselves from the needles of rain.

She spotted a flash of red on the other side of the river as she veered around the front corner of the hotel. She vaguely made out the shape of an old truck through the thickening of trees and undergrowth on the bank. Murray was standing close to the edge of the river. He raised an arm in greeting and hollered something she couldn't understand. She yelled a hello, which was swallowed by the storm and the sheer force of the moving water between them. Murray shouted, but his voice was again lost in the wind. Jane wedged the planter box against her hip and made a swooping hand gesture at her ears in the universal sign of *I can't hear you*. He gestured toward the hotel, presumably indicating they should try a radio call instead. She focused on getting the cats to safety.

Once inside, the dry, heated air in the lobby was a relief. She quickly made her way to the fireplace, where Sienna was still seated, her position nearly unchanged from where Jane had left her. The bowl of soup and the congealing liquid around it remained on the table. Sienna was laughing at something on her phone, but her expression changed when she saw Jane.

"What is that? Why are you so dirty?"

Jane was breathless after lugging the cats through the storm. She placed the dripping planter box close to the fireplace.

"It's Fraser—"

"Who?"

"The stray cat who lives around here—"

"Cat? Ew!" Sienna leapt from the couch. "I'm SO allergic. Get it out of here!"

"Let me finish, Sienna. The cat just had kittens. She needs our—"

"OH MY GOD!" Sienna hollered. "There's more than one? I'm seriously going to swell up like a balloon."

"I can't let them stay outside in the rain. They'll die if I leave them out there. One of them already has."

Jane roughly tugged a dove-gray throw blanket from the back of a nearby chair and laid it out a few feet from the low cement bench in front of the fire. She carefully scooped out the kittens one at a time, ignoring Fraser's warning sounds.

"Listen to it. It doesn't even want to be in here."

"She's scared. Animals are like this when they get frightened. Haven't you ever had a pet?"

Sienna's cheeks pinked. "Ummmmmm, no. I'm allergic, remember?"

"What's going on in here? Are those . . . kittens? Sienna, stay back, hon."

Dom hurried across the stone floor. His entire body was soaked—water funneled off his raincoat and baseball cap, leaving puddles in his wake. His mouth was turned down in concern.

"Jane, Sienna has a terrible allergy to cats. Is that the stray you were feeding earlier?"

"Yes, Fraser isn't a he! He's a she! And she has kittens," Jane cried enthusiastically.

"I don't think any of us care about misgendering the cat, Jane. I just don't want to have to live with it. Dad, you know what happens to me around animals!"

Fraser looked up from cleaning the unmoving kitten to meow her concern.

"Well, we're not going to let them die. I'll keep them in the kitchen. Sienna never goes in there. This poor cat has been through so much—"

"Obviously—look at it!"

Jane turned back to the creature. Her mottled coloration was dingier now that her fur was wet and standing up in hackles along her back. But her face was beatific—worn-out but proud of the little babies that surrounded her. She met Jane's gaze with her one eye that now seemed wise and knowing, as if motherhood had changed her in a profound way. She closed and opened it slowly before letting out a soft mew. She was begging for a chance. A small, unexpected movement made both Jane and Fraser turn. The runty baby beside Fraser lifted its head. Jane gasped in joy. Fraser gave another meow and began nudging the kitten with her pink nose.

"Look!" Jane cried. "Her kitten's revived—I saved its life!"

"She's a feral cat, Jane. She's not a pet," Dom said.

Jane looked at him in disbelief. "She was *Melissa*'s pet. She fed this cat every day. At the very least we can nurse them to health. I just want to give her a chance. Give them all a chance. They deserve it."

Dom seemed unmoved. "We can't prioritize this cat over Sienna. You understand that, right?" He walked toward her. Sienna stayed behind.

"Well, if you won't do it for me, how about for Melissa's memory? I'm telling you right now that I'm not putting them outside in this, and neither are you."

He closed his eyes and took a deep breath. "Okay, fine. Let's take them to the scullery. I guess they can stay there for now. Sienna, let Jane take care of your laundry, okay? I don't want you to get near these cats."

"Dad, no!" Sienna said, before forcing out a dry cough. "It's already starting. My throat is killing me."

Better you than Fraser and her kittens, Jane thought.

"I'll grab you an antihistamine after I help Jane."

Jane gathered the cats up in a soft blanket. She followed Dom to the elevator, staring straight down to avoid Sienna's scowl.

"This is so unfair," Sienna said. "Mom would never have done this to me!"

The elevator arrived and they both entered. Dom pressed the button for the second floor.

"Thank you," Jane said in a quiet voice once she was sure Sienna was out of earshot.

"You're welcome."

His tone was clipped, and he kept his eyes fixed on the elevator doors. In the mirror, Jane could see that his features were set hard as stone. The cats wriggled in the blanket.

"I'll let you take it from here," he said when they arrived at their floor.

"Wait! Are you angry?"

Dom rubbed his face. A few stray drops of water flew from his sleeve to her body. "No." His voice was monotone.

"Dom, please talk to me. I'm not sure what you expected me to do. Leave these cats to die?"

He shook his head. "No, of course not. I just—expected your priorities to be different. In my experience, good mothers tend to put their children first."

"And in mine, good fathers know when they're being manipulated."

CHAPTER | TWENTY-SIX

AFTER BUILDING A SOFT SPACE FOR FRASER OUT OF SEVERAL BLANKETS in the corner of the scullery near the short-wave radio, Jane coaxed the cat forward with a can of tuna and a fresh bowl of water. The sight of the wizened animal taking her tiny kittens in her mouth one at a time reassured her that she had done the right thing. Besides, it was nice not to be alone. She listened to the gentle sounds of them settling for a moment before her eyes landed on the small black filing cabinet under the radio.

Time to get to work.

Sliding open the drawer, she found chaos. Files were crammed haphazardly beside one another, many forced in so tight their ragged contents were shoved out the top. The first several she dislodged were from the current fiscal year—payroll, tax forms, employee benefit filings, and an itemized stack of invoices (all stamped *Paid*). From there, the filing systems devolved into a disorganized mess. Some were labeled, while others were blank or had poorly erased names. Many were from years before.

She sighed and furtively looked at the clock. It was hours until dinner. She wasn't sure how Dom was going to spend his time, but it didn't seem likely that either him or Sienna would come looking for her. Digging her hands between the tightly packed files, she began to slide them out one by one looking for payroll records, contact information, anything she could get her hands on about Melissa's renovation crew.

She stacked the ones from the previous year in a neat pile. Undated folders went onto a second pile. She placed all the others in a milk crate she found under the sink after emptying it of cleaning supplies.

A crashing sound from the kitchen made her leap away from the stacks. Someone was in there—right next door. Guilt bubbled through her body as she moved to the swinging door to ward them away from her research. She wasn't doing anything wrong, but she knew neither Sienna nor Dom would see it that way. In her battle of wills with Sienna, some-how she'd become the villain. As she gently pushed the swinging door open, she called out, "Hello? Are you okay?"

When she entered the room, she saw a copper pot laying upside down on the floor. The hook above it was empty.

"Hello?" she called again.

A rising sense of panic prompted her to check every cupboard. She flung open the doors wildly, searching for a reasonable explanation. Or an intruder.

Nothing.

She rounded on the dark corner by the pass-through to the dining room but there was only a collection of standing mops, stiffened by years of use. A hulking shape on the exterior wall caught her eye—it was a small dumbwaiter she hadn't noticed before. Something in her chest fluttered as she carefully slid the metal door open to look inside the small space. But it was empty too. She checked that the padlock she had attached to the walk-in cooler hadn't been disturbed, then chastised herself for her paranoia. Turning around, she bit her lip hard enough to make it crunch beneath her teeth. The pot had likely been carelessly hung. The hotel was full of nascent noises. It was an old building. There wasn't anything—or anyone—to worry about.

With trembling hands, she returned to handling the pages and folders. Her heart was still racing. She knew it was silly, but it was hard to shake the feeling she was being watched.

The fluorescent light hummed above her as she sorted and searched through the stacks of useless pages. Another glance at the clock made her swallow hard. Hours in, and she was no closer to locating anything of use. Despite her growing concern that there was no point to what she was doing, she pressed on.

Then a folder from the back of the drawer brought her up short. Its manila tab on top read *Payroll* and it was dated the year before. When she opened the folder and found an assortment of pay stubs, she sighed in relief. This was it. She thumbed through the contents of the list but was immediately disappointed when the names of Melissa's crew failed to appear.

The next file in the pile was marked *Contractors: External*. It was hopelessly disorganized. There were a dozen or so signed contracts with private businesses from various years: a laundry service, garbage removal, duct specialists. She spotted an agreement made with Dom's contracting company, Right Fit Construction, which she plucked up and read carefully. The contract was from two years ago—about a year before Melissa's death—and detailed the terms of the new build for the boathouse. Finally, something she could use.

Both Dom and his brother, Ted, were listed as signatories, with their cell phone numbers underneath. Peter Stanton had represented the hotel and had signed below their names. She wondered if Melissa's crew had interacted with Ted and Dom while they were on-site. Maybe Dom knew Dylan and Randeep as well. Or worse. Maybe he'd known a lot more about Elijah than he let on. She remembered what Lucy had told Mickey about Melissa's flirting—and Dom's jealousy when he was drinking.

She dug back into the drawer, fighting fatigue. Her earlier adrenaline was ebbing. She knew dead ends were part of every investigation, but once she began something, she found it difficult to let go. Her outstretched fingers grasped something sharp, and a blaze of pain ran up her arms. She tugged her hand out of the drawer, drawing it close to her face in panic. The tips of her index and middle finger were smeared with blood.

She rushed to the sink to clean her hand, wincing as the water stung. She gingerly patted them dry on a paper towel then examined her injury. There was a fresh horizontal cut across the pads of both fingers. The edges were clean. Had she sliced them on something inside the drawer? She looked inside the filing cabinet. An unfamiliar glint caught her eye.

Her body tensed when she saw the large carving knife placed squarely on top of the pile of dusty folders.

CHAPTER | TWENTY-SEVEN

HER PULSE POUNDED AGAINST THE FABRIC BANDAGES SHE HAD FOUND in the small first aid kit by the radio. She stared at the filing cabinet. The only reason someone would place a knife in a filing cabinet was for protection. Had it been Peter? The weapon had been buried deep under the files. Had he put the knife there to protect against intruders? Or to protect himself from someone in the hotel? Staff? Guests? The idea made little sense. Her thoughts turned to Sienna. The teenager could be playing a stupid prank. But it was Dom's name in the files. Could her husband be hiding something else?

Her phone pinged. Her heart sank when she saw the unknown sender had sent another file. This time, it was a transcript from her own film.

DOCUMENTARY—A-ROLL VIDEO LOG
EMBER PRODUCTIONS
FAILURE TO THRIVE

INTERVIEW WITH CAROL ROCHE
(MOTHER OF YOUTUBER RASCAL ROCOCO)
TAPE # 36
10/21/22
1:0:00 BEGIN TAPE

JANE: Hello, Ms. Roche. Thank you for agreeing to this interview about your son Rascal.

CAROL: Anything I can do to help. My son has been dragged over the coals for an innocent prank. It's silly nonsense.

JANE: Have you seen the YouTube video with Hailey Simon and her little boy, Bryson?

CAROL: No.

JANE: But you're certain that he meant no harm? That it was, in fact, an innocent prank?

CAROL: He loves that child. Ever since he started dating Hailey, he's been nothing but good to them both. I was worried when he got involved with a single mother, but Rascal is a stand-up guy. He's always been there for them.

JANE: Including their Christmas video? When he tells four-year-old Bryson that Santa fell down the stairs because he left his toys all over? So he won't be delivering presents this year? Hailey seems reluctant to participate. Many viewers have noted the pressure Rascal puts on her.

CAROL: It was a joke.

JANE: Do you think the Christmas video is funny?

CAROL: Yes, I do. My son would never hurt a child. I taught him better than that.

JANE: Do you want to see the other video? Decide for yourself?

CAROL: I trust my son.

JANE: See that laptop? It's queued up with the YouTube clip of Rascal's prank. I'm going to leave the room. This camera will stay on. Will you watch it now?

Footsteps thumped outside the door. Jane froze. The only sounds in the quiet room were the rasp of Fraser cleaning her kittens and the sluicing of rain down the solitary window. With a galloping heart, she tiptoed to the door and swung it open slowly to peer into the dining room.

It was empty. A small breeze lifted the hair on the back of her neck as she let the door swing shut again before opening the door that led to the kitchen. Also empty.

Jane no longer felt alone on the second floor of the hotel. And with that realization, she wondered if her suspicions about her stepdaughter hadn't gone far enough. Rather than giving out her number, could Sienna be the source of the harassment? Had she found a way to mask her phone number? Were these texts a veiled threat that she was about to reveal everything to Dom?

She was running out of time to tell Dom about her past before someone else did.

With hurried movements, she added Ted's number from Peter's files to her contacts. He'd been unable to come to the wedding so she'd yet to meet her brother-in-law.

It was time for an introduction.

Jane took a photo of the page then rifled through the remaining papers. A charter boat company called Fraser River Fish had signed a third-party operator's agreement in the spring to offer a "premier sports fishing experience." The signatories to the agreement were Randeep Gill and Dylan Musgrave, and Peter Stanton on behalf of the hotel.

Bingo.

She took several more photos, then returned the contract—which looked boilerplate to her eyes—to the file. After a frenzied search within the file, she found nothing else of interest. She returned to the cabinet and removed the knife carefully. A thick collection of wrinkled papers caught her eye. She let out a puff of satisfaction. It was a stack of waivers from Dylan and Randeep's guests over their fishing season. The names were unrecognizable to her until she reached the middle of the pile.

Sienna, Dom, and Melissa had all taken part in a "freshwater adventure package" in July 2022—three months before Melissa's drowning. She pored over each line of her stepdaughter's liability release form, stopping when she saw the name listed for Sienna's medical contact.

Dr. Abebe.

Jane snapped a photo, then added the doctor's name to her contacts list. Melissa's paperwork yielded nothing out of the ordinary—her medical contact was named Dr. Nikowsky. A quick online search showed she was part of a family health center. She scanned Dom's blocky handwriting before drawing in a sharp breath. Dr. Abebe was Dom's doctor as well. Why would Dom and Sienna list a mental health professional instead of a general practitioner on their forms? Did this have anything to do with Dom's prescription for antipsychotic medication?

Jane flicked through the rest of the undated folders but found nothing more of interest. She sent the photos to Mickey with a quick request to look into the fishing business. Then she packed up the files and jammed them back into the filing cabinet in a way that she hoped seemed just as disorganized as before. Her heart thumped in relief when she closed the filing cabinet. The knife sat menacingly on the vinyl flooring. She picked it up with two fingers and put it in the sink. She wasn't sure if it was a mistake to hide it from Dom—or the best decision she'd made since she met the charming man on a Spanish street.

After making sure the cats were all sleeping peacefully, Jane picked up the handheld transmitter on the radio and side-buttoned their signal— three long beeps—to see if Murray was around. A burst of static came across the line before she heard Murray's gravelly voice.

"Hi there, neighbor. Doing a little work around the property?"

"I was carrying a box of cats to safety. Fraser had kittens!"

Murray's laughter was both incredulous and pleased. "You're kidding me. That old tom is a female?"

Jane was gratified at his validation of the importance of the discovery.

"Yes! A mother with four beautiful babies. I thought only three survived, but she brought the runt back to life in front of me. She's a good mom."

"Well, the world needs more of those," Murray said.

"That's for sure."

"How about we name them after her? Call 'em Stuart, Nechako, Chilco, and Thompson."

"How is that naming them after her?"

"They're all tributaries of the Fraser. They flow into the larger river."

Jane laughed. "I love it. Your grandson likes Fraser, right? Maybe he'd like to come and see her when we get the bridge back in place. If this rain ever ends."

The silence stretched until Jane broke it. "You still there?"

"Yeah, I'm still here. Guess you touched a nerve. Joey would have loved to see that old scrappy cat taking care of her littles ones. But it's not possible, Jane. He died the fall before last."

The words sank into her stomach like a punch. Another death on the same crew?

"A year before Melissa's accident?"

"Yeah, pretty close."

"I'm so sorry for your loss, Murray."

"I appreciate that."

The rain dripped down the window. Jane's thoughts pooled and gathered like the drops. "Was it . . . suspicious?"

Again, there was a pause on the line.

"No, not suspicious, no," Murray finally answered. "He'd been miserable for a couple months. Wouldn't eat. Barely came out of his room. Told his poor grandmother that he'd rather be dead than alive. Few weeks later, I found the poor kid with the shotgun in his mouth."

"Oh god."

"Sorry to spoil your good news by bringing up the bad. You take care. I'll call you in two days to check in, okay?"

"Yes, thanks, Murray. I'm . . . sorry for bringing it up."

"You know, I do appreciate that but it's okay. I don't mind talking about him. It's nice to remember how much he loved that stupid cat. Gotta hold on to that stuff best I can. Talk tomorrow, all right?"

"Okay."

Jane hitched the radio back onto the small hook to end the call.

Five people had worked on the renovations crew in 2021: Melissa, Elijah, Randeep, Dylan, and Joseph Jack.

Melissa had drowned.

Joseph was dead by suicide.

Elijah, Randeep, and Dylan were missing.

What the hell was going on at the Venatura Hotel?

CHAPTER | TWENTY-EIGHT

THE DARKNESS WAS GATHERING WHEN JANE LEFT THE HOTEL FOR THE second time that day, after firing off a message to Mickey to find out more about Joseph Jack and do a reverse trace on the cell phone harasser. The wet landscape was stark and forlorn. Falling water had stripped the fall color from the trees and thick bands of dark clouds hid the mountains. The river was a moving mudslide lapping at the slippery edge of what was left of the lawn, but her curiosity was strong enough to battle the weather. She needed to see the boathouse. She wanted answers to what had happened to Dylan and Randeep, and she had a hunch that two guys who ran a fishing charter spent a lot of time close to the water.

Jane took a wide shot of the bleak setting on her phone, panning across the entire expanse of lawn to encompass the rising water and biting rain. Still actively filming, she retraced her steps around the front of the hotel and past the deck where she'd found Fraser, pulling her hood forward to protect from the cold rain. The wind picked up when she came around the eastern side of the building, gusty and sharp. Through the small screen on her phone, Jane glimpsed a trailhead tucked between creeping branches and lashing rain. According to Melissa's map, it was the way to the small grouping of cabins she had yet to explore.

The dimming light blurred the edges of things. She zoomed in with the video to solidify the confusing image of wobbling ground around the base of the tree trunks on the shoreline before realizing they were no longer standing on the ground at all. The water had submerged them like timid swimmers wading out past their depth. Her shiver shed beads of water from her coat. She nearly dropped her phone into a deep puddle.

Keeping the video going, she followed the gravel path that led toward the boathouse, promising herself that she would retrace her steps in better light to ensure she wasn't missing anything. Though she strained to hear anything that might indicate a threat to her safety—the huff of a bear, growl of a wolf, snarl of a cougar, or shriek of whomever had left the knife in the drawer—the only discernible sound was the churning current of the river carving new and deeper channels in the earth. It was loud enough to drown out the sound of her own footsteps.

It took ten minutes to reach the boathouse. Her throat tightened when she got to the long dock that stretched along the short edge of the building on the upriver side. The river was so high now that it had overwhelmed the wooden slats. In the dark gray light, she could barely see where the dock was under the inch or so of water flowing over the top. The wind nipped at her face, sucking away her breath as she tried to fill her lungs. Before she set foot on the watery surface, she glanced back at the hotel for reassurance.

With all its windows darkened and the light leaching from the sky, the building obscured the horizon. Its solid presence might have felt reassuring in the sunshine, but in the gloom of fast-approaching night, Jane found it threatening. Anyone could be standing at a window, invisible to her. The idea made her hurry to find shelter. On the dock, the submerged wooden boards swayed and slipped under her feet, while the river pulsed around her ankles. She placed each one of her steps carefully, knowing that an error would take her down.

Just like Melissa.

Up close she could she see the main building with the same ash-gray planks. The dusky light blackened the color to shadow in some places. There were four bays—three roughly the size of a single boat, and a fourth that doubled the others, presumably for a larger vessel—with barn-style doors on the dockside of each one. Her heart sank when she realized they were closed and padlocked. She tested each lock and cast another glance toward the imposing bulk of the hotel, wondering if her futile attempts were being watched.

Though the light was nearly lost, she took another panorama shot with her phone to show the river, the dock, and the boathouse. The darkness was atmospheric, almost palpable. Mickey would love it—creepy B-roll. She began taking still shots.

The flash of her camera caught an odd scratch by the first door. Kneeling onto the waterlogged dock, she trained her lens directly onto it. The outline of a heart had been carved into the wood. Within it, two letters were scratched into the wall just above the waterline: *E.S.* She traced them with a finger.

Elijah Stanton.

Again, her gaze darted to the large building looming on the rise of land above her. A shock jolted up and down her arms. The eastern side of the hotel was no longer completely dark. One window glowed. Room 401. The Sunrise Suite. Melissa's favorite room. She swirled her camera up to capture it. Something moved in front of the light, then was gone.

Someone was in there.

Jane shoved her phone into her pocket, sprang from her knees, and pushed off her back foot to sprint down the sopping dock. The soles of her shoes slid unnervingly. There was nearly no purchase on the submerged wood, but she pressed on, past the dock to the muddy trail. She looked up. The light was still on. She willed her thighs to work harder, to launch her forward, to get her there before—

Her right toe caught on something, but the rest of her kept moving forward. She fell hard, knocking the air out of her and splattering her face with mud. The small bones of her foot were on fire and her breath returned in a howl of anguish. Sucking hard in and out of her lungs, she unhooked her foot from the root that had tripped her, hugging her knee to her chest while sinking onto the saturated ground. Wetness traveled up her pants and she whimpered.

She wiggled her toes. Pain rocketed up her shin and knee. Something was very wrong. The short walk now seemed impossible. Shifting to one side, she wedged her phone from her pocket and dialed Dom.

No answer. She had to get back to the hotel by herself.

Jane filled her lungs then laid her bare hands on the seeping earth to push herself back up to standing. With uneven strides, she forced her protesting right foot up and down while urging her left to take as much of the weight as possible. Painful pins and needles traveled from the point of impact to the rest of her body. Her hip ached, her ass was frozen, and her brain screamed *Stop*.

But she didn't. She had to get to room 401. The Sunrise Suite.

One painful step at a time, she limped to the hotel, the muscles of her left leg cramping with strain as she pulled her injured foot behind her. A sob escaped her throat when she saw the side deck. She was almost there. Gripping the railing hard, she made her way around the corner. At the front side, she stumbled through the flower bed to use the wall for support, destroying the few remaining plants. Fighting through the mud and dead flowers, she made her way to the entrance before collapsing onto the stone floor.

"Dom? Dom?"

Her words rang through the empty lobby like an unanswered phone call. Why was no one ever around when she needed them?

"Sienna?"

There was no answer. She lay on the floor for a minute, savoring the warmth and quiet, letting gravity straighten her spine and pull down her hips. The new position made her foot throb in a different way. After a minute or two, she hoisted herself back to standing. She needed to find help. Unfamiliar noises came from her throat as she pushed forward. It was difficult to move at any speed across the huge first floor. She used her heel to relieve the searing pressure radiating from her toes. Finally, she reached the elevator in its bay. She stepped into the carriage. One look at her bedraggled hair hanging like strings around her face and her sunken eyes was enough. She averted her gaze until the elevator arrived on the fourth floor.

The hallway felt colder than it had been the last time she'd been up here, but maybe that was because she was drenched. Her teeth chattered and she clenched her jaw to still them. Slowly, she hobbled down the carpeted corridor past the closed doors of the rooms. Each peephole watched like a judging eye.

The door to the Sunrise Suite was closed but unlocked. She called out a greeting as she entered but heard no reply. Unsure of what she would find, Jane stumbled into the room.

"Dom?" she said. "Sienna? I'm hurt. I need help."

Her voice wavered and a deep wave of fatigue swept over her. She fought it with one hand flat on the wall to keep herself upright.

The room was identical to the suite she had shared with Dom. A large, luxurious duvet covered a beautiful big bed. Huge windows at the end of the room mirrored her movements. A tasteful chest of drawers below a wide-screen television lined the wall. She sensed an odd feeling. The room appeared as if a guest was still occupying the suite. It looked warm, cozy, and lived-in.

A suitcase lay half-open on a luggage stand left in the corner of the room. A bloodred throw had been flung over the back of the chair—Jane guessed it was cashmere from the rich-looking fuzz—and several lovely jackets and dresses hung in the closet by the door. Jane peered inside the bathroom to see cosmetics scattered all over the counter: lipstick, a pink blush, and several brushes.

But it was the mirror that caught and held her attention. Jane was transfixed by the ragged, rusty-brown letters scrawled across its surface:

GET OUT

CHAPTER | TWENTY-NINE

JANE RETRACED HER STEPS BACK TO THE ELEVATOR, DOWN TO THE FIRST floor, and through the lobby. She was weak with fatigue and numb with shock. Her body quivered with exhaustion and her throat was hoarse from calling for help. She stumbled down the hallway of the staff quarters. Voices caught her ear.

When she entered the shared space at the end of the hall, Dom stood up, swallowing a mouthful of something. Jane saw a box of crackers and a hunk of cheese. Sienna, seated at the table, looked Jane up and down then back to her plate without a word.

"Jane! Are you okay? You're shivering." A crumb was lodged in his mustache. He wiped his mouth with the pad of his thumb.

For the first time since they'd met, Jane felt no rush of attraction at the sight of Dom's face. He swept a ratty quilt off the back of the armchair before he came to her side. Dom tugged at the sleeves of her soaking coat, pulling it from her body, wrapped her in the quilt, and helped her to sit down. A whiff of cigarettes and body odor greeted her as she settled onto the busy pink-and-blue floral-patterned fabric.

"Where have you been?" he asked.

"Where were you?" she cried. "I called you!"

He looked upset. "I didn't hear my phone. I was downstairs checking the electrical panel. The signal gets a little choppy in the basement." He sat down on the corner of the couch near her chair.

"You weren't upstairs? In the Sunrise Suite?"

"What? No, I was in the basement. What happened? Are you okay?"

"Were you in there, Sienna?"

The teenager shook her head without looking up from her phone. "Nope."

"Jane, you're pale as a ghost. Are you okay?"

Deep weariness weighed her down. She looked back and forth between Dom and Sienna, trying to discern who was lying to her. Dom's eyes registered nothing but sympathy. Sienna was acting shifty. But accusing Sienna wouldn't convince Dom—or endear her to him—so she kept her suspicions to herself.

"I think I broke my toe," Jane said.

"Did you fall?"

Jane looked at him sharply. Had he been the one in the window? Had he scrawled the ugly letters on the mirror? He knelt in front of her, aware of her scrutiny. His hands tenderly encircled her ankle.

"Mind if I take a look?"

With Dom's gentle help, Jane gingerly eased off her wet sneaker, then peeled off her sock. Her foot was pale and wrinkled, save an angry three-inch bruise of deep blue and purple that ran across the base of her third and fourth toes.

"Damn," Dom said as he took her foot in his hands. "That doesn't look good."

"I hope you can still make us dinner," Sienna said, without looking up. "I'm starving."

"Thanks for your sympathy," Jane said, glaring at her. "When I was outside, I saw a light in the Sunrise Suite. Were you in there?"

Sienna screwed up her face. "What? No. What are you even talking about? Dad and I have been together since you brought those gross animals in here. I can only use this area now so I don't have an asthma attack."

"Sienna, enough. Jane is hurt," Dom said before catching Jane's eye. "You need ice for this. Keep it elevated. I'm going to grab you something."

Jane moved her foot out of Dom's cradled hands and onto the pillow he placed on the coffee table in front of her. Sienna pointedly moved the crackers and cheese to a side table. As he stood, she spoke again.

"What about you, Dom? Were you in that room?"

He shook his head before making his way to the bar fridge under the kitchen counter. "No. Sienna already told you. We were together. I wonder if I hit the wrong fuse and turned a light on up there by accident. I'll check the electrical panel again tomorrow. There shouldn't be any electricity in there at all. I wanted to close off that wing for the winter."

"Someone is living up there. I saw clothes and makeup." Jane watched him rummage through the ice-clogged freezer of the white-sided fridge. A faulty fuse didn't account for the shadow she'd seen moving past the window. Was he lying to her? "We need to go check it out together."

"You need to treat this injury first. Here we go," he said, pulling a bag of frozen peas from the freezer and placing them on her foot. "It's going to be sore for a while, but that will help. Broken toes are a bitch."

"You honestly think it's broken?"

He nodded. "I'm no doctor and no one can be sure without an X-ray, but yeah. Looks like it. I'm going to grab you some painkillers, okay? Be right back."

"Go to the Sunrise Suite first! You need to make sure there's no one else here."

He walked out the door without acknowledging her request. Jane wondered if he kept the pills in the same place as his medication. She took a deep breath to summon her strength before turning to Sienna, who finally raised her head to look directly at Jane.

"I'm sorry about what I did to your phone."

Sienna narrowed her eyes. "You should be."

Jane bit the inside of her cheek before answering. "You're right. I shouldn't have acted that way. I was . . . embarrassed. Humiliated, maybe. My work is important to me. I was worried about what publicity like that could do."

Her stepdaughter's expression didn't change.

"But more than that, I felt like I'd hurt your dad. And that's the last thing I want to do. But I think you wanted to hurt him. Why else would you give me your mother's necklace, Sienna?"

Sienna dropped her eyes to the plate of crackers. Dom returned— much too fast to have made his way to and from the fourth floor—with the over-the-counter painkillers. He placed a couple in Jane's hand along with a glass of water he'd filled at the sink. Jane was frustrated at the interruption—she needed to get to the bottom of this mess.

"Did you look inside the suite?"

Dom shook his head. "You are more important to me than a mess the housekeepers left behind. I promise you, Jane. There's no one in this hotel but us."

Jane paused. Both Dom's and Sienna's expressions had closed up, but she still had questions. The memory of the scrawled heart pressed her forward.

"How well did you know Elijah, Sienna?"

She rolled her eyes. "Like a little, I guess. He's six years older than me. It was sad when he disappeared but . . . I don't know. I don't remember much."

Jane leaned forward. The combination of painkillers and an empty stomach were effective. The pills had already begun to dull the sympathetic twinge in her tightened hamstring.

"Do you remember going on a fishing trip with an outfit called Fraser River Fish? Guys named Randeep and Dylan? I think Elijah was friends with them. They all worked with your mom."

Sienna stared at her blankly, then blinked. "Ummmm, maybe?"

"Dylan and Randeep responded to an ad for a truck for sale, shortly after your fishing trip. They never came home."

"Oh, that's so sad." Sienna got to her feet and joined her father. "Dad, I'm really hungry. Maybe I could try to eat a real dinner tonight?"

Dom nodded. "I'm hungry too. I'll make the meal tonight. Jane, you rest. But you're back on breakfast duty tomorrow."

"Thank you, Dom," Jane said. "But can we finish this conversation really quick? You might know something important."

Sienna rolled her eyes again. "Um, it's finished? I don't remember much about that fishing trip except it was cold and I hated it and we didn't catch anything. If you'll excuse me, *Jane*, I don't want to talk about my dead mom anymore tonight. I'm going to eat in my room."

Her thick ponytail bounced as she turned her back and walked down the hall. Dom sighed and shook his head.

"Listen, Jane, I really need this to stop. I know you're an investigator and I admire your persistence. But there's no story here. Elijah was wild—had a reputation for screwing every girl that came around."

"Like Sienna? Lucy said Sienna spent a lot of time with him, and that Peter had to intervene. Why Peter, not you or Melissa?"

He rubbed the side of his face and swore. "Lucy is not reliable. A lot of people—even Peter—think Elijah's laying low because he got involved with the wrong person. He'll be back at some point."

"That's not what his mother thinks."

Dom exhaled again. She was dismayed to smell alcohol on his breath—it was just after five p.m. She noticed an empty tumbler on the table with a finger of amber liquid left.

"Well, Lucy doesn't think much of Peter. She's never been one to agree with him if she can start an argument instead. I know she's worried about her son—we all are—but fueling rumors isn't going to change a goddamn thing."

"Rumors? What do you mean—"

Dom interrupted her. "Dragging up all this stuff is so triggering for Sienna. Can't you see that? She's struggling and you're making it worse. We can't afford to let her relapse. I brought her here to heal. I brought us all here to do that. Please, Jane. Drop it. For Sienna."

"I don't need healing. And if we're talking about your healing, I'd like you to stop day-drinking. For me. Think you can do that?"

Dom's face darkened and he left the room. She wondered if she was being gaslit. Did Dom really think that three disappearances in quick succession was normal? Not to mention a suicide and a drowning? She hadn't had time to mention Joseph, but surely news of his death would have reached Dom as well. And why wouldn't he check the suite? Why was she the only one worried that there was someone else in the hotel with them? Was Sienna playing another vicious prank? Was Dom in on it this time?

She picked up her phone to review the video and B-roll she'd taken that day, beginning with the still shots. The newest had poor resolution due to the dim lighting. She zoomed in on the trailhead near the dock to see if they'd be able to correct the graininess in post. Her body stiffened when she saw deep black marks in the muddy ground.

Footsteps leading directly to the forest behind the hotel.

CHAPTER | THIRTY

THE ACHE IN JANE'S FOOT DISTURBED HER ENOUGH TO WAKE BEFORE
the sun rose. Her mind immediately started racing in the early morning
darkness. Despite her injury, she managed to ease her way out of bed
without waking her husband. Using the light of her phone, she made
her way upstairs to document the disturbing message on the mirror in
the Sunrise Suite, cursing her broken toe for making her forget to take
pictures the night before.

Upon entering the luxurious room, she flipped on the lights. Dom
hadn't turned off the electricity like he'd said he had. The suitcase and
throw were gone. There were no letters on the mirror. All the cosmetics
had disappeared. The suite was pristine.

That rules out Sienna, she thought bitterly.

Jane closed the door to the suite and returned to the bed she
shared with Dom. Her body was still, but her thoughts swarmed.
Dom stirred.

"Good morning, honey," he said, resting his hand on the curve of her hip. "Sleep well?"

His soft eyes and pillow-tousled hair sent a burst of unexpected affection throughout her body. He was the face of innocence, yet she didn't trust him. Not with her worst suspicions. Someone was in the hotel with them, and either he knew (which would explain his refusal to check the suite) or he was ignoring her fear.

"Not great. My toe is still sore."

He brushed the hair out of his eyes with the back of his hand. "Sorry to hear that. How about taking the morning off? I'll fix something for us. You stay in bed."

Her eyes drifted to the fat blobs of water dotting the window. The storm was still beating against the building and the sight of it was enough to make her sink back beneath the covers. The bed springs squeaked.

"That sounds great."

"But back on for lunch, okay? I've got to take a walk around the property this morning. The water is getting high on the western bank just past the bridge washout. Last night, I checked the news. Low areas are flooding all over. I need to make some sandbags."

"Yes, of course. I can help with the sandbagging too. I don't mind getting my hands dirty. Do we need to do it at the dockside of the hotel as well? Were you down there yesterday checking it out?"

"No, it's the western side that's low. And I appreciate your offer. But I want to keep you safe inside. Your foot is a mess and we can't have you slipping in mud and rain."

Jane frowned. Someone had been on that trail, and it was hard to imagine Sienna trudging through the thick, slippery mud.

"What exactly are you keeping me safe from?"

Dom kissed the top of her head. "From anything coming our way. That's my job, honey. I'm going to take a shower."

He slid off the bed, grabbed a shirt from the back of the chair, then headed to the bathroom down the hall.

Jane stretched her foot cautiously. The stiffness from having it in one position overnight had made it tight and inflexible despite her quick foray to the fourth floor. Pain hummed up her right side. She grabbed her phone from the nightstand and saw multiple texts from Mickey. The first was a link to the obituary for Murray's grandson. It was nearly two years old—dated late November of the year before Melissa died.

> *Joseph Jack, age 20, died suddenly on Saturday, November 24, 2021. He is survived by his grandparents Murray and Rita Jack. He is predeceased by his father Anthony Williams, his mother Holly Williams, and his paternal grandfather and grandmother Bernie and Louise Williams. His life will be honored at the Yarrow Community Hall at noon on Friday, November 30.*

Mickey had followed that with two more texts:

Impossible to trace the phone # you gave me. It's a burner

Here's the link to the ChilBoyz channel

Before clicking the link, Jane sent Mickey the photos from the boathouse the night before, along with a nudge to find out anything they could about the fishing company.

She took a deep breath and clicked on the link to the internet platform she despised the most. The video-sharing forum often brought out the ugliest parts of people. Fame and adolescence were not a good match, and much of her last documentary had focused on the destructive combination. Anger flared as she remembered her argument had been lost in the furor around her tactics. She forced it away and turned to her screen.

As Mickey had noted, the YouTube channel was called ChilBoyz (@chilboyz). Jane recognized it as the second hashtag Sienna had used on her TikTok. She should have realized she'd seen it before—it had the nagging familiarity of overhyped content she'd attributed to a trending tag. The channel had over two million subscribers and had been posting for more than two years. The first video was titled *We Renovated a Hotel and All We Got Was Rat Shit*. It was dated October 1, 2021—seven weeks before Joseph's death.

Jane continued to scan the videos. From the descriptions, the collection relied on stupid pranks and unsophisticated humor for content, geared toward an audience Mickey derisively called "yo-bros" or "Joe Rogan's core demographic." The earliest videos looked painfully amateurish, but the most recent thumbnails from the year before—the last was dated a few days before Melissa died and Elijah disappeared—showed decent graphics and paid promotions for sports betting sites, energy drinks, and some product called Energy Bet that seemed to combine the two. They'd clearly begun to gain some attention. The presence of sponsors and the high number of followers was disheartening to Jane, but she shoved her professional resentment aside.

The earliest videos were focused on renovations. Thumbnails showed sweaty men in hoodies pulling stupid faces at the camera before the content deteriorated into more aggressive themes: *Prank a Dude: Halloween Edition*; *Trucks, Trucks, Trucks—WE LOVE TRUCKS*; *Savage Pranks 2018*; *We Hit On Your Girlfriend at the Club!*; and *In Through the Out Door Canada-Style*. As Mickey had mentioned, there were a few focused on the hotel, including *We Pulverized a Fireplace* and *Watch Dylan Eat a Dock Spider*, alongside even stupider fare like:

We Crash a Bar Mitzvah
Lippy Makes Deep R's Sister Eat Sh*t
Loudly Farting on People at the Grocery Store
The Time We Filled Lippy's Truck with Salmon

The last was accompanied by a thumbnail of a red vintage Ford with Elijah's horrified face overlaying the photo. Elijah was traditionally handsome, with tawny skin and thick light-brown hair worn long on top and shaved on the sides. He was tall like his father—but he carried gym-built muscles that made him look stronger and vainer. Apparently, Lippy was Elijah's nickname. Jane shuddered to think of the origin. She took out a notepad to piece together all the shorthand the crew used in their video descriptions. Nicknames were standard. Joseph—thicker-built and shorter, with deep black hair and dark eyes—was called Sharts; and Randeep—brown skin, brown eyes, and a mischievous smile—went by Deep R. Only Dylan was known by his real name. He was the sole blond in the crew, and his smaller frame and blue eyes gave him almost a feminine look compared to the others.

After gaining a solid overview, Jane dove deeper by clicking on the first reno video. It was poorly edited—jump cuts of the four guys she recognized as Elijah, Joseph, Dylan, and Randeep swinging a sledgehammer at a wall on the main floor of the hotel. Chunks of drywall rained down before the camera zoomed in on a squirming mass of rats. She flinched at the sight of their writhing bodies. The hoots and hollers of the young men were jarring, but as far as she could tell, there was no conflict between Joseph and the others. In fact, he seemed more enthusiastic than most, reaching in to poke at one of the scurrying rodents, eliciting a brutal squawk from the animal and several raucous cheers from Elijah and the others. They were so young—barely into their twenties. It was hard to reconcile their eager, adolescent behavior with their deaths and disappearances.

She opened the post called *Trucks, Trucks, Trucks* and immediately saw Elijah/Lippy, shirtless and tanned, leaning against a vintage red Ford. A young woman wearing only a bikini clambered onto the hood with a sponge in hand, while a small crowd of men gathered around. Jane could only watch a minute of the "car-washing" in real time before she sped the video up to the end. She clicked through the remaining content. The reno videos were silly and amateur as the crew tore up more interior walls with sledgehammers and took breaks to pose like bodybuilders.

The entire channel relied heavily on fast-paced edits and laughing young men pounding on stuff. She cycled through several posts that featured a popular theme. One or more members of the group would blow vape smoke directly into a stranger's face then run away. Another much-visited topic was asking a worker on a construction crew to move

206 | AMBER COWIE

their operations because this was the site where they usually got their "blowies."

Elijah/Lippy was clearly their leader. He was featured in most of the videos and often instigated the pranks. Even on a small screen, Jane understood the draw to his glowing skin and big smile, though he was the opposite of her usual arty type. Mickey had called the content "toxic masculinity in its most tedious form," and Jane had to agree. She was nearly ready to call it a day when she reached the Halloween video.

The gaudy graphics were replaced by eerie hand-drawn designs of torches and pained faces. There was none of the pulsing misogynistic rap theme used as a lead-in for the other posts. Rather than vivid color, this video was shot in black and white. The opening frame showed Elijah holding a flashlight under his face in a dark place.

"Is this a fucking snuff film?" he asked the camera.

Howls of laughter rose from behind him. On cue, figures lit torches in a circle just beyond his body, their faces distorted by the flickering flames and shadowed by the hoods of their coats. Elijah stepped aside and the camera zoomed forward to show Joseph's body face down on frozen ground. Leaves ringed in ice surrounded his prone form. As far as Jane could tell, he was not conscious. She looked beyond him and saw shadows of tall trees flickering in and out of the pale light of the wavering torches.

"I guess we'll find out tomorrow, hey SHARTS?" He picked up one of Joseph's arms, then let it fall heavily onto the ground.

"Sharts has had way too much to drink."

"With a little help from his friends!" cried a voice in the background.

Jane thought it belonged to Randeep but she couldn't be sure.

"And some drugs," said a girl from off-camera.

This time, Jane didn't recognize the voice.

"Sharts has volunteered to help us catch pesky spirits—the ghouls and goblins who haunt the forest on Halloween night!" Elijah burst into laughter. He had to calm himself before he could continue.

"But those little goblins are sneaky. We have to make sure Sharts is well-hidden."

The camera did a jerky spin. Jane recognized the outdoor oven from the cookhouse area. The shadowy forest seemed to lurch forward. She recalled the biting wind, haunted trees, and snapping branches from her visit. The memory of metal rubbing against metal set her teeth on edge. Jane brought the small screen closer to her eyes, trying to make sense of what they were doing there. The camera stopped on the stone structure and panned in fast. Jane sucked in a breath.

The door to the oven was open.

"Come on, boys," Elijah cried. "Oh . . . and girls."

As the camera recorded, the group of roughly eight people (it was difficult to count in the shaky lighting), wedged their hands under Joseph's body and lifted him. They shuffled their way to the yawning mouth of the gray concrete oven, then slid him all the way inside. Jane stiffened with terror as Elijah shoved the door closed with the flat of his hands, pulling the handle to lock, despite its screeching protest. The camera made another quick circle of the group. Some of their hoods had fallen away from their faces in their efforts. Jane squinted to make them out.

There was Dylan throwing up a gang sign with his fingers, while Randeep/Deep R was grinning at his side. "Yeaaaaah, Lipppy!" he shouted.

Their hooded eyes and rubbery mouths made them both look heavily intoxicated.

"Have a good sleeeeeeeep," Elijah called in a singsong voice as the camera spun back to him.

Jane heard more laughter. This time, she thought it sounded nervous.

The screen cut to black—then a title card appeared.

THE NEXT DAY

It was the same scene in the dim light of a fall morning. Icy branches whipped the lens as the camera image bobbed along the trail in a wooded forest. Within seconds, the open-air structure came into view. There was frost on its roof, thick as mold on a rotting orange. Elijah came into the shot. Jane saw the gnarled tree behind him, the darkened spot on its trunk yawning threateningly as the handsome young man walked to the out-door oven.

"Honey, I'm home," Elijah called while twisting the handle.

The door was forced open fast from the inside, bursting open so quickly that Elijah was knocked off his feet. Joseph scrambled out from the small opening, kicking and flailing, making inhuman noises. Once fully emerged, he fell to his knees, gulping at the cold winter air. His eyes were wide and darted from Elijah's face to the camera to the sky as if he couldn't quite understand what had happened.

Jane had seen that look twice before, and hoped never to see it again. It was shock—disassociation from reality. A mind protecting itself from the cruelty inflicted upon it. Horror wriggled through her. Like Joseph, the two people Jane had seen wearing the expression were now dead.

Both times, everyone had blamed Jane.

Her hands shook as she struggled to hold her phone up to see the last minute of the video. Elijah glanced at the camera with a worried expression before breaking into a wide smile as Joseph began to babble.

"Where was I? What happened? Holy fuck, I thought I was dead. The door was stuck. I couldn't get out. Couldn't you hear me? Where am I?"

Joseph was wild-eyed and confused. He tried to get to his feet, then collapsed again onto his knees.

"Hey Sharts!" Elijah's voice had lost much of its bravado. "Did you have good dreams? We let you stay in there for an extra-long nap."

"What? I'm freezing. Why didn't you come get me? I swear to god I thought I was dead. How did I—"

"Chill out, dude. It's not like we lit the oven. We're not Nazis! Here you go, man!"

Elijah produced a can of beer from his jacket pocket, shoved it into Joseph's hands. Joseph almost dropped the beer. His fingers seemed numb and stiff, and he stared at the can like he didn't know what to do with it. Elijah grinned and opened it for him before bringing it to Joseph's lips and pouring it into his mouth. A stream of beer ran down his cheek before he twisted his head away and threw up.

Elijah raised the can to the camera. "That's Sharts for you! Can't hold his liquor. But cheers to the ChilBoyz: Halloween stylez!"

The video changed to a neon graphic of a gnarled-looking cartoon man giving the finger to the viewer. Obnoxious music played as the credits rolled. Jane glanced at the header. The video had been viewed more than five million times.

Jane pressed the pad of her finger to the screen and slowly backed up the feed, frame by frame, until she returned to the moment when the camera scanned the group in the dark night. She examined each figure.

Dylan and Randeep stood closest to the oven. Their faces were frozen in expressions that looked wildly exhilarated, almost manic. Several other young men had furrowed brows. Two more people were standing at the edge of the circle, one step back from the group. A hood covered the face of one, and the other was staring at Elijah's back. Her expression was pained but Jane was still able to recognize her.

Sienna.

CHAPTER | THIRTY-ONE

AFTER FINISHING THE VIDEO, JANE COULDN'T SETTLE HER NERVES. SHE craned her ears for any sound from Sienna within the staff quarters. Her stepdaughter usually slept late and, as Dom had predicted, had picked a room as far away from them as possible. Still, the walls were thinner in this section of the hotel. The last thing Jane wanted was for her stepdaughter to overhear the phone calls she'd arranged.

Jane read the (mercifully) dwindling comments on her social media feeds, sent a handful of emails, then did a quick search for treatment of broken toes. As per the instructions, she slid her taped foot into a stiff-soled shoe, testing its weight-bearing ability with a tentative first step. The pain was more manageable. She opened the door of her room slowly before peering out into the hallway. Her exaggerated caution made her feel like she was doing something wrong. Something about the YouTube clip she'd just seen made it harder to shake her lingering shame. She reminded herself that the past was the past. There was nothing she could do to change it.

Still, it was hard to forget the torment on Joseph's face. Pain painted the same expression no matter what—or who—was the cause.

The hall was empty. She closed her door and walked toward the common room. In the light of day, it was even dingier. A wobbly side table and a lopsided standing lamp accompanied the dated couch and armchair. It smelled like stale beer and burnt coffee.

The door to the Bourbon Room squeaked when she pushed it open. She tensed, waiting to see if Dom or Sienna would come rushing in. The hotel remained silent save for the breath of hot air being forced through the vents. The Bourbon Room was far from her favorite place in the hotel, but it had two locking doors. After yesterday, it was clear that someone was trying to spook her. Jane hated to admit that the mind games were starting to work. She bolted the doors and sat at the elegant rolltop desk, ignoring Cary Grant's smirk. The narrow window below the thick ceiling trim on the exterior wall provided little light, and hulking animal heads blocked most of the rest of the beams. A thick oil painting above the fireplace depicted a hunting party. The entire room was dedicated to the celebration of death. No wonder she hated it.

She ran her hand along the underside of the desk. Bingo. An old-fashioned key had been taped to the bottom. She unlocked the desk, then rolled the dusty slats into place. The back housed a section of pigeonholes on one side and sturdy wooden shelves on the other. She ran a finger over the surface, disturbing the dust.

She cocked her ears again and heard no sounds of movement. This was a necessary betrayal. Dom was dodging her questions. Someone was sneaking around the hotel. She had to know the truth.

She pulled out her phone and dialed one of the numbers she'd recently added to her contacts. A smooth voice answered after two rings.

"Good morning, this is the office of Dr. Abebe. What can I do for you?"

"Hello, this is Jane Duvall. I have a call scheduled with the doctor."

"One moment, please."

The line clicked before a flutey rendition of a Phil Collins song came through the speaker. Jane listened while her other ear remained pricked to approaching footsteps. After a minute, another voice—older, female, and gently accented—came on the line.

"Hello, this is Dr. Abebe."

"Thank you for taking my call, Doctor. As you know from my email, Dom Lawrence and I recently married."

"Congratulations."

"Thank you. I'm calling because . . ."

Jane trailed off. Her eyes darted between both closed doors. She took a deep breath.

"We are currently staying at the Venatura Hotel with his daughter— sorry, my stepdaughter, Sienna—"

The doctor cut in. "Isn't there a lot of flooding in that region at the moment? What are you doing in the hotel?"

"We are working as the off season caretakers, and Dom is finishing interior renovations. I was told that you had recommended Sienna return here."

There was no response.

"Doctor?"

She cleared her throat. "Excuse me, I was just processing. Please go on. Tell me the reason you are calling."

"Well, since we've been here, about a week, Sienna's eating disorder has gotten worse. She is volatile—even hostile. I'm wondering if you can give me any professional recommendations as her guardian. Any treatment plan or guidelines to help her get through this?"

"What do you mean when you say volatile? Has there been any violence?"

Jane's pulse quickened. "Violence? Self-harm, I suppose," she said before considering the ugly letters scrawled on the mirror in the Sunrise Suite. "There was some property damage. And a nasty prank involving her late mother's necklace. A lot of emotional manipulation."

"Describe the prank to me."

Jane flushed at the memory. "She . . . gave me the necklace and told me to wear it to dinner with her father. I had no idea it originally belonged to Melissa." The name felt wrong in her mouth. "Dom was horrified. And she made a TikTok about it without my knowledge."

"I see," the doctor said. "Ms. Duvall, I think there is reason enough for me to schedule an online session with Dom and perhaps Sienna to discuss this behavior. I recommended that Sienna be brought to the hotel to help her get through the trauma of her mother's passing, but I had assumed that would happen during the peak season of its operations."

"Dom saw an opportunity to stay here for longer and took it—perhaps unwisely, as it's been harder than we expected. He wanted me to speak with you to ensure that we had your guidance and assistance in helping her."

Dr. Abebe's voice became guarded. "Please tell him to call my office. I'm assuming he has access to the internet and can set up the appointment with my assistant."

"I'd like to discuss it now."

"I'm afraid that's not possible. Dom has signed a formal agreement to act as Sienna's parental representative in therapy. I have nothing on record from you."

"Send me the form. I'll sign it now."

"Absolutely, yes. I'll have my assistant email it to you. I'll need a signature from both you and Sienna."

"Sienna?"

"It's a sign of good faith in my practice, Ms. Duvall. I ensure that my teenage clients understand what they are consenting to when they speak with me."

"Of course. Have your assistant send it, then," Jane said before rattling off her email address. "One last thing. Was Sienna having troubles during the spring *before* her mother died?"

Dr. Abebe paused before answering. "We've been working together for years."

"And you work with Dom personally as well? You were listed as his medical contact."

"Over the course of the last year, listing me as a contact would have been accurate for both."

Jane was confused. "So you're treating Dom?"

"I was working with the whole family. Melissa too. Peter asked me to." The doctor stopped herself. "I'm sorry—that is all I can disclose to you for the time being. Perhaps Dom can shed more light on this?"

"Yes, of course. Thank you for your time, Dr. Abebe."

"Have a good day, Ms. Duvall."

Jane said a quick goodbye before the line went dead. She didn't hesitate before dialing Ted, Dom's brother. As a result of her earlier emails, he was also expecting her call.

"Hi there, Jane," he answered, sounding slightly out of breath. "How are you doing? Been seeing some awful stuff on the news about the Fraser Valley. Should I get my canoe out of the garage and come rescue you folks?"

Jane laughed. He sounded like a more eager version of her husband—just the same as in their one rushed video chat when Dom had introduced her to him and shared their happy news.

"It's nice to talk to you again, Ted. I was sorry you couldn't make it to the wedding. I think we'll leave your canoe in reserve for now, but I'll call you if it keeps raining."

"Sure thing. Maybe I should look into renting an ark."

She laughed again; this time more polite than sincere. "So, I have a question for you. I was wandering around the grounds of the hotel. I saw the boathouse. You built it a couple years ago?"

"Sure did. Well, I framed it anyway. The moorings had already been poured."

"The concrete piers?"

"Yep. I just had to lay the wood on top and put in the walls and insulation. It was a tricky job working on the water like that. Got cold as hell out there."

"Did Peter hire you for the job?"

"Peter? No. It was all done through Dom. Never met Peter."

"Or his son?"

"Nope."

A moment passed and she wondered if the call would be a nonstarter. Neither of them spoke. Finally, Ted filled the silence. "You got snow up there yet?"

Jane glanced out the narrow window. The rain dripped down the panes.

"No, it's only rain so far."

"That's good."

There was another awkward moment. Jane decided to go for broke.

"My next question might be a bit weird," Jane said.

"Okay." He sounded nervous.

"I'm . . . worried about Sienna. She seems very high-strung."

"High-strung? The poor girl just lost her mother." He was tensing up. She could hear it in his voice.

"Oh, I know, I know. I didn't mean that. I mean . . . stressed. Agitated. It's just the three of us here. I want to try to support her as best I can."

A heavy gust of breath came across the line. "Isn't that something you should be talking to Dom about?"

"I have," she said, crossing her fingers to ward off the lie, a habit from childhood. "He told me to talk to you."

"Me? That's odd," he said. "Melissa didn't want a lot to do with me— with any of Dom's side of the family, really—after what happened during that fishing trip."

The fishing trip? Jane played along to keep him talking.

"Dom told me about that. Sounds like it was really hard."

"Yeah, it was. I mean, I saw Dom at work regularly after everything happened, but I missed Sienna. She's my little niece, you know. But Melissa? She could be . . . a bit much."

"How so?"

"Well, I don't want to speak ill of the dead, and I mean, she was a good person, don't get me wrong. Just . . . it was hard to enjoy stuff around her. She always wanted everything just so. It all had to be perfect or she made a stink. Had a real temper, that one. And Dom's so laid-back. A little too much sometimes. I'm sure you've noticed he's got a bit of a problem with the sauce."

Jane shifted in her seat, remembering the tumbler from the night before. Her mother's face flashed in her mind's eye.

"Yes, I've noticed."

"Melissa did all she could to keep him in check. But it was hard. Dom can get really stupid when he's had a few drinks. I mean, you know. That last screwup was one for the books."

Bitterness had crept into Ted's voice. Jane struggled not to interrupt the flow of conversation, though she was desperate to understand precisely what screwup Ted was referring to.

"On the boat, Melissa was all freaked out about something. She kept saying that Sienna needed to be honest. That she had to tell the truth."

"Sienna and Melissa fought?"

He snorted. "Fought? No. I mean, she slapped her hard, right in front of our whole family, but it stopped right there. Didn't go any further than that."

"Sienna slapped her mother?"

Ted's tone changed. "I thought you said you'd heard about this already. No, listen, I've said more than enough. Why don't you tell Dom to give me a call sometime? And, uh, maybe the two of you should have a long talk as well."

"But wait! How did Dom screw up—"

The line went dead. Jane's heart was pounding, and she tried to calm herself. She stared at the surface of the desk. A faint mark was visible on the corner of the pitted wood. When she ran her hand over it, she could feel it was deliberately carved. She shone the light from her phone to get a clearer look.

E.S. The same initials that had been carved into the boathouse moorings. Elijah Stanton.

There was a loud thud outside the room. She limped to the door that led to the staff quarters, pulling it open so hard she nearly hit herself in the face.

The common space was just as it had been when she'd walked through it.

She took one step inside, then stopped in her tracks. There was a cup of coffee sitting on the scarred table between the couches that hadn't been there before. Jane picked it up.

It was still warm.

CHAPTER | THIRTY-TWO

JANE FRANTICALLY TYPED A MESSAGE TO MICKEY AS SHE WALKED through the grand foyer, looking up after every word to make sure she wasn't about to collide with Sienna or Dom.

Call me, call me, call me

Within seconds, Mickey's name flashed onto her screen. She caught movement at the corner of her eye, so she spun around. The butterfly wings in the massive art piece above the fireplace glinted alongside the flickering flames in the hearth. Who had lit the fire? Dom was outside and she hadn't heard Sienna leave her bedroom.

Jane answered the call and her words tumbled out.

"Mickey! Sienna and her mother got violent with each other at least once. And that effed-up video from the ChilBoyz on Halloween? Sienna was there. She was part of that awful prank on Joseph Jack."

She lowered her voice as she walked up the staircase, grateful for the bird's-eye view it provided of the entire main floor. Neither Dom nor her stepdaughter were in sight, but there were so many places where a person could hide in this hotel. She hurried as fast as her injured foot would let her through the dining room before ducking into the scullery.

"Well, that makes the story a little juicer. Sienna is sus. Are you sure you're okay being alone with them? It's getting a bit *Orphan*, right?"

Jane ignored the reference to the creepy horror movie that featured a murderous older woman with a genetic condition that allowed her to pose as a young child. Her heart sank when she saw the sink and the surrounding counter. The pile of dirty dishes from that morning and the day before was nearly as high as the tall stainless-steel backsplash. Apparently, her broken toe excused her from cooking, but not cleaning. She wedged the phone between her shoulder and chin.

"Let's stick to the facts. Have you found anything that suggested Melissa and Sienna didn't get along?"

"What are we thinking? Matricide? No. Not exactly . . . but Melissa doesn't seem like mother of the year either. I did another deep dive into the ChilBoyz last night—you're welcome—and found this little gem."

Jane's phone beeped, announcing a new text with a link to a YouTube video called *MILFs and Barely Legal Babes Put on a Show*. It was dated two years ago—around the time when Melissa had begun to work with Elijah and the crew—a few months before Joseph had committed suicide. Jane's nerves jangled as she pressed play.

On a beach, a beautiful, long-legged woman with honey highlights and a shimmering rose-gold bikini strutted down a long stage fashioned into a runway. It was Melissa. The beach looked similar to the riverbank near the bridge before the storm had hit. At the back of the stage, black curtains had been hung with a hand-painted sign over the top: Mother/Daughter Beauty Pageant. Dozens of people—mainly young men—were crowded around the edge of the catwalk, leering up at Melissa with shouts of sexualized encouragement. She stopped at the end of the stage, jutted out her hip dramatically, and gave a salacious wink to the camera before blowing a kiss to the fans below.

They went wild.

Behind her, a teenage girl entered the stage from the black curtains at the back. It was a much younger Sienna—fourteen and beautiful, but visibly self-conscious. Unlike Melissa, her walk was timid, almost a shuffle. Her shoulders rounded forward like she was trying to hide in her simple black bathing suit. She looked uncomfortable—frightened, even—as Melissa turned back the way she'd come. When the two met on the stage, Sienna gave a half-smile as Melissa playfully bumped hips with her, eliciting more whoops from the audience. Suddenly, a young man jumped onto the stage in front of them. It was Elijah Stanton. Sienna paused awkwardly as her mother and Elijah began dancing suggestively, their legs scissored together as they gyrated to the thumping bass of "Pony" by Ginuwine.

Jane paused the video and found Dylan, Randeep, and Joseph Jack in the crowd. Melissa flashed them all a sparkling grin before tossing her hair, placing her palm on the back of Elijah's head, and pulling him in for a long, suggestive kiss.

"Wow," Jane said into the phone as the video ended. "Melissa was certainly extroverted."

"Sure, extroverted right into Elijah's teenage boner."

"Twenty-year-old," she corrected.

Mickey made a noise of contempt. "In any case, we're going to have to decide whether to include video footage of Melissa dry-humping the missing loser if we pursue this story. How do you think Dom's going to feel about that?"

"Don't worry about it," Jane said. "I'm more worried about Sienna. No wonder she's got a problem with food and body image. I would too if Melissa was my mother."

"Can't we be worried about both of those things simultaneously? This has officially entered the messed-up zone, right? I'm digging up videos of your new husband's dead wife aggressively flirting-slash–making out with a barely legal kid she's known since childhood, while you're stuck in a hotel with her widower and psycho daughter?"

"I don't know if she's psycho," Jane said, picturing the message on the mirror. "But yeah, that's pretty much what we're dealing with. Sienna's been a miserable, manipulative little shit since the moment we met, but for the first time in seventy-two hours, I feel bad for her."

"Tell me what happened between her and her mom."

Jane recounted her conversations with the psychiatrist and Ted.

"Yikes. I mean, the best thing to do is talk to Dom about this, right?"

"Right," Jane said.

"Okay," Mickey replied. Jane could clearly hear the disapproval in their voice. "Before you do though, I found one more video that seems relevant. Unless you think watching twenty-year-old maniacs snorting whiskey will help us crack our case? Because there's plenty of those, too."

"Snorting whiskey?"

"Yep. Up their noses. Fetish porn for frat guys. Elijah and his little crew were a bunch of winners. But this one is different."

Another text message alert beeped in her ear.

"*A Plea for R & D?*" Jane said as she read the title of the new link.

"Watch it."

This video was more somber than any of the previous ChilBoyz material. The lighting was unprofessional and dim. Elijah was seated on a couch—Jane zoomed in and realized he was in the staff quarters—with a collection of people around him both seated and standing.

"Today is a sad day for us here at ChilBoyz Productions. Two of our crew are missing. They were last seen three days ago on a hunt for the perfect truck. Last thing anyone heard from them was that they'd got a lead on a sweet seventy-three Ford and they were taking a cruise to check it out. They still haven't come home. Randeep and Dylan, we love you guys. Get back here soon."

As Elijah rattled off information on who to contact if the viewers knew anything that could help, Jane scanned the faces of the people gathered in the room. She didn't recognize any of them until she got to the back row and saw Sienna.

"Any follow-ups to this video?" she asked when it ended.

"I haven't found any yet," Mickey replied. "Maybe they didn't know what else to do. From what I can tell of the police briefs and news coverage, the trail went cold on Dylan and Randeep pretty fast. Took a long time before they were reported missing. Their families assumed they'd taken off and would be back soon."

"It doesn't make sense that we are the first people to connect these dots," Jane said in frustration. "All these people worked on the same crew, and no one noticed that they've gone missing or died since they worked together?"

"I know—it's weird. But Joseph's suicide happened well before Dylan and Randeep went missing, Melissa's death was ruled accidental, and how suspicious is it for a twentysomething guy like Elijah to move on? Not very. It must happen all the time. I'm guessing we *are* the first people to see the pattern here."

"All roads lead back to the Venatura—but if you didn't know much about the hotel, you'd never see that."

"Exactly. Elijah's mother had no idea who I was talking about when I mentioned the ChilBoyz and Randeep and Dylan. And apparently, Melissa's funeral was small and private. Lucy was estranged from Peter at that point—she didn't hear about it until months later and didn't make the connection between Melissa's drowning and Elijah's disappearance until I pointed out that it seemed suspicious. And . . ." Mickey trailed off.

"What?" Jane asked, dread dripping down her spine.

"The people who did know them all well enough to see the connections are not that eager to figure out what happened."

"People like Peter Stanton," Jane said.

"And Dom and Sienna Lawrence."

"Mickey!"

"You've just seen footage of Melissa practically making out with Elijah. I'm not sure we can exclude Dom from our list of suspects just yet. And based on what you told me about Sienna's relationship with her mom, I think she's got to be on the list too. She's clearly a mess."

"There is no list of suspects," Jane whispered, for fear of being overheard. "And if there was, Dom would never be on it."

"If you say so."

"I'm going to talk to him about this tonight, okay? I'll clear it all up. Our focus should stay on Elijah and his connections. There's something we're missing there."

Mickey's silence was pointed.

"Just keep digging, okay? It will be easier to talk this through with Dom and Sienna if I know the whole story."

"Sure thing, boss."

Jane said goodbye. As she pulled the phone from her ear, she saw another text from the unknown number. It was a link to a news story.

WOMAN, 41, DIES IN SINGLE-VEHICLE CRASH IN DON VALLEY

A 41-year-old woman has died in hospital of injuries suffered after a crash in the Don Valley late Saturday afternoon, Toronto police say.

The crash happened near Bayview Avenue and Pottery Road. According to witnesses, the vehicle was traveling at high speeds before veering off the road and rolling into the ditch.

Police's traffic services are investigating the crash to determine if alcohol was a factor.

Witnesses and those with dashboard camera video are urged to call police.

Story by Anusha Johal
Toronto Star
October 29, 2022

Her head swam as she set her phone down on the small shelf above the sink, then turned on the hot water tap to fill it. Several of the dishes were crusted with food and needed to be soaked and scraped before she ran them through the dishwasher. As the sink filled, she crossed the room to the place where she'd left the cats.

There was no sign of the blankets, Fraser, or any of her little kittens. Jane tensed. Had Dom or Sienna kicked the animals out of the hotel? She got down on her hands and knees, ignoring the twinge from her foot at the swift movement. The cats were gone.

The pounding of water flooding the stainless-steel sink matched the roaring in her ears at the idea of the cats being tossed into the unrelenting rainstorm. She turned off the water and reached for her phone to text Dom.

It had disappeared.

She patted the surface of the shelf, wincing as she stood on tiptoe to ensure the device hadn't slipped to the back, but there was no trace of it. The shelf contained an industrial-sized container of dishwashing detergent, a handful of wire scrubbing pads, and a desiccated roach. The insect carcass crunched unpleasantly under her searching fingers.

Buried disgust rose like bile at the memory of similar creatures scurrying from the bright light of the bathroom in the run-down rental her mother had secured after she'd left Jane's father. It had been an awful, hopeless time. Jane had believed their lives couldn't get worse.

She'd been wrong.

With shaking hands, she scrabbled along the shelf again, knocking over the soap in a clatter of plastic on metal. She yanked every item off in frustration.

No phone.

Jane bit back a howl of frustration. A bubble popped on the surface of the soapy water in the sink. Fear gripped her as she stared into the deep pool of hot water.

She plunged her hands into the sink, patting the bottom of the enormous basin with flat hands. The water was hot and deep enough to sting the skin all the way up to her elbows. The edge of the sink pinched her midsection as she leaned forward. Nothing but a jumble of plates and cutlery.

Her fingers reached into the farthest corner. There was something there. She wedged the pad of her fingertip underneath and pulled the object out of the water.

Her phone.

Destroyed.

CHAPTER | THIRTY-THREE

THE WALLS BEGAN TO SHAKE. THUD AFTER THUD MADE THE STANDING water in the sink bounce. She jumped away from the counter and laid a flat hand on the doorframe and felt the wood rattle low and deep. The noise was coming from inside the hotel.

She raced into the dining room. Empty. Her breath came in gulps. She froze. The thumping continued. Outside the windows, the river had forced its way higher up the grassy lawn toward the hotel. A paper birch on the far bank clung to the shore by its exposed roots. The ceaseless current tugged the dangling tendrils. Downstream, unluckier trees bobbed like drowning victims.

Thump, thump.

"Dom?" she cried.

With the useless phone still in hand, her heartbeat pounded in time with the noise. It was coming from somewhere above her. She hurried to the stairs, unsure if she could trust the elevator. The whitewashed stairwell was colder than the dining room. Her feet slapped the steps, sending

228 | AMBER COWIE

spikes of pain through her toes and up her leg. The booming grew louder the higher she rose. When she reached the third-floor landing, the sound made her ears wobble.

She thrust open the push door and found Dom standing in a pile of dust, sledgehammer gripped in his strong hands. A thick leather toolbelt hung low on his hips. His denim work shirt was coated in a film of white plaster. He looked at her in surprise.

"Jane? I thought you were making lunch?"

"What did you do with the cats?" she cried. "How could you leave them outside to die?"

"The cats?" He looked concerned. "They got outside?"

"Someone let them out! Or forced them out! Probably the same person who threw my phone in the sink!"

He brushed the heel of his hand across his forehead, lined with confusion. "What?"

"The cats are missing," she said. "They're not where I left them."

A wash of sorrow rose inside her. She had failed to protect them.

Dom's face was tender. The muscles on his forearms rippled as he leaned the sledgehammer against the wall. The toolbelt pulled at his jeans, making them grip his strong thighs. He cupped her cheek with his dusty hand.

"Oh, Jane. The cats are fine; I moved them into a new bed. Mother cats like to feel insulated—to have a space that's just their own. I wanted them to be comfortable. They deserve it after everything they've been through."

She swallowed a lump. "You did all that for Fraser? I thought you hated her."

"It was Sienna's idea. Neither of us hate the cats." He looked puzzled. "We just had to make sure they weren't going to activate See's allergies."

She allowed herself to lean into his warm palm. Tears pricked her eyes and she blinked hard to get rid of them.

"Are you okay, Jane? I'm worried about you."

Her jaw tightened. She pulled away. "Of course I'm okay. I wanted to protect the cats, that's all. Where are they?"

"In that big cupboard by the side door in the kitchen. I want to keep them safe. And you." He eyed her. "This place can be a little . . . triggering, right? Sometimes this old hotel gets the best of me. I often find myself more susceptible when I'm already upset about something. You know, something from the past."

Jane met Dom's sympathetic gaze while trying to quell her panic. What was he talking about? Had he broken their rule about researching each other just like she had? Or worse, did Sienna know about Ember's scandal? About what Jane had done?

"What do you mean?"

Dom smiled sadly.

"You lost your parents, right? Seems like you are doing everything you can to make sure those kittens don't lose their mom as well."

Jane's shoulders slumped in relief. He didn't know what she'd done. He didn't judge her, didn't assume the worst about her. He loved her. And for now, the kittens were safe. She could rest for a moment. Divert her anxious thoughts from the ChilBoyz and their relationship with Dom's first wife, Ted's bitter description of Dom's screwup, and Joseph's traumatized face to nicer thoughts, like Dom's brown eyes sparkling with desire as he leaned down to kiss her. There was a metallic taste on his breath, but her body responded anyway. His lips drove away her distraction, drawing her into the kiss.

She pushed herself against his hard body, letting him lift her shirt. He was moving fast, hungry for her, and she unfastened his buttons with eager fingers. His chest and stomach were warm and solid beneath her hands. He tangled his fingers in her hair, tugging at the roots as he kissed her neck. She took a step back and kicked a saw. The sharp teeth scratched the ankle of her good foot.

"Watch that," Dom said, placing his hands on her hips and lifting her to a clear spot in the crowded hallway. She caught flashes of the lurid fuchsia flowers and tangling vines on the carpet below his tools.

He pressed his long leg between hers. She traced a line down past his belt and he groaned in her ear.

"Oh, Melissa," he whispered.

CHAPTER | THIRTY-FOUR

SHE BROKE AWAY FROM HIS BODY, FLINCHING WHEN HE TRIED TO touch her again.

"I'm so sorry," he said, rubbing the back of his neck. "I didn't mean—"

"To call me by Melissa's name? Is that who you think of when you kiss me?"

Her earlier tears threatened to return, but she forced them down. She limped down the hallway, nearly kicking a bucket of plaster half-hidden by a drop cloth. Her toe ached as serotonin ebbed.

"No, never," he said, following behind her. "Please, Jane. I'm sorry. It's just this old hotel. There're a lot of memories for me here."

Jane wheeled on him. "Well, that's what you wanted, right? That's why we're here? So you can wallow, and Sienna can 'heal'? Great plan, Dom. All you've succeeded in doing is hurting all of us. I'm delighted I can enjoy this macabre retreat with our shitty little family!"

"Jane, I'm so sorry." The pain in Dom's eyes prompted her to dial it down.

"So tell me about the memories. Tell me what happened here."

Dom's eyes were shining as he looked past her shoulder as if afraid to meet her gaze. "It's hard to talk about. Melissa's death was the worst thing I've ever experienced."

She thought about Ted. "Did it affect your work?"

Dom's expression tightened. "At times. That's a whole different conversation."

"I'm listening."

"Please, Jane, I'm juggling a lot of things right now. This third floor is a disaster and I want to get more done before the end of the day. Can we put a pin in it for now?"

Fatigue overwhelmed her. She didn't know how to reach him.

"Do I have a choice?"

Dom shook his head in frustration.

"It can't all happen on your schedule, but I promise I'll tell you everything when I'm ready. You said something about your phone? The least I can do is help you with that."

Yes, that is the least you could do. Without another word, Jane led him to the second floor. She gestured to the deep sink and pointed to the narrow shelf above it.

"My phone was right there. Someone tipped it off the shelf into the water."

He frowned.

"Hold on."

She stared miserably at the sink's half-empty contents as Dom left the room. Only a few soap bubbles floated over the food-stained plates that had sunk to the bottom. Dom returned with a small object pinched between his index finger and thumb. He placed an olive on the back side of the shelf closest to the wall, then used the heel of his hand to pound against the supporting wall. The olive rolled down the surface before plopping into the sink.

Jane stepped to the side and eyed the angle of the metal shelf. It was noticeably slanted.

"My hammering was the problem, but this shelf is on its last legs. I'm going to add it to my list of tasks."

She couldn't take her eyes off the green orb at the bottom of the sink. She wasn't so easily satisfied. The hammering had started *after* the phone disappeared. Why was Dom so quick to come up with assurances about her fears, but unable to provide answers to her most important questions?

"I don't think this was an accident. I don't think any of this has been coincidence or bad luck. Sienna knew Elijah a whole lot better than you think. And so did Melissa."

Dom shook his head. "This again. Your work is making you see situations and people in the worst possible way. Everything is a threat to you. You have to trust us."

"Trust Sienna? After the stunts she pulled to hurt us both? No. Trust is a two-way street. I know I jumped to conclusions about the cats—"

"Let me show you something."

He entered the kitchen through the pass-through and Jane followed. He headed for a large cupboard close to the oven. The doors were ajar. He tugged them open all the way to show her a huge pile of blankets carefully arranged at the back of the space. A bowl of water and food had been placed at the front. Fraser blinked up at them sleepily. Her four kittens—the size of large hamsters in shades of gray, orange, and white—were nuzzled beside her and on top of one another. Dom gently half-closed the doors and Jane spotted a makeshift litter box made out of an industrial-sized cake pan stuffed with torn-up strips of newspaper around the corner from the cupboard.

"I promise to take care of you and them and everyone here. If you'll just let me."

"I'm not a princess in need of rescue, Dom. There's more to this story than you're letting yourself see. There was awful writing all over the mirror in the Sunrise Suite upstairs last night. And now it's cleaned up. I doubt it was Sienna, because she's incapable of picking up after herself. Nice parenting, by the way. Can't imagine what her host family in France had to put up with. What I'm trying to tell you is that there's someone here with us! And Sienna did know Elijah! They were friends. Or something more. It's hard to tell—"

Dom cut her off by pointing his finger in her face. His features were stern. "This is exactly what I'm talking about, Jane! You're fixated on this horrible reinterpretation of the past. And it's messing with your ability to see the present. This whole thing, with you and me and Sienna? It only works if you want it to. That's the thing about a family. Everyone has to believe in it. Or it doesn't exist."

Jane was stung. How could he accuse her of being stuck in the past after calling her by his dead wife's name?

"I do believe in it. Of course I do—I wouldn't be here if I didn't. But the truth matters, right? Honesty matters? Well, here's the truth: Sienna hates me. And she hates you for marrying me. Wake up, Dom! She's a messed-up bully who wants to make everyone as unhappy as she is."

"Your honesty is starting to look a lot like cruelty. Sienna and I need to move forward, not backward. I thought you understood that."

"Dom, you just confused me with Melissa! How is that moving forward?"

The lines around his mouth deepened, pulling down his expression into anxious sorrow.

"Jane, I am so sorry. I'm a wreck. Melissa . . . she was my first. We met in high school. I never thought I'd be with anyone but her."

"Why did you ask me to marry you?" she demanded. "Were you trying to forget her?"

"Forget her? No, of course not. I love you. You are not a replacement for—"

His words were interrupted by a high-pitched metallic screech. Jane looked around the room, wild-eyed.

"It's coming from outside," he said, dropping his shoulder to barrel into the dining room. She limped behind him, gasping at the sight outside the window.

The river had overpowered what remained of the bridge. Water rushed over its moorings in a torrent of muddy debris. Dom and Jane watched the surge force the heavy steel platform down the seething rapids like it weighed nothing at all.

CHAPTER | THIRTY-FIVE

THEY RUSHED DOWNSTAIRS. SIENNA WAS IN THE DINING ROOM FAC-
ing the windows. Even as they joined her, her eyes didn't leave the swollen
river.

"Dad, did you hear that? The bridge is totally gone!"

"I know, honey. This storm is the worst I've ever seen. All this water—
there's nowhere for it to go."

"Are we going to be okay?" Sienna asked.

Jane's heart twinged at the fear in her voice, in spite of her anger.

"Yes, of course," he said.

His phone blared an alert, and he pulled it out of his pocket, forehead
creasing as he scanned the text on his screen. He swore under his breath.
"There's been another slide—this one about fifteen kilometers from here
on the Coquihalla. The highway is closed to the north and flooded to the
south. Even if we could cross the river, the roads are washed out."

The Coquihalla was a major transportation corridor. Its closure would wreak havoc on supply lines across Western Canada and the American Pacific Northwest. They would have to repair it immediately, meaning all available crews would be diverted there.

Dom headed directly to the cocktail bar. He pulled out a can of beer. The hiss and pop made Sienna turn. She looked as miserable as Jane felt.

"Want one?" Dom asked Jane.

The clock behind him showed just past one thirty p.m.

"I'm not much of a day-drinker," Jane said.

"This has been quite a day."

He took a deep swig. Jane remembered the metallic taste on his breath. She wondered how many he'd already had.

"Maybe it's better to keep our heads clear."

Dom winced. "It's not going to do us much good. The Coq is completely blocked. It knocked out a bridge much bigger than this one. The footage is nuts. And farms in Abbotsford are all under an evacuation order. It used to be a lake before the city decided to bring in piles of earth and put houses on it. Guess it's decided to fill itself back up with water."

"What does that mean for us? Are we safe?"

"That's just what I was getting to. I walked the river edge this morning. We've got a low spot that's starting to flood in the western corner of the property. The water is coming for us too." He took another drink.

"How's your foot, Jane?" Sienna asked. "Ready to fill some sandbags?"

"It's still stiff but I can get around. I can help."

"No way," Dom replied. "I'm on sandbag duty. You need to heal."

Jane managed a grateful nod. What Dom had said was true—they were stuck here, together. They had to make it work. Maybe he was right. Maybe her dark thoughts were limiting her ability to accurately perceive reality. She had been wrong about the cats. Was she wrong about her phone too? And what about the pristine state of the Sunrise Suite? Could she have imagined the ugly writing while in a state of shock from her injury? She was so scared. Was the fear eroding her mind?

A loud growl came from her husband's midsection.

"Sorry. We haven't eaten lunch yet."

Dom and Sienna both looked at her with expectation. She began to balk before realizing she needed a minute alone.

"I'll find something," she said.

Jane walked into the kitchen, favoring her weak foot, and entered the walk-in cooler. She shivered as she searched for something simple. They were still well-stocked with fresh produce, though the edges of the greens were beginning to curl. She grabbed a block of cheese nearly the length of her arm and hastily prepared a batch of grilled cheese sandwiches. As the sandwiches began to brown, she found a sack of plain rice and filled a bowl. Nestling her phone within the grains to dry out, she prayed for a miracle.

A tiny mew from Fraser's cupboard was a comfort as she flipped the sandwiches.

Five minutes later, she placed the stack in front of Dom and Sienna, who had settled at a table near the window.

"They're kind of burnt," Sienna said as she reached for the plate.

"Still getting used to the equipment," Jane said.

"Looks great to me," Dom replied.

Two spots of pink had appeared high on his cheekbones. Jane noticed he had freshened up his beer. As the others chewed, Jane laid her sandwich on her plate and squared her shoulders.

"I would like to apologize to you, Sienna. I've been insensitive. Dom once said I was like a dog with a bone, and that's true. I've been that way all my life. My mom used to tell this story about when I was a kid and decided I needed to solve the mystery of the missing six-pack. I'd seen it in the fridge on Friday night. By Saturday morning cartoons it was gone. Mom and I'd fallen asleep on the sofa watching old movies, so I knew it wasn't her. My dad eventually had to admit that he'd finished the whole thing the night before. In front of my non-drinking grandparents, who were not too impressed. My dad was mad—he liked to be in charge, and he hated that I'd forced him into revealing more about himself than he wanted to."

Sienna cracked a small smile and looked at her father.

"After my parents died, solving mysteries became my way of making sense of the world. I liked problems that had answers, because mine didn't. Who knows, maybe if they were still alive, I'd be more polite."

"Less nosy," Sienna said, taking a big bite.

Dom squeezed Jane's hand under the table. "My parents were really traditional too—my dad worked as a highway engineer. My mom took care of me and my brother. It was nice to have that kind of stability. I always wanted the same thing for Sienna."

Jane looked up. "But Melissa had a job. You both worked."

"She was a stay-at-home mom until Sienna turned fourteen. Even after that, her business was part-time. This"—he opened his arms to gesture at the room around them—"was her first big project."

"And last," Sienna muttered.

"She must have had a work crew. Was Elijah on it?"

Sienna glowered and put down her sandwich.

"You did a few videos with him, right, Sienna? The ChilBoyz?" Jane pressed.

"I thought you weren't going to be nosy anymore," she said.

"I got the hashtag from your TikTok. I don't have to be nosy when you're broadcasting your business to the world. Listen, Sienna, I want to get to know you a little better. I need to close this circle before I can drop it. It's how my brain works. I think talking about your mom and Elijah will help you heal too."

Sienna pushed her chair back from the table. "Elijah was a jerk, okay? He used to pick on me. Dad never listened when I told him that I didn't like him!" She faced her father. "You always made me hang out with him and his stupid friends when you and Mom and Lucy and Peter were together, but I hated him!"

Dom looked bewildered. "Your mom always arranged that stuff. I didn't know you hated it. I thought you liked hanging out with the local kids."

"Well, you thought wrong! He was a total fucking loser."

Sienna stormed out of the dining room. Dom looked at Jane with a glassy stare that contained a confusing mix of emotions.

"I didn't know all that. I didn't know it bothered her."

"Well, maybe you should have known," Jane said gently. "I'm sorry I brought it up, but how am I supposed to get to know Sienna unless I ask questions?"

To Jane's surprise, Dom shook his head. "No, you were honest with us. I can see how hard you are trying. I've been a shit to you today, and Sienna's been worse. Tell you what. I'm going to get a few more sandbags in that low spot this afternoon. Why don't you whip us up something special for dinner? Make a tray that we can deliver to Sienna, and then the two of us are going on a proper date."

Jane cringed at the memory of the necklace during their last "date," but she didn't let it show.

"I'd love that. Should I set up a table in here?"

Dom winked.

"Nope. I'm taking you somewhere else. This old hotel's still got a few nice secrets to reveal."

CHAPTER | THIRTY-SIX

JANE STOOD TALL IN THE HIGH HEELS AND TEAL TWO-PIECE SET THAT
bared the top of her midriff. Her foot ached in the unnaturally angled position, but she needed to feel sexy after the confidence-draining encounter
with Dom earlier. Before she'd met him, this had been her favorite date
outfit, and it hadn't failed her yet—hopefully it was flashy enough to keep
the memory of his first wife at bay.

The ups and downs of the day had generated an odd intimacy between them. He had shown her the deepest part of himself—how raw
his grief really was. In turn, she had confided in him. She rarely spoke
of her parents to anyone but Mickey—who had seen her father fall
down the stairs drunk one night during a sleepover when they were
fourteen—but her mom had been on her mind a lot lately. Ever since
the Hot Docs festival. The thought of Mickey made her reach for her
phone, only to remember it was dead in the bowl of rice in the kitchen.
An hour before, she'd sent a message on her laptop to her friend to

explain what had happened. Jane was fully expecting a panicked reply when she returned to her inbox.

She pushed aside her worry about Mickey and took a moment to savor the anticipation of romance. Dressed in her own clothes in the sparkling lobby of the hotel with darkness pressing against the windows was almost enough to make this seem like a real date. She and Dom had enjoyed so few traditional evenings together over the course of their whirlwind courtship. It would be nice to be swept away from the anxiety of the meteorological and emotional storms.

But as she traced a finger on the smooth wooden surface of the desk, an unpleasant ripple crept up her neck. She caught a glimpse of herself in the mirrored panel behind the front desk. A shadow blurred and darted behind her. She whipped around to catch whatever was creeping up. Her eyes darted from one dark corner to the next for the source of the threat. She couldn't see anything, but she no longer felt alone. Jane took a step toward the stairs. In the half-light, blackness had gathered under them. The space was large enough to hide in.

The elevator pinged. Jane jumped at the sound, making her toe twinge. Footsteps came toward her, then Dom strode out from around the corner. He was wearing the same well-cut suit from the necklace night and a crisply ironed white shirt. He gave her a wide smile as he approached, pausing to scan her from head to toe.

"You look amazing," he said.

"So do you."

He kissed her long and deep. As she pulled away, she joked, "Should I wear a name tag?"

She was relieved when he laughed. Laying his hand flat on the small of her back, he pulled her into another kiss.

"Where are we going?" she whispered.

"Follow me."

He led Jane by the hand back to the elevator bay. As the doors closed in front of them, she watched him press a button labeled B. The elevator smoothly hummed its way downstairs to the basement.

Dom's eyes were warm, if a little unfocused. She winked. Her endless reflection in the mirrored walls did the same.

"It's taking everything I have not to rip your clothes off right now," Dom said.

She brought her hand to her throat, which had flushed at his words.

"Please tell me there are silk sheets and a hot tub waiting for us."

"Even better."

As if on cue, the elevator glided to a stop and the doors opened to a decidedly unimpressive industrial space. She stepped out onto a concrete floor and gazed at a shabby off-white wall in desperate need of a coat of paint after years of scuff marks and general abuse. To her left was a long hallway piled with large boxes, wooden crates, and plastic-covered mattresses—and a metal safe that must have been the gun storage area Dom had mentioned. On her right was a stack of dollies, large brooms, and other equipment tucked into a storage alcove. Dom tugged her down the cluttered hallway on the left. They had to turn sideways to get past two dark-green leather armchairs which had been stacked top to bottom.

"This is not exactly what I was expecting," she said.

"Have faith, my darling."

They arrived at a nondescript door, which looked like a janitor's closet. Dom swung it open with a flourish, and Jane followed him into a place she never would have dreamed possible. Dom was right—the hotel still had secrets.

The room was slightly more than half the size of the fourth-floor suite, with six crescent-shaped cherrywood tables circled by deep red tufted stools. The walls were covered in a midnight-blue wallpaper etched with a golden geometric pattern that made her think of the Empire State Building. Looking up, she saw a tin ceiling punched out in a concentric square design. The entire room looked as if it had been transported from the elegant and edgy Art Deco period.

"This is incredible," she said. "But I thought this hotel was built in the 1950s? This looks like it came straight out of the Roaring Twenties."

"*Rebuilt* in the fifties," Dom said. "The original hotel was constructed in the mid-1920s by a wealthy and wild countess. It was partially destroyed in a fire in the late 1940s, then created again using what was left of the remaining structure. This room is an homage to the entire history. Wait until you see the best part."

He grinned, then made his way to the dark marble bar at the back of the room. Behind it were intricately carved wooden shelves stocked with gleaming bottles of absinthe, gin, and vodka. Jane half expected a red-jacketed bartender to materialize.

"Tell me about this countess."

Dom grinned. "She was the heiress to a huge but scandalous fortune. Her mother had married the richest man in England after a long affair. The countess brought the money to Canada after her own divorce. She bought a ranch and ran cattle before deciding to create this luxurious hotel in what would have been wilderness. She raised her daughter here. The poor girl died in the hotel fire I mentioned. The countess never recovered. She sold the land and moved to southern Italy. By all accounts, she lived life on her own terms. Just like you."

"For better and for worse."

The tragic death of a young girl disturbed her more than she let on. Another of the Venatura's victims.

"Always for better, Jane. Your fire is what I love most about you. Can I make you a drink?"

She slid onto a stool, letting his words fill up the hollow that had been created when he called her by the wrong name. Her faltering faith in herself strengthened again. She could trust her instincts. This hotel was creepy as hell. Dom was still grieving Melissa, but that didn't mean he didn't love Jane. Grief was complicated and messy—she knew that more than most. Finding Elijah would give Dom the closure they both needed.

"How could I resist a cocktail in our very own speakeasy? What do you recommend?"

"How about a French-75? Specialty of the house."

"You're on."

Dom began to assemble cocktail glasses, a lemon, and mixing tools. She watched in amazement as his large hands moved nimbly between filling measures, zesting lemon, and shaking ice. He presented her with an elegant flute filled nearly to the brim with pale yellow liquid. A slice of lemon sat jauntily on top.

"Cheers," Dom said as he touched the lip of his glass to hers with a delicate *ting*.

She took a sip and winced. The strong cocktail took a sharp turn at the back of her throat before heading straight down into her empty stomach.

"This was a popular drink in the twenties," he said after downing nearly half the contents. "Named after the fastest-firing gun the French army used during the First World War. Watch out—it packs a punch."

He was right. His words had begun to run into each other. The cumulative effects of his drinking throughout the day were beginning to show.

"I can tell. This tastes like straight gin mixed with lemon juice," she said. Heat rose in her cheeks as she attempted another sip. The cool, citrusy booze was smoother the second time around. A pleasant glow warmed her chest and limbs.

"And a splash of champagne," he said with a loose wink. "Now for the pièce de résistance."

His accent was exaggerated but still sexy, and the drift into French reminded her of their first meeting in Barcelona. They'd been tacky with tourism and sweat when they'd stumbled upon a gorgeous mosaic covering the front of an apartment building. It was by Gaudí, and it was exquisite. Like this speakeasy, it had offered a moment of unexpected and startling beauty. He motioned for her to follow him before moving to the back corner of the wall farthest away from the bar.

"Check this out."

Jane was perplexed when she saw dead bolts affixed to the top and bottom panels of the wall. Dom reached for the top one then made a small sound in the back of his throat.

"What's wrong?" she asked.

"Nothing. Just thought it would be locked."

"Locked?"

"Never mind—the summer staff must have missed it when they were closing down for the season. Peter doesn't show many people this place. He likes to keep it a secret. And here's why."

He patted the wall at waist height, then applied pressure. She gasped as a panel swung open to reveal a hidden doorway. A cold draft of musty air pushed her hair from her face as she leaned in to see a set of concrete stairs leading up. He took her by the hand and they climbed the cold staircase. He pointed up to a panel above them with a visible hinge.

"This is a trapdoor. It leads outside to the walking path on the western side of the hotel. Real speakeasies always had a getaway," he said with a lopsided grin.

He was soused.

Dom unlatched a sliding bolt and pushed the trapdoor open. Rain fell on their heads. The wind caught hold of the door, and Dom struggled to pull it closed. They headed back down the stairs and he sealed the hidden door once again. The bar seemed cozier after their trip into the storm raging above.

"So, this was built to pay tribute to the hotel's origins during Prohibition?" she asked.

Dom nodded. "Melissa loved the authenticity—" He stopped.

"It's okay to talk about her, Dom. She's going to come up, one way or another."

Dom seemed relieved. And Jane felt a little better. The only way to establish their new family was to get Dom to release his emotions about his first wife. Holding on to grief held people back. No matter how painful it was, they had to be honest. She still believed that, despite what it had cost her.

"She devoured everything she could find about the countess. It was her idea to honor her. There was a little speakeasy down here during the countess's time, but it was nowhere near this grand." He frowned at her drink, which was still close to two-thirds full. "Get that drink down, honey. There's more where that came from."

She fetched it from the bar and took another sip. Her stomach rolled. "I should carry down our dinner," she said.

"No need. That's the other cool thing about this secret space."

Dom moved to a small metal panel at the end of the bar. The hinges creaked as he opened it. He pressed a button. Slowly, an open-sided box, large enough to fit a small child, descended. Two plates domed with silver room-service lids had been placed upon it. Dom had prepared servings of the dinner she'd prepared. She was touched at the gesture.

"This is where the dumbwaiter leads?"

"Man, nothing gets by you. I didn't know if you'd seen it. It's in a weird spot—behind the shelves where the big pots are kept. Melissa didn't want people to know about this place, so she made sure it was discreet."

A slosh of courage prompted her to speak. "Did Melissa keep a lot of secrets?"

Dom's face contorted into a grimace. Jane regretted the clumsy words when she heard the irritation in his voice. "Are you sure you want to keep talking about her? After everything that happened this afternoon?"

Blotches had appeared on his cheeks again.

"Please, Dom. We need to be open with each other. You're remembering her because she's a part of this place. You can't let her go unless you're willing to speak about who she was. I told you about my parents this afternoon. About my father's drinking problem."

"That's true," he admitted.

She seized her chance. "Is it okay if I ask you a few more questions?"

She fumbled for her phone before remembering it was lying lifeless in a bowl of rice. When Dom met her eyes again, his gaze was off-center and his expression had changed. He looked morose. "Your grief is different though," he said. "That's what I need you to know. That's why I brought you here. Okay?"

Alcohol was affecting his speech. She pushed her own drink aside.

"I'm not sure what you mean by that. How was Melissa's death different from my parents'?"

"We're different people. We went through different things." He nodded emphatically as if the matter was settled, then began to fiddle with their food, dramatically lifting the silver lids to show a plate of listless spaghetti doused in plain tomato sauce that hardly deserved the elaborate place settings. As he set the pasta down in front of her, the plate hit the marble bar hard enough to knock a noodle loose from the pile.

"How are we different?"

Rather than answer, Dom spun around in an exaggerated circle. "Babe, have you seen my fork?"

A spike of annoyance pierced her body. She had never seen her husband this drunk.

"How is it different for me?" she repeated.

After an excruciating wait, while he wolfed down his food, he finally mumbled a few more words. "I shouldn't have said that."

"But you did."

"Every death is different, right? Your parents . . . it was a car accident. My dad, a heart attack."

He slid his plate—which was already empty save for a smear of red sauce—back into the dumbwaiter with an unpleasant clank.

"And Melissa's?"

Dom spoke his answer to the floor. "That was a hard one. Seeing her like that. Her body . . . so broken. I'll never forget it. She was just pulverized, you know? Mangled and torn up. All that blood." He nearly choked on the last word.

Sympathy swelled inside Jane. She picked up her plate then walked around the bar to Dom, who took her into his arms after she placed her dish on top of his in the dumbwaiter. The world swam around her: his warm body, the soft lights reflected in the colored glass, and the pleasant geometric patterns of the antique wallpaper.

"Oh, Dom, I'm so sorry. You've been through so much."

"So have you. That's why we work. That's why we found each other."

He ran his hands up the curve of her hip and over her breasts, prompting her to eagerly grab his hand and pull him into the hallway where she led him to the elevator. He pinned her to the wall, pressing the button while kissing her. When the car arrived, they stumbled inside, their mouths barely missing a moment. She opened her eyes as he pressed her against the back wall, his lips on her neck, her ears, her mouth. He put his hand between her legs, stroking her above the thin fabric of her pants.

"Oh god, I want you," he whispered.

She kissed him hard in response.

When the elevator stopped, the doors opened to the fourth floor. She had thought they were heading to the staff quarters.

"The Sunset?"

"Come on," he said from behind.

They hurried down the hall. As she reached for the handle of the door, he leaned against her, pinning her, stroking her neck as she arched backward. His mouth was hot on her skin. With his other hand, he pushed open the door. She turned to face him in the small hallway, and he looked at her questioningly as he closed his large hand around her throat.

"Is this okay?" he whispered.

She nodded, overcome with the physical sensation of one powerful hand on her neck and the other between her legs. He squeezed gently, then pushed her against the wall, nudging her legs open with his knee before lifting one up to press against her. She moaned.

The sound of his belt buckle unclasping was followed by the rasp of a zipper. He hooked a finger under her waistband and pulled her silky pants off with a rough tug. The cold breeze on her skin was forgotten the moment she felt the warmth she had been craving inside her body. His hand tightened as their breath quickened. His strokes were long and powerful.

"Jane, oh god."

The sound of her name made her melt. "I love you so much," she whispered as her body tensed and fluttered.

Afterward, he led her to the huge bed, which she slid into with a soft groan. The pillowtop mattress and thick white duvet were heavenly compared to the springy coils they'd been sleeping on downstairs. He fit his body behind her and laid a heavy hand on her hip. Within seconds, his snores began. Her own eyelids were heavy. The pull of sleep was too much to overcome, despite a small thought flitting like the flash of a minnow below the surface of a stream.

How could a drowning victim be covered in blood?

CHAPTER | THIRTY-SEVEN

JANE JERKED AWAKE TO AN UNFAMILIAR SOUND IN THE COLD, DARK room. Sledgehammer, bridge destruction, a tree falling on the hotel? Her mind tried to fill in the blanks in her half sleep. The boom echoed in her ears again. She reached for Dom, calling his name as she patted his side of the bed.

She found nothing but a bunched-up blanket.

"Dom?"

No answer.

"Dom?"

Still nothing. She clicked on the lamp, cringing at the painful burst of light, then gathered the puffy duvet around her naked body, which was now covered in an unpleasant layer of cold sweat. Where was her husband? She walked toward the small entryway. Dom's clothes were missing from the hasty pile they'd left on the floor. She needed the toilet.

Jane slipped inside the bathroom, leaving the door partially open in her haste. As she began to pee, a black shape rushed past, heading toward the door to the hallway.

"Dom?" Her voice was raw with fright. The bathroom door slammed shut.

She struggled to finish so she could follow. Wrapping the blanket around her body, she sprang out the door. Her foot screamed in agony. The unheated hallway made her fingers stiff and her cheeks tingle. She could barely see a thing. Why was it so dark? She cursed the loss of her phone, which could have been her flashlight. Now she was empty-handed and alone in the night.

She began to call for her husband again, but the sound died in her throat. Who had been in their room? It couldn't have been Dom. He would have answered her.

Right?

There were no windows in the corridor. She kept one hand on the wall, while clutching the fabric around her chest. She slid her bare feet forward, one by one, trailing her fingers along the nubbly wall covering, ignoring the pang of pain each time her injured foot hit the floor. The high heels had been a bad idea. Her breath was ragged and deep as she strained to hear something, anything, to tell her Dom was near.

Finally, the corridor reached the T-shaped turn. On her right, a faint glimmer of moonlight through the window by the elevator bay offered a tiny respite to the darkness. Ahead of her, a deep pit of blackness led to the Sunrise Suite. She continued down the straight path toward the darkness.

She wondered what she'd find this time.

As she passed through the dim portal of light, Jane considered calling for Dom again, but something stopped her. The soles of her feet rubbed against the spongy carpet as the folds of the blanket rustled behind her like the train of a wedding dress. With each step, her eyes strained to discern recognizable shapes within the lightless passage. Her fingertips found a ninety-degree angle. She had reached the door. Adjusting the blanket, she stretched out her hand to turn the doorknob.

It was locked.

She pulled back. The hotel hummed and creaked in the dark. No sign of Dom. No way to get into the suite. She had no choice but to retrace her steps. This time, she pushed herself to walk at full speed, laying her palm flat against the wall and listening to the fabric tick against her smooth skin. The hair on her scalp crawled, but she squared her shoulders. She had never been afraid of the dark. She was Jane Duvall. She had never been afraid of anything. Except how far she would go for the truth—and how much people hated her for it.

"DOM?" she cried when she reached the intersection of the halls again. "Where are you?"

Her voice was rough and sharp like a crow's call. Cold air forced its way under her wrappings, making her shiver. She pushed herself to move toward the elevators.

When she reached them, the dim light from the large window helped her find her bearings. With the blanket dragging, she ran toward the silver glint of Sienna's former room where the number on the door caught a tiny shaft of moonlight. She turned the handle and tumbled inside, using her flat hand to click the light on. The room was still in a horrible state. Dirty plates, smeared cake, and half-empty coffee cups littered the surfaces. A jagged burst of pain rose from the sole of her good foot. She cursed as she bent to pick up a discarded fork. She did a quick, thorough search of the room, under the bed, behind the curtains, even in the bathtub.

It was empty and cold like the rest of the fourth floor. Sienna must be downstairs. Or had she been in Jane's room? And where was Dom?

Quick steps back through the hallway brought her to the elevator area. She thrust her hand out to call a car before stopping with her finger outstretched in midair. The movement of the elevator would be loud in the silent hotel. She carefully opened the door to the stairs.

The unforgiving surface below her feet sucked the remaining warmth from her body. Her teeth chattered as she gripped the icy banister. In the closed space, each breath sounded like the panting of a scared dog. On the second floor, she pushed the emergency exit open. The metallic clunk made her heart seize. The dining room was mercifully dappled with clouded moonlight. It too was empty.

She had to find Dom.

The lobby glowed with soft track lighting as she descended the grand staircase, searching for movement or a hint of Dom's presence. Her frustration bloomed when she reached the empty main floor.

"Dom?" she called, louder than before, not caring if it woke Sienna or attracted unwanted attention.

She was bolder now that she was downstairs. If worse came to worst, there were places to hide.

Her cry bounced around the room without response. She rushed to the huge windows by the butterfly artwork, pressing her face against the glass to see if the intruder had run outside. The draft from the window sent a shiver from her forehead to her spine. Rain pelted the glass, obscuring anything beyond the surface of the window. She swore again as she realized the best vantage point was at the top of the stairs.

Jane limped back up the stairs to the windows in the dining room, through the doors that led to the balcony and out onto the main deck, which was now empty save for furniture Dom had stacked in the corner. She approached the large pile cautiously like a small animal searching for sign of a predator. The pouring rain drenched her blanket. She peered out into the endless darkness, calling her husband's name in a shriek.

"DOM! Where are you?"

She stopped at the eastern edge of the balcony. The wind whipped her hair as the rain drove into her eyes, ears, and mouth. Then, a flash of silver. She peered through the darkness.

Her husband was walking toward the hotel from the path that led to the boathouse.

He was carrying a shovel.

CHAPTER | THIRTY-EIGHT

JANE RAN BACK DOWN THE STAIRS TO THE MAIN ENTRANCE. HER FEET throbbed. The deep prints she had seen at the trailhead leading to the cabins must have been Dom's. What was he hiding? And why did he have a shovel?

"Where the hell have you been?" Jane demanded as he came through the doors.

Dom looked at her with an unreadable expression. The whites of his eyes were visible above and below his irises. Red lines scored their surface. His dark hair hung in wet, lanky strands across his forehead.

"I thought you were sleeping."

"I was. Something woke me up. It was loud, like a door slamming closed. What were you doing?"

"You did hear a door," Dom said, running his hand through his hair to shake out the water. Drops fell to the floor and hit Jane's feet. She edged away as he continued.

"The boathouse . . . the wind must have pulled it open. I heard it slamming. I didn't want to wake you. I'm sorry."

Jane shook her head. "Don't lie to me. Those doors were all padlocked shut. And we were sleeping on the opposite side of the hotel. Where were you?" Her voice shook like the wind-battered trees outside the window.

"You're freezing," Dom said.

He tried to reach for her but she dodged his hand.

"Get away from me."

"At least let me warm you up."

He crossed the lobby, giving Jane a wide berth as he passed behind the stairs and headed to the fireplace. For a moment, she stayed in place, watching him shed water on the stone floor as he removed his wet coat and boots and propped them up by the fireplace. Clumps of black mud fell from the soles. She stared at them in silence as he knelt before the fireplace and flicked the hidden switch below to ignite the flames before turning back to her.

"Were you on the eastern trail? The one you told me to avoid?"

"Come here, Jane. You can warm up as we talk."

She expelled the air from her lungs in an angry sigh, then stalked over to the fireplace. The glass plate atop the butterfly wings reflected a shadowy version of her movements. She averted her eyes and focused on her husband.

"Tell me what you were doing with that shovel."

"What?"

His face fell in what appeared to be genuine confusion. Was he still drunk? Her head felt thick.

"The shovel you were carrying. Just now." She forced the words out one at a time through a tight jaw.

"Oh," Dom said. "I left it down by the boathouse earlier when I was filling sandbags. I was bringing it back to the tool shed."

"Stop lying to me!"

"What are you talking about? I haven't lied to you."

"You've done nothing but lie to me."

"About what?"

"About Melissa. About Sienna and Elijah. And about yourself. Why are you on antipsychotic medication, Dom? What did you screw up at work? Who the hell are you? Why did you bring me here?"

His face became drawn, and he stared at her for a moment before moving to a set of built-in shelves to the left of the fireplace that Jane hadn't noticed before. He slid a panel open. Behind it was a tray with two heavy tumblers and a beautiful crystal decanter full of an amber liquid. He brought it to the coffee table and poured them both a generous two inches. Jane refused to accept the offered glass. Dom set it on the table before taking a long swig from his.

"No more alcohol. I don't want another drink. I want the truth."

"I have told you everything I could."

"What the hell does that mean?" Jane snapped.

Dom swore. "You know, I've been so patient with you. But you are nothing like the woman I thought I married. I was carrying a shovel, for god's sake. It's not exactly a capital offense."

Jane stepped toward him. He took another huge drink.

"Me? You have got to be joking—"

"Yes, you. Jane, you're heartless. You don't give a shit about Sienna and what she's been struggling with. You're obsessed with the past. You're selfish. You're irrationally attached to feral cats. You have no respect for my privacy or my wishes—"

"Sienna is awful, Dom. Every overture has been thrown in my face, and she treats me like the fucking maid. You're in denial about her and your dead wife. And the only thing I'm obsessed with is figuring out what you're hiding—"

"And you're a god-awful cook."

She glowered at him. He grimaced in return before refilling his glass.

"And you're drunk, again. Do you really think that's a good idea?"

"The best," he said, nearly side-swiping the couch as he swung his body back to face her.

"You're nothing like I thought you were either."

He laughed. "We should start a club."

His glib response made her tense. "Tell me why you had the shovel. What are you hiding? What DID YOU BURY?"

She hadn't meant to scream, but the words bounced around the room.

"Stop yelling! Oh my god, what is wrong with you?" Sienna had emerged from the staff quarters.

Her usually perfect hair was tousled as she stood behind the front desk. Her expression was cross and sleepy like a grumpy toddler. Dom gave Jane a dark look before approaching his daughter and slinging a protective arm around her shoulder.

"Did we wake you?"

"*You* didn't," Sienna said with a scowl in Jane's direction.

"Sienna, go back to bed," Jane said.

"Why do you always have to be such a bitch?"

"That is inappropriate," Dom said. He sounded insincere.

"Why did you bring me here?" Jane demanded. She was close to tears.

"I've been asking him that question since we arrived," Sienna said.

"Can you please be quiet?" Jane said to her stepdaughter.

"You have to calm down, Jane. For Sienna."

"Sienna can handle herself. I'm talking about you, Dom. Am I in danger? What the hell is going on here?"

Dom's eyes bulged as Sienna's widened.

"Slow down, psycho," Sienna said. "You're not in danger."

"I'm not a psycho. And I'm tired of being lied to."

"You're such a nutjob. I wish my father had never married you. You are the worst person I've ever met. You're not a mother. You're a bitch."

Jane clenched her fists. Fury rose inside her like vomit. She walked toward the fireplace, desperate for calm, but her stepdaughter kept talking.

"You're not the person you pretend to be," Sienna said. "I know all about you. I know all about what you did to that woman—"

"And neither are you, you little troll!"

Jane grabbed the sparkling decanter by the neck. She walked toward Sienna with purposeful strides, feeling a flash of satisfaction when fear

THE OFF SEASON | 259

pinched her stepdaughter's face. As she raised the decanter to shoulder height, the round topper of the glass bottle plummeted with a splintering smash. Alcohol poured from the opening. Fumes filled the air.

The brown liquid arced as Jane launched it toward the desk with a raw howl. The bottle shattered on contact, spraying glass and liquor.

In the silence that followed, Jane stood frozen in place, staring at the results of her savage act. For a split second, she wondered when she would wake up from this horrible nightmare. This was not who she was.

Sienna's voice broke through Jane's shock. "Daddy?" She sounded like a child. "She cut me, Daddy. Help me. I'm bleeding."

CHAPTER | THIRTY-NINE

JANE WOKE AT SEVEN A.M. FROM A SHORT AND SHALLOW SLEEP. HER mouth was dry. Shame gurgled in her stomach. There was no forgetting her actions from the night before: Sienna's cut had left a spatter of blood on the floor. After her outburst, Dom had quietly told her to sleep alone. His lack of emotion had scared her nearly as much as her loss of control. Jane had collected her personal items from their room and retreated to a new room down the hall. In the early morning darkness, guilt scratched at her conscience like an animal.

She reached for her laptop. A wash of desperation made her snap it shut again almost immediately. Her messages to Mickey had not gone through. There was no Wi-Fi.

Placing her feet on the cold floor was a tiny agony. Her toe was tender, and a deep purple bruise had spread down the entire right side of her foot. She donned a warm base layer, thick jeans, and a sweater from a bag, wincing as she pulled on her boots.

Jane stilled for a moment, listening. Then, with laptop in hand, she eased open the door and tiptoed to the end of the hallway before entering the lobby. She was deliberate with her movements—heel, toe, heel, toe—to avoid unnecessary pain and noise.

Though the sun had begun to rise, it was obscured by the flat gray light of the low clouds and endless rain. The interior was dim, and the corners of objects lacked definition. Once she reached the stairs, she kept her feet as flat as possible as she raised them one step at a time. On the second floor, she quickened, looking longingly at the coffee bar as she passed. She didn't dare risk the time or the disruption, though the thought of a warm cup made her twitch with desire.

After passing through the swinging doors to the kitchen, she pulled her phone out of the rice. Still dead.

With an eye on the door, she opened a can of tuna and placed it in a bowl for Fraser. The cat blinked sleepily. Her kittens raised their heads and let out little mews. In honor of Murray, she'd named the biggest Thompson—a white, fuzzy creature with a threading of orange fur on his tail. He stood up and regarded her with curiosity. Both his green eyes were open. Beside him, the beautiful baby calico she called Chilco wobbled to her feet. Her face was comically lopsided: only one eye had opened.

Jane left the door of the cupboard slightly ajar so Fraser could access the litterbox, then walked to the exterior door. Too late, she realized she hadn't grabbed her rain gear hanging on a hook in the room she had been sharing with Dom. The thick knit of her sweater would be a liability in the storm—wet wool was the worst layer—but she had no choice.

Someone had made those footsteps in the mud that had showed up in her photo, and she had to find out what Dom was doing with the shovel. In the bleak dawn, it felt like a matter of life and death.

Jane headed outside in the pounding rain, bracing herself as the cold drops found her exposed skin. She descended the stairs gingerly, aware of the noise her heavy boots would make if she wasn't careful. At the front of the hotel, the reflection of the gloomy clouds made the windows opaque sheets of gray. It was impossible to see inside, but she knew that those within could track her clear as day. Jane crept low and slow past the glass.

She grabbed the shovel from the place Dom had left it the night before. Once she was on the eastern side of the hotel and away from the glaring glass eyes, she stopped to examine it. The rain had washed it clean of anything incriminating.

Using the shovel as a cane, she moved across the saturated ground. After a few steps, she paused and searched for any disturbance that would indicate a recent dig. Low points of the lawn were filled with brown pools of water.

She continued down the trail where she had fallen and spotted two small sticks protruding from the ground. She knelt, ignoring the cold suck of water on her knees. Fishing line had been strung taut between the two poles.

It was a trip line. She hadn't accidentally caught her foot on a root. Someone had placed this here deliberately.

Fury, fear, and vindication simmered inside her as she made her way down the flooded dock. The boards were completely underwater now—past the ankles of her boots. The pressure of the currents pushed and pulled on her as she moved. One wrong step would sweep her into the wide, swirling mass of water surrounding the dock.

The doors of the boathouse were all firmly closed and locked. The entire area looked the same as it had the last time she'd seen it, apart from the rising river licking the bottom of the bays.

With careful steps, she returned to the solid ground of the path. Jane traced the tree line with her eyes, staring at the trailhead about ten meters away from where she stood. Snarled and stunted pines with trunks the size of her bicep quivered in the cold wind. Their spindly branches twisted toward one another, partially blocking entry to the path, which had been cut close to the edge of the bank. She could see streams of mud running off the eroded edge. Hungry waves chewed the sodden bank, eating away the earth that supported the trees above.

She darted a quick look back to the hotel. The massive building loomed against the overcast sky. The balconies were empty and there was no movement on the grounds. As she walked toward the shaking stand of trees, the mud pulled at her feet. Her makeshift cane sank deeper into the earth with each step. Rushing water filled the little pockets almost immediately.

A deep pop split the air. Jane's heart pounded. She spun in a wide circle in search of the sound, but she could see nothing but falling rain and suffocating sky. She blinked water from her eyes. Another pop sounded and mud erupted from a puddle about five meters to her left. In a flash, her mind made sense of it: someone was shooting at her.

And that someone was standing in the trees.

She flung herself down on the soft ground beside the river. The ooze of mud and water soaked through her sweater and pants. She lay frozen, her chin sunk into the earth, her eyes trained on the snaking branches. Seconds passed. Jane counted to ten, twenty, thirty, sixty. Waiting for the shot that would end her life.

A cry came from the opposite direction. She heard her name, then a wet, thumping rhythm. She turned her head to see Dom running toward her from the hotel. He was calling out. Her throat clogged at the sight of him. He yelled again. She could barely make out the words.

"JANE! GET AWAY FROM THE EDGE!"

She felt the stomach-dropping sensation of something shifting under her hands. She leapt to her feet. A tree from the small stand at the water's edge toppled into the river. Its trunk and roots were sucked under the churning rapids the moment it touched the water. As she watched in horror, the others fell like dominoes into the seething current. She whirled on her heels and raced toward Dom, stopping just shy of his open arms. A rushing sound made her spin around in the direction she'd come.

The river was wrenching away the entire point she'd been lying on. Sand, stone, and bushes tore away from the bank. The hurtling mass of plant and soil was swarmed by waves before it disappeared in the chaos of white-capped water. She stilled, unable to take her eyes away from the place where the shooter had taken aim at her. It was now a writhing mass of water, indistinguishable from the rest of the river. Gone as if it had never existed.

She turned back to Dom. The thin fabric of his long-sleeved shirt clung to his chest and arms.

"What are you doing out here?"

"Where did you come from?" she demanded.

"I just woke up. I went looking for you but your room was empty. I thought I might find you out here. What were you doing on the ground?"

Jane was frantic. "Someone was shooting! At me!"

Dom looked at her, incredulous. "I didn't hear a thing. All I saw was you on the ground close to the edge."

Jane stared at him in shock. He was scolding her for dodging a killer? "I was on the ground because someone was shooting at me. There's someone else here, Dom. I know it!" The gunshots had been so loud—there was no way he could have missed them. She tried to calculate the length of time that had passed between the last shot and his warning cries. Was he lying? Had there been enough time for him to have fired, then raced back to the hotel?

Had Dom pulled the trigger?

CHAPTER | FORTY

JANE FOLLOWED DOM ON THE SLIPPERY PATH BACK TO THE HOTEL, slowing down when he tried to walk alongside. She needed to keep him where she could see him. Once inside the lobby, her wet shoes squeaked with unpleasant friction on the floor. She peeled off the wool sweater, which now smelled of dog. The two of them moved to the fireplace.

"Where is Sienna?" Jane asked.

"Still sleeping, I think. It was a rough night for her."

Jane barely noticed the jab. "Why were you outside?"

Dom cursed. "I already told you I was looking for you."

"What were you doing with the shovel last night? What's down the eastern trail? Is there someone living in those cabins?"

"Do we really need to rehash this again?"

"Give me a straight answer."

"I've been honest with you about everything you've asked."

Jane's mouth dropped. "I've had more luck getting information from legal teams than I have from you. Someone just shot at me from where you were shoveling last night. And I found a tripwire."

He closed his eyes and sighed heavily. Jane ignored the water dripping from her hair down her collar.

"You're delusional, Jane. You knocked out the internet with your stunt last night. That bourbon fried the router and the storm seems to have done the rest. Our cells are down. The internet is messed. If you're right about the shooter, the only way we can get in touch with anyone is through the short-wave radio."

Fear prickled down her limbs. "I am right about the shooter. Someone has been sneaking around this hotel, writing on a mirror. My phone was deliberately destroyed. There was a person in the suite last night after you left. Someone is sending me threatening texts. I'm breaking our pact, Dom. If you won't tell me the truth, I'll find out myself."

"Goddamnit, Jane." He huffed out a breath like a bear about to charge. "After Melissa died, I was left alone to raise Sienna. She wasn't doing well. It was hard, and I didn't"—he looked at the ceiling and his eyes welled up—"handle it well. I started drinking too much. I was screwing up at work."

"That's what Ted told me. What happened?"

"Stop rushing me. I messed up a few quotes. Ted and I had to work double shifts for weeks so we could keep our shirts on. I was distracted. Thought I had my shit together but I wasn't thinking straight.

"Ted and Peter encouraged me to get help. It wasn't easy to admit how much I was failing, but I did. I began to meet with Dr. Abebe twice a week. After a few sessions, she prescribed a low-dose antidepressant/anti-anxiety med, which I've been taking ever since. I was close to weaning myself off it . . . until I married you."

"Right. It must have been a real burden to have to keep your lies straight. When you say Sienna wasn't doing well, what do you mean by that?"

Dom's expression darkened. "Can you at least pretend that this is a civil conversation and not an interrogation?"

Jane responded with a fixed stare. Dom rolled his shoulders before answering.

"She started losing weight. I couldn't get her to eat anything. And there were . . . a few incidents at school. Nothing major, but her guidance counselor was concerned."

"Tell me about the incidents."

"Bullying, I guess. A fight."

"Somebody was violent with her?"

Dom broke eye contact. "No."

"Sienna was violent with another student?"

"I knew you were going to twist it. She's just a kid."

"And the more you excuse her the worse she gets. I'm not twisting anything. I need information."

"Fine, yes. Some kid was shoved into a locker. She said Sienna had been the one to do it, but there were no witnesses. Sienna swore she wasn't even there, but the school was concerned."

Jane's mind whirred. "Tell me about the fishing trip."

"Are you serious? You've already grilled Sienna about that. How the hell did you even find out?"

"I'm a researcher. It's my job."

"Your job is to dig up shit on your husband?"

Jane's temper flared. "If it's the only way to figure out what's really going on with him, yes. You act like I married you just for a story. But that's not true, Dom! I've been asking you to tell me what's going on and all I get are blank stares and 'never mind's. Tell me the truth and you won't have to worry about what I uncover. Keep lying and I'll keep going."

The two of them glared at each other.

"Peter was right," he said.

Jane's neck stiffened at the mention of the hotel owner. "About what?"

"That you are not who you seem to be. That it was dangerous to rush into a marriage. That I don't really know who you are."

"Likewise. And Peter's a cold prick who cares more about his hotel than his family."

"I should have learned my lesson the first time," Dom said.

"What do you mean? When you married Melissa? Was she different than you thought she would be?"

Dom let out another long rush of air. "I can't say a thing without you making it fit whatever narrative you want to believe. That's not a partnership. You're nothing like I thought you were."

"I know—you've made that very clear. But here I am and guess what? I'm stubborn as hell. What happened on that fishing trip?"

"Nothing. We fished. Randeep and Dylan were useless. We didn't catch a thing. Everyone had a few beers. And then we went home."

"That's not what your brother said."

Dom's face was a mix of impatience and hostility. "Ted was the one who told you? When did you speak with him?"

"Yesterday."

Her husband shook his head before responding. "What did he say?"

"He said Sienna and Melissa got into a fight. He wasn't sure what it was about."

Dom's shoulders drooped. "Right, I forgot about that."

Jane hoped her disbelief wasn't showing. But it was. Dom's expression grew frustrated.

"I'm not lying. It wasn't a big deal. Sienna is a teenager. Her and her mom used to fight—it wasn't exactly newsworthy. But yeah, I remember the two of them arguing now. I was casting off the back of the boat when I heard them yelling. It was hard to understand why they were both so angry. I'm not sure what started it and neither of them wanted to talk about it after. . . ."

Dom trailed off and his eyes became sad.

"After what?"

"I wish I could tell you this without it becoming a huge issue."

"Tell me what?"

"Sienna was going through a tough phase. Her mom kept asking about a video—Elijah and his crew used to shoot these really dumb YouTubes. We all thought they were silly, but you know. Social media is a whole thing these days. We all do stupid stuff when we're young. And not so young. I've always tried to forgive and forget. But you and Melissa are the same. It's all about outing people. Finding the truth, no matter what the cost."

"I know the cost, Dom. I've just always been willing to pay it. And I think other people should too. Why was Melissa asking about the videos?"

"She wanted to know who had the idea for one of them. Something about a Halloween prank? I don't know the details."

Jane's heart raced. She remembered Joseph's pale, traumatized face. That dazed, hurt expression. Jane knew it well. She'd seen it on her mother's face too.

"Randeep and Dylan dodged the question, but Melissa wouldn't let it go. She was hounding Sienna for an answer. But Sienna . . . she refused. Got quiet. Wouldn't say anything until Melissa took it too far."

"Too far?"

"Melissa slapped her."

Jane's mouth dropped. She had been wrong about the fight. Sienna had been the victim.

"Melissa could be . . . she could be intense. She started yelling that she was going to get the police involved. An empty threat, the kind you make when your kids won't tell you the truth. I mean, it was an online prank. They used to pull each other's pants down on camera. Nothing the police would be interested in. But it worked."

Jane looked at him aghast. "Would you be okay if someone pulled down Sienna's pants, filmed it, and posted it? Never mind. I don't want to know the answer. What did Sienna say?"

Dom shook his head again before looking away. His jawline was tight.

"Dom, what did Sienna say?"

"She told Melissa it was her idea, okay? Sienna was the one who came up with it. Trying to impress a boy."

CHAPTER | FORTY-ONE

FRASER PURRED UNDERNEATH JANE'S HAND AS SHE STROKED HER long warm spine. The cat's affection brought tears to her eyes. Everything had changed in light of Dom's damaging revelations about his daughter. Her husband wasn't being reticent to protect himself—he'd been trying to keep Jane from learning the truth about his daughter.

Sienna wasn't just cruel. She was dangerous.

And Dom kept making excuses for her.

After a quick change into dry clothes, Jane had returned to the scullery. Dom was on the third floor again, which gave her the opportunity she needed. After a moment with Fraser and her kittens, she picked up the handheld mike on the radio, looking over her shoulder as she tapped out her signal to Murray. To her relief, he answered immediately.

"You missed our call this morning. I was worried," he said.

The tension in her jaw dissipated a little at the sound of his voice.

"Murray, I'm scared." She wanted to tell him about Sienna, but she knew from experience that bad things happened when people learned too much, too fast.

"This storm is bad," he said. "I'm not surprised. How are you holding up for supplies? Got candles? Batteries? The power could go out at any moment. I'm guessing you've got a generator over there, right? Natural gas? Is the pilot light on?"

The barrage of questions nearly overwhelmed her, but she stayed focused. "How well do you know Sienna and Dom?"

Murray didn't answer immediately. When he spoke, he sounded concerned.

"Why? What's going on over there, Jane?"

"I'm not sure yet. He tells me everything's okay, but I've learned some awful things about them. Between Melissa's death—"

"What have they told you about that?"

"That's just it. They won't talk to me about it at all. Dom changes the subject every time I bring it up, and I have to fight for every scrap of information I get. And last night . . . I caught him coming back to the hotel with a shovel. He was covered in mud. He told me he was returning it to the tool shed. Then this morning, I went outside to see if I could learn more. And someone shot at me. But there's more. I know what happened to Joseph—"

"Listen to me. You need to get out of there. The river's wild but you can still make it. There are kayaks in the boathouse. You just need to paddle across the river to my place. It's a straight shot."

"What? I've only been in a kayak once."

She remembered a blue sky in Deep Cove. An instructor who smelled like weed and wet suits. The overwhelming upside down of an underwater exit.

"Ever canoed? It's the same thing, but easier. Please, Jane. Get out of there."

"No! I'd be risking my life if I tried it."

"Sounds like you're risking your life if you stay."

"What are you saying? Do you know something about Dom? About Sienna?" The words caught in her throat.

"I can't talk about it on the radio."

"About what?"

Static buzzed between them.

"Tell me!"

"Okay, okay. That morning . . . the day Melissa drowned. I heard shouting. A man and a woman. Screaming, really. Sound carries over water. It roused my horses and brought me to the shoreline. I couldn't make out what they were saying, but it was clear enough to know it wasn't anything good. The man's voice . . . it sounded like your husband."

"But Dom wasn't here that day. He got called later. After Melissa went missing."

"Is that what he told you?"

"Yes."

"He's lying."

Jane gripped the edge of the counter to stop her head from swimming. "Murray, Sienna hurt Joseph. Dom is covering it up. I'm not safe here. But I can't leave. I'm trapped. I'm all alone."

"No, you got me. I'm going to find a way to get over there, okay? The motor on my boat is hooped or I'd be there right away, but I'll get it going. I'm not going to leave you on your own, hear me?"

Grateful tears sprang to Jane's eyes again. "Thank you."

Murray's voice gathered force. "Do me a favor, Jane. Check on that generator right now. I'm going to give it everything I have, but if I can't make it there before sunset, the last thing you need is to be stuck over there in the dark. This storm is going to get worse."

"I will."

"I'm going to call again at four p.m. Be at the radio. If you don't answer, I'm getting the police involved."

"Okay."

"Jane. Whatever he says to you. Don't trust him. Talk soon, okay?"

"Okay."

Jane replaced the radio with shaking hands. She had no idea where the generator was. The basement? The idea of going into that cold, dim hallway all alone and empty-handed made her skin crawl. She slid off the stool and headed to the small utility closet in the kitchen where the broom and mop were kept. It was dusty and smelled faintly of rodent and trapped food odors. A dented toolbox had been placed on a low shelf. Inside were a handful of rudimentary items: a hammer, measuring tape, screwdrivers. She picked up a flattened chiseled-tip screwdriver and slid it in her pocket.

Fraser howled from the kitchen.

Jane went to see if everything was okay.

Sienna stood in the center of the room. There was a large white bandage on her arm where the shattered glass of the decanter had cut her. Fraser was pacing anxiously outside the cupboard, crying for her lost kitten. Jane lunged for the small creature who was snuffling helplessly a meter from the cupboard.

"Sienna! What are you doing with that kitten?"

"Nothing. I'm allergic, remember? I was looking for you."

"Did you do something to Fraser?"

"What? No, of course not. She's been like that since I came in."

"Why are you here?"

The teenager glared at Jane. "I came here to tell you to stop. You have to stop. Elijah and my mom are none of your business."

"They most certainly are. And you are too. I know what happened on Halloween night in 2021; that it was your idea. Your little prank drove Joseph Jack to suicide."

Sienna interrupted her. "I know the truth about you too." Her voice shook on the last word. "My dad doesn't understand social media. But I do."

Jane stared at her stepdaughter in horror.

"What do you mean?"

"Stop asking questions about us. Or I'm going to tell my dad about the woman you killed."

CHAPTER | FORTY-TWO

JANE WAS OUT OF BREATH WHEN SHE GOT TO THE BOURBON ROOM, her laptop in hand. She dead-bolted the locks on both doors, darted to the corner, rolled up the desk's cover, and hid her screwdriver in a pigeonhole.

She'd managed to wipe most of the blood off it.

Outside the window, the storm raged. Scatterings of sodden leaves and small branches flew by. Fierce gusts of wind forced trees to bow down, nearly touching the ground as their trunks curved into unnatural shapes. Jane wondered how long it would be until they snapped.

How long before she snapped? Or had it happened already? Panic, anger, and pain bashed around in her head. What had she become?

She stiffened as she heard a sound from the hallway connected to the staff quarters: the slam of a door, then footsteps halting a few feet from where she stood. She watched, her stomach twisting, as the handle rotated once, twice. Heavy footfalls tramped off in the other direction. A moment later, the handle on the other door, the one leading to the sitting area, rattled in its casing.

Jane held her breath. She was safe in here. For now. But how long before Sienna told Dom the truth? She found a yellow legal pad in the top drawer of the desk and began furiously recording the facts.

A woman died after the production of my last film. But I didn't kill her.

Her writing scrawled across the page in nearly illegible letters. Once her confession was complete, she began to lay out the strange events at the Venatura Hotel, beginning the summer the renovation began.

Melissa had formed her crew of Randeep, Dylan, Joseph, and Elijah in 2021, a little more than a year before she died. Prior to that, they'd known one another (perhaps peripherally) at least a year, as shown in the MILF pageant video. Sienna hung around with the crew.

The five of them had worked together over the course of the first off season while the ChilBoyz continued to film short videos. The prank where they'd locked Joseph in the oven on Halloween night of that year had been Sienna's idea. Dom admitted that Sienna was a bully at school, too. Bad enough to involve a guidance counselor. Murray had said Joseph was depressed and anxious. The video had gone viral, and Joseph had committed suicide in late November of that year.

Knowing that it was Sienna's idea to trap Joseph made her sick. The girl was unhinged. What had just happened in the kitchen proved it. Jane hadn't had a choice. Her actions had been justified; she knew it. She wiped a hand on her pants, trying to rid it of the blood that remained.

Jane kept writing.

After Joseph's death, the rest of the "boyz" had continued to make videos—lots of them—but none referenced Joseph's death. Dom's company—primarily his brother, Ted—had rebuilt the boathouse in December of that year. In the spring following Joseph's suicide, Randeep and Dylan had taken Dom's family out on a fishing trip, where Melissa discovered that Sienna had masterminded the prank. After Melissa learned the truth about her daughter's cruel nature, about her role in the suicide of Joseph Jack, she'd struck her.

Shortly after the fishing trip, Randeep and Dylan left to meet someone to check out a truck for sale. They never returned. A few months later,

Melissa died in a kayaking accident—Jane underlined the last word and put a question mark after it—and later that day, Elijah disappeared.

She was reviewing her notes when something white in one of the pigeonholes caught her eye. She reached for it, careful to avoid touching the screwdriver she'd placed beside it. It was a scrap of paper with a line from a recently popular song written in messy masculine block printing.

IF WE GO DOWN, WE GO DOWN TOGETHER. I'M NOT GOING TO LET THEM HURT YOU.
I LOVE YOU.

ELIJAH

Jane gasped, poking her fingers into the rest of the desk to make sure she hadn't missed anything else. There were no other notes—but she kicked herself.

It was all so obvious now.

Elijah had written someone a love letter. She flashed back to the MILF video, and the way Melissa had kissed him on the makeshift stage.

The dots were connecting. Melissa and Elijah had been having an affair, and someone must have discovered it. According to Lucy, Peter's ex-wife, Sienna was always hanging around trying to impress Elijah with her pranks. Now she hated the very thought of him.

Had Sienna known about her mother's affair?

A loud knocking on the door interrupted her thoughts.

"Who is it?"

"It's me." Dom's voice was more anguished than angry.

"What do you want?"

"Open the door."

Had he found Sienna? She couldn't trust him.

She looked at the bloody screwdriver. She couldn't trust herself, either.

"Did you and Melissa have an argument on the day she died? Was Peter here?"

"Goddamnit, Jane. We are in a serious emergency right now. I don't have time for another conversation about Melissa. What's wrong with you?"

Jane began to answer but Dom spoke over her, through the door. "Our main power's gone. The generator can keep the essentials on for now, but it runs on gas. It won't last the night. It's going to get really cold, really fast. I need your help if we want to get out of here alive."

CHAPTER | FORTY-THREE

JANE CRACKED THE DOOR. DOM HAD TUCKED A FLASHLIGHT INTO HIS work belt, where it hung like a weapon. His face was a mix of concern and compassion—or a very good facsimile. "What happened?"

"Who knows? Tree on the line or the rising water is getting into the transmission station. The power crews won't be here for days, maybe weeks. There are outages across this whole area and the city. Hey, what happened to your face?" Dom peered closer at Jane, and she touched her cheek gingerly. When she looked at her hand, it was dotted with blood.

"One of the kittens snagged me. Their claws are sharp as needles. What were you saying?"

"The elevator will run on backup power for the next ninety minutes or so, but we've got no lights and no heat until we get that generator going. I need your help."

"My help?"

Dom widened his eyes in frustration. "Yes, your help. Listen, I don't

know what is going on in your head right now, but we need to work together. I can't find Sienna anywhere. Can you help me, please? Can you
come with me downstairs so we don't freeze tonight?"

"No, Dom. I don't trust you. You keep lying to me. You told me you
weren't at the hotel when Melissa died."

"I *wasn't*."

"Murray heard a man arguing with Melissa. He's sure it was you."

"Murray? Is that where all this stuff is coming from?"

"Who was with Melissa that day?"

Dom turned on his heel and called over his shoulder, "I'm not doing
this with you right now. I need your help in the basement. It's going to be
dark in an hour. Let's go. Now. First, we work. Then we'll talk."

He walked quickly through the lobby while she considered her options. A chill was creeping into the air. They needed power. But it was a
huge risk to be alone with Dom. What if he was luring her into a trap?
Did he know what she'd done to Sienna?

"We'll take the stairs," Dom said gruffly when they met at the elevator
bay.

"You go first."

He shouldered his way through the door. The cement stairwell was
colder than the lobby. Colder than it had been the night before. Dom
took the landing in one step before barreling down the last half flight of
stairs. Her breath heaved as she fought to keep up. Her foot and thigh
ached. The scratches on her face stung. She gripped the railing. When he
stopped abruptly, Jane banged into him, cringing at the wrenching pain
that shot up her leg.

"It's wet."

He pointed toward a darker patch of cement directly under the door.

"Water's getting in here. That's not good. Be careful, okay? Follow
me closely."

Dom shoved open the door, his flashlight bobbing. Darkness yawned
from the hallway. She took one step forward and icy water flowed over
the soles of her boots. Up ahead, her husband swore. Another step and the

water seeped into her socks. Her feet ached, but the pain didn't last long. Within seconds, they were numb. The water lapped at Dom's tan pants, splattering the material.

"Shine the light over there," she said to Dom, gesturing at the hallway wall half a meter in front of him. "We need to mark the level."

She found a scuff on the wall slightly above the six inches of water already on the cement floor. After five slow breaths, the mark was engulfed.

The basement was flooding. And the water was rising fast.

CHAPTER | FORTY-FOUR

TO HER SURPRISE, DOM GRIPPED HER HAND.

"We can do this, okay? Together. We have to find that generator. If it's underwater, we're screwed."

"What do you mean?"

"It's a natural gas system. If the water comes up above the pilot light, it's useless at best. At worst, it could cause a carbon monoxide leak."

"So, what do we do now?"

He released her hand to pull out a pocketknife, then moved forward to score the wall at the level of the water. Her stomach flipped at the sight of the weapon. When he locked eyes with her after he rose to standing, his irises were surrounded by white.

"The water is coming in hard." His voice was tight with strain. "The backup generator might be the least of our problems. If this place floods, we've got nowhere to go."

"Oh my god."

"This hotel was built on a floodplain. We're on a low point in the land—a risky site from the beginning. Water has been diverted from this whole area for years with dikes and dams." Dom squeezed her upper arm gently.

She tensed. The knife was still in his other hand. He slipped it in his pocket, then twined his hand with hers. He raised the flashlight. The small circle shimmered on the standing water all the way down the length of the hall. Objects floated on the surface: a pillowcase, a sleeve of plastic cups, a basket, a length of slim white baseboard trim. The gun safe was half-submerged. Pulling her forward, Dom moved down the hall in the direction of the speakeasy, creating a wake in the filthy water.

"I am going to get you somewhere safe, but first I need your help. Okay?"

Jane nodded stiffly. Any port in a storm. She swallowed hard as she trained her eyes on the beam of Dom's flashlight. The water on the floor looked almost as deep as it was in the hallway—over her ankles and rising up her calves. She heard a low rippling coming from inside.

"That's where it's getting in. I knew it. That side of the bank was so weak. It needs a construction crew, not a guy with a shovel." Stress strained his voice. He pulled her past the door and down the hall. "People are drawn to the lowlands. Food grows well here. Lots of water. But that water finds a way. We need to get to higher ground as fast as we can." Dom stopped outside an institutional-gray metal door close to the end of the hall. "The generator is in here."

He passed her the flashlight and released her hand. Using his arm and shoulder, he forced the heavy door open against the water. He swept the light around the contents of a storage area. A few tall metal shelving units stood in front of them. The contents of the lower shelves—extension cords, toolboxes, and cardboard boxes—were underwater. Several cot mattresses leaned against the wall to her left, their bottoms waterlogged and stained.

"It's in the back corner. Here—take the light."

Jane accepted the heavy flashlight, keenly aware of the faith the gesture conveyed. There was no way he'd found Sienna yet. She trained it a few steps ahead of him as he waded through a watery space filled with floating debris. She kicked away a bobbing badminton birdie and several life jackets so she could stay close to him. The water was colder and deeper in here. Its iciness lapped halfway up her shin.

Her light found the squat cylinder shape of the generator. Dom crouched in front of it, leaning forward.

"Shine it over here," he said, before prying a small door open with an agonizing creak.

Jane closed the distance between them and peered into the opening. A funnel-shaped roof was positioned around a hose facing up. Dom clicked a long lighter at the base of the opening. It spit out a flame, which failed to catch.

"Damn. The pilot light is out. It doesn't look like there's any gas getting through. The line must be damaged."

He straightened up with a deep frown on his face. "There's a backup generator outside that will keep the ground-floor heat and elevators going for a few hours, but it won't last long. We're going to be without heat tonight and there's still a whole lot of water to worry about."

Jane didn't need the mark on the wall to know he was right. The level was above the middle of her calf now. In the time they'd been down here, it had risen at least two inches.

"If I can find the spot where the water's getting into the speakeasy, we might be able to prevent the hotel from flooding tonight."

"But what about tomorrow?"

Dom's voice was distracted. "I'm hoping Peter gets here by then, that his boat can make it through."

Jane froze. "What did you say?"

He didn't seem to realize she had stopped until the flashlight failed to light his way. "Jane? Come on."

"Peter is coming? Why didn't you tell me?"

Any trace of trust for him dissolved. Peter—the man who refused to look for his own son, putting profit ahead of everything else—was coming here? Murray had heard a man's voice the day that Melissa died and had assumed it to be Dom. But what if it wasn't?

What if it was Peter? Did Peter know Melissa was having an affair with his son?

"I just did. Let's get moving. Hand me the flashlight."

"I've got it."

"Okay, then let's go. Fast."

She moved forward reluctantly. "Why is Peter coming to the hotel?"

He retraced their path to the speakeasy with her close on his heels. "He's the owner! He knows we are in trouble. He comes whenever there's a problem. That's what he does."

Jane didn't respond. Peter was part of what had happened to Elijah and Melissa—she knew it. According to Lucy, "Peter had to step in a couple years ago to keep Sienna from hanging around Elijah and his friends too much." What was that about? Was Peter *protecting* Elijah, or protecting him from *consequences*? The thought of him in the hotel with them made her spine creep.

Dom was moving too fast for her to stay close. Her legs and injured foot ached with cold and exertion, and the water resisted all her movements. He disappeared into the doorway of the speakeasy. The sound of flowing water was louder than it had been. A quick circle of the flashlight found him at the side of the room where he'd shown her the exit.

"I think it's coming from here," he said.

"Did Peter come to help when Melissa died?"

"He didn't have to. He was already here." Dom put his hand on the panel of the exit door as Jane struggled to process the new information. Before she could ask another question, Dom began to speak rapidly.

"This is it; I can see it coming in. There's water gushing. Come on back with the light. We need to stop this."

Jane pushed forward with the flashlight held at shoulder height. As she neared Dom, a silvery glint came back to her from the locking mechanism Dom had shown her the night before.

The dead bolt had been released.

"Didn't you lock this door last night?"

"Jane! Focus. Bring that light over here. Better yet, can I hold on to it? I need to get something to stop this water. Did you see any tarps back in that storage area? Duct tape?"

Jane stayed where she was. "Were Peter and Melissa close?"

Dom's face tightened in the harsh glare of the flashlight. "You have got to be kidding!"

"Answer me. Or I'm taking the light. Were they close?"

"No," Dom shouted. "Melissa worked for Peter, but they weren't friends. The two of them—didn't always see eye to eye."

"Because Melissa cheated on you?"

Dom's jaw tensed. "What are you talk—?"

"I found the letter Elijah wrote to her. I know the two of them flirted for years—there's a video of them all over each other. She wasn't a good wife to you, was she? But Peter's convinced you he's a good friend, right?"

Dom didn't speak. For a moment, there was nothing but the sound of water.

"Did Peter kill Melissa because she was sleeping with his son?"

Dom took a step toward her, and she instinctively took a step back. She held up the flashlight with one hand while the other reached into her sleeve for the screwdriver she had removed from the pigeonhole before opening the door to Dom. She brandished the tip toward him.

"Good lord, Jane. What is wrong with you?"

"There are things you don't know, Dom. That fight between Sienna and Melissa? It was about the Halloween prank that drove Murray's grandson to suicide. It was all Sienna's idea. Elijah must have been close enough to Melissa to tell her the truth. Maybe it was pillow talk."

"Goddamn you, Jane. Just fucking stop it."

But Jane was relentless. "Tell me what you know about Melissa and Peter! Or I swear to god I'll—"

"Melissa was unfaithful."

Jane's mouth dropped.

"She slept with Elijah. Even though he was like a son to me. To both of us, I thought."

The rushing water became a roar.

"What happened to Melissa?" she whispered.

Dom's face cracked in despair.

"Peter—he took care of everything—"

A loud groan made the room shake. Her sternum vibrated. She darted the flashlight to the door. Water was pouring in from all sides.

Dom looked behind his shoulder.

"GET OUT," he shouted, wading toward her with jerky knee-high steps.

Behind him, the door bulged.

It was the last thing she saw before a wall of muddy water walloped Jane off her feet.

CHAPTER | FORTY-FIVE

EVERYTHING WENT BLACK. THE WATER WAS FRIGID. JANE'S LUNGS burned as she thrashed through the black water, fighting to find air. Objects bashed against her, knocking her senseless. Her chest tightened and she spun in a wild circle. The thin beam of light was overwhelmed by liquid. She couldn't make out anything. Her lungs screamed for air.

She banged her forearm against a sharp corner. Round smooth shapes rolled against her legs and feet, making it hard to gain purchase. She touched something solid—the floor—and tried to push up, but her head crunched against a hard surface, rattling her teeth. Her legs ached. The darkness was as deep as the water.

Where was up? She flailed her arms and struck something unyielding. Another lightning strike of pain shot through her and white sparks danced in front of her eyes. Though her limbs stopped responding, her mind shrieked: FIND AIR. FIND AIR. FIND AIR.

But all she could feel was water. Cold, immense, black. Everywhere she turned was a wall or a rolling barrage. FIND AIR. There was no up or down. Only freezing black liquid. She couldn't hold on any longer. Her lips parted.

Something gripped her. Her body was wrenched upward. The surface was a mercy and she gasped for breath. A mottled face appeared. Brackish, frigid water ran from her hair into her eyes, and out of her mouth. She vomited. She had to keep moving to stay up. She was now roughly a foot away from the ceiling and rising. She gagged again, her legs failing. She sucked in another gulp of air.

"Jane, hold on!"

Dom circled her underarms from behind to keep her afloat. The flashlight was still clenched in her hand. Her body spasmed several more times as she heaved. She wiped her mouth roughly with the back of her hand. Dom's voice was low in her ear, barely audible above the water pouring in from the doorway.

"Are you okay?"

"I'm okay."

"Can you swim?"

Exhaustion was not an option. "Yes."

Dom stroked around to face her, his arms dropping momentarily to aid his movement. Her face dipped below the waterline and he grabbed her again.

"Lay on your back. Can you keep hold of the flashlight?"

"Yes."

"Don't drop it."

"I won't."

He returned to the rescue position, angling his body so his front aligned with her back. She held the flashlight tightly, her hands aching. Among the splintered boards and dissolving chunks of drywall, maraschino cherries bobbed beside them like bloody eyes. Her husband grunted as he forced their way through the door, letting go with one hand to grab the frame and drag her through after him. He headed for the stairwell.

To safety.

"This door is going to be heavy. Can you hold on to my back?"

He dove down before she could reply. His watery form stretched out long, then bunched up again. Under the water, he was holding the handle with both hands, forcing it open by jamming his leg against the wall for leverage. She willed her arms to rise and her fingers to curl around his shoulders. Her legs were blocks of fleshy ice, but she forced them to kick. Forward, back. The eggbeater thing she'd learned in swimming lessons at a chilly community pool as a ten-year-old. Keep it simple. Stay alive. Forward, back.

The door shuddered open an inch, two. Water gushed into the stairwell. The new current forced them through the small opening like a hard shove. Dom was knocked onto his face in the water pooling at the base of the stairs. He lay there, unmoving.

"Dom!"

One second, two seconds, three. Jane screamed his name again, hauling on his shoulders, shaking his frame.

But Dom didn't move.

CHAPTER | FORTY-SIX

JANE GRIPPED THE FRAME OF THE DOOR WITH ONE HAND TO STAY upright and shoved the flashlight into her waistband with the other. The water was rising fast, lapping at the third step of the concrete staircase. She lunged for Dom's body face down in the rushing water, grabbed a handful of his hair, and yanked up with all her might.

Liquid streamed from his nostrils and open mouth, and he gasped for breath. She grabbed hold of his sopping collar to tug him onto the stairs. With her help, he slumped onto a dry step halfway up and coughed deeply. Jane dragged him to his feet and draped his arm around her shoulder. He was heavy; her knees buckled as she took his weight. Her numb toes caught the edge of a step as she staggered toward the landing. She lurched to grab the metal railing to pull them up the next half-flight of stairs. Her body ached with the extra effort of keeping Dom upright—her movements were frantic and clumsy—but she knew if she didn't keep going that they'd die there.

Suddenly, the weight of his body lessened.

"I'm okay," he muttered. "I can walk on my own." He began up the steps two at a time, dragging her with his hand. She tripped. The edge of the concrete stair broke the skin of her shin.

"Are you okay?"

"I can walk," Jane said, tightening her hold on him.

"I'm going to keep you safe. I'm going to get you out of this. I'm going to save us. I'm going to save you." Dom's words filled the dark stairwell.

She had been ten years old when her father had lost his job and her mother had been forced to clean houses. Ten years old when she had vowed never to depend on a man who would let her down. Taking care of herself had been well worth the cost, so how had she ended up here?

She had to rely on Dom or die alone.

Teeth chattering, she freed the flashlight from her waistband and shone it upward. With her light and his strength, they moved together up the steps to the landing and the door. The main floor opened to them. They stumbled, dripping, onto the blessedly dry stone floor.

Jane collapsed to her knees, letting the flashlight roll onto the floor beside her. Delayed pain flooded through her legs and body as her shock ebbed and the warmth sunk in. She pressed her hands flat against the dry surface of the floor to reassure herself of safety. The floor vibrated with movement. Jane raised her head. Someone was walking toward them from the front desk. She blinked hard to force the shape to make sense.

It was Sienna.

"Dad! Where have you been? How can you be with Jane after what she did to me?"

Jane had never wanted to hurt someone so badly.

"What I did to YOU? You attacked me!"

"Who was the one holding a screwdriver?"

"I was defending myself! You stabbed me in the thigh!"

"Who was the one that killed—"

"ENOUGH!" Dom yelled. "Sienna, get a grip! The hotel is flooding.

The foundation in the basement has been breached—I don't know how bad the damage is, but the water is coming in fast. We've got to get to higher ground."

Sienna glared at Jane with a reddened face. She didn't seem to hear her father.

"It's true, Sienna. The wall downstairs is close to caving in. We can't stay here," Jane said, her voice pitchy and raw.

"Dad, she murdered someone on her last film! Why won't you—"

Sienna's accusations were lost to her father's determination. He strode toward the main doors. "I've got to reinforce the bank. If I can repair the sandbags, we'll be okay."

Jane wheeled on him. "No, Dom, no. You can't go out there. You have a head injury!"

"I'm fine."

"Daddy, don't leave me with her. She's a monster! She tried to lock me in the freezer!"

Dom's face was rigid. "STOP IT. We're in danger. If we don't stick together, we won't survive. That's all that matters."

"She's dangerous," Sienna pleaded again.

But Dom was already at the entranceway. "Radio Murray. Tell him what's going on."

Before either she or Sienna could speak another word, Dom was gone.

Sienna's expression turned instantly hateful. "How could you let him go?"

"How could I have stopped him?" Jane replied.

"Get him back here." Cords strained in Sienna's neck as pink blossoms rose on her cheeks. "He's going to die, and you don't even care!"

"Me? You drove Joseph Jack to suicide for YouTube views! You are a mentally unwell little girl," Jane hissed.

"And you made that woman see things she should never have seen. You killed her!"

"That's not what happened!"

Sienna turned to the door. Jane reached for her arm but Sienna dodged, jerking her bandaged arm out of Jane's reach. Jane made another move, this time catching hold of Sienna's wrist.

"Get off me! Let me go!"

Sienna's face was almost purple now, twisted in emotion. She tried to tear herself from Jane's grip, but Jane held on.

Sienna slammed her heel down hard on Jane's broken toe.

CHAPTER | FORTY-SEVEN

BLACK DOTS PULSED IN FRONT OF JANE'S EYES. SHE FELL TO HER KNEES on the hard floor with a thud that echoed across the gray-lit lobby. Sienna raced to the elevator. To Jane's surprise, the car dinged its arrival almost immediately. They still had backup power—for now.

Jane's stomach heaved. She vomited water. Pain drove up her leg like shards of glass. Her swollen foot was too tight for the boot. Burning heat throbbed up her ankle and shin.

She fought the sobs clutching her throat. How could Sienna do this to her? The teenager's hate was deeper than anything she'd experienced before—and Jane knew how it felt to be hated. The newspapers, the Hot Docs audience, even her own production partner had shamed her for her decision to show Carol the footage of her son pranking his girlfriend's toddler. And then they had all blamed her for the result. She'd almost become used to seeing the contempt in the eyes of strangers. But she'd never wanted her family to look at her like that. She'd come here with them to find a place to belong.

Jane placed her good foot flat on the floor and pressed down hard on her wounded thigh to force herself to rise. She looked around the lobby, her face taut with pain. Her eyes stopped at the front desk. She hopped toward it and the basket filled with Venatura-branded umbrellas.

The golf umbrella was nearly the same height as a cane. Its pointed tip dug into the stone floor, leaving satisfying gouges as she hobbled her way toward the elevator. The hotel had beaten her down; the least she could do was scar it in return.

Sienna had a head start. By now, she could be anywhere in the hotel. The panel at the top of the elevator showed a car stopped on the fourth floor. Part of Jane wanted to leave her there all alone. But no matter how horrendous her stepdaughter was, she was still a kid. And Jane was still the closest thing the little demon had to a mother.

Jane hated the idea of climbing into a waterlogged mechanism that could fail at any moment but her foot wouldn't allow her to climb the stairs. When the elevator arrived, she hobbled inside, jamming the button to the fourth floor.

The mirrored walls showed her a nightmare. Her hair was clumped in sodden strands around her haunted, colorless complexion. Hollow, blood-shot eyes were underscored by black shadows. A deep gash had chiseled out a chunk of skin above her eyebrow, making the upper part of her face pull oddly toward it; purple-red bruises had bloomed around the cut. Her lip was split in two places and blood had dried to black welts. She raised her forearm and saw yellowish fat oozing out of a deep wound caused by her underwater flailing in the basement.

The sudden halt of the elevator signaled she'd arrived. The doors opened. Sparse light from the gathering dusk came in through the window by the elevator bay, but the rest of the floor was dark. She shuddered at the idea of another walk through the shadowy corridors of the godforsaken hotel. Clicking on the flashlight, she willed herself to be strong. Jane couldn't risk another surprise attack. She had to find Sienna and keep her safe—whether the miserable girl wanted her help or not.

Following her instinct, she headed to Melissa's favorite room.

Suite 401. The Sunrise Suite.

The jewel of the Venatura Hotel.

The thump of her umbrella and the slow drag of her battered body were quieted by the cushioning of the ugly hall carpet, but fearful thoughts screamed in her brain. Sienna was frightened, maybe delusional with fear, and she wouldn't think twice about lashing out. Jane's skin puckered with goose bumps at the thought of what Sienna was capable of, and her soaked clothes felt colder and heavier than before. Her mind was working against her now; draining energy from her limbs and core to stop her from heading into danger.

But she continued.

Turning the corner, she saw a thin band of light under the door of suite 401 and almost smiled. But her triumph was short-lived. How was the suite lit up in the middle of a power failure? Was the backup generator connected to this room as well as the elevators? She stopped, blinking hard, then turned off the flashlight to make sure she wasn't imagining things. The light was real. A glowing strip at the end of the dark hall, faint and flickering. She turned the handle and the door swung inward. She stepped into the room.

Every surface glittered with lit candles. The desk, the table, even the nightstands were dotted with tiny wavering flames. It looked like an altar.

"Sienna?" She held her breath, braced herself, and looked into the bathroom.

It was empty. She exhaled loudly.

"Sienna?"

There was no answer. No sound at all but the thud of her umbrella as she moved toward the bed.

"Sienna?"

A slight breeze flitted against her cheek. She turned back toward the entry only to see the door swinging shut. The slam was as loud as a gun.

Jane almost jumped out of her skin.

She hobbled her way back to the door and tried the handle, pulling it hard.

The door wouldn't open. She was locked in.

She pounded against it with a flat hand, then a fist. Had the power outage messed up the locking device? Was it an electronic glitch?

She heard laughter.

"I knew you couldn't resist. Did those candles make you think there was a ghost in here? A spooky mystery to investigate? God, Jane. You're so predictable. I bet you didn't know there's an override for all the doors. In case of emergencies—like an active shooter, or some hunter flipping his lid up here—a manager can ensure everyone is secured in their rooms. Wouldn't that be great, Jane? You could make a documentary about the massacre, then force some poor mother to watch her son taking out tourists with an AR-15. That's your MO, right?"

Jane pressed her forehead against the door and tried the handle again.

Sienna laughed. "You're such an idiot. I just told you about the override. That was my mom's idea. She thought of everything. She was so much smarter and prettier than you."

"Sienna! Please let me out."

"Not a chance. You've been messing with my dad's head since you got here. Since you got married. What kind of woman carries the purse of a dead woman on her wedding day?"

Jane felt sick. Dom had given her Melissa's clutch as her something borrowed?

"What kind of woman would marry a man who just lost his wife? You're here for Ember. For a new story to exploit. You're not here for us."

"That's not true, Sienna. I swear to you."

"I know why you're here," Sienna continued. "We all do. First you go after Rascal Rococo. And then you set your sights on Elijah, right? You've got a real rage for online pranks, don't you? But you're guiltier than anyone! I figured it out. I know why you're here. You've been searching the hotel for it, just like me. Where'd you find it? And where have you hidden it?"

"What are you talking about?"

"Fuck off, Jane. Tell me where the phone is and then leave me and my dad alone. He doesn't love you, you know. He told me. He said marrying you was a big mistake."

"I know you think you hate me, Sienna. But it's grief. Your mom—I know what she did, Sienna. To you and your dad. It's making you do crazy things like writing horrible things all over the mirror in here."

Jane was startled to hear peals of laughter coming from the other side of the door. "Number one: take my mom's name out of your mouth. Number two: you are such an idiot. That wasn't me. Elijah did that. He's the crazy one."

"Elijah?" Jane reeled as her brain struggled to make sense of this new information.

Had the awful, scrawled letters on the mirror been left there, un-touched, for over a year? That made no sense. Peter would never have allowed that. Or had Elijah returned to set the stage and make her feel like she was losing her mind? Was Elijah in the hotel with them now? Was it his presence that she felt lingering, watching, just out of sight?

"Sienna? SIENNA?"

There was no answer. Jane craned her head to hear any sound outside the door. She heard a sharp metallic click, once, then twice.

"Hello? Sienna, please let me out!"

A sweet acrid scent wafted up. Smoke. She looked down in alarm. Gray wisps were curling under the door. She gripped the door handle, then pulled away with a sharp cry. It was searing hot, painful to touch.

The sound of Sienna laughing on the other side of the door again made Jane tremble. She had to find a way out of the room.

"I know where Elijah's phone is, Sienna. I can show you!" Jane lied.

CHAPTER | **FORTY-EIGHT**

"WHERE IS IT?" SIENNA YELLED FROM THE OTHER SIDE OF THE DOOR.

"It's on the third floor," Jane said. She heard the lock click and Sienna swung open the door.

The girl's eyes were wild as her gaze darted from Jane's face back down to the garish carpet. Her cheeks were mottled with red splotches. In one hand was a half-scorched piece of paper. The other held a lighter. Jane fought off a twinge of respect for the girl's ingenuity. When Sienna raised her chin again, her expression was hardened with resolve.

"Give me the phone. Now."

"It's downstairs," Jane said.

Sienna made a sweeping gesture with the lighter. "After you."

Jane started down the hall, softly whimpering every time her foot hit the ground. This was going to be harder than she had realized. She grabbed Sienna's arm for stability. Sienna pushed her off, then relented when it was clear Jane couldn't walk without support.

"Take me to the elevators," she said.

On the third floor, Jane shut her eyes. Adrenaline was dumping from her system. She held the wall to summon her remaining strength, then followed Sienna out of the elevator car just before the doors slid shut.

"How long have you had it?" Sienna said in a monotone.

"Awhile," Jane lied again.

"I knew it was here. The night Mom died, Dad hustled me away from the hotel so fast that I didn't even have a chance to say goodbye. Elijah left too—but he told me to text, and I did. I sent message after message, but he didn't reply. I pinged his phone's location when we got back to Vancouver. It was here, but by the time we arrived this fall, the signal was gone. The battery died. He must have left it by accident. It's got everything on it. I have to find it."

Sienna was shaking now. Tears streamed down her face and her nose was running. Once again, Jane could see the child she'd been not so many years before.

"I thought you hated him."

Sienna gave a long, shuddering sigh. "I don't hate him. I love him. He was my boyfriend."

Jane bit the inside of her cheeks as the words sunk in. The heart with his initials inside it. The letter she had found.

"He wrote that note for you."

"He wrote me lots of notes. He loved me. He loved my ideas."

"For his YouTube channel."

"Yeah. And other ones too." Sienna sounded defensive. "Not just those."

"Elijah loved the idea of trapping Joseph in the outdoor oven? Of leaving him there all night? Of filming him? That's psychological torture, Sienna. A young man died because of what you did."

"And a woman died because of what you did! I wasn't trying to hurt Joseph! You sound just like her!" Her voice had become loud, unregulated.

"Your mom?"

"Yes. She didn't understand anything about me!" She sobbed. "No, no, no. You can't make me say bad things about my mom. She was amazing. My dad will never get over her. She was beautiful and funny and had incredible taste."

Unlike me, Jane inferred.

"Dad loved her so much. He's been a wreck since she died. I couldn't stand it. I came home from a party one night and he was drunk on the couch. Like, slurring-his-words, couldn't-stand-up drunk. He kept talking about how he should have protected her. How he screwed up by not making enough to provide for her. That taking the design job at the hotel was the worst thing that could have happened to her. He kept saying that he'd failed as a husband and a father. That men were supposed to provide, and women were supposed to nurture, and that they'd both failed me. It was scary. All that gender-conforming bullshit."

"It sounds awful," Jane said, suddenly understanding Dom's confusing sexism.

"You've made it even worse! You keep bringing up all this stuff about my mom. It's making him feel like he's worthless. He's always drinking. Because of you. He doesn't talk to Dr. Abebe anymore. I think he stopped taking his meds."

Jane remembered the Seroquel. And the shovel and the gunshots. Did Dom know that Sienna was dating Elijah before he disappeared? Where was Dom now? Where was Elijah?

"Grief is a horrible thing," Jane said. "It can change the way you think."

"It can make you rewrite the past, too. Every time Dad talks to me about Mom, he makes it seem like she was an angel. She wasn't. Honestly, sometimes my mom could be a bitch."

Jane swallowed. Finally, Sienna had lowered her snide, contemptible defenses. She nudged her stepdaughter down the narrow hallway cluttered with loose boards and power tools. Sienna didn't resist. She was acquiescent now. Jane wished she could trust the girl to remain that way. She kept her eyes on the carpet and didn't say a word. After a few steps, Sienna filled the silence.

"They were fighting all the time that summer. It started with the fishing trip. My dad struggled a lot with what I had done to Joseph. He told my mom it would never have happened if he was able to support us and give her the chance to be a stay-at-home mother. He blamed himself . . . and her. But she blamed Elijah. Said he was a toxic influence, but she didn't know the whole story. Randeep and Dylan were supposed to go back and get Joseph out after like an hour, but they kept drinking and passed out! Mom and Dad couldn't understand that we'd never meant for it to go that far. It was an accident. They were so fucking serious about the whole thing."

Jane had to swallow her objection. Sienna may not have meant to keep Joseph entombed overnight—but the ChilBoyz had. The entire structure of the video relied on the intensity of Joseph's reaction.

"My mom made me send Mr. and Mrs. Jack a card to say sorry. I didn't want to hurt Joey. It was stupid. I was trying to impress Elijah. I wanted him to think I could do what he did. I hate myself, okay? You get that, right? I hate what I did to him. I just have these thoughts. I don't know how to stop them. You know what I'm talking about, right?" Her voice was edged with hysteria.

Jane nodded. "I know about that. About hating yourself, and not being able to stop those bad thoughts."

Sienna sniffed and wiped at her eyes with the heel of her hand. "All summer, it was bad. My mom told my dad that she didn't want to sleep in the same room as him. She moved into the suite alone. She wanted a divorce. Because of me! My dad asked Peter if we could stay an extra two weeks after the hotel closed. Try to patch things up when the hotel was quiet. My mom really didn't want my dad around while she was working, but somehow he convinced her to let him stay."

Jane was struggling with Sienna's version of events. Why had Melissa blamed Dom for Sienna's behavior? How did that make sense? But more importantly, Sienna had just confirmed that Dom had been here when Melissa drowned. Jane's stomach sank.

"You were all around the day your mother . . . died?"

"I was in my room. I heard them screaming."

"Who?"

Sienna's features twisted in a tortured combination of pain and rage. "Oh god, I hate you and all your stupid questions. You are so self-righteous. You're not better than me. I know what you did. You forced Rascal Rococo's mom to watch his prank. And look what happened to her."

Blood pulsed in Jane's temples. "I didn't do anything to that woman. In our interviews, she insisted her son was innocent, that it was a harmless prank, but she admitted she had never watched the video. All I did was leave her alone with the footage. It was her choice to view it. To see the truth. To learn who her son really was."

Mickey had been against it. They thought it was too cruel. But Jane had viewed the YouTube video of Hailey Simon's blond, brown-eyed toddler, Bryson, too many times to let Rascal's mother, Carol Roche, defend him. Hailey's son had a habit of grabbing his cat too roughly. Rascal—Hailey's boyfriend of less than six months—had decided that smearing the kid's hand in fast-acting glue would teach him a lesson. He had gleefully recorded the small kid's panicked struggles to free himself from the snarling, hissing cat for his channel.

It was just another funny cat clip.

Until the toddler's cuts and scratches got badly infected and the tender flesh on his arms swelled up like he'd been poisoned.

Child protective services got involved.

Hailey had temporarily lost custody of her son.

Rascal had gained thousands of followers in the aftermath, hundreds of furious comments and thousands of supportive ones. It had led to a sponsorship deal for a weight-training supplement also endorsed by a MMA fighter recently charged with domestic assault.

Jane would never know if the footage had been the reason Carol Roche drove her car off the road at high speed, killing herself on impact. But it was hard to imagine it being unrelated to Rascal's last lines in the YouTube clip.

Stop crying, kid. This is nothing compared to what my mom used to do to me.

Jane took a deep breath. Mothers got blamed for everything.

Her father had been an ugly drunk—not violent, but insulting and cold. Jane had been fourteen when her mother had finally summoned the courage to leave him and move into a dilapidated trailer with Jane in tow. There were rats in the walls and mold growing in the corners. Jane had hated it. After being refused twenty dollars to go to the movies, she had told her mother in a fit of rage that she would never be able to make it without the help of her husband. The light had left her mother's eyes. Two months later, her mother had returned to her father. Four years after that, her mother had been thrown through the windshield when her father got behind the wheel drunk.

Again.

"I get it, Sienna. More than you know. Joseph killed himself after that night trapped in the oven. So did Carol after she watched that video. I have to live with that. And so do you."

Sienna paled. Her body shuddered, and a moan escaped from her lips. "I'm sorry, okay? I'm so sorry. I didn't mean for him to die. You think I wanted this? They all died because of me! I want to die too. I hate myself for what I did. I killed them all. I don't deserve to be alive."

Her sobs became retches, and she crouched down to the floor as if her legs couldn't hold her. Jane sank to the floor with her and opened her arms. Sienna crawled into them. Her body jerked with powerful and terrifying emotions.

Jane's mind raced. What did Sienna mean? Had she lost control with her own mother like she had in the kitchen when she'd lunged at Jane? She'd been stunned at Sienna's animal strength as she'd fought for control of the screwdriver. The girl had overpowered her, gripping her hand so tightly that she'd been forced to jab the sharp point into her own thigh.

Had Sienna killed Melissa?

"Did your mom forgive you?" Jane whispered.

The question prompted another round of guttural sobs. Finally, Sienna choked out an answer.

"Yes. But she never forgave Elijah. I told her that we were running away together."

"When did you tell her that, Sienna?"

Sienna looked at her with anguish in her eyes. "The day she died."

"Oh my god," Jane whispered.

Sienna was gasping through tears. "She was so mad. She said she hated him. We got into a big fight. She told me that Elijah was wrong for me. That evening, she locked me in my room." She drew in a rasping breath. "I heard them screaming outside. I don't know what she threatened him with, but he left so quickly, he didn't bring his phone. I've been looking everywhere for it, all over the hotel."

A puzzle piece clicked into place. *Sienna* had been the unseen presence Jane had felt in so many rooms.

"Elijah's whole life was on his phone. Now that you've found it, we can charge it. I can figure out where he is. Where he went."

Jane had never heard someone so young sound so bitter or so heartbroken. She weighed her next words carefully. "I don't have his phone, Sienna. I never did. I didn't even know it was here."

Sienna's face crumpled. "How could you lie about that?"

"I needed to get out of that room, Sienna. I can help you. But you have to tell me the truth. What happened to your mother?"

In the darkness, Sienna raised her head. The flashlight glinted off the tears in her eyes, making them appear strange and unseeing. "I pounded on the door for hours for her to let me out of my room. She never came. I got so tired. I fell asleep. Early the next morning—like really early—my dad came to my room. To tell me my mom was dead. Wanna know the last words I said to my mom?"

Jane nodded. Already knowing.

"I hate you."

Jane looked down at this child in so much pain and searched inside for some instinct to guide her. They both carried the wound of inflicting deep harm on their mothers. There was so much to process. But she didn't know how to comfort Sienna. She didn't even know how to comfort herself.

Finally, Sienna calmed on her own. Her next words were robotic.

"Peter was so worried about me. About all of us . . . It was super hard for him. He didn't want people to say awful things about the hotel that would keep them away from seeing the incredible work my mom had done. We had to honor her, right? He got me to sign an NDA to keep everything quiet. He told me to take the exchange trip to France to clear my head. In return, he set up a trust fund for me to live in Paris as soon as I graduate."

"A trust fund? I thought that came from your dad?"

"No. It's all from Peter. I lost my mom but got a future. That's what he said."

Sienna broke down again as Jane's thoughts raced. Why would the hotel owner offer that to Sienna? A sign of guilt?

"Did Peter or your dad know about you and Elijah?"

"God, no. I would never tell them. Are you kidding? When I'm done with school, I'm going to find him. I know he's out there somewhere."

But Peter *had* known about her and Elijah. Lucy had confirmed it to Mickey. That meant Sienna only knew part of the truth. Jane nodded but didn't say a word.

Sienna wiped the back of her hand roughly across her nose. "I just need to find Elijah."

"When your dad comes back—"

Sienna snorted before she could finish. "You still believe him?"

"Why wouldn't I?"

"Um, maybe because he's been lying to you this entire time?"

Jane waited, hoping for more but not daring to ask.

Sienna filled the gap.

"First of all, you didn't break the router when you threw that glass bottle at me. We lied. Neither of us wanted you to be online. We don't trust you. I knew you were going to keep collecting info for your next documentary, so we turned it off. Before the power went out, it was working just fine. Convincing you that you broke the router was Peter's idea."

The muscles in Jane's jaw were rigid. "Your dad has been talking to Peter? About me?"

This time, it was Sienna who let the silence stretch.

"I could have messaged for help this whole time?"

"I mean, you could have tried. But nobody's coming here." Sienna's voice changed. She sounded sad. "It's just us now. Elijah used to call this place no-man's-land. The end of the world."

Jane shook her head. She wasn't wrong about Dom—she had to be able to trust him. "No. Your father told us he was going to get us out of here, and I believe him."

Sienna shook her head. "He's telling the truth about that. It's everything else. You know he doesn't have a job, right? My uncle told him to go clear his head."

"What?"

"Ask him. And while you're at it, you might want to get him to tell you who's staying in the cabins down the trail from the boathouse."

Jane froze.

"Spoiler alert. Peter never went back to the city. He's been here the whole time. And he thinks you're dangerous."

The elevator panel suddenly brightened, and Sienna and Jane both jumped back.

Someone was on their way up.

CHAPTER | FORTY-NINE

DOM STEPPED OFF THE ELEVATOR. THE LIGHT OF HIS HEADLAMP BOBBED sickeningly with each step, blinding Jane. Sienna began to cry again at the sight of him.

"We're going to be okay, See, I promise. Take this and go and pack a bag—bare essentials, okay? Warm change of clothes, your headlamp, and anything else you need. The water is coming up too fast. I've hauled boats to the shore. We have to make it across with kayaks. The engine of the motorboat is seized."

"What motorboat?" Jane asked.

At the same time, Sienna asked, "We're going to be okay?"

"Yes. As long as you listen to me. Take that flashlight and go."

Sienna gave a sidelong glance at Jane.

"Take care of Jane, Dad. She . . . just doesn't know . . . how to be a mother."

Jane was oddly touched by the insult.

"We don't have time to talk about that, See. Get your stuff and hurry back," Dom said. The two embraced. He passed Sienna a large flashlight.

The window was still black. It was difficult to gauge the time. The night had been long and hard, but it must have been close to dawn. And Peter was out there somewhere in the darkness.

"Where is Peter? Is he by the boats? Is he waiting for me? What are you planning to do? How did you know where to find us?"

"What? Jane, you're hysterical. I'm here to get you out. Peter wants to help."

"Peter is not your friend. He shot at me! Why won't you believe that? Listen. Melissa and Elijah weren't having an affair—"

"Enough! Enough with this bullshit. We are in a life-or-death situation here. Leave your theories. I need to get you to safety. We can figure out the rest later."

She wouldn't yield. "Not until you tell me the truth—all of it. Why did you bring me here?"

"I already told you why! Dr. Abebe recommended it for Sienna. A way to face the trauma and get past it. She said I had sent Sienna away to France too quickly. She hadn't processed her loss. People need time to mourn. Peter was desperate for a hand around here and Ted wanted me to take a break from the business."

"Peter sent her to France, not you. He was trying to get rid of her."

"Who told you that?"

"Your decisions were unsound. You were grieving too. You still haven't gotten over Melissa. We have to talk about it. You have to get it out." She remembered that Dom believed that Melissa was unfaithful with Elijah and soft-pedaled her next question. "Who told you about the affair? Was it Peter?"

Dom hurled another curse word at the ceiling. "You're pathological! Yes, Peter saw them together. It all made sense. Melissa had been acting strange for months, starting with the horrible fight with Sienna on the boat. I thought she was distracted by the hotel design. Her work was so consuming she barely had time for me or Sienna. Then I realized her attention was focused on someone else. Elijah." He scowled.

"But Dom, Peter lied. Elijah"—she took a deep breath as he stepped toward her—"was with Sienna."

All expression dropped from Dom's features. The light from his head-lamp shone at her in a sharp, blinding beam. She ducked her head to avoid it.

His words were monotone. "God, you're sick. Sienna was like a sister to him."

"No, that's not true—"

"Shut up!" His voice was distorted by emotion. "The night she died, I heard Elijah yelling at Melissa, telling her not to say anything. That it was all over. That he'd never do it again. Melissa was enraged, she got violent. She pushed him. I ran to help but it was too late. He had to get her off him. He was defending himself. She lost her balance. She hit her head on the dock. She died instantly."

"You saw Elijah kill Melissa?"

Jane watched his face collapse in sorrow. "I didn't see it, but I heard it. Then Elijah told me everything. That the affair was a mistake, that Melissa's death was an accident. She slipped. She was dead before I turned the corner. I couldn't save her. She was gone."

"But why did you cover it up? Make it look like a drowning?"

"I had no choice. Melissa started the fight. I knew what she was like when she got angry. She'd been violent with me before, and Sienna too. I couldn't bear for my daughter to know that her mother died like that. Be-traying me, trying to hurt someone else. Elijah was so scared to admit that he'd slept with my wife, but how could he deny it? I heard everything. And I didn't want Sienna to know that her mother had taken advantage of a young man we considered part of the family."

As he looked down, the beam of his head lamp pooled on the floor. Jane was left in darkness.

"Elijah called Peter. He explained everything to me while we waited. She . . . It started the night of that stupid beach fashion show that Lucy arranged. It was supposed to be fun, but Melissa drank too much. Elijah showed me a video. She was all over him."

Jane tried to interrupt, but Dom wouldn't let her.

"When Peter arrived the day Melissa died, he—we worked it out together. We couldn't let Sienna find out about the affair. It would have killed her. And Peter . . . the hotel was everything to him. Lucy would have leapt on any chance she could to tarnish the reputation of the place, try to force a sale so she could split the proceeds in the divorce settlement. The last thing I wanted was to end Elijah's life with a prison sentence for an accident. I forgave him for betraying me. He was just a kid. When he drove out of here in that old red Ford, I knew Peter was right. Staging a kayaking accident was the right thing to do. When you started talking about it again, I panicked."

He sighed and continued.

"You might as well know now. I was the one who told Peter that I needed him. He's been staying in a cabin on that side of the property to keep an eye on you. He helped me."

Jane had to set the betrayal aside to focus on what Dom had done to his first wife.

"You threw Melissa in the river. You covered up her murder because Peter told you to."

"It was what Melissa would have wanted. She would never have sent Elijah to prison. She loved him . . . in her way. That's the thing about mothers. Sometimes they sacrifice themselves for others."

He jerked his head up and she shrank from the glare. His eyes were glittering in a way that scared her.

"Dom—"

"You would do the same thing, right? To save Sienna?"

"There's so much you've misunderstood. Elijah and Peter manipulated you into believing a story that's not true. Melissa wasn't cheating on you. It was Sienna who was with Elijah. Ask her yourself. Melissa was flirty in that fashion show, but she was faithful to you. You have to believe me."

Dom stared at her with a blank face worse than anger. He looked disassociated. Dangerous.

"No. Elijah and Peter told me the truth."

"No. Elijah told you he was sleeping with Melissa because if he told you the truth, that he was sleeping with Sienna, you'd have killed him on the spot. Melissa had discovered that Sienna was planning to run away with him, and she put a stop to it. Elijah killed her to cover his own crime—statutory rape of a minor—and he needed you to cover for him. Easiest way to do that was to make you feel ashamed that you weren't enough for your own wife. To keep it all a secret because of your shame."

Dom shook his head. A jangling treble cut off the conversation, stunning her into silence. His cell phone still worked? They had lied to her about that too. She wanted to rip it from his hands to call Mickey. He reached into his deep jacket pocket and pulled out the chunky satellite phone. She kicked herself for having forgotten all about it.

"Hello? Yes, okay. We'll try. But it's going to be—"

Jane heard a muffled voice on the other end of the line.

"Okay. We'll get there." Dom pressed a button and looked at her. His expression was hard.

"That was Peter. He wants us all at the boathouse in twenty minutes."

Jane took a step back onto her injured foot and nearly lost her balance. She had to give him one more chance.

"Go check on Sienna. Make sure she's okay. Ask her about what I said. I think . . . I think she's ready to tell you the truth now."

Dom grimaced at the mention of his daughter's name. He rubbed the heel of his hand roughly against his cheek. "I am so tired of your theories about my life. I don't need to talk to my daughter and open old wounds. I know what happened to Melissa. I did what I had to do to keep my daughter safe. Just like I'm doing for you now. You have to come with me. Peter is here to help." Impatience sharpened Dom's words.

Jane's unease grew. Peter thought she was a threat—he had been hiding out for days to make sure she wouldn't discredit his hotel. And Dom had been willing to stand by and let Peter cover up the murder of his wife, while hiding Peter's presence from her. He had gaslit her when she told him about the shooting. Rage clogged her throat. Was Dom siding with Peter? Were they both planning to get rid of her now that she knew the truth about Melissa?

"Okay, I'll come with you. But first, I have to make sure the cats are safe."

"Those goddamn cats—I swear they mean more to you than Sienna and me. I wish I could believe what you say, but I can't. You've lied to me over and over about respecting my wishes and dropping your research. And now, you're asking me to trust you not to do something stupid? I don't, Jane. You're not the person I thought I married. I'm not letting you out of my sight."

He moved forward. There was a glint of silver in his hand. It looked like a knife.

"You are not the person I thought you were either."

She hit him over the head with her flashlight.

CHAPTER | FIFTY

A FEW MOMENTS LATER, JANE WAS IN THE KITCHEN, UPENDING A BUR-lap sack of potatoes on the floor. With shaking hands, she shoved the wriggling cats inside. The kittens' cries were small and pitiful, but their mother's protests were full of spitting rage. She ran down the stairs as fast as her damaged foot would take her. A coating of rain made each step as smooth as glass, so she clung to the wooden railing, sliding her hand along its surface. At the bottom of the stairs, she blinked hard. The river was louder now. Water drove down from the sky. The line of the horizon was faint but present. The darkness was beginning to gray.

The night was almost over. Sunrise was coming.

She lifted the heavy sack to her chest and squared her shoulders to the river. She willed her weak body to find a reserve of strength.

Just get to the boats, she told herself, though she had no idea what she would do if Peter was waiting for her there. Her mother had always told her to take it one step at a time.

So she did.

Jane forced her toes to clear the ground, because a stumble now would be the end of her. She had no idea how long Dom would be incapacitated, and her skin crawled at the idea of him sneaking up behind her—under cover of the roaring river. Or would it be Peter, firing a shot from the woods? She spun backward. The stairs were empty in the muted dawn.

No one was following her.

Yet.

She turned back to face what had once been the rolling green lawn stretching from the front of the hotel toward the Fraser River. Now, its bloated and bubbling surface was as thick and brown as a chocolate milk-shake, frothing over everything it touched. She could smell it—cold and damp and deadly. The mud was unnervingly soft beneath her feet. Nothing was secure. Nowhere was safe.

Then she saw them. The bright colors—green, orange, yellow, and red—were dull beacons in the gaining light. The four kayaks were lined up about two meters from the lip of the curling rapids. She ran in a shuffling, awkward gait with the sack jostling violently against her body. The cats were silent now—either petrified or worse, but she didn't have a moment to check.

At the boats, she shoved the sack under elasticated ropes coiled around the bow to allow boaters to carry small items. Trying to be gentle, she guided the rough fabric under the tight bands, then positioned herself at the back of the boat and pushed it forward, fighting the shifting sand and wet ground beneath her feet.

A muffled yell made her look up. Across the river, Murray Jack was waving, both arms flailing like a windmill. She could hear his voice, but it was impossible to make out the words. She raised her hand like a visor to protect her eyes from the rain. He was holding something.

Her heart leapt. A rope. Murray had a rope. Something large and ungainly was tied to the end. She raised her hands high and stretched out her thumbs in a doubled gesture of understanding.

He nodded, then like a cowboy from an old movie, began circling the object tied to the end over his head, feeding length to gradually expand the circle wider. The rope twisted and spun into a wobbling circumference above his head. She held her breath as it danced, exhaling when he released it. The object tied to the end splashed down about twenty meters away from where he'd thrown it, roughly a quarter of the distance between them. There was no way she could reach it.

Murray yelled something and pointed downriver. She struggled to hear him.

"Go to the eddy! The rope will get caught up! GO!"

Eddy?

She didn't try to understand. Whatever was downriver, it was the only chance she had. Leaving the cats on the boat, she limped to the place he indicated—a curve of the bank before the boathouse and the dock—quickly scanning the grounds for any sign of Peter or Dom. The old farmer fed more rope into the river. She gasped and pumped a fist hard into the air as the object she'd been chasing came closer, bobbing in the wild waves about half a meter from shore.

She laid on the sopping ground to extend her reach. The deep mud squished under her body and she remembered the chunk of land the river had already eaten. She stretched, her muscles twanging. Her fingers were swollen and frozen. It hurt to close them. Touching the object—it looked like an old bleach jug fashioned into a makeshift lifeguard's throw—her grip failed. She only managed to brush it, pushing it farther away. Again, she thrust her shaking hands into the rushing water to get purchase. And her second attempt failed. Jane dug her aching fingers on one hand into the soft ground, knowing she couldn't trust it to bear her weight but doing it anyway. She used the extra two inches gained from the traction to roll her shoulder, then bat the slippery object toward her. It came closer. She willed her frozen hands to grasp its handle.

She sobbed as she pulled the weathered white plastic container to her chest. Fighting for purchase on the slick ground, she held the object over her head in victory. Murray also raised his arms high, mimicking her earlier double thumbs-up. The rope attached to the jug tugged against her as she struggled to pull it upriver toward the kayak.

A motorized hum began grinding, barely discernible under the growl of the river. Her head snapped up, and she frantically searched the seething surface for Peter's boat. Then, she felt the rope begin to tighten. Murray was waving her forward, urging her to move in the direction of the rope, which had become taut enough to be raised out of the water into a line between her and him. The low hum stopped when she reached the kayak. He had fashioned some kind of pulley system.

She wedged the jug under the ropes for stability as she clambered one leg into the rubber-skirted opening of the kayak, pushing against the mucky grit below with her other foot to launch the craft. From behind, a ragged voice shouted her name.

"JANE! DON'T DO IT! IT'S NOT SAFE!" Dom yelled.

It was too late. The tip of the boat sank down into violent water. Jane tucked her other leg into the rubber skirt and felt a queasy wobble as the waves began to bash against her, rocking the narrow boat from side to side. With waxy hands, she clung to the tubular handle of the jug. The motor began again. The rope jerked and the jug slid an inch forward. She nearly lost her hold.

Walls of frigid water slammed her uncovered head and face. She gasped and sputtered but held on. As the rope fought the churn, her muscles strained and her bones were bounced by the cruel drops and bumps.

The river swept over her once again, a slap of frothing ice against her face, neck, and shoulders. The boat landed hard on a hollow of water, jostling her tailbone. She cried out but the current was louder. The endless wash made it impossible to see anything beyond the pointed tip of the boat. Another hit, this one harder. The kayak tipped impossibly far to one side. She was going over. Her aching hands grabbed the burlap sack as the boat lost its fight with gravity and listed hard. She took a rasping last breath before realizing her shoulder had sunk into sand.

Strong hands grabbed her. She let the bag fall to the ground and looked up into Murray's triumphant face. They both wept as he flung his arms tight around her body, bursting open the breath she had held in her lungs. A panicked mew came from Thompson as the gray bedraggled kitten poked its head out of the opening of the rough-hewn sack. Fraser followed with a menacing one-eyed glare. Her hackles stood up in dark spikes. She jerked away from Jane's reach and ducked back into the bag. When she emerged, there was another kitten in her mouth. Chilco!

Murray looked at Jane in astonishment as she helped Fraser out of the opening, pulling it wide to release the third and fourth kittens, who rewarded her with small but forceful cries. They had all survived.

"Good god, Jane. You saved the cats!"

"*You* saved the cats!" she cried.

"That old winch saved you all," Murray said, pointing up the hill to a grouping of trees.

Laughing and crying, Jane gathered up a furious Fraser and one of her babies, ignoring the scratches and squirms. Murray picked up the other three and tucked them under his thick coat.

"Let's get them warm. I've got the truck running. Up here."

He placed a heavy boot on the sandy beach, following a trail that shot directly up through the thick forest that lined the edge of the bank.

With no hands available to avoid the rain-weighted branches hanging low over the trail, she had to drop her shoulders and push the trees away to avoid being pelted in the face with needles and leaves. The rope that had pulled her across the river was attached to something at the top of the trail. Its thick braided cord continued to retract up the path, and the hum of the motor grew louder with every step she took. Rivulets of water ran alongside the depression it made in the center of the trail, forcing her to walk in a wide, bow-legged stance that made her broken toe flame. She followed Murray's mint-green flannel coat like a lighthouse, pushing herself forward despite the powerful urge to stop, to sleep, to heal.

The trees thinned out into an overgrown pasture with weeds as high as her shoulders. Murray stopped just shy of a rotating wheel mounted on the front of an old truck. A vintage red Ford. Jane could see the rope spooling a little thicker on the coil with each rotation of the mechanism.

For a moment, she was so struck by the simple but ingenious design that she didn't see the bullet hole in the windshield.

Murray moved swiftly to the passenger-side door and hauled it open with a shriek of rust. He gently placed the three kittens on the front seat while Jane watched, frozen in horror. When he turned, he glanced at the shattered windshield then back into her eyes with a knowing look.

"Many rivers lead to the Fraser," he says. "But I'm sure glad this one led you straight to me."

CHAPTER | FIFTY-ONE

A DAY AGO, AN HOUR AGO, A MOMENT AGO, JANE WOULD HAVE
heeded the voice screaming inside her head to flee, run, escape. But she
had reached the end. She had nothing left, no resources to fall back on.
She dropped to her knees on the cold, wet ground. As her body sank into
the muck, she smelled manure.

Murray's truck was a vintage red Ford. She should have put it together when she first glimpsed it between the trees. It matched Dom's
description of the one Elijah had driven away from the hotel the night he
disappeared. Why would Murray leave it in sight?

Fraser growled deeply then sprang from her arms into the sopping
grass. Jane placed the small kitten beside her mom. After another glare,
Fraser took the baby into her mouth and leapt onto the passenger seat beside the other three mewling kitties. The gray light of the early morning
reflected off the shiny silver object on the dash.

Elijah's phone.

Jane smiled wanly as Fraser began aggressively bathing her babies. What a lovely sight for sore eyes, Jane thought, even if it was the last thing she'd ever see.

A mother caring for her babies.

"Up you go, girl. Let's get outta this rain." Murray hoisted Jane up and into the passenger side of the truck beside the kittens. Then he walked around the front, opened the driver's door, and got in behind the wheel. The interior smelled of diesel and weed. The truck engine purred. An unfinished can of Energy Bet rested in the console between them. The windshield began to fog as the rain fell on the glass outside. It was a surprisingly cozy place to be murdered, Jane thought. "You know, the moment you showed up, I knew things were going to change. A true crime investigator at the Venatura Hotel? Finally, the truth was going to come out."

She blinked, struggling to remember their first conversation. She'd never spoken to him about her films.

"You knew who I was?"

"I may be an old man, but I can find my way around a search engine. Or at least, I figured it out after several lessons from my wife and Joseph a few years ago. Now that they're not around anymore, I don't find much use for the computer, but it sure helped me get a bead on you. Never knew how much I needed you until you arrived."

He chuckled, and Jane almost felt as if they were having a normal conversation—one of their chats over the radio that had made her so fond of him. It was difficult to reconcile his kindness with the bullet hole in the windshield.

"Why is Elijah's truck on your property?"

"Well now, that's a good question."

Jane scanned his hands for a weapon, then looked over his body for the bulge of a gun. He was sitting with his head tipped back on the headrest, relaxed, almost jovial. Murray didn't look like he was about to murder her. Curiosity overcame her fear.

"You've been feeding me information this whole time. You must have known there was a chance I'd figure it all out."

"I was hoping so. Truth is, I've been waiting a long time for someone to puzzle through what happened that day. That whole year, I guess. All I know is my side of it. It never made sense to me. I spent many sleepless nights since you arrived, trying to figure out how they killed Melissa. I was worried that the same thing was going to happen to you."

Jane shuddered. The cold water from the ground had worked its way into the material of her pants straight to her skin, but that wasn't the source of the icy chill traveling up her spine. Murray noticed and leaned forward to turn on the heat. As a blast of dusty air hit her, she cursed her own blinding stupidity. She'd gone from forcing a woman to bear witness to her son's hateful indictment of her, to marrying a man who was duped into covering up the murder of his own wife. And then she'd trusted Murray Jack.

She had been wrong so many times.

Murray looked down at Fraser and the kittens, who were making snuffling sounds. He leaned over and whispered a few words to the mother cat, who interrupted her grooming and met his eyes with a long, slow blink. Murray gently picked up the smallest kitten, fitting the tiny animal into the palm of his hand. He began stroking the cat's spine with two fingers.

"Was this the one you thought wasn't going to make it?"

Jane nodded. "I call her Nechako."

"She's having a tough time shaking off the cold," he said. "But I'll get her back."

The two of them sat in silence as he continued petting the little kitten. Jane was grateful for a moment to get her thoughts in order.

"Why would you worry about me dying like Melissa?"

Murray's eyes were soft. "Because you're my friend. Just like Melissa was. She was a lot like you. Hellfire at the core. Always sticking up for the underdog. Never willing to let a crime go unpunished. She asked questions. She drew that map for me so I would know where it all began. That damn prank at the cookhouse. That's why I gave it to you, Jane. I knew you were the one who could finish what she and I started."

"What did you start?"

"It was my idea. Not hers." He gave her a searching look.

Jane nodded. It satisfied him enough to go on.

"I used to drop eggs off for Melissa, just the same as I did for you. Not that she used them. She wasn't much of a cook. Another thing you had in common, I guess."

The little kitten in Murray's palm lifted its head. Both of its eyes were open now. It butted against Murray's fingers.

"There you go. Now, let's keep you somewhere warm."

With careful movements, Murray eased open his jacket and tucked the small cat into his breast pocket. The rain had eased enough so Jane could hear its small thrum.

"Joseph was like a son to us. My daughter had him real young—too young to take care of him proper. She went back to school for nursing after we agreed to take him in. When Joey was five, she moved back east after she finished her degree—got married, was doing good. Came back to visit every Christmas. Then, she lost control of her vehicle on a patch of black ice. Head-on collision. Dead on impact."

"Oh, Murray."

A ripple of sorrow at the loss of her own parents made her swallow hard.

"Yeah, it was rough. My wife was devastated. But we put all our love into that little boy. After Joseph died, my wife went downhill fast. She'd been battling cancer for a while but we thought she was going to pull through. With Joey gone, she didn't care anymore. She let the disease eat her up. She passed away three months after Joseph did. February of last year."

"I'm so sorry."

The man's mouth quirked up at the side. "Maybe save your sympathy for a minute. There's more to tell and you may not look at me so nicely once you hear it all. But thank you. Your kindness is the thing I like the most about you."

He bowed his head, then started talking again.

"That spring, Melissa paid me a visit for the first time. I always came to her, so it was a surprise to see her walking across that bridge. It wasn't a happy afternoon though. She wanted to tell me the truth about what had happened to my grandson. Watching that video was one of the hardest things I've ever had to do."

He broke off and stared into the middle distance for a moment. A stark image of the outdoor oven flashed in Jane's mind.

"I knew then that I couldn't sit here and let that crew of dipshits keep pulling their dangerous pranks. Melissa felt the same way. She'd been working with them for a while by then and she was fed up. She hated the way Elijah was always sniffing around Sienna. Could see how he was manipulating her—grooming, I think they call it nowadays. Giving her a little praise, a little opportunity. Making her think she was part of the gang. Egging her on to be one of the boys, then pulling the rug out from under her. Tricking her, making her look foolish. Melissa was worried Elijah was going to hurt Sienna the same way he hurt Joseph.

"I don't blame Sienna for Joseph's death, mind you. She was fourteen, and desperate to impress that crew. And now she's gotta carry that weight around for the rest of her life.

"That's what those kinds of guys are like, right? Pack mentality. Pick on the weakest—the young, the disenfranchised. Joseph was a little overweight, not the most social guy. They made him trust them so they could hurt him."

Jane closed her eyes out of respect for his grandson. No one deserved to be treated as he had. Certainly not for YouTube views.

"Anyway. It wasn't hard for me to decide what I wanted to do to those pricks. The one good thing about a pack of dogs is that they are easy to lead. Those guys had a thing for vintage trucks. And I had more than enough bait. Melissa was the one who told them I had a truck for sale. I agreed to let them take it on a test drive—so long as I could follow in my vehicle. Randeep and Dylan went way out in the bush. When we pulled over, I shot them both and left them in the ditch. I thought for sure some trucker would find them eventually. But nope. They're still out there."

332 | AMBER COWIE

Jane kept her expression neutral, but inside she was reeling. Melissa baited the crew so Murray could pick them off one by one? That was a fierce, fearless, and frightening mother.

"Elijah—well, he was tougher because he was smarter. Melissa came up with a way to lure him over to me, but something happened. The day they were supposed to arrive, nobody showed up. I waited for hours before I went down to the riverbank with my binoculars. I saw your man Dom shoving Melissa's lifeless body into a kayak, then pushing it into the river. The three of them all watched like ghouls. Your husband, Peter Stanton, and Elijah.

"I knew then that it had all gone wrong. When that little fuck came driving across the bridge without a care in the world, I was ready. There's a high point on the road about fifty feet from here. I was waiting there with my shotgun. One blast, through the windshield, and he was done. I did to him what he did to Melissa. Threw him right into the river."

Jane closed her eyes. Sienna would be devastated. Dom, too. She shook her head to get rid of the pang of sympathy she felt for her husband. She felt nothing for Peter's loss.

"Since then, I've been sitting here, waiting to get caught. Never thought it would take this long to find all the bodies. I've been holding steady for a knock on the door for more than a year. I don't care if they take me off to jail. It's why I'm telling you all this. I've seen and dealt enough death. It's time for me to face my punishment."

"And that's why you rescued me?"

"That and I couldn't bear the thought of losing another amazing woman to the awful men of the Venatura Hotel."

"Amazing?"

"Hey, I told you I know my way around a search engine. You're a hotshot filmmaker. You stand up for what's right. They made you a villain for casting light on what happened to that little boy, but I think you're a goddamn hero. I've watched everything you've made. You're real talented—"

Murray stopped short, lowered his window, and tilted his head toward the trail they'd come up.

"Do you hear that?"

Voices rose and fell on the wind, muted by the rushing of water. Jane recognized them as kin. When Dom and Sienna burst from the trees, her heart soared. After everything, they felt like family.

Then she saw the brutal expression on the face of Peter Stanton, close on their heels.

And the gun in his hand.

"That's my son's truck," Peter said, approaching slowly.

Murray nodded once, opened his door, and stepped out. He locked eyes with Jane. In his expression, she saw peace. Forgiveness. Completion.

The gunshot was deafening. Murray buckled over, clutching his chest, as she screamed.

CHAPTER | FIFTY-TWO

MURRAY'S BLOOD BLOOMED ON HIS MIDSECTION, SOAKING THROUGH the green flannel. Dom and Sienna froze in place.

Jane tried to scoot across the bench seat to help her friend, but Peter trained the gun on her and she stopped short.

"You were supposed to help me find him—alive. I thought you were going to lead me to him. Not to his murderer." Peter turned to Dom. "This is Elijah's truck. This is the vehicle he drove away in. The one I thought I'd see someday out of the corner of my eye and know my son had come home. But it's been on this bastard's farm the whole time."

On the ground, Murray moved.

Jane's heart leapt in hope. But Peter saw it too. He jerked his head toward the dying man. A rumpled, bloodstained kitten crawled out of Murray's jacket.

It was her only chance.

Jane lunged from the passenger seat, bolted from the truck, and ran.

She stumbled down the muddy path, sliding on her hip and backside when the mud took her feet out from under her. At a level section, she pushed herself up into a stumbling sprint. Branches clawed at her eyes. She raised her forearms to protect her face from the rough wood and whipping leaves. Again, she lost her purchase and flat-footed down the slope like she was skiing. A rock halted her slide, tilting her forward and down in a sudden, gut-punching fall.

The impact took her breath away. Her cheekbone struck rock. Warmth gushed from the point of impact. She pushed herself up again, willing her depleted limbs to move, to ignore the pulsing pain, to over-come her exhaustion. She floundered forward, gripping the long grass at the edge of the trail as a guide. Another fall would be fatal. Her body would not rise again.

Thick mud slowed her footsteps when she reached the water's edge. She caught a whiff of campfire smoke, acrid and dry at the back of her throat. The front half of Peter's boat had been heaved onto the gravelly shore. Already, it had been knocked sideways by the force of the rising river. Even if she knew how to drive a boat, it was too treacherous to try. The swollen river could toss it in any direction.

And Jane was tired of being pushed around.

She heard the slippery squelch of footsteps, wet and deep in the satu-rated earth, seconds before Peter, Dom, and Sienna rushed down the trail. The gun was still in Peter's hand. He trained it on her chest.

Peter's face was an unnatural color, patchy gray with rings of blanched pink around his bulging eyes. The tendons in his neck stretched taut.

"Was this all just a *story* for you? How could you not tell me what happened to my son? How could you keep it from me?"

"I didn't know," Jane said, instinctively raising her arms in the sign of surrender. "I didn't know until Murray confessed."

"Always play the innocent, don't you? First with the death of Carol Roche—yes, I know all about that—and then my son. You killed her, just like that slut Melissa killed my son with her wild accusations. Has Dom seen your latest documentary, Jane? Did he see the moment after

Carol hears what her son says about her? She looked like a dead woman walking. No light in her eyes. No reason to live."

Jane nodded. He was right. The deadened expression on Rascal Rococo's mother's face had been exactly like the expression her own mother wore when Jane told her she was going to fail without her husband. She had unknowingly repeated the pattern. Her legs weakened as Peter continued to berate her.

"You've been communicating with that old bastard this whole time! Dom told me about your radio sessions. You've been in on it since the beginning. I knew you couldn't be trusted to leave well enough alone. But, my dear, you are a terrible investigator. Who do you think was sending you those messages?"

As if on cue, Dom and Sienna rushed forward to block Peter's aim.

"Peter, please. Put the gun down," Dom said. "Jane's innocent."

"Innocent? Please. This woman has you whipped. She's been jerking your chain since you married her—just like Melissa used to. How can you believe a word she says?"

"Peter. I've done everything you asked me. I threw her phone into a sink, for Christ's sake. I tricked her into thinking we were offline. I cut her off from the world just like you wanted. I lied to her about your warning gunshots. I didn't do all that just to watch you kill her."

"She covered up my son's murder. She knew what that miserable old man did, and said nothing."

"Peter, be reasonable. Jane's been focused on Melissa this whole time—she didn't care about Elijah. You're wrong about why she's here. She's after a story, but it's not the one you think." His face creased in pain. "Is it true what Jane says? Did Elijah kill my wife?"

"You're a fool, Dom. A useful idiot. Jane's last project was an awful exposé of that other YouTuber. She's got a bloody theme! She's going to turn his cold-blooded murder into a posthumous public shaming. Just you wait. People like her hide things until the right moment, then they cash in. She is going to humiliate us all and take down my hotel with her. She's a no-good bitch." Peter said the last word like it tasted good in his mouth.

He eyed Dom before continuing. "She's always been out to get you. All she cares about is herself."

"Just like your son," Sienna said.

Her voice was shrill. She tugged on Peter's arm and the gun dipped alarmingly, but he was strong enough to shake her off. Jane watched the muzzle dance, hoping it wasn't the last thing she'd ever see.

Sienna couldn't keep her balance. She fell hard on the rough rocks and cried out in pain. She pushed herself up to her elbows, her young face contorted in misery. "You're acting like Elijah didn't deserve to die."

All three adults turned to her as she fumbled her way to standing. Though Dom was close enough to help her, he seemed immobilized by her words.

"Jane is the only one who knows the truth. She realized who Elijah really was. And what he was capable of."

Peter's eyes protruded from his drawn face.

Dom didn't take his off his daughter. "But, See, I heard them fighting. They were breaking up. He was telling her it was all over. That it would never happen again. It was an accident. Elijah told me everything."

"He lied," Sienna said. "Mom hated him. She blamed him for Joseph Jack's suicide, and she hated what he was doing to me. She said she didn't like the person I'd become, and she told me to stay away from him. When he told her he was going to stop, he wasn't talking about sleeping with her, he was talking about sleeping with me. But he was lying about that, too. We weren't going to stop. We were going to run away together."

Lines carved across Dom's handsome face. "The kayak, the cover-up . . . we did it all to protect you, Sienna. Peter and Elijah convinced me that it would kill you to know the truth about your mother."

Peter's eyes darkened. His jaw was set.

Tears slipped down Sienna's cheeks. "She was a good mother. She was trying to protect me, but I hated her for it. Elijah told me where he was going that night. I've been looking for his phone since we came back. I wanted to show you, Dad. I wanted to show you the texts between them. They hated each other. Mom wasn't sleeping with Elijah. It was me, Dad."

Peter exploded. "You despicable little whore. How dare you lie about my son?"

She rounded on Peter, her adolescent bravado like a shield against the gun he aimed at her. "Elijah killed my mother because she was trying to protect me! You lied for him. You lied to me. You lied to my dad. You let Elijah get away." Her voice was venomous.

Dom finally looked away from Sienna. When his eyes met Jane's, they misted. She was surprised to feel hers doing the same.

"You were right," Dom said to her.

Peter gave him a foul sideways glance. "Dom! For fuck's sake, use your bloody head. How can you believe this charlatan? This second-rate *film*maker? How can you entertain the idea of Elijah being anything but a good son, a good man, when we've just learned of his murder? What has this woman done to you? Why do you keep letting these sluts lead you around by your balls?"

Sienna laughed. Her ill-advised courage made Jane shudder. "A good man? Would a good man try to drown his girlfriend for views?"

"What the hell are you on about?" Peter said.

"I know why Elijah was out there at the boathouse. So did my mom."

A wave crashed over the boat, dragging it farther into the seething water.

"She died protecting me," Sienna said again.

"Protecting you from what?" Dom asked.

"Don't believe a word she says. Your new wife has poisoned her mind. And yours, by the looks of it," Peter said through a clenched jaw.

Sienna scowled at Peter. "Mom died protecting me from him! His stupid pranks. Elijah carved his initials in the pilings when the boathouse was all ripped apart. When Uncle Ted was working on it. He told me his next video was a way for me to prove my love. That day—the day my mom died—I was supposed to swim down and carve my initials under his. But it was all a prank. Mom overheard him telling someone that he was planning to pretend he didn't know who I was when I came out of the water. Like I was just some stupid teenager trying to make him fall in love with me. She told me about it but I didn't want to believe it. I told her I hated her—but it was really Elijah I hated." Sienna choked on her tears. "He didn't want anyone to know he was dating me. I wasn't good enough to be his girlfriend, but maybe I'd be good enough to get him half a million views on a stupid YouTube channel."

"What utter shit. You were a child. Like a sister to him. He would never have hurt you."

"I don't care if you believe me, Peter. But you believe me, right, Dad?"

A moment passed. Jane held her breath. Dom finally closed the distance between them and wrapped his arms around her.

Peter grew exasperated. "Your mother was a whore! She died because she seduced a young man."

"Melissa was not a whore," Dom said, releasing Sienna but keeping a hand on her shoulder.

But Peter couldn't be dissuaded. "Get it together, man! Your wife was a pain in the ass. She would do anything to get ahead, like shaking her ass at that fashion show. She probably fucked that old farmer as well. She could get people to do whatever she wanted. Just like this one."

He gestured toward Jane with the gun.

Dom shook his head.

"No, Peter. That's not true." Dom let go of Sienna and took a step forward.

Rage distorted Peter's face. "You married two worthless women hell-bent on destroying everything I love. My son is dead, but I will be damned if I let you take my hotel. You'll be better off when your second wife is dead and buried."

His finger twitched as Dom dropped his shoulder, ramming into Peter's midsection. The older man gasped, losing his balance. Peter stumbled backward, pinwheeling his arms, dropping the gun into the water. His body lurched toward the river and panic blighted his face. He toppled into the muddy river.

THE OFF SEASON | 341

The three of them stood on the bank, stunned and silent, as his head was pulled below the surface.

Suddenly Sienna shouted, "The hotel!"

Jane jerked her head up, digging her heels into the soft ground to keep upright. Across the raging river, plumes of smoke billowed from the east side of the fourth floor. The Sunrise Suite. Thick smoke formed a cloud above the hotel, purple and black like a bruise.

CHAPTER | FIFTY-THREE

THE SNOW FELL IN LOOSE CLUMPS OF FLAKES OUTSIDE THE WINDOW
of Jane's favorite dim-sum restaurant on Hastings Street.

"Merry fricking Christmas," Mickey said, tapping their warm teacup
against the one in Jane's hand. "I had to pull some serious strings to get
this *Home Alone* snow for you."

"Merry Christmas to you," she replied with a laugh.

The Chinese server gave them a wide smile as she deposited three
more steaming wicker baskets of dumplings, vegetables, and pork buns
to their table.

"You're hungry!" she said with a small laugh before speedily pushing
her cart to a large Jewish family seated nearby.

"They're late," Jane said. "Maybe they decided not to come."

Under the table, she extended her foot to ease the ache. Her injuries
had been healing for nearly two months now, but cold weather still made
her foot feel tender. Her bruises had faded after three weeks.

"The roads are probably pretty bad right now. Vancouver drivers can't handle the snow."

Jane smiled. "That's true."

"Listen, before we head back to the apartment, remind me that we need toilet paper desperately. Don't let me forget."

She nodded. Mickey had offered her a room after their rescue from Murray's farm. The enormous hotel fire had bumped them to the top of the triage list, and a helicopter had airlifted them from the swollen banks of the river to the Chilliwack RCMP detachment where they faced hours of emergency services and police questioning about the deaths of Murray Jack and Peter Stanton, whose body had washed up on shore the day after his fall.

As they left the detachment, one officer said it was a mercy that Murray Jack didn't have to face trial for murder. Jane agreed.

The investigation had been closed shortly after they returned home. Jane had attended his funeral a few weeks later, held at the community hall. He was buried beside his grandson, his daughter, and his wife, in a mossy, peaceful place.

"Before they arrive, can we pin down the subject of our next project? I've got an idea."

Jane nodded reluctantly. Mickey squeezed her hand.

"As long as we're not mentioning anyone or anything involved with the Venatura Hotel."

Mickey's expression became respectful. "Absolutely not."

"Good."

Mickey beamed. "Awesome."

The door chimed and both Mickey and Jane looked toward it. Sienna and Dom were stamping snow off their feet and brushing flakes from their shoulders.

"You think you're ready for this?" Mickey whispered, as Dom spotted her and waved.

"I do," said Jane.

ACKNOWLEDGMENTS

I WRITE DARK BOOKS BUT MY LIFE IS FULL OF LIGHT (MOST DAYS).
Adrienne Kerr, your talent, grace, and grit are what got me through this wild ride of ravaging self-doubt and punishing five a.m. mornings. This book would not exist without you because you are an excellent editor and an enormously awesome human being.

Laurie Grassi, I'm so glad you found me and saw what we could do together. I thought about you every time I opened this manuscript.

Karen Silva, authors around the world lost a lot when you pivoted careers, but libraries gained a hero and I (begrudgingly) agree that is a fair trade.

Brittany Lavery, it was brief but fantastic to get your insights.

Cayley Pimentel, you are seriously rad and I was so glad to share a little bit of my wonderful town with you in real life.

Gordon Warnock, thanks for sticking with me through thick and thin.

Ben, thank you for taking me by the arm and settling down upon the farm. We are raising our kids as gently as we please, and you still make me go shaky at the knees. I know this has been a tough year, but we've got each other and that's a lot. You can lean on me when you're not strong. God knows how many times you've held me up.

Eve, you are a beautiful braid of fire, beauty, and intelligence that I'm honored to tend and kindle as you grow and glow.

Thompson, you are my little baloney face and I love being part of your Jon Rigo, chicken marauders, Joe Pesto, spumoni-filled, mini-man world.

Mew and Clover, your fuzzy bodies and ridiculous antics make our family complete.

Morgan, I would be lost without you. Your confidence, courage, and all-around smoke show are a guide to all the beautiful ways to be, and I would feel like less than I am if I didn't have you.

Marc, you are the smartest man I know and the funniest person at every party.

Jasper, you are the coolest middle-schooler I know. My kids (especially Thompson) think you are a champion already and I know you're just getting started.

Emmerich, your wisdom and knowledge are something we all admire. My kids think you are a legend, and they always ask me to see if you know the answer to things I don't.

Kim, it's an eternal ride-or-die with you and me. I'm grateful we get to show our daughters and son that not all families are connected by genetics, and though it sometimes takes a long time to find them, when you do, it's forever.

Nate, you are my viceroy and a man who understands the value of a good garage session.

Olivia, you are a sparkle of sunshine and a bright light in every room.

Siryn, thank you for allowing me into the early stages of the artistic and creative life you are creating. Phoenix, thank you for giving me a place in the audience to see your bright light shine onstage. Griffin, thank you for being generally rad and for getting through some very awful stuff. Natasha, you know more about me than most people, and I know you too, and I love the strength and commitment you have given to me and to the incredible kids you raised. I really believe Lucas thanks you too.

Ava Perraton, Deryl Cowie, Darlene Cowie, Jeff, and Joanne, the front page is meant for you. Thank you for doing the hardest job for me and Ben, and for caring for the next generation.

Joan Jacobsen and Chris Cowie, you survived a fire this year and I'm so glad the house from my childhood remains standing—but the most important thing is that you stayed safe and got through a horrible summer.

Thank you to my family, Auntie Donna, Auntie Carla, Helen and Myron Smith, Auntie Linda, Uncle Dale, Cousin Sherri, Linda and Ulrich, and Lee and Marjorie.

Love to my writing family, Karen Dodd, Mahtab Narsimhan, Sonia Garrett, Diana Stevan, Shoshona Freedman, Caroline (Rae Knightley), Tatiana Lee, Rebecca Wood Barrett, Stella Harvey, Deborah Wade, Jan Redford, Ali Vefive, Antonia Reed, Carolyn & Christina (The Mom-Babes), Samantha Bailey, Robyn Harding, Roz Nay, Christina MacDonald, Sarah at Armchair Books, Feet Banks, Charlotte Morganti, Winona Kent, Erik D'Souza, and Julie Wilkins at Little Bookshop (thank you for leveling up our town and my life).

Huge gratitude and joy to my talented and beautiful singing and dancing friends Shannon Handley, Jessica Kelly, Ashala Mah, Lindsay Leathem, Deb, Johanna Samuel, Mara Halayko, Leanne Roderick, Megan, Anna Davies, Lara Funa, Allan, Liesl, Carmen, Hannah Sheppeard, Drea, Kelly Farrell, and the incredible Troupe group.

Thank you for being a friend, traveled down the road and back again to: Maple, Teena, Graham, Neva, and Brea Downes, Kate Rose and Jon Bennet, Abigail and George, Carol, Heather Jean, Sarah and Russ, Tasha, Julie and James, Danielle, Christine Lee, Shauna and Ian, Charlene and Steve, Mel and Jamie, Celia and Dave, Zoe, Grant, Alison, Leo and Casey, Daniel, Nancy and Georgia Stubbe, Troy Cochrane, Alyssa Murdoch, Kim Haxton, Orane Cheung, Ayton Novak, Kim Haxton, and Alison Dasho (always).

Enormous thank-you to the creators of *The Louds*, *Modern Family*, *The*

InBestigators, and *Life on Earth* for keeping my kids occupied during long days at my computer.

Thank you to the volcanoes for not erupting and the rivers for not rising. Thank you for the peace and love that still exists in human hearts and for the kindness that we give to the world.

May cruelty be overcome so our stories can be told.

ABOUT THE AUTHOR

AMBER COWIE IS A NOVELIST LIVING IN A SMALL TOWN ON THE WEST coast of British Columbia. Her work has appeared in the *New York Times*, Salon, the *Globe and Mail*, CrimeReads, and Scary Mommy. Her first novel, *Rapid Falls*, was a Whistler Book Awards nominee. She holds a history degree from the University of Victoria and is a mother of two. She likes skiing, running, and inventing stories that make for a questionable internet search history. Visit her at AmberCowie.com or on Twitter/X and Instagram @AmberCowie.

"A haunting claustrophobic, unpredictable thriller...
A bewitching read teeming with fascinating characters,
this book is an absolute standout."

#1 internationally bestselling author
SAMANTHA M. BAILEY

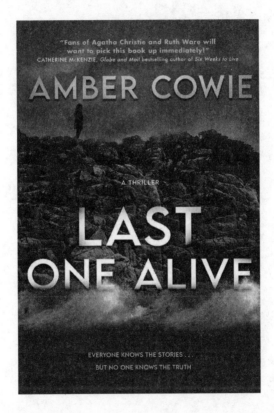

"Cowie has done Agatha Christie proud in this
stay-up-all-night, keep-all-the-lights-on mystery."

Globe and Mail bestselling author
CATHERINE MCKENZIE

SIMON &
SCHUSTER